THE FORGOTTEN LYRIC

The Creed of Gethin Book II

CAROLINA CRUZ

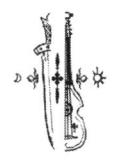

Copyright © 2023 by Carolina Cruz

All rights reserved.

No part of this book may be reproduced in any form or by any electronic or mechanical means, including information storage and retrieval systems, without written permission from the author, except for the use of brief quotations in a book review.

This is a work of fiction. Names, characters, places and incidents either are products of the author's imagination or are used fictitiously. Any resemblance to actual events or locales or persons, living or dead, is entirely coincidental.

Cover Art: By Lyrica Costello

Cover Design: By Fancypants Design

Map Art: By David Cole

Additional Artistic Elements: By Carolina Cruz

To music: I'd never have written a word without you

CONTENTS

PART I: THE ANTIDOTE

1. Kennet Peders Makes a Friend — 3
2. Learning the Stakes before Making Our Bets — 27
3. Bad at Telling the Truth, Bad at Lying — 41
4. An Apathetic Herbalist — 53
5. The Golden Bard — 70
6. A Terrible Tale Told to a Terrible Tail — 88
7. The Things We Do for the Sake of a Child — 107
8. The Journey Back — 122
9. Distillation and Clarification — 136
10. Far from Over — 147

PART II: THE ASSASSIN

1. Asa Attempts to Determine What Counts as an "Adventure" — 171
2. A Philosophy Reinforced, the Dedication to it Challenged — 189
3. Asa of the Isles Makes a Friend — 211
4. A Ballad for a Bastard — 230
5. Asa Gets Their Answers — 252
6. The Inevitable — 269
7. Asa Sings a Song — 287

PART III: ASA

A Letter to Lucien — 305
1. The Singer and the Storyteller — 309
2. Demonstrations of Knowledge and Power — 328
3. Chaos — 344
4. Coming to Terms with Conditions — 359
5. A Moment of Respite — 374
6. Sticks and Stones — 387
7. Fire, Pain and Rebirth — 400
8. The One to Make It — 418
9. The Heart of the Matter — 435

Epilogue	452
Short Story: The New High Priest	459
Acknowledgments	479
About the Author	481
Also by Carolina Cruz	483

BLADLAND
Solstice Summit
Lange's Hut
Brandmora
Hagertrask
Grankoping
Guldfjord
Ornhult
Osternas
Vindmora

PART I: THE ANTIDOTE

CHAPTER 1

KENNET PEDERS MAKES A FRIEND

THE SOUNDS OF BOOTS AGAINST THE STONE WALKWAYS OF the keep echoed and filled the anxious minds of all who could hear them. They knew who was here—knew he was coming. They all knew why. Most thought it was a measure too far, taken out of desperation rather than necessity. Some thought it was a mistake. Others viewed it as their last possible hope, no matter their personal opinions on the newcomer.

And the newcomer? He looked on this as he looked on most of his meetings. It would be needlessly stressful. Things like this always were. But, god willing, it would be over as soon as possible, and he could begin his assignment in earnest with the groundwork out of the way. This was the part of his job he'd never been especially good at.

It was usually easier when the client wasn't rich. If all they had was whatever scraps they could scrounge together to hire him, he could look gracious when he refused some of their pay. He could look like a hero. He liked looking like a hero.

Some jobs were almost impossible to come out of looking like a hero. Impossible for Kennet, at least. There were people who could spin any job to make themselves look good. Kennet was not one of them.

Luckily, this particular job didn't need spinning. Despite the client being especially wealthy and powerful, it was the job itself that would make him look good. Not because of who had hired him, but because of who he was doing it for—and in this case those two things were very different.

"Here we are." The young man who had been leading Kennet through the halls of the keep stopped in front of a door. "His Lordship is waiting for you inside."

Kennet nodded graciously to the man, a servant who had met him at the gates of the keep. He had been half expecting the lord himself to greet him, but when the door opened, Kennet quickly saw why that hadn't happened.

Lord Hagen, a man with dark hair and sad brown eyes, barely glanced up at Kennet's entry. His gaze was fixed on the bed before him, and what was lying in it: a young girl. Kennet had been told that the lord's daughter had fallen ill; that was why he was here. But he hadn't been told just how . . . young the daughter was. How small.

Kennet inclined his head slightly as he stepped up beside the lord, not focusing on his client but instead on the daughter, considering her curiously. She couldn't be older than nine. Her face was pale, unearthly pale. If Kennet hadn't had her father's light but far more lively complexion to compare her to, he might not have been able to imagine what she looked like healthy at all. Her breathing was ragged. Dark bags had formed under her eyes, and her hair was clinging to her forehead in a layer of sweat.

He felt saddened immediately, though not the deep sort of sadness he thought he probably should be feeling. He imagined it might be different if this were a child he knew personally. No, this sadness was hollow. It was more pity than anything else. But still, it was there, and it moved him to speak softly as though his words could disturb her if they were too loud.

"How long has she been like this?"

For a moment, the lord stood still, staring at his child. It took a second to register that the words spoken had been meant for him. He blinked hard as he snapped back into the present and the matter at hand, and a tear fell down his face. The tear was wiped away by a shaking hand, smeared across the lord's cheek as he turned to Kennet with a sad smile.

It struck Kennet, now that he got a good look at his client, how young this man was. One of the youngest he had worked with in some time, without a single streak of grey in his hair. This was in direct contrast to Kennet's own appearance. He wondered if he was truly that much older than the lord, or if the difference in their appearance was due to their vastly opposite lifestyles. If Kennet had been a noble by birth, would he still have the grey streaks through his otherwise mousy brown hair? Would his skin bear the weathering it did, or was that all from exposure to the elements?

He only wondered this for a moment, until he met the lord's eyes, and saw that the grief there had aged them in its own way. Lord Hagen finally answered Kennet's question slowly, as though it had only taken so long to answer because he was finding a way to hold back further tears. "It's been nearly a full moon cycle," he said. "She'll swallow broth, if we're careful, but she's lost so much weight, I—" His voice cracked. "I don't know how much longer she'll last. It isn't as though she'll pass away tonight, but after a few more weeks of this . . ."

Kennet clicked his tongue and returned his attention to the bed. "And you've ruled out any natural causes of illness?"

"As much as we can. We've had every doctor we can afford, they all said the same thing. They said that if it was an illness, they couldn't determine which. Nothing they'd ever seen before, at least."

"That doesn't necessarily rule anything out," Kennet murmured to himself. He had little faith in doctors—so many were of the opinion that if they hadn't heard of an illness personally, it didn't bear looking into, or trying to cure. Sometimes they'd even call it a curse, an affliction of the gods. Anything rather than admit their ignorance.

"No, it wouldn't necessarily," Hagen agreed, to Kennet's surprise. "But as much as I've tried to ignore it, I can't help but be drawn to the only alternative I can consider: poison."

There it was.

The phrase had been present in Hagen's summons to Kennet, but he had wondered if the lord would be confident enough to say it out loud.

"Poison," Kennet repeated. "And who would poison your child?"

"That's the problem, isn't it?" Hagen replied, his voice soft and tense. "I don't know. Who would do something this awful, and in a way that it wouldn't kill her immediately, but instead leave her suffering? Not quite dead but not quite alive and having these fits—gods, the fits she has, Sir Peders. They're violent, and she cries out as though she's in terror. I'm afraid she might injure herself."

"Perhaps you ought to restrain her," Kennet suggested, only realizing after he'd already said it that it might be an insensitive thing to say. Indeed, the lord looked pained to have heard it.

"I can't bring myself to," he said. "She already looks . . . well, look at her!"

Kennet didn't want to. He had already looked at her, and he had felt everything he wanted to feel about the matter. Nevertheless, when asked to, he looked again. Her feebleness struck him once more, along with the sudden realization that he was about to be responsible for her well-being. It was a situation he hesitated to shoulder, but if he didn't, who would? The doctors hadn't been able to help, and if the money of a lord couldn't solve this problem, what could?

Indeed, what could? What could Kennet Peders do that they couldn't?

He wanted to ask Hagen exactly that. He had to know who Kennet was, didn't he? He had hired him knowing what he was capable of, though Kennet wasn't sure where he'd gotten the recommendation. So had he been hired to save the child, or had he been hired to avenge her? He was hardly known for saving children. Taking revenge—that, he was well suited for.

However, when he went to ask the question, he fell silent at the sight of the lord's face. He knew that the sentiment would do no good. It was more than possible that even Hagen didn't know his own true intentions, honestly. Whether Kennet had been hired as an assassin or simply as an investigator, the answer would come when he found whoever had hurt this man's daughter—and it would entirely depend on whether or not it was, at that point, too late to save her.

"I can see that this is hard for you to talk about," Kennet said slowly. "I was told you'd written a report for me. If you wish, I can simply fetch that and read over it tonight, and try to prepare some sort of plan. Tomorrow, we can meet and discuss things further."

Lord Hagen nodded, his face written over with a mixture of relief and gratitude. "Yes. Yes, that will do very well. Thank you."

"Of course, my lord." Kennet gave a shallow bow, then quietly made his way from the room. The lord stayed behind. It seemed like he was terrified to leave, in fear that he may miss his daughter's final moments if he did so much as go and get a drink of water.

The thought made Kennet sick to consider, but he didn't get to dwell on it long, as a servant diverted his focus by handing him a stack of papers. "Your report, sir," he said.

"Thank you." Kennet nodded as he accepted the papers and tucked them under his arm. The servant watched him, and Kennet thought he could detect a hint of awe in the young man. "Can I help you?" he asked, finally, when the man did not move to leave.

"Sorry, sir," the servant said. "It's just, I heard you were coming, and I've heard a lot about you—about the Hawks—just never thought I'd be standing in your presence, that's all."

Kennet raised an eyebrow. "Is that so?"

"Begging your pardon, of course."

Kennet looked the servant over. He almost looked to be a child himself, but for the patch of barely noticeable blond hair that had sprouted from his upper lip. It registered with Kennet that while he and the lord had been speaking, this young man had been rushing to and from the room, doing little things like drawing the curtains as the sun set, or carefully checking that the pillows propping up the lord's daughter up were clean and comfortable. He hadn't slowed down until right this moment. Kennet could see bags under his eyes that rivaled the ones he'd seen on the lord's daughter herself.

An idea occurred to Kennet, one that he wasn't sure was quite appropriate given the circumstances. Nevertheless, it was impossible to shake it after he had thought of it, so he voiced it out loud to the young man next to him.

"You look like you need a drink," he said, with a smile that did its best to shake away all the sadness he'd seen that day. "Join me for one?"

~

DRINKING ALONE WAS PATHETIC, even on the best of days, but today it would've been entirely unacceptable. Luckily, Kennet had now acquired a companion. The young manservant, whose name Kennet had learned to be Gerrit, had jumped at the opportunity to take a break. After a brief aside to let his supervisor know he was leaving, the two had made their way into town. Kennet was happy to know that his authority was enough to grant the boy at least one night of rest. He'd wondered if they would argue, but it seemed nobody was eager to oppose the lord's last hope of saving his daughter. Whatever Kennet wanted, Kennet got. Within reason.

Gerrit was helpful beyond just being someone to take the edge off drinking alone. He also knew where to find the best ale in town, and it wasn't at the inn Kennet had been staying at.

They walked past that inn, toward the southernmost side of town. There was a tavern there that Kennet hadn't even noticed when he'd arrived. That was likely because he'd arrived in Osternas during daylight hours, when the town seemed almost sterile, empty except for the normal hustle and bustle of everyday life. Now, though, after the sun had set, it was far more lively. Outside the entrance of the tavern, a few patrons lingered, talking loudly with each other and greeting newcomers. None of them paid Kennet and his companion particular mind as they walked in—he could hear his name mentioned in the gossip they were taking part in, but it quickly became clear that none of them connected the assassin in their rumors to the man who was walking past them.

That was preferable. If he was immediately recognizable, his job would be a good deal harder.

Gerrit didn't even seem to register the chatter, completely focused on the drink he'd been promised. "Come on, it's this way," he told Kennet, and began to weave through the crowd of people that took up the space between the doorway and the bar.

There wasn't an empty table in the place, Kennet realized. He had rarely seen an establishment so busy. It was the hallmark of a healthy society, even in spite of the anguish their leader seemed to be in at the moment. Kennet made an internal note to ask the people of Osternas how they felt about their lord. At the moment, it was hard to imagine that any of these people harbored ill will toward him, but at the very least, maybe they would know who did.

Gerrit, also, would likely be helpful for that. If only they could find a place to sit and talk . . .

"I'll get the drinks," Gerrit said presently, cheerfully. "I know the tavern owner, so she'll help us out. Why don't you find us a seat in the meantime?" He suddenly seemed to remember that he wasn't talking to an old friend, but rather to a seasoned sword-for-hire. "Sir," he added hastily.

"Wonderful idea, Master Gerrit." Kennet clapped him on the shoulder with the warmest smile he could muster. It would be useful to have the young man feel comfortable—that was how he'd be able to get the best information. Not to mention, he genuinely did want the boy to relax. There was nothing to be gained from keeping him stressed. Some might thrive on exercises of power, using their reputation to keep others cowering, but it was hard for Kennet to see the use for that.

As Gerrit made his way toward the bar, Kennet turned his attention to the room around him. Most of the seating came in the form of big wooden tables that were arranged in rows and were completely occupied. Against the wall, however, were more secluded booths: round tables with benches that wrapped around them, and wooden separators. These were also occupied, mostly by groups, except for one. One had a single person sitting in it with a big mug of ale, a lute as their only companion.

Best bet that I've seen, Kennet remarked internally, and set his bearing. He made his way through the tables and toward the booth in the corner.

The table's sole occupant looked up as he approached, raising one bushy eyebrow and looking him over. Kennet allowed the examination. He attempted another warm smile, and gave a slight nod as a greeting.

"Hello, friend," he said.

"A friend, am I?" They cocked their head to one side. They were considering Kennet with such an idle curiosity, he wondered if they would instantly dismiss him. Then, completely contrary to his expectations, a smile broke out over the stranger's face. "Well! What kind of friend would I be if I didn't invite you to sit? Please, sit," they insisted, gesturing to the bench across from them.

"Thank you," Kennet said brightly, and he slid into the seat, grunting as he finally felt the relief of sitting after a long day on his feet. He could feel the stranger's eyes still on him as he did so.

"If we are friends, I think I should know your name," they said.

Kennet almost used a fake name—reflex, at this point— but he remembered it would be nearly impossible to maintain that level of privacy with Gerrit around. So he told the truth instead. "My name is Kennet Peders," he said. "And you, then, how should I refer to you?"

"Your friend's name is Asa of the Isles."

That caught his attention, the mention of the Isles. Could they mean the eastern Isles, all the way across the sea? Now that he looked at them, that made sense. They had dark curly hair, and a deeper skin tone, both features that were common to the island nation of Lucien. Beyond that, there was their accent. It was strong, and they paused on some words—they favored flowery language, but it wasn't coming easily to them. Bladstongue was certainly not their first language, and though Kennet had only ever met Luciens in passing, the accent was consistent with what he remembered. So Lucien it was. Why someone from the Isles would come this far west was anybody's guess—and likewise, none of Kennet's business.

Once he had determined that much about them, he began to notice a few more things about their appearance. Not their innate appearance—golden brown skin, deep brown eyes, dark curls as he had already remarked on to himself—but rather, their clothes. They were a bard, he realized. They must be. The coordination of their clothing gave it away. Everything was warm oranges and yellows, from their doublet to the striking yellow liner that they wore under their eyes. This styling was purposeful and meticulous. It matched the detailing on what he had first assumed was a lute, but now saw was something slightly different, with a more hourglass shape than the typical teardrop structure of a lute. The filigree on the instrument brought the entire thing up from an outfit to a costume, and the person themself from a musician to a performer.

"Lucien?" Kennet circled around to the first point. The second seemed so obvious now he was surprised at himself for not picking up on it immediately.

"Ah, so you know of it." Asa of the Isles seemed almost entirely unsurprised. "You seem to be a well-traveled fellow. I assume you aren't from around here, then."

Before Kennet could say anything about their rather uncharitable impression of the people in this town—however correct they may have been—Gerrit had returned with a pint of ale in each hand.

"Sir Peders!" he said cheerfully. "And . . . friend."

"I really am everyone's friend, aren't I?" Asa said, their voice betraying a bit of bitterness from their solitude being interrupted further, but they gestured for Gerrit to join them.

"You're a bard?" Gerrit perked up when he noticed the musical instrument next to them. "Oh, excellent! It's so quiet in here, it's borderline maddening."

Apparently the clamoring conversation from all the other patrons meant nothing to Gerrit, since Kennet would have hardly called the environment quiet. He could, however, admit that some music would be nice. Unfortunately, Asa shook their head at Gerrit's observation.

"No, I've not been permitted to play here," they said with

a roll of their eyes. "I don't know enough popular drinking songs for these parts, apparently."

"Oh," Gerrit said, and his attention was immediately diverted from the bard back his drink. Kennet, on the other hand, became intrigued.

"You've offered already?"

"I've been here for a couple days at this point, and I've tried to pick up on the local favorites, but . . ." They shrugged. "So coin has been hard to come by. Some people appreciate songs from my country. Nobody here, though."

"Quite unfortunate."

"'Twould be less unfortunate," Asa said as they stretched their arms out over their head, "if the man they *did* have playing wasn't such a . . ." They struggled for the word, abandoning their stretch to gesture with both hands as though they would be able to pull the term they were searching for out of thin air.

"Buffoon?" supplied Gerrit, looking up from his drink finally.

"Yes, that's it."

As if on cue, a loud, dramatic riff on a lute demanded the attention of the entire tavern, including those in its corner booth. Asa didn't so much as flinch at the sudden instrumental, while Gerrit and Kennet both tried to trace the sound to its source. Eventually, Kennet located the stage, and saw the man on it. He was drab, with dirty blond hair and a much less composed costume than the bard whose table Kennet had found himself at. This man sang loudly, without so much as waiting for the crowd's full attention. No captive audience here—at most, they seemed to be tolerating his shaking, weak voice as it warbled just above the notes of the lute.

Kennet cringed, but tried to be gracious in his phrasing. "He's . . ."

"Awful," Gerrit finished for him, with feeling, and Asa

cracked the first genuine smile Kennet had seen from them since they'd sat down.

"Honestly," they agreed. They crossed their arms, and leaned back in the booth with satisfaction. "I'm glad my friends have some taste."

The noise was almost unbearable, but Gerrit seemed to have found a way to deal with it—burying himself in his drink. Kennet decided to join him, taking a heavy swig of his own ale. Luckily, unlike the entertainment, this tavern held its own when it came to drinks. It was smooth, and went down easy, and he found himself halfway through the pint before he knew it. With some relief he noted that the ale had taken the edge off the music, and he was able to relax finally. He propped himself up against the wall of the booth, and gave a contented sigh.

Asa had started to ignore their new tablemates the moment they had stopped talking to them, which was fine. It was just as well, on top of that, that the bard wasn't from the area. That meant they were likely not a threat, and he could talk freely to Gerrit with them around. Likely. It didn't mean for certain that they weren't connected to this; there was always a chance.

But that was a chance he would have to take, because if he let Gerrit keep drinking, it would become harder and harder to get the information he needed.

"Gerrit," Kennet said, under the shrill tones of the music, "I've been meaning to ask you some questions about all this."

Gerrit looked a little confused. "About the bar?"

"No, about Lord Hagen and his daughter."

The color that had been rising in Gerrit's face as he drank suddenly drained a fraction, and his eyes widened. "Don't you have the report for all of that?" he said weakly.

"The report is a fine start, but you've been present for all of it. I'd much rather get perspective from a direct witness."

Gerrit sighed. "I suppose I shouldn't argue. I just don't know if I'll be of any help."

"I'm sure you'll be surprised," Kennet said reassuringly, and Gerrit visibly relaxed. "I won't ask anything too hard, and if you don't know something, just say you don't know. I'm not looking for you to solve all my problems over a drink and a chat."

"I'll do my best, then," Gerrit said with renewed confidence.

Kennet nodded. He started his line of questioning with an easy one. "Did the girl complain of any strange tastes in her food the night she took ill?"

Gerrit gave an eager nod. It seemed this was something he knew without effort. "She said her food tasted wrong, though she didn't mention exactly in what way."

"Do you not have tasters at the keep, anything like that?"

"No, we never saw the need. And on top of that, His Lordship disapproves of putting others at risk for his own sake."

"A good man, His Lordship," Kennet muttered to himself.

"A very good man," Gerrit agreed with feeling. "He's been very good to all of us, which is why this is so distressing."

"And confusing," Kennet added. "If he's so well-loved, this makes even less sense. Tell me, does Lord Hagen have any enemies?"

"Oh, plenty," Gerrit said, taking another swig of his ale, "on account of he's the king's son and all."

Kennet, who had been in the middle of a sip himself, almost choked on his drink. "What?" he sputtered, and glanced over at Asa. The bard didn't seem to have heard anything, but nonetheless, Kennet grabbed Gerrit by the shoulder and pulled him closer, repeating his question in much more hushed tones. "What did you say? The prince?"

"W-well, yes," Gerrit stuttered, dropping his own voice.

"I thought the prince was disowned."

"Not quite. That's what the king told everyone, but Hagen left of his own accord. Wanted to get away from the pressures of princehood."

Kennet's expression must have betrayed exactly what he was thinking—that this would have been nice to know sooner—because Gerrit became immediately caught up in trying to explain himself.

"He's never told anyone, outside of the staff. Nobody knows."

"Surely that's not true. Somebody *must* know, or this wouldn't have happened. Have you told anyone?"

"No! No—and I wouldn't have told you, either, if it weren't important to your investigation."

"So nobody knows."

"Nobody that shouldn't!"

Gerrit seemed to fully believe what he was saying, but it wasn't the boy's honesty that Kennet doubted. It was his logic. Kennet knew better. Information that rich didn't stay off tongues for long. Rumors spread quickly.

While Lord Hagen—the prince—might not have enemies, the king certainly would. Any number of the targets on the king's back could very easily be transferred to the king's only son, no matter how estranged that son was.

Important information indeed. Kennet would have to scold His Lordship for keeping it from him.

"Should I give my friends some privacy?" a voice called from across the table. Asa had finally noticed their strange behavior.

"No." Kennet straightened up. "He just delivered me some . . . news. Slightly personal, but nothing we need to kick you off the table for."

"Good. I was here first, after all." They paused as the song that had been playing died down, and the beginning of a new one took its place. "I can't take much more of this."

"Are you really that much better?" Gerrit teased. Kennet

shot him a look, surprised that the ale had taken the manservant to this level of confidence.

Asa seemed equally surprised, but also slightly impressed. "I am," they said.

"Too bad we'll never get to hear you and know for sure." Gerrit poked them further.

"Is that so?" Another smile began to pull at Asa's lips, revealing a gap between their front teeth that Kennet noticed now for the first time. "Well." Before either man could make any further comments, Asa had risen to their feet, their hand on the neck of their instrument. They leaned in over the table toward them, and said in a conspiratorial whisper, "Watch this."

Gerrit seemed grateful for a break from the interrogation, and while Kennet didn't exactly feel the same way, he could admit to being intrigued by the bard's intentions. He watched them as they made their way across the room, with their instrument in hand and a steadiness to their step.

The bard stepped up to the small stage and stood at its base, watching the other performer intently. Kennet realized that he and Gerrit were the only members of the crowd who had noticed this movement, but that didn't stay the case for long. One by one the bar's patrons noticed the golden character at the stage and their hawk-like focus on the man singing. Eventually, the singer himself noticed, too.

At first he seemed to try to ignore them and carry on singing, but his already weak voice faltered. In an effort to save face, he stopped his playing abruptly.

"Can I help you?" he asked.

"Yes!" Asa replied brightly. "Get off the stage."

"What?" the other bard sputtered.

"It would be a great help." Asa's tone was falsely innocent. "Since you offered."

Kennet's gaze flicked back and forth between the two bards, wondering if the one would give up his stage easily, or if he would pick a fight. Asa hardly seemed a physical titan, but Kennet had learned not to judge people by their stature, and there was this lingering sense about them. Whatever it was, it made Kennet hesitant to make any bets against them. Perhaps it was their pure confidence.

"You've been told they don't need your services here," the singer said, "so take your songs and find somewhere that does."

"I think I've found it. You might say I'm not needed, but I say they simply don't know what they're missing."

"And they never shall. Be on your way, friend."

Asa's eyebrow twitched, enough that Kennet could see the motion from where he sat. "Now, I've been called 'friend' by a good many tonight, but you're the first one who I don't really believe means it."

"And how did you figure that one out?"

Asa considered the question. Then they took a step up the stairs to the stage.

"Hey now," said the singer. It was incredible how quickly his voice filled with panic. "What do you think you're doing?"

"Take a break, friend," Asa replied, taking another step. "Have a drink. I'll hold the stage for you in the meantime."

"This is my stage. This is my night!"

"And so it shall remain!" Asa said soothingly. "I promise I won't take a cent of your earnings."

"Get off the stage now, I'm warning you—"

SMACK.

Kennet started in his seat as the golden bard let loose with the back of their hand, striking the man on stage across the face before they had so much as fully laid foot on the platform.

The man staggered back. His face was white as a sheet, and Kennet could see that tears had started to form in his eyes. Had Asa really struck him that hard? Then, the man onstage began to shake. Kennet's expression remained unchanged, but internally he was shocked. He had seen enough men get slapped in his day to know that most don't react with immediate tears and trembling.

He also knew that nobody as indignant as this man had been would immediately surrender after a single blow. He fully expected more to follow, a full-blown bar brawl headed by the bards. But instead, his intrigue only grew as the man continued to stumble backward until he had backed off the stage entirely, holding his hands up the entire time in a pitiful display of defense and surrender.

The bar was silent. Kennet's gaze snapped back to Asa, who was looking directly at him. They were grinning as they winked, and took the last step up onto the stage full of the same confidence they had approached it with.

Everyone watched them as they readied their instrument and, with one look over the crowd, began to play.

The difference between the two musicians was instantly noticeable. The bard before Asa had barely been worthy of the label of "competent." He had been about as good as one could expect from a small town, but Asa played differently. They played like Kennet had never heard, a style he knew had to be Lucien in influence. The newness of it washed over him like the first few drops of a spring rain. He relished in it—the melody had more variance. Their fingers moved quickly on the neck of the instrument, flourishing where flourishes were hardly needed.

Their fancy playing died down with a soft, trilling embellishment before they paused their playing entirely, letting their voice take their instrument's place in the ears of the patrons.

"*Eu conheci uma garota nas margens de um rio.*"

They played again, the same strings, and then stopped again to sing the next line.

"*Ela carregava um pacote de plátanos maduros.*"

This time when they launched back into the instrumental,

they sang along with it. Their voice was strong and clear, ringing out over their masterful playing in a way that Kennet found captivating. One quick glance around the bar and he found that the same could be said for most of the others there, his companion included. Gerrit was watching, enraptured, his mug of ale pressed to his chest.

So, the bard did well to have such pride in their playing. It was well-founded.

But Kennet's mind kept coming back to the blow they had struck on their rival bard, and what had followed. As he replayed it over and over in his head, he wondered if he was reading too much into it. Perhaps the other bard had truly been a coward, unable to cope with being struck first. Perhaps Kennet had only imagined the tears in the man's eyes. Perhaps Asa had simply struck the man really, really hard.

Or . . .

Or what?

What was the other option?

There wasn't one, so he put the thoughts out of his mind, and refocused on the music.

Most of what he'd heard of Lucien customs and music had been from a distance at docks, or secondhand from a friend who had lived near the country, not in it. Though that friend had only had favorable things to say of the island country and its people, she hadn't offered many details beyond the food she enjoyed and their colorful clothing.

Honestly, description wouldn't have done this music justice.

It was a treat to hear it for himself.

There was also something to be said about watching an artist who had perfected their craft. It was infectious, and attractive. The bard hadn't been unattractive to begin with, of course. Kennet wasn't blind. But the way they performed only added to the allure, and Kennet found himself leaning in, propped up against the table. For a moment, he let himself get lost in the music. Then he remembered why he was in the tavern in the first place.

That little girl, lying in pain in her bed.

It hit like a wave of ice cold water, shocking and sobering.

He had to focus on his job.

The fact that the lord was a prince by birth was important, but knowing the motive wouldn't get him very far. Having not read the report he'd been handed, he still didn't know whether his objective was to find the culprit. He highly doubted it. His focus needed to be less on the motivation, and more on the cure.

And for a cure for poison, there were only a few people he could think to reach out to for help. He didn't particularly want to talk to either, and it didn't help that only one of them was likely to ever want to speak to him again, even slightly. Nevertheless, he would have to swallow his pride and approach her. She was already on his mind, with the bard and the mention of the continent across the sea—perhaps this was meant to be. She didn't live far. He'd likely be able to make the journey in a few days. Any of his other resources were much farther away, and time was of the essence.

His choice had been made for him.

This job was going to be one inconvenience after another, wasn't it?

He looked back up toward the stage, almost absentmindedly, noting that the song seemed to be coming to a close.

Just in time. Asa caught his eye and held his gaze as they bowed. They smiled widely, and Kennet felt as though the expression was meant just for him.

He felt slightly guilty for having practically ignored the last half of their performance, before he realized that every member of the audience likely felt as though it had been played just for them. Asa was a talented performer, and even performers with the littlest amount of talent knew to charm an audience that way. He scolded himself for letting himself feel special, then sighed inwardly, crediting the emotion to the artist. He didn't need to be ashamed—it just meant their whole display was effective. Like a colorful bird.

The eyes of every person in the room followed Asa as they, true to their word, relinquished the stage once more.

Their predecessor seemed hesitant, approaching the stage as though it might bite him, as though Asa had somehow laid a trap. Upon resuming his place in front of the crowd, though, he found that the only thing waiting for him was mild disinterest. Asa had stolen the hearts of the crowd, and they weren't so willing to give them back. When he began to sing, it was like the color that Asa had lent to the room was drained out once more. The conversations that had paused for the striking performance resumed now, and the tavern returned to normal.

Asa took their place across from Kennet at the table again.

"So, how was that?" they asked, getting comfortable once more. "Was I that much better?"

"And more," Gerrit said emphatically.

Asa beamed. "I thought so," they said matter-of-factly, but Kennet could see the proud glint in their eye at the approval. A barmaid approached with a mug of ale, stopping at Asa's side with a smile on her face.

"That was somethin', good bard," she said. "For the record, I told Missus Lauer that you ought to be allowed to play."

"Well, maybe now that you know what I can do . . .?" Asa took the ale and gave her a hopeful look. The barmaid sighed.

"We'll have to see," she said. "I make no promises, but if more folks keep buying you drinks, she'll see it's good for business."

"Wonderful!" Asa grinned and pulled a coin out of the purse that hung at their side, handing it to the barmaid.

"That's for you," they added, and turned their attention to their drink.

The tip made the barmaid smile wider, though she hovered for a moment, probably wondering if Asa would ask who the drink had come from. They didn't. Kennet assumed it must be a cultural thing, or perhaps Asa was so used to receiving drinks for their efforts that they had learned to save time by not asking. Or perhaps they were just cocky. Or any combination of the three, honestly.

The barmaid eventually slipped away, leaving the three alone in the booth again. Kennet sat lost in thought as she walked away, wondering if now would be an appropriate time to excuse himself from the table to work more on his assignment. He glanced out of the corner of his eye at Asa, who was immediately occupied by the ale in their hands. Gerrit's gaze was still glued to them. Kennet couldn't blame him. If he didn't have work to do, he'd likely feel the same way.

"What was the song about?" Gerrit asked. "It was beautiful."

"Ah, thank you." Asa wiped a mustache of foam from the ale off their upper lip. "It's an older song from the Isles. You'll probably find this funny—it's really just a list of foods. The narrator meets a girl and she makes him dinner, and the song is about what she cooks for him. It's catchy, and the lyrics are harmless if someone unfamiliar with them finds themselves singing along. Though"—they paused, considering their ale—"it's always funny to sing a dirty one, and have foreigners sing along thinking it's about love or something." They gave a little snicker at their own mischief.

Gerrit laughed along with them, but Kennet couldn't find it within himself to join the merriment. Asa noticed this.

"Did I not please you?" they asked, their accent nearly overshadowing the words themselves as they sat up straighter. "Was that not impressive?"

"Oh, no, very impressive," Kennet said. "I just have . . . more pressing matters on my mind, I suppose."

In truth, it was all he could do to focus on the "more pressing matters" in the presence of the bard. The battle between enjoying their company and thinking about a dying child was not a battle Kennet wanted to keep fighting, so he began to slide out of the booth, and stood up, giving a mild bow.

Asa raised an eyebrow, visibly put out by his attitude. "Well! Don't let me keep you, then."

"I don't mean to be rude," Kennet sighed.

"Then don't be! And you haven't been," they added. "I promise, I'll only take it personally until this mug is empty." They winked at him, and raised the mug. "Good luck with your 'pressing matters,' whatever they may be."

Kennet finally smiled again, taking their words as a promise and giving them another little bow before he turned and made his way out of the tavern.

He'd gotten information that he needed, that's what was important. It was crucial information, too. The fact that the food had tasted off was particularly significant. He wished that the child was conscious to give him any further details—though, if she were conscious, he wouldn't feel so much pressure. God, did he feel pressure.

He said a soft prayer under his breath as he made his way through the empty streets in the moonlight. He hadn't worshiped the god for very long. He hadn't felt the need to, but as of late it was becoming more and more important. If his god cared about life as much as he said he did, then he would lend some goodwill to Kennet's assignment. Perhaps even a divine gift, some kind of helping hand.

Or not.

Honestly, just asking for a little help made him feel better. Even if he wasn't sure the god would listen, or even if he cared, asking was better than nothing. Had more of a chance of working than if he didn't ask at all, at least.

The god's direct help wasn't the point though. Kennet worshiped Gethin, god of Life and Death. Well, worship was a light term. More accurately, he knew that the religion existed and he knew the creed it followed.

I will do what I must

To celebrate life

And prevent it from ending

If I must die

I will die

If I must kill

I will kill

Those were the only words Kennet knew when it came to the god, but they were words he'd chosen to live by. And whether or not Gethin was going to step in and help him directly, the creed itself was what drove him to help the child in the first place.

So, in a way, hadn't the god already helped?

Kennet was starting to get a headache.

There was a reason he'd never been religious before. It was all a little too philosophical for him. Best to focus on what he was good at: problem solving.

He reached his inn just as he was about to have a religious crisis. Perfect timing. The street-level rooms were bustling, and a cacophony of drunk voices sounded from down the hall. Kennet counted himself lucky that he was staying on the second floor as he passed a particularly noisy room to get to the stairs.

When he was finally in his own room, he shut the door behind him and breathed a sigh of relief.

The report was still in one of his pockets, folded neatly. And so it would remain—he had the thought to read it, but when his fingertips brushed the paper he felt overcome by exhaustion at the idea. There would be time to read it before he went to the keep tomorrow. Even better that he wait, so it would be fresh in his mind when he spoke to the lord—the prince.

For now, he fell back into the rough wool pad that the inn passed off as a mattress, and sighed.

A long day over. Tomorrow promised to be just as long.

He hoped that at least the night would be long and resting enough to make up for it.

CHAPTER 2

LEARNING THE STAKES BEFORE MAKING OUR BETS

Kennet rose before the sun, as he usually did. He found that waking before sunrise gave him time he sorely needed to get right with the world before he had to face it. It also gave him time to perform his little morning routine—something that kept him grounded no matter where he found himself. It wasn't much, and it certainly wasn't ratified by any church. There was a church for the god he worshiped, yes, but Kennet knew next to nothing about it. And really, whose business was it how he practiced his religion, or even if he knew how to? It was his, and nobody else's.

He got dressed first. It was important to him that he not meditate in his sleep-clothes. That, of all things, seemed irreverent. Surely one should count meditation as one of their important day-to-day activities rather than just rolling out of bed and into it. So he got out of bed and washed his face in the basin of cold water that was set up by the door. There was a rough towel lying next to it to dry his face with, but he opted to use the front of his sleep shirt before he pulled it over his head and dug through his belongings to find a clean shirt to wear for the day.

Keeping appearances had been hard when he'd first

started traveling, but he'd gotten used to it. He'd found that having one consistent piece of clothing made everything else he wore matter a lot less. In this case, it was a long leather coat that doubled as armor with its thick padding on the upper arms and chest. Bladland's weather never got particularly hot, but it could get bitterly cold, so the coat was invaluable for warmth as well as for the intimidating flair it lent to his appearance. And on top of that, it covered up everything he wore underneath, so as long as his shirts were comfortable, he found nothing else really mattered.

Satisfied that he had found a clean shirt, he pulled it on over his head, slipped into his pants, and laced up his boots. That was clothed enough for now, so he finished this step in his morning routine by tying his hair out of his face with a leather strap.

Finally, he was presentable enough to start his day.

He got back into bed.

Not to sleep, of course, but to meditate. He crossed his legs underneath him, and folded his hands in his lap.

It wasn't quite praying. He'd never learned how to pray properly, and honestly, he didn't feel that it was crucial to know. Really, he thought it was enough to take a little moment each day to remember the creed and reflect on it. Reflect on his recent actions, and whether or not they aligned with his morals—or at least, the morals he was trying to keep up with.

So far, he thought, *I think I'm doing pretty well.*

He had found that different parts of the creed stuck with him on different days. Oftentimes it was the lines about dying, or killing. But not today. Today, it was the very first line.

I will do what I must.

Because arguably, what he *must* do this time was worse than killing, or dying. He had to revisit old wounds, wounds he wasn't sure had ever healed.

Hopefully he wouldn't *have* to. Maybe it wasn't a must. Maybe it was an "I *might have to* do what I must," instead of a "*will*." Ideally that would be the case. He wouldn't be able to waste much time looking for an alternative to it, but he could at least check a few other apothecaries on the way to his old . . . connection.

Maybe he wouldn't have to go all the way there after all.

Maybe, maybe, maybe.

Kennet clicked his tongue as he realized he'd been clenching his jaw and tensing his shoulders. He forced himself to relax. If he had to go to those lengths, then he would. It wasn't a question. In order to protect the girl, Marna, he would do what he had to do.

With his mind made up, he decided that the meditation had served its purpose, and opened his eyes. The sun had risen by now, and rays of light peeked through the window behind him. Kennet stretched and sighed. No use holding things up any longer. It was time he went to talk to Lord Hagen about their options.

The report hadn't had any new information, really, Kennet reflected as he pulled his coat on and buckled it shut. No, the report Hagen had given him had actually been next to useless. It hadn't told him of the odd taste the girl had reported, or of Hagen's birthright. Of course, he wouldn't have expected the latter to be included. He still hadn't decided whether or not he ought to bring it up today.

He would probably have to.

Not looking forward to that, he remarked inwardly as he made his way out of the inn and into the streets. The air was cool but not cold. Spring had recently given in fully to summer, but Osternas was a coastal city, and that kept it considerably less hot than it could have been—cool enough that he didn't have to abandon his coat at all, most days.

He was looking forward to summer's end, though. Autumn was his favorite of the seasons, and he hoped that he would finish this job in time to be able to fully enjoy it. The warm hues that the leaves would take, the crisp air . . . it all seemed so close.

The color of the changing leaves was still on his mind as he neared the keep, and he saw those same colors in the form of a vaguely familiar figure who was standing at the gates. They were arguing with the guards, loud and animated, gesturing with their hands in apparent annoyance. While most of their words were in Bladstongue, he noted as he approached that with their increasing irritation came a string of Isla, the language of Lucien. He didn't understand any of it, but he guessed that they were punctuating their frustration with the curses of their native tongue.

He only stood behind them a moment before the guards caught his eye and relief wrote itself over their faces. Kennet interrupted the display before they could greet him.

"Asa?" he said, loudly enough that they would hear him over their own mutterings.

The bard spun around immediately when they heard his voice, and lit up. "Kennet Peders!" they said brightly, an abrupt change of tone. "Fancy meeting you here!"

"I was about to say the same thing." He looked at the guards, then back to Asa. "Some kind of trouble?"

"Oh no, nothing you need to worry about," they said with a sigh. "I just heard that the lord's daughter was in pain, having fits at night and such. Your friend last night, young Gerrit—he told me."

Kennet cringed. Of course Gerrit hadn't been able to keep his mouth shut. "Ah, and that brought you to the keep to . . . what, play her a song?"

Asa scoffed, their expression immediately falling into an unimpressed glare. "No. I do believe in the healing power of music, but I actually have something far more potent at my disposal—which is what I was trying to explain to the guards here before you arrived." They turned their glare from

Kennet back toward the guards. "But! Enough about me. Why are you here?"

Anyone else would have connected Kennet's name to the girl's mysterious illness at this point, realizing it had to be more than a simple sickness. But Kennet realized that Asa's lack of familiarity extended beyond just the popular songs of the country—they had no way of knowing his occupation, or the reputation that came with it. "I'm here to see Lord Hagen, actually."

For a moment, Asa seemed confused by this information. But rather than question him, they quickly turned to optimism. "Oh! Perhaps you can help me, then. Speak to the lord, get me to his daughter's side. I promise I can help."

"Is that so?" Kennet tried to hide the skepticism in his tone. "And how is that, exactly? I'm afraid I'm still a little unclear on that point."

"That's what I was trying to get out of them, sir," one of the guards interjected, "but they won't say."

"It's too hard to explain." Asa waved their hands. "But I swear, I mean nothing but goodwill toward her. I just want to ease her suffering. Won't you allow her that?"

The guard looked over Asa's head, toward Kennet. The expression on her face was clear, though she couldn't say it out loud. The girl had been poisoned. If someone was this desperate to get to her side, there was an equal chance—no, maybe even a majority chance—that their true intent was to finish what the poison had started. It would be foolish to trust such a vague claim. The guards would not let Asa in.

Kennet couldn't blame them. "That's not much to go on, friend," he said, aware that he sounded patronizing. Asa took it that way, too, scowling at his words.

"Ah, so you're no help either," they said, adding another string of muttered Isla under their breath. "Fine! Let your precious lord's precious daughter die in pain, for all I care! I can't say I didn't try!"

Kennet blinked in surprise at their harsh words, and tried to reach a hand out to console them, but they were already walking away. In their wake, they left the guards and Kennet stunned to silence. For a moment, they all stood still.

"What an odd duck!" one of the guards said finally. "Sorry about that, Sir Peders."

"No, no, it's not your fault. I met them at the tavern last night and they seemed just fine then. It's possible that they're telling the truth."

"They're either bad at telling the truth or a bad liar, because they certainly aren't convincing," the guard replied, then stood aside, unlocking the gate. "His Lordship is waiting for you."

Kennet nodded to her his thanks, but cast one last look over his shoulder toward the bard's vanishing form before he went through the gate. Whatever that was about, it would have to at least wait until after he had met with the lord. Selfishly, though, he was a bit happy that he had an excuse to seek them out. They had been intriguing from the start, and now on top of that, they were part of his investigation. This behavior had been shifty enough to make sure of that.

He hoped to god that they were just bad at telling the truth. Otherwise, he might have to kill them, and he really didn't want to do that.

Gerrit was standing by the door to Marna's room. With the way his face looked, Kennet was astonished to find the young man was standing. He must have kept drinking long after Kennet left—while he was sure that Gerrit had needed the relief, it had been a foolish decision on his part. Not only had he let too much information slip, but it seemed that the hangover was treating him terribly. His long blond hair was tied back haphazardly, framing his bleary-eyed face at random. He quickly tried to pull himself together when he noticed Kennet.

"Good morning, Sir Peders!" he said with false cheer.

"Good morning, Master Gerrit!" Kennet matched his energy with equal sincerity, though there was a note of teasing in his voice. "Sleep well?"

"Oh, absolutely, sir." Gerrit's lie was followed by a particularly wet belch that he tried and failed to hide behind his hand. "Sorry."

"I ran into our friend from the Isles at the gate this morning," Kennet said. "I handled it, but perhaps you shouldn't drink so much if it makes you prone to telling tall tales."

Gerrit's face flushed. He opened his mouth to defend himself, then clapped it shut again. "Yes, sir," he said in shame.

"Good man." Kennet smiled. "Like I said, I handled it. Perhaps you ought to buy the guards something nice, or throw a few coins their way. They'll probably keep it all between us if you play your cards right."

"Yes, sir."

"Gerrit." Kennet ducked his head to catch the eye contact that Gerrit had been avoiding. "I'm not angry, you know."

Gerrit looked immediately relieved. "You're not?"

"No, I'm not. You're young, it happens. Just don't do it again."

"I won't, sir."

Kennet was sure he wouldn't, not after a lecture from someone like himself. That was one thing he loved about this profession. He got to look intense and intimidating, and then when people least expected it . . . he got to be kind.

The door swung open slowly, and Kennet saw that the lord was sitting by his daughter's bedside again. He wondered if Hagen had moved at all since the night before. Probably not. Kennet cleared his throat as he approached, and Hagen looked up.

"Sir Peders." He greeted Kennet quietly. "Did you read the report I gave you?"

Kennet nodded. "I did."

"And . . .?"

"Respectfully, Your Lordship, I think you should have included your relationship with your father in the report. I had to find out from your staff."

Hagen's expression shifted first to anger, then understanding. "I didn't think it was relevant."

"It's incredibly relevant, Lordship. It widens the pool of suspects a great deal."

"And how does that matter in finding a cure?"

Kennet tried to think of a way to explain it simply. "If someone doesn't like you, a lord, then they're likely one of your subjects. Your particular subjects are well enough off, but they still have very limited resources. Their access to poisons wouldn't be all that vast, and I wouldn't have to worry. But let's say the person who did this is not after you, or your daughter. Let's say he's after the king. Not only that, but he knows who you are to the king. What kind of person would know all that?"

Hagen seemed to be getting the picture. He furrowed his brows and crossed his arms. "A rich person," he said slowly.

"Right. So, the list of possible poisons, and by extension possible antidotes, has now tripled. The solution may be much more complex. If I hadn't found out about your lineage, I might have missed something very important simply because I didn't know to look."

Kennet was used to scolding his clients over stuff like this. They always thought their secrets were unimportant no matter how huge they were. But there could be no secrets between them, not if Kennet was going to be able to work. And there was no way to politely and respectfully tell them that, even if they *were* a lord.

Luckily, Hagen clearly understood the gravity of his mistake as he nodded, and his next words carried a tone of apology. "I'll not keep anything more from you," he said. "You're right, my father has many enemies and most of them are rich. I hadn't thought that any of them would go this far, but now that you mention it, assumptions like that are risky in these circumstances."

"Then I'll need as much information as you can give me so I can work quickly on this. We don't need to waste time on speculating who did it; I've made as many inferences as I can based on that. What I need to know is what kind of poison it was so I can find a cure."

"Everything we know is in the report," Hagen said tiredly, his momentary apologetics slipping into the same despair he'd had before.

"Not quite. Did she complain about any flavors? Any symptoms before she slipped away?" Kennet knew this couldn't be easy for Hagen to think about, so he paused. "If it's too hard to talk about, we can always write another—"

He was cut off by movement from the bed. For a brief splinter of a second he wondered if by some miracle the child was awake. Those hopes were quickly dashed by reality as Hagen jumped to his feet and Kennet realized this must be one of the fits he'd been told about.

Not many things would cause a man like Kennet to freeze and lose track of what needed to be done in any given moment. He prided himself on being a quick thinker. But nothing he'd seen in his life thus far was quite as shocking or upsetting as seeing this small girl convulse, her eyes snapping open to show nothing but the whites. Her father grabbed the cup off the table near her, just in time to avoid Marna hitting it. As if to bring Kennet back to reality, she screamed, a shrill and panicked sound. He couldn't make out any words, just her voice and a sense of terror.

When Kennet finally broke out of his haze to try and hold her down, he was stopped by the surprisingly strong arm of Lord Hagen holding him back.

"Don't!" he said, breathlessly. "The doctors said not to hold her down. They said it could do more harm than good."

"Can we do nothing more than watch?" Kennet asked.

The lord did not respond, but Kennet could hear that he was saying something under his breath—counting. When Marna finally lay still again, he didn't relax. He set the cup back down and scooped up a piece of paper from the ground. "Check her pulse please," he said, leaning on the bedside table as he wrote something down on the paper.

Kennet did as he was told, pressing two fingers to the girl's wrists. "She's still alive. And breathing," he added, checking the latter vitals. "God, I'm sorry. That's even worse than I'd imagined."

Hagen was quiet for a moment, finishing his writing, but when he registered what Kennet had said he gave a little scoff of laughter. "I'm sorry too," he said, as he straightened up and looked toward Kennet again. Kennet stole a glance at what he had been writing and saw that he had simply added a line to a growing list of numbers. His heart sank even further.

"I will do whatever I can to help her," Kennet said, not moving from her side. He looked back down at her and the fresh sheen of sweat that had appeared on her brow. Her dark hair was slick with the stuff, and though her eyes had closed, he could see they were twitching under the lids. "I promise."

"Thank you. I'm sorry I haven't been more helpful. But to answer your question . . ." His demeanor had shifted just slightly, as though the danger of the fit had brought him to his senses in some way. Sure enough, when Kennet met his gaze, it looked sharper. "She ate the same thing as I did, she usually does. She's not the type to complain, but she did mention—not to me, but to the cook—that the food tasted funny. The cook and Marna are good friends, almost like sisters. She invited Marna to come down to the kitchens and tell her what she should change for the next time. Likely she's the one you should talk to about it."

Kennet nodded seriously and stepped away from the bed.

"I'll do that. Thank you, Your Lordship. I'll get what information I can, and move out as soon as possible."

Lord Hagen nodded. Finally, he allowed himself to look back down at his daughter again, and almost immediately Kennet watched him fade back into despair. Well, that was unfortunately all that could be expected of him. Kennet left the room quietly and almost ran into Gerrit as he did.

"Good morning again, sir," Gerrit said as the door shut behind Kennet.

"Good morning, Gerrit," Kennet chuckled. "Say, you know your way around the keep, don't you?"

"Very well, sir, lived here my whole life."

"Can you tell me where the kitchens are?"

∽

KENNET HAD ALWAYS FOUND KITCHENS the most pleasant part of any house, large or small, that he found himself in. Usually there were pleasant smells, and pleasant people to go along with them. The keep's kitchen was no different.

The cook was a shockingly small woman named Britta. Shockingly small, and also shockingly young. Thirty at the oldest, Kennet thought. Probably not even that. She moved with purpose, but her expression and tone of voice kept the same mourning in them that the rest of the staff had. As Hagen had mentioned, Britta seemed to have been very close to the girl. Not only was Kennet extremely reluctant to add her to his list of suspects (though he did anyway), he could also tell that no small part of her blamed herself for the incident.

"It's not as if I'm not safe, you know!" she said, talking while she worked at chopping up a bunch of carrots one by one. "I'm extremely safe. Even more so now."

"I believe you," Kennet said sympathetically. "I believe whoever did this is incredibly intentional and clever. You would have likely already had to know what they were doing to catch them."

Britta paused in her chopping to shoot him a grateful look. He could tell she felt a little better for his words. "She's always a critic, that little one." She continued her train of thought. "But I welcome it! She's the one I'm cooking for after all, not Jan. That man would eat dirt if you served it to him. He has the discerning taste of a goat."

"Jan?"

Britta's eyes widened at her mistake. "Lord Hagen." She corrected herself. "Sorry, I've worked for him for nearly half my life. He's like a father to me. Hard to call him Lord Hagen all the time, you know?"

"And he lets you?"

"He doesn't 'let' us do anything. As long as we get our jobs done and we act proper in front of guests, we're like a family here."

Kennet wondered how much of that was Hagen being purposefully benevolent, and how much was a result of him being rather absentminded. Though it was possible that when the lord wasn't on edge about the health of his only child, he was much more responsible with his duties as a leader. The description of his eating habits certainly hadn't strengthened the image of him as a vigilant ruler, though. "So she comes to you to talk about the menu from time to time?"

"Yes. Not after every meal, but it's not unusual. And it wasn't unusual the night of, either. She just said she had some notes, so I told her to come to the kitchen before bed."

"Did she mention any specific flavors? Anything can help, even if you don't think it's important."

Britta paused in her chopping again to think. "Well, yes. I made a stew, a bit hot for the weather but it's Marna's favorite. It was fairly well-seasoned so it would be hard to notice any unusual flavors but she did complain of there being a taste of . . . well, she described it as being like sour milk—which was interesting, because I hadn't added any milk or cream to the stew at all."

Kennet nodded, and pulled a notebook from the inner pocket of his coat, opening it and recording the relevant information. "Good," he said. "That's very good. What was in the stew? Anything unusual? Any new ingredients?"

"No, just beef, carrots, potatoes, some barley, and mushrooms."

Kennet perked up at the last word. "Mushrooms!" he said. "Do you remember what kind?"

"They looked like normal mushrooms to me," Britta said, slightly defensive. "Why?"

"Did you leave the room while the stew was cooking?"

"Stews tend to take a while, so yes," she admitted, "I did leave for a while, but only to do a couple other chores around the keep."

"Then since the stew already had mushrooms, someone might have been able to slip in and add more without you noticing, and without changing the appearance of the stew."

"But Jan—Lord Hagen—ate the same stew," Britta said. "So that can't be it."

He considered that. "Did you serve the stew and bring it to them yourself?"

"No, I dish it out down here, and then one of the other servants brings it up."

"Then that's likely when it happened."

"You know, that makes sense!" Britta said. "Since she did complain about the soup having crunchy bits in it! I wondered if maybe I'd undercooked something, since I decided to add more carrots near the end, but perhaps it was raw mushrooms!"

"Or something else entirely, but the ideal situation would be mushrooms, since it's the simplest answer—and I've found that often, the most obvious answer is the correct one." He jotted the new information down. "Anything else?"

"No, just the milk and the crunch."

"Excellent. Thank you very much, Britta."

"Thank you yourself, Sir Peders."

∼

KENNET WALKED BACK into the town with a notebook full of new information, and a small sack filled with treats from Britta. He had considered sticking around longer, questioning more of the staff, but it was unlikely there would be anything else to gain from that. He doubted that whoever had done it was part of the staff—or at least, not working alone. More likely, it was someone like him: an outside party who had been hired to do the deed, then get out again. Integrating into the staff was risky, too risky. What kind of person would be able to work alongside a young girl and maintain the desire to poison her? Well, then again . . . enough money would make even the most loyal servant do unthinkable things.

He had to remind himself again that wasn't the point of his assignment. He had the information he needed to be able to work out a cure, or at least get someone else to work out a cure for him. That meant the only thing left to do was pack his things and head off in the direction of the help he needed.

Well, there was one other thing left to do.

Curiosity still lingered in his mind when his thoughts turned to the bard and their interaction at the keep's gates earlier that morning. Time was of the essence, undoubtedly, but it was after noon and there was no way he'd make it to the next town before the sun set. He would set off tomorrow.

Tonight, he would do a little investigating for himself.

CHAPTER 3

BAD AT TELLING THE TRUTH, BAD AT LYING

Kennet found Asa where they had been the night before, except that this time they were sitting at the bar rather than in a booth. They had a mug in front of them that Kennet could tell, even from a distance, was half-full of mead. Their instrument was propped up on their seat, and one of their hands rested on it protectively as they nonchalantly watched the rest of the bar from their perch. They saw Kennet as he approached them.

"Kennet Peders," they said, lacking any of the energy they'd had in their last interaction, "again."

"Asa of the Isles," Kennet replied and took the seat next to them at the bar, "again."

There was a pause as they looked each other over. "So you work for Lord Hagen or something?"

"Something like that." Kennet nodded. "I was summoned here on his orders. The lord was in need of an expert in certain subjects."

"Ah. A mercenary!" Asa said with understanding. Kennet started to try and correct them, but they cut him off. "I should have known, looking at the way you dress. Don't you get hot in that?"

"I'm not . . ." No, honestly, that would do just fine for the time being. To explain the difference between a mercenary, an assassin, a jack of all trades if the trade was fixing dirty little problems—it would take too long. Mercenary would do just fine for the moment. "That's actually what I'm here to talk to you about."

"Fashion advice? Wonderful! Of course, what you have going on right now works very well for you, but I could probably give you a couple things to change that would make a huge difference."

"No, I meant what you said at the gates this morning. What did you mean when you said you could alleviate the young lady's night terrors?"

Asa fell silent, pursing their lips as they looked up at the ceiling and rattled their fingers against the bar top. "Hmm. It's . . . very hard to explain," they said reluctantly. "I wish I could, but it would take a lot of time. That's why I didn't get into it at the gates."

"I have time," Kennet said, "and if you help me to understand, I can help you in return. I have a direct audience with Lord Hagen, and he trusts me a good amount. He at least trusts me to have his daughter's best interests at heart."

Despite their comments about his dress, this appeared to be the first time Asa had truly seen him. They turned their head toward him, looking down their nose as they considered him with warm brown eyes in a way that made him feel deeply scrutinized. When they were done, they crossed their arms, apparently not satisfied with what they had seen there. "So you're saying that if I convince you, I'll have an audience with Lord Hagen?"

"I'm not promising that, but I am saying I'd like to help you."

They frowned. "Why?"

"Well, I'd love to say it's because of my job, and that I've grown to care for the young lady, and I want to help her find comfort any way I can. And that may also be true, but the main reason is more selfish." He leaned in a little, resting an elbow on the bar as he did. "I'm curious."

"Curious?"

"Very. About you. If you'll remember, I watched you perform last night."

That earned a soft scoff from the bard. "Oh, and my performance was so compelling that now you're willing to put your job on the line for me?"

"Is that so unbelievable? You put on quite the show." Kennet was aware he was flirting, and lying at the same time, but he still wasn't sure if the slap had been anything important. If it hadn't, he didn't want to look like a fool by bringing it up.

"Well, that's very kind of you to say," they said smoothly, "and I can't deny that I'm flattered. And if you and I have the same goals, I suppose your motive shouldn't matter all that much."

"If your goal is to help the girl, then we are certainly in this together."

"Then I suppose I'll make an attempt to explain, at least." Asa pulled one leg up into their lap, holding it by the ankle. "I . . . see, it's hard to talk about it, because even I don't know the details, but . . . for most of my life, I've been able to affect people's emotions by touching them. It can be very brief—as little as brushing my hand against theirs as we pass in a crowded street, it doesn't matter. As long as my skin meets theirs, in that moment I can shift their emotional state wherever I would like it to go."

"Brief, you say? As brief as a swift slap across the face?" Kennet suggested.

For a moment, Asa had the decency to look surprised by the implication, before a knowing smile took up on their face. "Well, I suppose that would be possible, though I don't know why you'd give such a specific example."

"Purely hypothetical," Kennet said, and he found himself smiling as well. "But that's fascinating."

"So you believe me?"

"I don't know if I'd go that far."

"Most people wouldn't," Asa said, and the smile disappeared once again. "I wish there was a way I could be clearer, but honestly, there's nothing more to it."

It was impossible to believe, of course, and they obviously knew that themself. There was no world in which he could bring them before Lord Hagen without some level of proof that what they were saying was true. And there didn't seem to be any way to actually obtain that proof, really. As much as the slap had been interesting, he'd hardly be able to cite it to the lord, and he didn't dare ask them to demonstrate like that again. So it was likely that he would just have to be content with buying them a drink and keeping this curiosity in his mind, as something he would likely think about once a month for the rest of his life, unless . . .

Unless.

He sat up straighter in his chair, scratching the stubble on his neck as he considered his next move. Asa watched him with one eyebrow raised.

"What?" they asked. "What are you thinking?"

"What if you showed me?" Kennet said.

Asa blinked in surprise. The suggestion wasn't shot down immediately, but he could see by the look on their face that it wouldn't be approved of immediately, either. "You already connected what I said with what you saw last night," they said, "but you still don't believe me after that. And as a general rule, I don't like to do it to people who don't know it's being done to them."

"Unless the person is a prick," Kennet pointed out.

"A prick and a bad musician, yes." Asa refused to acknowledge their hypocrisy.

Kennet chuckled at that and considered them further, still

unsure of whether or not he was willing to commit to his idea. Then he said, "No, but I would know if you were doing it to me, wouldn't I? So." He held out a hand, and looked up to meet their eyes. "Try it on me."

"What?"

"You want to help the girl, don't you?"

"You have no idea what you're asking me to do."

"And you can't get into the keep until I do have an idea, for certain. Why would I let you do to a young child what I wouldn't let you do to me?"

They bit their lip, chewing it thoughtfully for a moment before nodding slowly. "Quite noble for a mercenary."

"Just thorough."

"Very well, then." They collected themself, correcting their posture. They seemed less put off by the concept of what he'd asked them to do in principle, and more just shocked that he had offered in the first place. "I feel compelled to warn you, it may not be an exceedingly pleasant experience."

"I imagine it could feel quite violating," Kennet agreed calmly, "but my line of work comes with all sorts of unpleasantries. I've learned how to process such things. So don't worry about me."

He knew that what he was saying could raise questions he wasn't particularly keen to answer, but honestly with the amount of intrigue they were bringing to the conversation, he was desperate to level the playing field and seem even a tenth as interesting as his new companion. They looked mildly impressed but unsurprised by the statement.

"Very well," they repeated. "But you have to remember that I warned you."

"Of course," Kennet said, trying and perhaps failing to hide the pleasure he felt at having gotten his way, and the excitement over what might come next. Whether it would be pleasant or not, he imagined he was about to experience something very new to him, an opportunity that was becoming more and more rare these days.

Asa looked a good deal less excited, with the expression of a parent who knows their child is about to burn themself trying to touch a hot pan. "What would you like to feel?" they asked, and began to remove a pair of brown leather gloves that Kennet only now realized they were wearing. They hadn't been wearing any last night, now that he thought about it.

"I think it would be best if it were something I wouldn't naturally feel in this situation." Kennet answered Asa's question thoughtfully. "That way there's less of a chance I'd ruin the test by making myself feel the way I want to."

"Makes sense." Asa nodded as they laid their gloves on the bar. "What are you least likely to feel right now, then?"

Well, that was a good question. And what was the answer? Fear? No, that wouldn't work, he already felt his nerves sparking with energy at the concept of the experience in general. That would be too easy to mess up. Joy? No, same issue. Love? Well . . . no, that would likely create plenty of problems for the both of them.

The answer became apparent suddenly.

"Anger," Kennet said, and Asa nodded.

"All right," they said, "but that's a dangerous one. If you get angry enough to try and hurt me, I'll do what I need to in order to keep myself safe."

He hadn't considered that aspect, though he should have. Would they be in danger? He hadn't been properly angry in quite some time; he didn't even know what he was capable of. But before he could open his mouth to tell them that perhaps they should try a less volatile experiment, it was too late.

They reached out and touched his hand.

And the anger he began to feel . . .

Again, he hadn't been properly angry in quite some time. And this . . .

This was proper anger.

He was angry at everything, all of it at once. At the injustice of the world that would lead to a little girl being poisoned. At the fact he had so little evidence to go on. Angry at himself for wasting time, angry at himself for . . . for being here, for having gotten himself to this place and for not being better yet. Why wasn't he better yet?

Why did he still hate himself? He was angry at himself for hating himself. He was angry that he was holding himself back—angry that he knew exactly who could fix this, exactly who could save this little girl's life, but he was too afraid to go to her. He was angry at himself for being afraid.

Overwhelmed by anger, he tried to turn it somewhere productive, but there was nowhere for it to go. So suddenly, it turned on the one who had created it. Suddenly, he was angry at Asa for making him feel this way.

"What . . . the hell?" he growled, and was surprised to hear that he was speaking through tears. When had he started crying? He pulled his hand back from theirs sharply.

Asa's eyes had widened. It seemed that out of every reaction they might have expected from him, tears hadn't been part of the equation. Immediately apologetic, they reached out as he withdrew. "Wait, don't, I can make it stop—"

Kennet got up from his chair and stumbled, the anger giving way to confusion but not completely. The confusion mixed with the anger, and he felt something new. Fear, but not the fear he had thought he would feel. He wasn't afraid of Asa, or what he was feeling, but of himself. He took a step back, unsure of where to go. He couldn't run from himself, could he? The room was almost spinning as he tried to find his bearings.

The bard's hand was still outstretched toward him, and as he backed away from them, they faltered. It seemed that for a moment, they were considering just letting him go. Then, their face set itself with determination, and they lunged forward as quickly as they had lashed out the night before. Rather than slap him, however, they grabbed his hand and pulled him back toward them. The moment their hand touched his for the second time, every negative feeling subsided. Only a fairly reasonable amount of confusion remained.

As quickly as they had taken his hand, Asa dropped it again, and the two stood across from each other. Asa's chest heaved with panicked breath, and their eyes were as wide as saucers. Kennet knew he couldn't be in much better shape than them. He could feel the tears still running down his face, and when he looked down at the hand that Asa had just let go of, he realized that it was shaking.

Neither of them spoke for a while, until Asa broke the silence.

"I'm sorry," they said. "I didn't know it would be like that."

Kennet blinked hard, squeezing his eyes shut in an attempt to reset his mind. It almost worked, and he leaned against the bar hard as he forced himself to take a deep breath and smile at Asa in an attempt to reassure them both. He let out a strained laugh. "No, no, it's not your fault," he said. "It seems I'm not as well adjusted as I thought I was."

Asa joined his laughter with equal strain and gingerly resumed their seat at the bar. He saw that their immediate move was to put the gloves back on, and that they made this move with haste. He wondered how dangerous he must have made them feel.

"I can assure you," they said as they finished buttoning their gloves at the wrist, "the effects on Lord Hagen's daughter would be much . . . gentler."

"I have to imagine so," Kennet replied.

The silence that followed was palpably tense.

"I'm sorry," Asa apologized again, after a moment, "but I hope . . . I hope that was enough for you."

"Asa, my friend," Kennet said, "that was more proof than I could have asked for. I've never felt like that in my entire life, so there's no world in which I would have felt it without your influence."

The meaning of his words took time to register with Asa, but after they had, their eyes lit up. "Then you'll help me?"

"Tonight, if you like. I leave town tomorrow, so there's no use wasting time."

"Tonight it shall be, then."

∼

LORD HAGEN and Kennet stood back from the bed, watching as Asa examined Marna's motionless form. They had taken their gloves off, and laid them on the side table next to the cup of water. Gerrit stood at the door as well, pretending to stand guard though Kennet could see that his eyes wandered back into the room every few moments as he glanced over his shoulder.

"Are you certain this is a good idea, Sir Peders?" Hagen asked. It was the third time he had asked the same question since they'd entered the room.

"I trust them with my life, my lord." Kennet made another attempt to reassure him. "If nothing else, all they'll do is lay hands on her. Even the worst-case scenario is simply that nothing happens."

Asa stood up straighter and took a step back from the bed. "It's likely that might be the case after all," they said, "but I want to try. Even if it works, it may not last for long."

"Even just the chance that she may have some peace is better than anything I can do for her."

"Nonsense, my lord," Asa said with a soft, genuine smile. "You're the one doing this. You're the one who let me in."

Kennet saw that Lord Hagen was smiling as well, though there was far more sadness in his smile. He stepped up to stand next to Asa and stood quietly for a moment before he said something under his breath. "Perhaps," he said, "the one who truly needs your attention is not the child, but her father."

"I'd had the exact same thought," Asa replied, equally soft. "I didn't want to do it without you knowing, but since you brought it up . . . I'll make a move when we leave, I'll shake his hand."

The two nodded conspiratorially.

"What's that?" Hagen asked, craning his head as if he would be able to see what they were talking about.

"Ah, I simply have to be in a specific state of mind to be able to do this," Asa said with another smile over their shoulder at the lord. "Sir Peders was offering some encouragement. I'm ready now."

With that, Asa reached down and rested their hand on the little girl's bare arm as it lay limply on the sheets. They closed their eyes and took a deep breath, only staying there a moment before they lifted their hand again. In that moment, Kennet noticed a small but marked change in the girl's breathing. It slowed, and though that was the only difference, Kennet looked back to see that Lord Hagen seemed to have noticed it too, by the relief on his own face.

Asa took a step back away from the bed. "There you go," they said, picking up their gloves. "I've done what I can. Again, it may not last long, but—"

Where Kennet had been expecting the lord to be hesitant to thank Asa, hesitant even to shake their hand, he found himself completely incorrect as tears had sprung to Hagen's eyes, and he threw his arms around Asa in an embrace. The bard's eyes widened, but then their smile grew, and they patted his back somewhat awkwardly. When Hagen drew away again, he clasped one of their hands in his, and though his expression had started out giddy, Kennet thought he could pinpoint the exact moment Asa's influence took effect.

"Bless you," he said, breathlessly. "I don't know who you are or how you've done it, but I believe you're the first person in this place who's actually done some good for her." He let out a long sigh, and his smile turned relaxed and more calm. "I feel . . . I feel as though I can finally relax, even for just a moment."

"My pleasure, Lordship." Asa gave a slight bow and pulled their hand back from his.

"Surely I can reward you somehow?"

"Absolutely not." They shook their head. "I only wish that you are able to fully heal her soon."

"That duty, unfortunately, lies heavily on my shoulders alone," Kennet broke in, with a bow of his own. "And on that note, we ought to leave."

"Yes, of course. You must rest for your journey." Lord Hagen nodded and gestured to the door, where Gerrit snapped back to attention in a vain attempt to look as though he hadn't been paying attention at all.

Kennet snorted softly. He began to make his way out, waving for Asa to join him.

As they passed Gerrit, he threw them a sheepish smile. "Safe journey, Sir Peders."

"Safe staying-put, Master Gerrit," Kennet replied. "Don't get into too much trouble."

"I'll do my best, sir."

Kennet and Asa made their way through the rest of the keep and out through the gates mostly in silence, only stopping when they had entered the town again. Asa turned to Kennet and smiled, extending a once-again-gloved hand.

"I suppose this is farewell, Sir Peders."

He wished it didn't have to be. He hadn't even begun to question what they were capable of, their reason for coming to Bladland, their purpose in wandering its countryside. But he couldn't justify that curiosity. The sun had set, and his time was up. He had to say it.

"I suppose it is." He took their hand in his own and gave it a firm shake. "Farewell, Asa of the Isles. Gethin guide you," he added as an afterthought, mostly because it seemed like the right thing to do.

They made a face. "I'd rather he didn't!" they said brightly. "But if you wish, may he guide you instead."

"That will do, I think," Kennet replied. He added something new to his list of questions about them. "Safe travels, then."

"Safe travels, Sir Peders."

For a moment they stood, and Kennet wondered if they'd keep walking in the same direction, but then they turned on their heel and continued on without him. Though he'd known they had to, his heart still sank a little as he made the lonely walk back to his own inn.

He'd been working alone for so long, he'd forgotten what it was like to have someone to conspire with, an equal with the same goals. Even though it had been brief, the moment of partnership between him and the bard left him wanting more. More partnership? Or more of them?

They'd only known each other for a day! It had to be the partnership he was craving.

As he tried to convince himself of his own apathy, he felt a gnawing at his mind, a reminder of his past partnerships. Perhaps it was for the best that they had parted ways now, before they had even begun to get to know each other, before things could get messy.

Even though he tried hard to believe it, he knew wholeheartedly that it was a lie.

CHAPTER 4

AN APATHETIC HERBALIST

Travel was not Kennet's favorite part of any assignment. Seemingly endless hours alone with nothing but his thoughts was unbearable at all times, but as of late it had only gotten worse. It didn't help to know where he was going—the thought that he might have to go the entire way there.

He wished this was the kind of job that came with social gatherings. Parties he could stand at the back of and look aloof and superior. The kind that brought interesting people to him, instead of sending him searching for them. Those were always fun. Then again, those kinds of jobs usually came with the assignment to kill someone rich. Usually, those jobs were messy.

Not that this one was clean, especially if . . .

There was no use keeping it out of his mind any longer. He had to seriously consider his options, and dancing around the most promising one wasn't going to help anyone—not his own sensitivities, nor Marna's health.

Hana was his best bet.

And who could tell, maybe she wouldn't be unhappy to see him? How long had it been? Nearly three years? Certainly a lot could have changed for her—it had for him. Not to mention, out of the two people who had a problem with him, Hana had less of one. He was lucky that she was the one he needed.

Honestly, if there had been even the slightest chance of the *other* one being involved, he wouldn't have agreed to the job in the first place.

He'd make a couple stops on the way to where she was staying—or at least, the last place he knew of where she'd been staying—and by the time he got there, he would have figured out what to say.

"She'll be happy to see you, at least," Kennet said jokingly to his horse, Starling. "She always liked you better than me."

The horse didn't react. She never did. She hardly listened to his directions, much less his small talk.

Kennet sighed and looked up at the sky, watching the sun overhead. Not even a full day's distance from Osternas, and he'd already been forced to shed his coat as they moved inland. The shade of the rather dense forest they rode through certainly lent a bit of relief, but not completely. The heat brought with it a myriad of smells, the scent of evergreen branches and dust that was kicked up as the horse's hooves hit the dirt road, their muted steps mingling with bird calls as Kennet remained lost in thought.

He tried not to think of Hana any further. As much as he planned to think of the right things to say, he knew that it would likely all escape him in the moment. There was really no use trying to come up with anything at all. It would all depend on how she reacted to seeing him again, and there was no way to predict *that*. And he'd already gone over the information he knew for certain, multiple times, even. He knew it was likely a mushroom—the flavor of sour milk and the texture that Britta had described made him think so, at least. He thanked god that he had paid attention in his time being friends with Hana. All his knowledge of poisons had come from her in the first place. But because of that, his knowledge was limited, and there was only so long he could dwell on that.

So . . . what to think about instead? That was simple. It had been hard to keep his mind from settling back on the same topic, over and over again, since he'd left Osternas. Asa. There was no use in it, he couldn't seem to help himself. Though, he was having a hard time narrowing down exactly what it was that had him so hung up on them. Was it simply their existence? Perhaps it was, more specifically, this odd influence they had?

Truthfully, it *was* their strange abilities that he was thinking about the most. This kind of thing wasn't unheard of, certainly, but it had to come from *somewhere*. What? Or maybe the question was "who?" Though Asa hadn't spoken of any specifics, and in fact didn't seem to know the answer themself, Kennet had started to try and divine an answer. And to his knowledge, there was really only one way that a human could do something like what Asa had done, and that was through a god.

He hadn't read much of Compendium, the holy text of Gethin, but he was aware of how some of it was written. There were people who had been touched by the god and subsequently were blessed with abilities most people couldn't even fathom. He knew of one who could heal the sick, and one who could see the future. It didn't seem unbelievable that the same touch could awaken the kind of thing that Asa was able to do. He wished he'd thought of that while they had been together. It was simply a theory, and a theory he couldn't even confirm with them unless they happened to still be in Osternas by the time he got back. As unlikely as that was, he allowed himself to continue hoping for it as he rode on.

His attention turned to his surroundings, after a while. Between trees he could see that the underbrush was mostly bushes, and he was surprised to find the bushes weighed down by berries. It seemed a bit early in the season for them—but, what did he know of berries? Not much besides which kinds were good to eat.

Looking back up at the sun he remarked to himself that he still had a good ways to go before he reached the next major town. And he'd been riding for a while. He gently pulled on the reins, bringing his horse to a halt. He could spare a moment for some berry picking, and Starling would likely enjoy a moment's rest too. He led her off the road and tied her to a tree out of sight of it, leaving her to graze in a clearing nearby as he turned his attention to the bushes.

The berries nearest the road would be too dusty, but the fact that there were still some near the road at all meant that this crop was mostly unpicked, missed by birds and ignored by passersby. Kennet shouldered his way through thorn bushes carefully, rearranging tangled branches and vines until he had a safe path to what he deemed a desirable patch of berries.

He reached out to pluck a few and let them fall into his hand—they fell off so easily, he knew even before he popped them into his mouth that they were very ripe. They were still warm from the sunshine when he bit into them, and he took a moment to savor their flavor. It was nice to eat something that wasn't the tough dried meat that he'd bought back in Osternas. He would always welcome some cured meat, and it certainly staved off hunger, but it wasn't fresh berries either.

As he picked, he began to wish he'd brought a sack or something with him, but it wasn't as if he had something like that to spare. He could use his shirt, but then he might stain it with the dark berry juice, and he was already low on shirts without stains as it was. So he was going to have to deal with this being a temporary treat.

Having picked through the area he was in, he pushed a little farther into the thicket. He could swear he heard some rustling. Likely a bird, he thought at first, until he pushed into a new clearing and found himself face to face with another person.

A woman, he realized, with greying hair and dark eyes, who yelped as Kennet broke into her view. Kennet started as well, then laughed at his own actions.

"Oh, gods," he breathed. "So sorry about that."

She laughed too. "You almost lost me all my hard work!" she said, and gestured to a basket that rested on her hip. Kennet could see it was half-full of the same berries he'd been picking.

"I'm so sorry," he repeated. "I didn't expect anybody else to be out here."

"Me neither!" the woman said. "You traveling?"

"Yes, from Osternas."

"Of course." She nodded, and returned to picking berries, giving him hardly another glance but continuing their conversation. "Headed to Ornhult?"

"First, at least," Kennet said. "Grankoping is my final destination."

"All the way to Grankoping! Well, you have a ways to go! Don't let me keep you."

Kennet looked around the clearing and saw she'd picked over most of it already. "No, I was just stopping to rest, you're hardly interrupting anything. If anything, I'm the one keeping you."

"Hardly. It's been quiet out here, which was nice at first, but it gets lonely. I tried to convince my daughter and her children to come out with me, but I suppose they had better things to do. No time to help their poor old grandmother."

Kennet chuckled, and noticed another basket at her feet, this one empty. "I can give you a hand for a moment," he offered. "It would be a nice distraction."

What was he talking about, a distraction? A distraction from saving a dying child?

The woman smiled. "I would appreciate it, Sir . . . ?"

"Andersen." Kennet used a fake name. No need for an old lady to find out a few weeks from now that she'd been chatting with someone of his reputation. Save her the heart attack.

"Well met, then, Sir Andersen. You can call me Ingrid."

"Well met, ma'am." He picked up the empty basket and quickly located a spot that hadn't been picked dry yet. As he began to harvest the berries, he began to justify it to himself. He needed a break anyway. No use in tiring Starling out. Not to mention, if this woman knew Ornhult, it was possible she could help him find a local herbalist or apothecary more quickly. "So you're from Ornhult?"

"Not quite," said Ingrid from her spot a few feet away. "Almsby."

"Oh! I think I have a cousin from there. It's near a river, isn't it?"

"No, no, that's the other Almsby," she replied. "Farther south, closer to Vindmora. Easy mistakes, though, people make them all the time. *That* Almsby is bigger, more notable. Our Almsby is a nothing town. To do 'most anything you need to take the road over to Ornhult."

"I'm from a nothing town myself," Kennet said idly. "Honestly the name isn't even worth remembering, that's how nothing it is."

Ingrid laughed. "Just two folks from nothing towns, picking berries. This is the way a summer afternoon should be spent."

He wished he could enjoy it in that context. But to continue making any use of this time, he found himself pushing for more. "So you find yourself in Ornhult often, then."

"Quite often, at least once a week. Why?"

"Do you know of any herbalists in town?"

He heard a pause in the rustling of leaves as she stopped picking berries to think over his question. "I do," she said.

"He's very good, he helped a friend of mine through a near-deadly illness, but he doesn't really advertise himself. He's a chef."

"Are there none who are herbalists by trade? No apothecaries?"

"Not in Ornhult, no. If you're looking for a proper apothecary, you're doing the right thing heading toward Grankoping."

Kennet hummed at that. "Well, I should try whoever I can. Would he be willing to talk to a stranger?"

"Possibly," Ingrid answered. "Why? Are you in need of some kind of specific herb? I know plants all right myself, maybe I could help."

Kennet smiled, and he felt that the smile was tight, and likely looked forced. "No, that's all right," he said. "It's . . . rather complicated. But I appreciate the offer."

"Of course."

Kennet slowed in his picking, and looked down at the basket. He had completely covered the bottom, at least. It was likely time to move on.

"Here you are," he said, making his way back over to her and putting the basket down at her feet. "Thank you for the help."

"Same to you," she said with a bright smile. "When you get to Ornhult, go to the Wilting Dove. The owner is my brother, actually. Tell him I sent you, and you'll be well taken care of."

Kennet bowed his head in thanks, and left her behind in the clearing. Starling didn't so much as look up as he approached, as usual. He paused at her side and inhaled deeply, looking up at the sky. If only he could spare more time for berry picking, and chatting, and enjoying the summer sun. If only Marna could do the same, he added. This was about her in the end. She was more important than any fleeting moment spent with any stranger, whether the bard in the tavern or the woman in the forest. He was doing this so *she* could listen to music, eat berries, and see her father smile.

He untied Starling from the tree, and climbed back onto her back.

Marna would be able to do all of those things very soon, he was certain.

He was going to ensure it.

∼

ORNHULT WAS a fair bit smaller than Osternas, and that was quite fine by Kennet. It did mean, however, that he likely would have ended up at the Wilting Dove either way. It wasn't the only tavern in the town but it was certainly the only one that anyone seemed to want to be at. In fact, as Kennet entered, he remarked that he wouldn't really be surprised if the entirety of the town was in this one room. The sun had set and anyone whose day was ending had decided that it should end here—Kennet included.

He immediately picked out Ingrid's brother behind the bar, though. The man had the same dark eyes and when he saw Kennet, he smiled a similar, inquisitive smile.

"Evening, sir," he said, moving from serving another customer to greet this stranger. "How can I help you?"

"I'm mostly passing through, but I met your sister Ingrid and she told me this was the place to be in town—and it seems like the rest of the town agrees," Kennet replied, which earned a hearty laugh from the man.

"She's always saying that," he said. "Never sure if she really means it, or if she's just trying to find some excuse to claim a share of my profits. But please, make yourself at home! Let me get you something. What do you fancy?"

"If you have a house mead, I'm always interested," Kennet said, leaning against the bar though there were no empty seats to settle in. Neither patron on either side of him seemed bothered by it, at least. One even chimed in with her own opinion.

"Best mead this side of the lake if you ask me," she said.

"Like you would know," Ingrid's brother retorted. "You've never been farther east than the edge of the forest."

"Don't need to go any farther to know what good mead is." She sniffed.

"That's high enough praise for me to at least want to give it a try. I'll take one—and a room, if you have one," Kennet interjected.

"That I do!"

And so Kennet found himself with a mug of mead, a room for the night, and a moment to think. He'd made it here with plenty of time to spare, in spite of his detour, though he still felt a nagging guilt about that. If he'd arrived even earlier, perhaps he could have tried to find the herbalist tonight.

"Say." He stopped Ingrid's brother the next time the man walked by. "Ingrid mentioned a chef in this town who also has some knowledge of herbs and medicines. Would you happen to know who that is, and how I could find him?"

Ingrid's brother frowned. "Now, she mentioned someone like that a while ago—you remember, when Laurie got sick?" He addressed the second part to the woman next to Kennet.

"Wasn't that Torger?"

"Oh, it would be, wouldn't it?"

"I'm sure it was." The woman turned to Kennet and addressed him directly. "Torger's the closest thing we got to a doctor in a day's journey."

A small town "excuse" for a doctor was hardly the best option for finding a cure, but it was a better use for his time than *not* talking to the man. If he was incredibly lucky, then he might have even a slight idea for a cure, or even the identity of the mushroom. At the very least he would have a better frame of reference than Kennet, whose knowledge was entirely secondhand.

"Where can I find this man, then?" he wondered. "I'm in need of an opinion on some herbs, and Ingrid seemed to think he could help."

"He'll do his damndest, that's for sure," Ingrid's brother said, craning his neck to look across the room. "Looks like he's at his favorite spot tonight—table down on the left back there, the man with the red hat."

Kennet followed the man's directions, and quickly homed in on who he was talking about. He wasn't wearing the red hat, but it sat on the table in front of him, along with a plate of food that made Kennet's stomach growl. He'd order something after he talked to the man—this conversation probably wouldn't take very long anyway.

"Thank you, I'll be back for more," he said as he picked up his mead and pushed off the bar to approach the man at his table.

Torger looked up at Kennet's approach. "Hello! Can I help you with something?"

"I hope so!" Kennet replied, relieved to find the man friendly. "I hear you're something of an herbalist."

"Something of one," Torger snorted. He took a bite from a thick slice of bread, speaking again before he had finished chewing. "Not much of one though."

"That's all right, I'm even less of one."

He laughed. "S'pose that's all right, then. Tell me then, what's your story?"

Kennet sighed. "Well, it's not a very nice one. There's a little girl, one in my charge, and she's very sick. We think she might've eaten something poisonous."

Torger's eyebrows shot up, and he set down his bread. Immediately, any lightheartedness seeped from his expression, replaced by a deep sympathy and sadness. "I'm sorry to hear that. She nearby? You're not from around here, are you, so she can't be."

"No, I'm on my way west to Grankoping, thinking I might

find a cure or a doctor who knows one there, but there's no harm in asking who I can on my way. Maybe I'll get lucky, save us both some precious time."

"Terrible situation indeed." Torger nodded seriously. "Well, I'll certainly do my best to help."

"I thank you," Kennet said.

"So the best way to know what happened is to know how she's feeling. What's this illness like, exactly?" Torger allowed himself to turn back to his food, though he seemed less enthusiastic to eat it. Kennet could understand where that was coming from; this conversation was making him lose his appetite as well.

"She's fallen into a deep sleep, that's the most pressing thing," he said.

Torger's round face scrunched up at that. He shook his head, as though to indicate that the description was too general, too little to go off of. Kennet continued.

"She has these fits—horrible fits. I saw one myself, it was . . ." Kennet shuddered against his will. "Harrowing." He winced. "It was like she wasn't in control of her whole body, every muscle tensing and shaking. I would give every cent I'd ever earned to keep her from experiencing one again."

Kennet noticed that the man had stopped eating again completely now. He was staring at his own hands, as though deep in thought, as though contemplating whether or not to say something. Kennet wondered if he was reading into things too much—but when the man began to speak again, he wasn't meeting Kennet's eyes.

"Doesn't sound like anything I'm familiar with," he said.

"Well, even if you don't know the symptoms, perhaps you're aware of the kind of poison it might be if I describe what she ate? I know sometimes, especially if you're a chef who harvests their own ingredients, knowing the signs of a poisonous food can be important to avoid accidentally using it," Kennet prodded.

"Perhaps," Torger admitted, but his tone seemed shorter. Kennet noticed the man's hand was trembling a bit as he picked up another piece of bread.

Something was wrong here. Very wrong. Surely this man couldn't be *involved*? A small town like this? What were the odds of that?

. . . not zero. In fact, he'd been taught while in his early days as a Hawk to consider allies from low places, places none would expect. Certainly he himself wouldn't have expected this. Now that he had the idea in his head, it was hard to shake it. The town was small, but it wasn't far from Osternas. It was convenient and accessible if nothing else. Kennet tried to hide his suspicion as he continued, telling himself that he was being wildly assumptive. He was being silly.

"The girl mentioned tasting something sour, like spoiled milk, in her food the very night she fell ill. Is that something you would think—"

"Doesn't sound familiar," Torger repeated, shrugging his shoulders. He made eye contact with Kennet now, decisively. Kennet told himself he couldn't be imagining it—the man was forcing himself to look at him. "I fear I'm just not knowledgeable enough to help you."

"I hadn't finished," Kennet said with a small huff. "But I fear you might be underselling your knowledge. This girl is sick—very sick. She might die if I can't get this cure for her."

"I wish I could help you," the man said, then he leaned in slightly. "But I can't."

Kennet blinked. There was a weight to his tone that implied something. The conversation they were having had shifted to the unsaid, and with it, Kennet was certain that he was speaking with a man who had been complicit in the very crime they were discussing. "I know it was a mushroom," he supplied, an attempt to give the man an opportunity, an excuse to give him something more. "I'm not interested in finding out who did this," he added more brazenly when

Torger didn't reply, knowing that he was making a dangerous implication. But desperation was starting to set in. This man knew something. This man could save the girl right now if he wanted to, but he wouldn't. Why wouldn't he?

"You think it was intentional? Not just a mistake one of the chefs made, perhaps?" Torger responded after a while of silence. Another slip—not a question a man would ask if he was innocent, not a question he would ask if he was mostly worried about the health of the girl.

Was he afraid of Kennet? Of what would happen if he were caught? But Kennet had stressed that wasn't a concern of his right now. "Perhaps," he said slowly, "but as I said, we aren't worried about who did it. Only about her health. Please," he added. "Please, she's sick, if you have any ideas that could help me, I'm begging you. I'm *begging* you, you must tell me."

There was sweat beginning to bead on Torger's brow, and Kennet almost felt as though he could hear the man's heart beating. "I can't help you," he repeated, his tone turning harsher with each new word, "and I don't like how you're speaking to me."

"Damn you, man," Kennet hissed, "can I not make myself more clear? A child is going to die! What could be more important to you than that? What is keeping you from helping me?"

The man looked as angry as Kennet felt. He wondered if he was about to get in a fight—if he was going to have to beat the truth out of this man, though that would hardly gain him anything in a busy bar like this. He might have found a lead but he had put himself in a corner at the same time. He was at a loss—what else could he do but back off? If he stayed and tried to press the man in a more private location—find him at home, perhaps—then he risked failing again. If Torger held fast his secrets, then Kennet would waste time he didn't have, time he could use to find a cure for certain in Grankoping. If he left now, then Torger could run—would run, if he was smart.

As he turned his options over in his mind, wishing time would stop to give him the opportunity to consider every angle, he noticed a flash of bright golden fabric behind Torger. And in an instant, the man's tongue was loosened.

The stress turned to fear and tears sprang to his eyes, anger replaced by a blubbering mess of guilt and terror. "I'm sorry," he said softly, tersely, quickly. "I want to help, but she'll kill me, she'll kill me."

There it was. *She?* He wanted to ask but that would be the worst thing he could do. Instead, he forced himself to stay on task, to ignore the chase and focus on the cure. "She'll never find out," he said soothingly. "I'll never tell her. Nobody will ever know, I swear, please just tell me anything. ANYTHING that can save me time."

"I can't. My family—"

"You *must*, or I will make your life hell. I will hunt you down, I swear to god I will. I'll make you regret this night and your silence. I already know what you've done—so tell me how I can fix it," Kennet said.

That seemed to get through to him, as much as Kennet despised the threats that had come from his mouth. "It was a sun-cap, that's what she asked me for, asked me to find some for her. I'm sorry, I'm sorry," he added, wiping tears that welled up as quickly as he could dab them away. "If I had known it was a child—and if I knew the cure—I swear—"

"Don't tell me more." Kennet stopped him. "If you're worried someone's going to kill you because you talked, stop talking now. I believe your intentions weren't for this to happen. I want you to live. So shut up."

Torger nodded and Kennet looked around the bar as surreptitiously as he could manage. Nobody seemed to be watching them—perhaps one or two people might have been when their conversation started, curious about the stranger from out of town and what he wanted from Torger, but he had kept things calm enough for long enough that they had lost interest.

He wished he could promise Torger protection—that as long as the girl was safe, Lord Hagen would assure his safety. But Kennet wasn't in the position to make such promises. Even if he had been, he wasn't sure Torger deserved it. What had he done it for? Money? Had he been forced to under the same threats he cowered from now? Kennet didn't really care, if he was being honest. He had to look to the real solution, now, the solution that lay another day down the road.

Marna would be able to last that long, he hoped.

He prayed.

"I'll make sure your name is kept out of it," he said by way of parting from the man as he pushed out from the table.

"Thank you," Torger said with feeling.

As Kennet stepped away, his mind was still reeling from the information he had collected, as little as it had been. Even though he had stopped himself from pursuing the poisoner, now that the conversation was over, it was all he could focus on. Whoever had done this had seen fit to rope this poor man into their scheme. Perhaps they had started the operation out of loyalty to whichever noble had plotted the whole thing, but things had escalated from there as the noble realized the danger of a nonprofessional being in possession of key information. Perhaps Torger had been hired before they'd realized they would need a professional. No matter what the case was, he had learned two things for certain.

Firstly, the poison had been identified, a sun-cap. That would speed things up for Hana immensely, at least.

And, secondly . . .

Whoever had orchestrated this, or at least whoever was in a position to threaten Torger, was a "she."

That narrowed the suspect list a little.

Having written all of this down in his notebook, Kennet

made his way back to the bar, and ordered another mead. "No." He stopped himself and glanced across the room to see if his eyes had deceived him. They hadn't. Asa of the Isles was sitting, watching him from a spot near the back of the busy tavern. "Two of those, please."

Having acquired the mead, Kennet approached Asa, who bowed their head towards him in greeting.

"For you," Kennet said, setting one of the mugs down in front of the bard.

"Thank you. I hope I wasn't interrupting anything, but you seemed to be talking that poor man in circles."

"No, you were very helpful. I hit a dead end, but I was at least able to get something."

"Glad to hear it!" Asa said, taking a small sip of their mead to test the flavor before deciding they liked it, and taking a wholehearted swig. "Also glad to see we happen to be taking the same road!"

Their smile was infectious, Kennet found, and he chuckled. "If I had known that, I would have suggested we travel together."

"Are you suggesting that now?" Asa cocked their head.

"That depends. Where are you headed next?"

"Where's the next big city?"

"Grankoping. It's where I'm headed."

"Well, then it comes down to convenience! You're the one with the important agenda. I'd hate to get in the way if you thought I'd be a bother."

"You've been nothing but a delight so far," Kennet reassured them. "The real question is whether or not you'd find my company dreadfully boring."

"Sir Peders!" Asa said. "Traveling alone is like performing for an empty room! No company is always worse than boring company."

"I do note that you didn't bother to tell me I'm not boring."

"I've only known you for a day, Sir Peders. Not even that."

Kennet grimaced, but didn't argue the point as he raised his mug in their direction. "Then, to knowing each other for longer than a day?" He offered a toast.

"To knowing each other for at least two days!"

CHAPTER 5
THE GOLDEN BARD

THE MORNING SUN STREAMED INTO THE WINDOWS OF THE Wilted Dove as Kennet peeked out of his room and into the hallway. He had already meditated, and dressed, and even packed his things, feeling well-rested despite the fact that he and his new traveling companion had stayed up quite late chatting. Asa had been talkative, describing their journey to Ornhult, which had been surprisingly eventful.

The bard had been doing a lot of traveling since they arrived in Bladland, Kennet found, so it was unsurprising that the two had ended up on the same path. They'd started their journey from the south, the closest port city to the eastern continent's shore in Vindmora, and Osternas had just been another stop in their travels. Where they were going was anyone's guess—even they didn't seem to know.

But inland was as good a direction as any, so they would travel together.

Kennet paused at the bard's door when he heard that there was the sound of a soft instrumental coming from inside. He had been certain that he would have awoken long before them, being used to being the earliest riser in any group. When he knocked, however, the music stopped abruptly and their voice answered as strong and bright as though they'd been awake for hours.

"Yes?"

"It's Kennet."

"Oh! One moment." There was a shuffling noise, and then the door opened to reveal Asa's smiling face. They weren't wearing their full costume, lacking the gold doublet and the bright eye makeup, and their hair was wrapped up in a silk scarf. "Sorry, I didn't expect you to be up so early."

"I was going to say the same thing to you," Kennet said. "I was afraid I'd have to wake you."

"Oh, no, I know you're on a strict time limit, so I planned to be up early." They motioned for him to enter the room. "Please, I'll just finish getting dressed, and we can leave immediately."

Kennet nodded and stepped into their room, shutting the door behind him. Their instrument was laid flat on the bed, and Kennet wandered over to look at it as they pulled their doublet over their undershirt. They noticed him reaching out to touch it and turned to him sharply.

"Hey hey! No touching, please."

"Sorry," Kennet said sheepishly, but continued to examine it out of curiosity. It was rounded on the top and bottom, but had points where it curved inward, giving it the almost hourglass shape he had noticed the first time he saw it. Six pairs of strings ran up a short neck, crossing frets and a decorative embellishment in the middle that was shaped like a clover. "What is it? It looks a bit like a lute, but I've never seen one shaped like this."

"*Vihuela de Mão*," Asa replied. When they were satisfied that he wasn't going to touch it, they turned away again, facing a bit of polished metal that was propped up against the wall to function as a mirror. They pulled a small tin out of their pocket, popping it open to reveal three thin yellow sticks in different shades. Their fingers danced over them for a moment before they picked out the darkest of the three, and snapped the tin shut again. "You can call it a vihuela, though—the 'de Mão' part just means I don't use a bow for it. It's basically a lute, tunes the same way."

"Is it Lucien?"

"Well, obviously." They snorted, leaning toward the mirror and pulling the chalky substance across their lower lash line, leaving a bold streak of color. "I bought it myself. It's the most expensive thing I own."

"It's beautiful," Kennet remarked.

"Isn't it? Sometimes I think I should name her, but she's transcended the need for a name."

Kennet smiled at that. It was an odd statement, but it made sense to him. "Some things do that," he agreed.

They wiped at the edge of their eyeliner, cleaning it up before they nodded in satisfaction with their work and came to meet Kennet by the bed. They picked up their gloves from where they were resting on the pillow and slipped them on. With care, they slung the vihuela over their back, and then faced Kennet with a grin. "All right, then!" they said. "On our way we go."

∼

Kennet had experienced a moment of panic when he realized that Asa may not have a mount, making their travel arrangement a sight more difficult, but the panic had quickly been resolved when he met Emilio the mule.

As they rode side by side, Asa recounted how they had come across Emilio in the first place. "When I got here, I'd sort of had no plans for travel. I grew up in a city, you know," they said. "So I got here, and I didn't have nearly enough money for a fine horse. Luckily at some point while I was staying in Vindmora, a farmer died, and they auctioned off all his livestock. Nobody wanted poor Emilio!"

The mule swiveled his ears, turning them to face Asa inquisitively, and they patted the side of his neck.

"He seems like a trustworthy steed," Kennet said, remarking internally how ironic it was that the mule was so much more well-behaved than Starling.

"He's been a gem for the few months I've been on the road—but now he has competition! We'll have to see if you usurp his position as 'best traveling companion.'"

"I feel like I have my work cut out for me," Kennet said.

"Well, you already have a leg up because you listened to me when I told you not to touch my vihuela," Asa said. "He almost put me out of business two days after I got him! I guess it just looked tasty."

"It's very colorful."

"Right. It's very colorful, and he's very stupid, so he tried to give it a nibble. Luckily I managed to get him to leave it alone, or else I would've had to put him down." They patted his neck again.

For a moment, the two rode in silence. They'd been riding and talking for a while, and had made it all the way out of the town and its surrounding farmland, now coming to a rather thick area of forest that Ornhult lay on the outskirts of. The forest was full of interesting sounds, so there was no true silence in the absence of their voices. Nevertheless, Kennet found that now that he had the option to talk to someone, he couldn't hold his tongue for very long. But what to talk about? There was the obvious, of course, but somehow he felt that would be rude.

"You grew up in the city, then?" he prompted, and Asa sighed.

"Come on now," they said, "stop dancing around it. You want to talk about what happened in Osternas."

Ah, damn. "Yes."

"Then ask! I wouldn't have come with you if I didn't want to talk about it. It's unavoidable at this point. And honestly, it'll be a relief to have someone to talk to about it at all." They paused, and when he didn't speak, they continued. "Did you know that you, Lord Hagen, and that little servant man are the only people in this country who know I can do that?"

"I had assumed it wasn't something you advertised to everyone you met."

"It really isn't, no." Asa nodded. "And it's not even that I trust you as some kind of exception, it's more that I figured nobody would believe you even if you tried to tell them."

"Oh, certainly," Kennet agreed. "Nobody even believes *you* when you tell them, why should anyone believe me?"

"Well!" Asa said, but they laughed. "I can't blame them for it. It's unbelievable."

"Especially since it seems like even you aren't sure how it works," Kennet said.

"I don't! It's not something I've ever known, it just . . . happens. I don't know if I was doing it before I realized it was something I could do, either, it's entirely possible I've been doing this my whole life without knowing. One day I figured it out, though, and since then I've been more careful."

"So you really have no idea how you do it?"

"No, I don't. But I've sort of learned not to question it."

Kennet clicked his tongue at that. "I suppose that means you won't be interested in my theory, then."

They straightened up in their saddle at that. "Theory?" they repeated.

"Oh, or maybe you are interested."

"Interested? My dear Sir Peders, I can't begin to tell you how interested I am. Nobody's ever had *theories*, or at least not serious ones. My own parents were at a loss, they thought I was making it up. I've always been very fanciful. I honestly don't know if they ever really believed me in the first place, that's part of why I . . ." They paused and shook their head. "Why I left," they finished the thought. "But you know, that's not really important. What I want to know is what *you* think it is."

Kennet acknowledged their statement regarding parents with a sympathetic incline of his head, but decided they would probably appreciate it if he ignored it and addressed their curiosity instead. "Well, it sounds almost like what Gethinism describes as 'prophets.'"

"Bah!" they scoffed, throwing up a hand.

"Oh, I'm sorry?" Kennet wondered what he had said that was wrong, but they didn't leave him with just the scoff.

"No, no, it's not you, it's Gethinism," Asa replied, somewhat apologetically. "I've never been fond of it."

"Why not? Is there something wrong with it?" Kennet wondered, suddenly worried that he was part of some abhorrent religion, ignorant to its faults when he had joined.

"No, not particularly, I've just . . . never liked it much, you know? The people back home who practice it, they're not the type of people I enjoy being around. Besides that, I've always found it . . ." They shuddered exaggeratedly. "I don't know! I don't know what it is. It's nothing about the religion itself or its beliefs, it's just me. It's definitely me."

"Does that negate my theory immediately?"

"Well, that depends. Is the theory directly connected to Gethinism?"

"Not quite," Kennet said. "It's not specific to Gethin at all."

"Then please, continue."

Kennet nodded. "Well, prophets are people who have been touched by a god. Most of the documented examples were Gethin, but I feel like I've heard a story or two about other gods doing it. Folk tales, mostly, they might not even be true, but . . ."

"I think if I'd met a god, I'd remember it," Asa said thoughtfully, "but it's not the worst guess I've heard. One person once told me I was cursed, and another told me I must have been born during a certain season, on a certain day —as though I was the only person to be born at the exact right time. Absurd! Very odd theories. Honestly, yours is the most believable one I've heard yet."

"But you've never met a god?"

"Not to my knowledge."

"Well, then, so much for that."

Asa shrugged. "That's part of why I came here, you know."

Kennet glanced down at them—Starling was a hand or so taller than Emilio, so they sat a bit below him—and saw that they were staring off into the distance. "To find out why you can do this?"

"More or less. I don't know why, but I felt like I was more likely to figure things out if I left. It felt . . . like a pull, just a deep desire to get out. You know? I felt like I wasn't learning anything by staying. Nothing about myself, nothing about the world. Everyone back home acted like they already knew me, and here I was, discovering that I didn't even know myself. Discovering that I had . . . that I could do things nobody else could, and they didn't believe me, because they had 'known me all my life.' Well, I've known me all my life too! Imagine how *I* feel!"

Kennet hummed softly at that. He could relate to the feeling, in no small sense, but his solution to his own similar crisis had been Gethinism. Though he had only known Asa a short while, he was *fairly* certain that wouldn't work for Asa the way it had for him. "But you're learning things here?" he asked.

"Oh!" Asa snapped out of the annoyed haze that had overcome them. "Oh yes. I've learned that mules are beautiful, friendly creatures. I learned that I can use this influence to be useful to others—before now, all I really used it for was my own benefit, a prank here and there. But over the past few days, I've helped a girl sleep, and a grieving father rest . . ."

"And you got some very good information for me back at the Dove," Kennet interjected.

"Oh, did I? I wasn't sure if that had worked at all."

"He didn't know anything that would help directly, but what he *did* say will make things easier down the road."

"Well. Good, then." They puffed their chest out a bit in pride.

Something occurred to Kennet, and before he could think better of the idea, he said it aloud. "Asa—"

"Hmm?"

"I know we had just planned on traveling together a short while for convenience's sake, but I was wondering—"

"I hope you know where you're going with this, Sir Peders," Asa teased. "I'm not that kind of bard."

Kennet laughed, so loudly that it startled his horse a bit. "Oh, I wasn't propositioning you. Well, I was, but not that kind. I was going to ask if you wanted to work with me."

"Oh?" They raised an eyebrow at him.

"Like you said, your ability to influence people has been very helpful. And it might continue to be—would you like to accompany me in my investigation for Lord Hagen?"

Asa considered this. "This is to find a cure for the girl?" they asked.

"Partially. That's the focus at the moment, but it might go beyond that, depending on if we're too late or not."

Asa's eyes widened. "What do you mean?"

"I mean, if we can't save Marna." He paused, hating that he had said those words out loud. "We might have to hunt down her killer."

"Lord Hagen doesn't seem the vengeful type," Asa said doubtfully.

"He's too busy worrying to be vengeful."

They shrugged. "That may be true. So, then, would I be on the hook until Marna is cured, or until the job is done either way?"

"You're on the hook until you don't want to be. But if you leave before I'm paid, you won't get paid either."

"Oh, there's money involved?" The innocence in their voice was very obviously feigned, coated in a thick layer of sarcasm. "I was just doing this for fun."

"I'd be happy to share the profits with you," Kennet said. "Emilio needs to eat, you know."

"Ha!" Asa rubbed the neck of the mule again, then turned to look up at Kennet with a smile on their face. "Very well then, if you think I can be of help, I'd be happy to."

So he had a partner again. Kennet found that he had done this mostly without planning, without meaning to fill that void he had noticed days ago. That was all right, he decided; it wasn't a selfish action. It was solving more than one problem. To have Asa was more than to just have a partner in the way he was used. He'd had partners before. They were helpful, but most hadn't been able to do anything Kennet couldn't do himself.

Asa, on the other hand, was capable of things Kennet couldn't fathom. They had already opened a few doors he wouldn't have been able to without them. What more would they be able to accomplish now that they were officially working together?

He was anxious to find out.

~

KENNET SAT cross-legged in front of a fire that was just starting to burn properly, one that he had spent far too long building. Even now it threatened to give out on him, flickering weakly as the small branches in the center burned, refusing to move toward the larger logs that he had carefully stacked on top so as to not smother the small flame. Eventually, though, he noted with satisfaction that the flames were spreading, and he allowed himself to turn his attention away from the fire and toward his horse.

Starling and Emilio were hitched to some trees, close to each other. The two were getting along shockingly well. Perhaps Starling would learn a thing or two from the mule and Kennet would have a more obedient horse by the end of this. Perhaps not, though. Kennet stepped up to the two, giving Starling a loving pat on the nose before he felt a nudge at his back from Emilio.

"Hello there." He laughed and gave the mule a nose pat as well.

"If I find out that he likes you better than me I'm going to kill you in your sleep," came Asa's voice as they emerged from the small tent they had just finished setting up.

"I'd like to see you try that," Kennet replied.

He moved away from the horses and back into the camp, joining Asa by the fire. Asa had shed their doublet and was in the process of wrapping their hair up in a silk scarf again. When they had finished, they began to wipe the makeup off from under their eyes with a small kerchief.

"You went to all the trouble of putting that on and nobody even saw you wear it," Kennet remarked.

"You saw me," Asa pointed out.

"Oh." He hadn't considered himself the target audience.

They picked their vihuela up from where it was propped up against the tent, and sat down in front of the fire. With their legs crossed, they began to strum at the instrument quietly. Kennet sat down as well and allowed himself to enjoy the music, staring into the flames which had now become quite strong and were crackling away under the soft tones of the bard's song.

"Do you mind if I sing?" Asa said after a while of this.

"I've never known a bard to ask before they start singing," Kennet said. "Usually they just go for it."

"I'm not just a bard right now, I'm your traveling companion. If you want some quiet, it's only polite for me to shut the hell up."

Kennet chuckled, shaking his head. "Please, sing," he said. "I'm sure I'll enjoy it. I've had far too much quiet lately."

Asa bowed their head to acknowledge that, and picked up the pace of their playing, falling into a distinct rhythm. They continued to play without singing for some time before speaking again, rather than starting to sing. "I'm trying to write something in Bladstongue," they said. "I think after a year of being here, I'm finally getting good enough that I can try."

"I can help, if you need it," Kennet offered. "I've spoken the language my whole life."

"Wonderful, I'm definitely afraid of getting something wrong, and just . . . not knowing. I've heard some do the same with my home tongue—we get a lot of travelers from the north and many of them don't catch on easily to the nuances of Isla."

"Ah, nuance. Well, Bladstongue has some, but not enough that I'd get bogged down in worry if I were you."

"I won't," Asa reassured him, "especially since I'll have a second opinion."

"How did you learn Bladstongue, anyway? Did you know any before you came here?"

"No!" Asa laughed, playing a short melodic phrase to punctuate their statement. "Oh no, and that was likely the most stupid thing I did, or rather didn't do. The first . . . what, six months? Six months of my early time here I spent with this very kind family in Vindmora—a mother and her two children. They were very patient with me, and I learned most of it from them."

"Six months is a lot of time to spend in Vindmora. How did you like that?"

They shrugged. "Out of everywhere I've been, I would consider it perhaps the closest I've come to a home since I left Lucien. But I didn't come here to find a home, did I? I came here to explore."

"To learn things," Kennet repeated what they had said earlier.

"Right," they agreed. "And now I'm going to learn how to write a song in Bladstongue. Well, that's not quite true. I've already written it, actually. This one's mostly a translation of one I'd already written in Isla. It's my most repetitive song so I thought it would be the easiest one to translate. Maybe you can listen to it, tell me if I did all right?"

Kennet adjusted himself to face them and gestured for them to play, which was met with a smile and a new rhythm from the bard, a new song.

Their voice was clear, and each word was carefully enunciated, unlike when they had sung in Isla and Kennet had been unsure where any one word ended and the next began. The song maintained a great deal of the Lucien stylings both in their play style and the melody. This mixed interestingly with the Bladstongue lyrics, creating a unique atmosphere that Kennet was so wrapped up in observing that he almost forgot he was supposed to be listening to the lyrics themselves.

> I wrote a song about you
> And you, you painted your muse
> My body on your canvas
> In golden tones and hues
> Between the two of us I found
> No space and nothing new
> A comfortable quiet
> The painter paints his lover
> The lover sings the painter's song

I wrote a song about you
And you, you painted me still
I saw myself once again
Painted with the same skill
Between the two of us I found
No space and nothing new
A comfortable quiet
The painter paints his lover
The lover sings the painter's song

I wrote a song about you
And you, what did you paint now?
I did not see myself there
No gold, nor orange, nor brown
Between the two of us I found
Some space and something new
Uncomfortable questions
The painter paints a painting
The lover sings the painter's song

I asked about your painting
And you painted on without care
A flower bright and blooming
Your answer for me was a vacant stare
Between the two of us I found
Myself suddenly alone
The painter paints a flower
The lover sings the painter's song

> I wrote a song about you
> I can't seem to write anything else
> Your lingering presence haunts me
> I can't seem to be free of your spell
> There is no two of us, I've found
> I'll have to make it on my own
> The painter paints what he pleases
> The lover sings the painter's song

KENNET APPLAUDED SOFTLY as the song faded out. Asa's face, which had been gently mournful to reflect the tone of the song, quickly snapped back into a smile as they bowed to his applause.

"So! You liked it?" they asked, falling back into the soft instrumental strumming they had been playing before they started singing.

"It was very good," Kennet replied. "Heart-wrenching story. Inspired by someone?"

"No, not really," Asa said, "but audiences love it when they think that the singer is singing about themself. They almost write their own stories about you in their head."

Kennet knew he was absolutely guilty of doing exactly that. "It's very easy to do, in this case."

"Good, then I've done my job!"

"Do you ever write about personal experiences?"

Asa thought about it for a moment. "Well, yes, everyone does," they said. "But I've sort of run out of interesting experiences to write about. Luckily, I figure that traveling with a mercenary is a wonderful way to see new and exciting things."

"I'm not a mercenary," Kennet said tiredly.

They paused in their playing, resting their hand against the strings to quiet them. "Oh? Then you're just someone who has a lot of knives and scars, and gets paid to travel around for fun?"

"Firstly, I don't have that many knives," Kennet said. "Just four."

"That's three more than I have."

"Secondly, mercenaries fight in wars," he added, completely ignoring their interjection. "I've never fought in a war before."

"Oh, I didn't know that's what that meant." Asa blinked. "See, I'm already learning things! Then . . ." They considered what he had said. "What's the word for someone who does the same thing a mercenary does, but not during wars?"

"Assassin." The word tasted sour in Kennet's mouth. He let it sit for a moment before clarifying. "But I'm not that either."

"It seems like you are, by definition."

"I don't kill people for money anymore."

Asa was quiet, looking Kennet over as they drummed their fingers against the vihuela. "Anymore?" they prompted when he didn't elaborate.

Kennet shook his head. He didn't really want to get into it, but it was going to be hard to get around it if they were going to continue to travel together. If he didn't tell Asa himself, someone else likely would. "I used to be one of the most sought-after assassins in the country," he said slowly. "But that kind of work is hard on your mind and body, so I stopped taking those kinds of jobs. These days I try to help people who can't help themselves, in a way. Whether it be bounty hunting, debt collection—or investigations, like what I'm doing now, just . . . no killing anymore."

"Why not? Not that I think you're wrong or anything, I just know people don't make those decisions on a whim."

"This coming from the person who left their home country to come to a land whose language they didn't know a lick of."

"That's a completely different kind of decision." Asa waved their hand dismissively. "A career like that requires time and effort to build, especially to gain a reputation of trust that awards you the title of 'most sought-after assassin.'"

"I may have been exaggerating that part."

"Nevertheless."

Kennet stared into the fire again, propping his head up on his hand. "Well, what would make you stop playing music?"

There was silence from Asa that lasted a few minutes this time. They seemed to be taking his question seriously, mulling it over until they finally said, "Honestly, I would only ever stop if I was no longer able to do it at all, or if it stopped being fun."

"So, killing people stopped being fun." Kennet latched onto their example. "It was bound to happen at some point."

"I find it hard to believe you were ever the kind of person to find it fun in the first place," Asa said, and Kennet gave a rueful chuckle.

"Oh, you've met a very different Kennet than I was even just a few years ago," he said. "But you should count yourself lucky for that."

Asa was quiet again. Then, slowly, they broke the silence with more music, and Kennet hoped he hadn't said anything wrong. He knew this was a hard topic to broach, not just for him, but for people who wanted to like him. He was trying to be a better person now, but it was impossible to do that without acknowledging his past, especially when that past seemed intent on following him around—even more especially considering who they were going to Grankoping to see.

Even if he hadn't told them himself, Hana would say something that would give it away almost immediately. This conversation felt like it had gone poorly, but at least it had come from him. At least they were prepared.

Was this some kind of self-sabotage, he wondered? Was there no way he could let them get to know him without front-loading the relationship with all the bad things he'd done? Or was this a necessary precaution?

Honestly, it felt like a safeguard. If he told them as much as he could bear to tell them now, then if they decided to hate him, at least it would happen before he got attached.

He was already attached, of course. It was hard not to be with how shockingly easy the two of them were getting along. He hadn't found someone this easy to talk to in some time. However, he knew he could get further attached if he let himself. Best to give them a chance to think about it seriously first, to properly decide whether or not he was worth the risk.

He wouldn't blame them if they decided he wasn't.

Before he could try and breach the silence again, try and figure out a way to ask if he had gone too far, they beat him to it.

"If there were no assassins in the world, would little girls still get poisoned?" they wondered aloud. "Would those who wanted to hurt people simply find a different way to do it? Would they do it themselves? Are people like you not just an excuse, someone to blame for the intent of the harm that they would cause either way?"

Kennet had often wondered the same things himself. "I don't know," he said. "Perhaps we make things too easy for those who wouldn't have gone through with it if they had to do more than throw money at those of us who are willing to get our hands dirty."

"Or perhaps you're simply a middleman of a process that would come to pass either way," Asa said. "I'm not trying to justify what you've done; I'm saying at least you didn't do it out of hatred."

"Some would say that's even worse."

"Some might!" Asa agreed. "Anyway, it's simply a philosophical question. I think you were right to stop, obviously."

"Or you might not have stayed?" Kennet said. "If I had still been in that profession?"

"What?" They frowned. "Remember, Sir Peders, I *did* think you were of that profession until mere moments ago! Not to sound immoral, but as long as we're not on our way to kill someone right this second, I wasn't going to get bogged down in the details. I know what you're being paid to do right now, and it's as noble a job as anyone could hope to take."

"Well, I can agree with that much."

Asa nodded, seeming satisfied with the conclusion they had reached, and their melodies became more complicated. Kennet took this as a sign that their mind had shifted from the matter at hand and toward their practice, so he let that be the end of it. Their musings had given him a little relief. Of course, they didn't know the details. Maybe if they heard how things had ended with the last people who had dared to work alongside him, they wouldn't be so quick to give him a chance.

It was almost not even worth thinking about that possibility though.

For now, he knew where they stood. And with any luck there would be plenty of time for him to elaborate. In their own time.

At their own pace.

CHAPTER 6

A TERRIBLE TALE TOLD TO A TERRIBLE TAIL

G RANKOPING WAS EASILY THE BUSIEST CITY KENNET HAD ever found himself in. Certainly Guldfjord, the capital of Bladland, was *technically* larger, but something about it had always seemed very contained, very official. Nothing as frantic as this market town.

Asa seemed right at home, however, looking about excitedly as they entered the town proper after dropping their mounts off at a stable. Kennet had been planning on leading the way through the town, since he was the taller of the two, but he found out quickly that they were a natural citymover. They slid between crowds in the middle of the road as though it were second nature.

They *had* mentioned growing up in a city, hadn't they?

The sun was beginning to set as they walked through the streets, moving through groups of people getting off work and heading toward taverns. They passed the infamous market itself, and Kennet paused for a second to watch a stall tear down. A good many were empty, and looked to have been for a while now—he guessed they had to be left early for the farmers to make it back to their land before the sun set, and that journey couldn't be short. Artisans who lived in town could likely afford to keep their wares up a little longer.

Asa stopped next to Kennet, their hands on their hips, watching the stall take down its display with him for a moment. "So!" they said, when they could no longer stay silent. "Where are we going?"

Kennet snapped to attention at that and looked up at the sky. Judging by the colors streaking across it, they should likely find a place to stay before exploring any farther. "Let's find ourselves some rooms," he suggested, "and I can ask where we can find our contact."

"Who is this contact, exactly?" Asa wondered as they started to walk again and Kennet started to scan the streets to try and identify an inn.

"Her name is Hana Oh," Kennet said. "She's an old friend of mine who's very good with herbs and poisons."

"Her name sounds Anjeonese," Asa observed. "That's not something I expected in Bladland."

"She's the only person I've really known from the southeastern coast before I met you," Kennet replied, "apart from a few merchants, and I didn't talk to them long. Hana—she hasn't been in Anjeon for years, though, I should note. Left because of some sort of plague."

Asa raised their eyebrows. "Oh, that long ago? The plague was . . ." They paused, seemingly doing the math in their head. "What, somewhere around fifteen years ago now, I think?"

"It hit your country as well?" Kennet asked, surprised.

"Oh, did it ever. Everyone along the coast was affected, as far north as Byvar. I was too young to remember anything about it, but countless of my elders were left scarred."

Kennet nodded, familiar with exactly the kind of scars Asa was speaking of. When he had met Hana, they were the first things he had noticed about her, in spite of himself. "It sounded to me like an awful time. I'm glad it never made it out this way."

"Me too," Asa agreed seriously. "You're all very lucky that the voyage is so long. Any plague-infested ship would perish at sea before they even caught a glimpse of Bladland's shore."

Kennet shuddered at that. Hana had never been one to talk about the plague, and he hadn't been one to pry, but Asa painted a grim picture with their artistic language. No wonder Hana hadn't ever wanted to speak about it.

"But you said she knows herbs and poisons. Did you used to work together?" Asa prompted in an attempt to bring the conversation back around.

"We did," Kennet said.

"And is that what didn't end well?"

"It didn't," Kennet admitted after a brief pause, "but not as poorly as some other relationships. I think when she hears why I've come to her, she'll understand."

"Well, if she doesn't, I can always make her."

Kennet's expression caught itself somewhere between amusement and surprise. "I suppose you can!" he said. "I'd almost forgotten about that."

"Oh, you flatter me. If only my personality were interesting enough for you to forget about the *real* reason you asked me along." Asa laughed.

"I asked you along for several reasons." Kennet stopped suddenly, having identified an inn, and opened the door for Asa. They bowed in thanks.

"Oh, like what?" they said over their shoulder as they entered in front of him.

Kennet found himself stumbling over his words as he tried to think of a way to answer that question. "Your singing," he said as smoothly as he could manage, stepping into the room behind them. He knew the statement was weak, and could tell they were unimpressed with it by the look on their face.

"My singing?" they repeated skeptically. "So you asked me along because I'm so good at my job?"

"Partially."

They considered him in the unnerving way he was now aware was just a habit of theirs, allowing their eyes to slowly travel over his face and dress before they snapped up to his own eyes again, and a smile lit up their countenance. "Well," Asa said, "I suppose I am very good at it."

Kennet snorted, recovering quickly from whatever had caused him to lose track of his words. "And very humble, too," he added, and brushed past them on the way to the bar. He heard their laughter like a bell behind him before they caught up to him once again. They reached the bar together.

The bartender was busy, so Asa leaned against the bar and took the time to look over the rest of the establishment. Kennet followed their gaze through the crowded but not packed room, and saw that they were particularly interested in a group of performers that was gathered on a small stage in the corner. The music they were playing was pleasant enough, in Kennet's opinion, and judging by the slight frown on Asa's face, they agreed with him.

"Seems like there's no need for my services here," they observed with a somewhat sullen tone. "That's all right! Means I have plenty of time to relax and rest my voice for when we get back to Osternas."

As they said this, the bartender freed up, coming to their aid. "Can I get you anything?" She was a tall woman with straw-blonde hair tied back in a tight bun, and in contrast to her apparent musculature, she had a soft face. "I like your makeup," she added to Asa. Kennet saw the bard's face bloom with a smile once again.

"Thank you! I didn't have a mirror to put it on in this morning, so it's not my best work."

"It's better than I can do," the bartender lamented.

"Never had a steady hand, afraid I'd poke myself in the eye. Never mind that, though. Can I get you some ale?"

"And two hot meals, whatever you think is good," Asa said. They pulled money out of their purse and slid it across the counter to her.

As the bartender accepted the coin and turned away to get their food and drink, Kennet turned to his companion. "I'll pay you back for that," he said, and Asa scoffed.

"No you won't. I won't let you."

"You really won't, will you?"

They grinned. "Nope." They tugged at the edges of their gloves, pulling them on more snugly. It was a tic Kennet had noticed, even though the gloves never seemed to actually be loose.

The bartender returned once more, and Kennet addressed her. "I have a question," he said as he accepted the ale and food from her. "If I was looking for someone in town, where should I ask?"

The bartender raised an eyebrow. "Depends on why you're looking for them."

"It's an old friend of mine," Kennet said, "that's all. We used to work together, and I know she lives here. I'm just passing through but I know she'd kill me if she found out I came by and didn't say hello."

The bartender considered his words, then the way he looked, then who he'd come in with. Finally, she shrugged. "Well, you can ask me."

"Better than nothing." He felt almost certain that this woman wouldn't know Hana, but honestly, it wasn't impossible and he had to start somewhere. "Hana Oh, a woman from across the eastern sea."

"Well, you don't see many from the east this far inland," the bartender said thoughtfully. "I can't say I've seen anyone by that description recently."

"I thought as much, but that's all right. Thank you for trying."

The bartender inclined her head in apology and returned to her work, leaving Asa and Kennet alone once more. Kennet sighed roughly.

"It was a bit of a long shot." Asa's tone was soothing. "I suppose a better place to ask would be an herbalist's shop or something similar? Though I guess a lot of those would be closed by now."

"Ah, a lesson in my trade for you." Kennet stretched, finding himself smiling again. "After close is often the best time to question a shop owner. Privacy."

"That makes sense. I don't suppose you'll want me along for that?" They wiggled their fingers to suggest the use of their influence.

Kennet shook his head. "It's been a long day. You should eat and get some sleep. I doubt anything I do tonight will get us anywhere."

"If you're so sure, then why not join me? We already have the food, it'll go to waste," they added as they noticed him pushing off the bar, and adjusting his coat to make his way back out onto the street.

"I feel like I've wasted so much time," Kennet said softly, honestly. "Even if I know it's not going to help, I won't be able to sleep if I don't at least try to do something."

Asa looked concerned at the way he said this. "I can help you sleep," they offered. "If you know logically that you can't do anything to help, I can give you a way to feel at peace with that, and you can get some rest."

Kennet considered that. It was tempting, but he couldn't shake the feeling that he would be doing the girl a great disservice. He might miss something if he let his guard down for even a second. So he shook his head again. "No," he said, "but thank you."

The bard sighed. "Suit yourself. I'll get lodgings squared away."

Kennet nodded in thanks and gave them a pat on the shoulder as he stepped back toward the door. "I'll be back before long," he said.

"If you aren't back by morning, I'll assume you're dead."

Kennet laughed, and for a moment he almost responded. But it was a terrible response to say, and it would only worry them—there was really no use in telling them it'd honestly be a fairly accurate assumption to make.

∼

THE STREETS WERE STILL BUSY, even after the market was closed. There were more shops open than Kennet had anticipated, including a good few apothecaries and herbalists. While that had made his job considerably easier, it had not yet yielded any results. Most didn't know what a sun-cap mushroom was—none knew of a cure. Even though he had expected as much, he couldn't help but feel discouraged.

And that was only half of the issue. His second line of questioning wasn't working out any better than the first. He had been hoping that even if he couldn't find Hana directly, he would at least get an idea of where to start, because he didn't have much more of a plan. Surely she frequented *one* of these shops. Even if she was going by a different name, she was impossible to mistake for someone else. But it was a big city, and she had always liked the more hole-in-the-wall type establishments. Come morning, he would have to get more incisive, get into the nooks and crannies of the city itself.

The sun had fully gone down, and Kennet was beginning to get frustrated with the city's crowdedness. Nothing had calmed. If anything, there had been a short lull when they first arrived, but now things were renewed with the passion of nightlife. It made walking through the streets borderline impossible if one was the type of person who didn't like being bumped into.

This kind of bustle would usually be the perfect place to follow someone, if someone needed to be followed. Even a novice would be able to tail someone without being noticed in a crowd like this.

Whoever was tailing Kennet, though . . .

Worse than a novice.

He'd noticed the man in the second shop he'd stopped in. This man had come in shortly after Kennet, hung around for a while. Left before Kennet did. This was all quite normal, except he had also been hanging around outside a bar by the next shop. There he'd been talking to people—again, very casually, very normal. Nevertheless, this exceedingly normal behavior had done anything but put Kennet at ease.

He could feel the man walking behind him. There was something about the way that the crowd was shifting that told him that he was being followed closely. Too closely.

He stopped in the middle of the crowd, and bent down to tie a lace on his boots that wasn't loose. Behind him, he could hear a few men yelling at someone to keep moving. Someone else had stopped too.

The crowd continued to flow around Kennet. He stole a glance between his legs at the ground behind him to see a pair of black boots. They stood still in the street, flickering in and out of view through the herd of other feet that stepped between them and Kennet.

When the crowd got particularly thick between them, and for a split second Kennet could not see the boots, he moved.

Not much, mind you. He had stopped near a well, and quickly ducked past a group of people walking to slide behind it. Then after a moment to catch his breath, he peeked up over the well to see if he could get a good look at his new friend.

The man was standing still, looking lost. He could not have been more obvious if he had tried, glancing around like a child who had been left behind by their mother. Kennet cocked his head slowly and took stock of his new enemy. He was short and wore dark clothing. He dressed like Kennet did, Kennet realized. Which was funny—if this man was a member of the same guild that he had been a part of, Kennet would expect him to be better at his job.

Still, it might make sense. What better way to fight fire than with fire? So. Someone knew Kennet was on this job, and they were trying to make sure he didn't complete it. He was suddenly glad he had found this man before he found Hana. It gave him a chance to shut this down before he put her in any undue danger.

The man started to walk again, looking defeated, and Kennet felt a small smile creep onto his face. The tables had turned. It was time to show this fool what a real stalker looked like.

As his would-be pursuer started on his way back, Kennet slipped out of his cover and back into the crowd. Unlike him, Kennet kept his distance. He walked casually, weaving in and out of the people with renewed energy—where the jostling had bothered him before, now he took it as an opportunity to blend in. He jostled back.

The man walked with clear purpose, but kept scanning the crowd in front of him as if hoping that Kennet would miraculously reappear. He didn't look behind him, not once, which Kennet counted as lucky for himself. Not that he couldn't have handled it if the man *did* look behind. In fact, he sort of wanted him to look. Kennet wanted this man to see him standing there, he wanted that moment of pride and surprise.

But the man didn't look. He stayed on the main street for a while, eventually giving up trying to relocate Kennet and instead peeling off into an alleyway. Kennet took this as his moment to strike.

Once they had entered the alley there was no more pretense to be had. The man noticed Kennet almost immediately.

"Gods!" the man shouted. He stumbled back as Kennet advanced on him, but he didn't move to run.

Kennet closed the distance between them and with a simple maneuver he had the man by the throat, slamming him into the wall of the alley. A fierceness entered his expression as he lifted the shorter man to stand on the tips of his toes. Finally, he could get a good look at the man who had dared to tail him. He was older than Kennet, with streaks of grey at each temple, and similar streaks in his well-groomed beard that grew beneath a hawkish hooked nose. His eyes were close together, and he held Kennet's gaze with a surprising ferocity of his own as calloused hands flew up to attempt to claw Kennet's grip away from his throat. Kennet did not relent. In fact, he pressed harder. The man gagged at the pressure on his windpipe.

"Why are you following me?" Kennet demanded. "Who sent you?"

"You—who—?" the man stuttered, his voice hoarse.

"Answer the question!" Kennet barked. "Who sent you?"

"I don't know what you—"

There was the sound of a door opening, and both Kennet's and the man's head swiveled to see who had interrupted them. Into the alleyway peeked a child—a young boy. He stared at Kennet and the ongoing interrogation with wide eyes.

Kennet tried to calculate what would be best to say. How he could best respond to this. He should tell the child to go back inside, he thought, but before he could say anything the child said something that stopped him in his tracks.

"Pa?" The child's voice trembled, as though he was about to burst into tears.

"Heeeyyy, James." The man Kennet had pinned to the wall stopped struggling, holding his hands up to seem as nonthreatening as possible. "It's all right, boy, don't be scared."

"Is it all right?" Kennet wondered aloud, stunned for words as he looked at the boy. The man's demeanor had shifted entirely. Kennet let up the pressure on his neck in his confusion, trying to put together the puzzle that was laying itself out in front of him.

The man seized upon his mistake immediately and smacked his arm aside. With a second, quicker move, he planted a knee in Kennet's gut. Kennet wheezed for breath, cursing himself internally for letting his guard down as the other man slammed an elbow into his back as he was doubled over in pain. Over the sound of his ears ringing, he could hear the child screaming in terror as his father unleashed hell on this strange man.

Kennet let himself fall to the ground at the man's attacks, using the momentum to sweep his opponent's legs out from under him. The man landed on his back with a thud. After a pause to spit blood onto the stone pavement, Kennet rolled over and straddled the man. He grabbed the man's wrists, pinning him to the ground—the child was still shouting, now calling for help. Kennet's heart started to race.

Then a voice broke through the blood rushing in his ears —clear as day and deadly familiar.

"Kennet?"

Both men froze. Kennet slowly turned toward the voice without letting go of the man's wrists. The child stood, teary-faced, holding the hand of a woman who stood behind him with an unimpressed look directed at both of the men on the ground.

"Hana." Kennet breathed a sigh of relief. He looked back

down at the man on the ground, suddenly more curious than angry. "Do you know . . . ?"

"He's a friend. An idiot, but a friend. Get off him, please, you're scaring James."

Kennet obliged immediately, standing up and stepping over the man on the ground toward Hana. The child flinched at his approach.

"It's all right, James." The boy's father repeated his placation as he got to his feet as well, his voice still hoarse from Kennet's attacks. "This is the friend your auntie and I were talking about earlier. We just had a misunderstanding."

"Auntie?" Kennet raised an eyebrow at Hana. She sighed.

"It's a very long story," she said. "You both should come inside."

∽

KENNET SAT on a long wooden bench across from a small fireplace, holding a mug full of warm tea. The boy James had not stopped staring at him since he arrived, and he could hardly blame the child. He knew he had frightened him, and he'd have felt bad about it, if the child's father hadn't been such a buffoon.

The buffoon in question entered the room as well now, a mug of his own in his hands. He stood by the fire, and Hana joined them shortly after. The three adults had been mostly silent other than to ask niceties like whether anyone wanted anything to drink, or anything like that. Now it was time to talk business.

"James, maybe you'd better go play in your room," Hana said softly.

James didn't need to be told twice. The boy scurried off up a narrow staircase behind them, leaving the adults alone. For a moment, things stayed quiet. Kennet finally let himself get a good look at Hana—she looked the same as she always had. Same dark hair she wore braided, same patchy scar that started at her neck. This was the most he'd seen of her scars. She no longer wore the full-coverage dark clothing she'd worn when they worked together, now sporting a simple tunic with rolled up sleeves, showing that the scars trailed down her forearms and stopped just before her hands.

All the same, beyond that small change she looked healthy. Not happy, though. Just healthy.

"When Stefan said someone was looking for me, I really hoped it'd be anyone else," she said after a long silence.

"That bad, is it?" Kennet replied sheepishly.

"What do you think?" Hana said. Her face was still stony calm, her mouth a straight line. "You can't have thought there was another way this could go."

"Well, I didn't expect you to have someone follow me. Sorry about all that, by the way," Kennet added toward Stefan, who raised his mug in acceptance of the apology.

"Just wish it hadn't happened in front of the boy," he said. "But all in all, that was my fault. I led you here."

"It was both your fault, and mine for taking my eyes off him for thirty seconds. Gods damn me for trying to get some time to myself, I guess," Hana said. "Stefan overheard you asking about me at a tavern and came home to check and see if I knew who you were. It sounded like you, but I couldn't believe you'd have the audacity to show your face anywhere near me. So I had him try to figure out what exactly you were after. Apparently he did a shit job of it."

"I'm out of practice," Stefan said, leaning on the wall.

"Stealth was never your strong suit," Hana countered. "You're a fighter first and foremost, I've always known that. When I needed stealth, I went to Kennet."

"Likely why the two of us haven't met before," Stefan acknowledged. "Stefan Bergstrom, by the way."

"Kennet Peders. You're a Hawk?"

"For a while, yes. Before James."

"Not that it matters anymore," Hana added. "After the stunt you pulled, Kennet, the Hawks no longer exist."

Kennet's eyes widened. He had expected Hana to have retired—that's why he hadn't reached out to the guild in any way. That, and the fact that he hadn't exactly been on good terms with them last he checked. But to hear they had disbanded completely . . .

"You say that like it was my fault," Kennet said slowly.

"Not entirely," Hana admitted, "but it was the beginning of the end. I left shortly after everything happened with you, and luckily Stefan's been out for some time, living a normal life out here with his son. So I decided to do the same."

"I didn't take you for the motherly type," Kennet said.

"Not a mother, no. James's mother left not long after he was born," Hana said with a soft incline of her head toward Stefan, who suddenly seemed very preoccupied with the mug of tea in his hands. "But as an aunt, I think I do quite well."

"So the two of you aren't . . .?"

Hana scoffed loudly at that, then glanced at Stefan again with a hand raised. "No offense, of course."

"Oh, no, of course," Stefan said, "I know I'm not your type."

"No, not by a mile."

Kennet shrugged. He didn't know enough about Hana's personal life to assume one way or the other. Sure, the last time they'd spent any time together, she'd been deeply in love with a woman. But Kennet had been deeply in love with a man at the time, and that didn't mean he didn't still fancy a woman here and there.

"They gave me a place to live, Stefan and James. And I do my best to give back by caring for the boy—he's a good one, you know," she added with a sigh, "and I think it's good for a child to have more than one influence in their life."

"And you're a far better influence than I am," Stefan agreed.

The lull that the conversation found itself in now seemed almost pleasant until Hana remembered she was angry at Kennet. For a moment, he had hoped she'd forgotten.

"So. How dare you?" she said suddenly, casually, turning toward him with a little bit of ire underlying her tone. "How dare you interrupt my calm life with your chaos? I thought you had at least *some* shame."

"You thought right," Kennet said. "I wouldn't have come if it wasn't important—and it is, very important. I need your help."

Hana didn't respond. She raised one eyebrow and looked toward Stefan as if to ask, "Are you seeing this?"

"I've been hired on an extremely sensitive job," Kennet continued when nobody prompted him further. "A child has been poisoned, and I'm in search of an antidote. I have some ideas, but—"

Hana's expression had shifted. "A child?" she asked. "Why?"

"I don't know. Her father is a lord, it seems like she may have been poisoned by mistake when her father was the target. Or, perhaps I'm being too generous to this villain, and the intent was to be especially cruel all along and kill the child herself."

She hesitated. The shift in her expression had gone from stern to almost understanding, which was echoed by her tone when she spoke again. "The girl is young?"

"Near James's age, I'd say." Kennet knew it was underhanded to bring the boy into this, but it had the desired effect, sending a shockwave of nervous energy through the room.

Stefan was staring daggers at Hana. Kennet could tell he had immediately decided what the right move was.

Hana didn't seem to agree. Not right away, at least.

"So let me see if I understand you correctly," she said. "You ruin my life. You destroy the only good thing in it and leave me lost, broken and alone to recover. Then, you decide to clean up your act. You better yourself. Now you only take good jobs, the jobs that help people. You think that will fix you. And you think that since you're fixed, and since you help people now, you can come to me—still broken, mind you!—and you can ask me to help you now. Because you're fixed."

"Hana, I'm sorry."

"You cannot be sorry enough." Hana's face had become a blank slate again, and she crossed her arms. "You can never atone, and I won't help you try."

"Hana . . ." Stefan broke in, but she held up a hand to shut him down.

"So when I say I'll make you an antidote, know that it's not because I believe your motivation is pure. Know that it's because I have my own—and mine is to keep a child safe. It's nothing to do with you. In fact, the child would have been better off if anybody else had been the one to ask me."

Kennet hung his head in shame, but he felt relief wash over him at the same time in an ugly slurry of emotions. He found himself wishing he had brought the bard after all, if only for them to calm him down like they had offered. "Thank you," he said softly.

"Get out of my house now," Hana added. Her tone was stiff. It was clear she had a lot more that she wanted to say and was barely holding back. "It's too late to do anything tonight. Come back in the morning and we'll figure out what we need to do next."

"Thank you," Kennet repeated. "I—ah, I should warn you, I'm not traveling alone. I'll be bringing my companion with me in the morning, if that's all right?"

"Traveling with . . .?" Hana seemed surprised. "I suppose you may, as long as they know how to behave themself."

"They do. More than me, I think."

"That's not hard." Hana's expression softened slightly, and she sighed. "You certainly know how to keep my life interesting, Kennet. I'll give you that. Now leave my house, and don't come back until tomorrow, all right?"

"Yes ma'am." Kennet stood and gave a little bow to her, and then to Stefan, who raised his mug again in goodbye.

As Kennet stepped out of the small row house into the alley again and heard the door shut behind him, he felt himself starting to shake. A combination of nerves and the night breeze, he was sure, but he hated it either way.

It could have gone worse, he told himself, but he wasn't sure how. He had known she would say yes—at least, he hadn't allowed himself to imagine a world where she didn't. All the same, he hadn't expected this. He'd thought she'd be living alone, as hurt as she had mentioned she was, but strong and stoic and all of that. And she was! But she had a family now.

And he was pulling her away from that.

Again.

He felt intensely guilty.

But he was only doing that for a moment, wasn't he? All he needed was an antidote, and then he'd be on his way, and she could forget he ever existed.

He hoped, at least, that she would be able to. It seemed like she was much happier in a world like that.

∽

HE ARRIVED at the tavern to find it mostly empty. A few stragglers still hovered at the bar, and the same bartender as before stood behind it. She smiled when she saw him walk in.

"Your friend said to tell you they've got a room for you. Yours is the first door on the left, right next to theirs. They said they'll let you fetch them when it's time for you to leave tomorrow."

Two rooms. Certainly it would've been cheaper to buy one with a couple beds, but perhaps they wanted the privacy. That was fine. With the state he was in, Kennet rather wanted the privacy himself. He was too tired to think about it much more than that, accepting the information from the bartender and making his way up the stairs. He felt them creak under his weight and felt as though he was carrying a bag full of bricks with the way his heart was sagging in his chest.

She was right to be mad at him. And he'd known she would be. And he'd gotten what he needed.

But . . .

He wanted to go back and plead with her, to tell her he knew. He *knew* there would be no redemption. Deep down, he did know. Deep down he knew that under every prayer he spoke, behind every job he took, there was nothing but the same depraved old soul that had hurt her. He wasn't as delusional about it as she thought he was, he knew it well and good.

He entered the small inn room. Shut the door behind him. Sat down hard on the bed.

And found he was crying.

Of course he was crying.

He let himself cry an angry, ugly cry, the cry that had perhaps been begging to be released since it began with the bard's touch three days ago.

Part of him considered going to Asa again, knocking on their door, waking them up. Begging them to hold his hand in theirs and give him some semblance of peace so he could sleep.

But he didn't want to bother them. They deserved their peace, a full night's rest, and he deserved this. Not peace. Not *them*.

What a fool he was.

He sucked a breath in through his teeth and forced the tears to stop, holding them back with shuddering sighs. This was all a waste of time, all things he already knew, had already cried over, and already damned himself for. There was no use going through all that again.

Tomorrow he would go back to Hana. They would save this child.

And then she could go back to hating him, and he could go back to trying to lie to himself.

CHAPTER 7

THE THINGS WE DO FOR THE SAKE OF A CHILD

Asa was already dressed and ready to leave by the time Kennet dragged himself out of his bed and made it to their room. He figured he didn't have the time to meditate, and the conversation with Hana had made the action feel slightly hollow, and almost meaningless. It felt like a sham he was putting up. It made more sense to him to push on without it and get this next part over and done with.

"You look awful," Asa remarked the moment they saw him.

"God, do I?" Kennet hadn't taken the time to look in a mirror.

"Yes. You're all puffy." They leaned against the frame of the door, and their eyes narrowed in suspicion. "Did something happen last night?"

"Well, yes," Kennet admitted, "I found Hana."

"Oh! How?"

It was hard to take offense at the disbelief in their voice. In their position, Kennet likely would have felt the same. "A friend of hers overheard me asking around for her and brought me to where she's staying. Pure luck." He abridged the messy parts.

"Oh, well! Excellent. We could use a little luck, I think. You spoke to her?"

"Briefly. Only enough to explain the basics of the situation."

"And?"

"She said yes."

Asa looked pleased by this. "And I didn't even have to do anything," they said. "Just the way I like it."

Kennet could feel his spirits rising just from being around them. "Well, it was nice to have that trick up my sleeve, even if I didn't have to use it. Anyhow, I told her I'd be by again today with you, to go over the details. So, if you're ready—"

"I am!" Asa nodded. "Should I bring my vihuela?"

"I suppose there's no harm in it. They have a child, but he's old enough to know not to touch it."

"I certainly hope so." Asa sniffed and fetched their instrument from near the bed. "It would be a shame if I had to hit a child; it would fly in the face of everything we're here to achieve."

With laughter, the two made their way down through the tavern and into the streets. It was late enough in the morning that the market was in full display, and they had the luxury of walking right by it as they made their way to Hana's home. Asa stopped at one of the stalls, only for a moment, to ooh and ahh over some freshly baked pastries. With the flick of a coin from their gloved fingertips to the stall owner, they had purchased a few small rounds of shortbread, and handed one to Kennet. Kennet accepted the sweet with a bow of thanks, and turned his attention toward the streets as he took small bites, letting the delicate and well-made shortbread melt in his mouth.

Even in the state of distress he had been in the night before, he had been careful to pay attention to which streets led him back to the inn. It wasn't going to be a long walk, especially now that he wasn't winding through the shopping district looking for leads. It took them almost no time at all to find themselves in front of the small house, at the front door this time.

With a short, curt knock, Kennet announced their arrival, then stepped back. After a moment, the door opened and they were greeted by a smile, a salt and pepper beard, and a deep purple bruise that had bloomed on a high cheekbone. Kennet cringed at the sight.

"Stefan," he said.

"Sir Peders!" Stefan said, unfazed and apparently holding no grudges. "Welcome back. We were afraid you might not be able to find the place."

"I have an excellent sense of direction. We just slept in," Kennet replied.

"Ah, right. Your friend." Stefan opened the door wider, stepping outside fully to get a better look at Asa.

"Asa of the Isles. Pleasure to meet you." Asa gave an elegant bow that looked polished by practice. At first, Stefan seemed a little put off by their bright costume and dramatic behavior; nevertheless he gave a small bow of his own in return.

"Stefan Bergstrom. Welcome to my home—er, please. Come in." He stepped aside to allow them to enter.

As they stepped into the house, Kennet immediately caught sight of Hana leaning against the back wall by the fireplace to watch them. Her expression was almost impossible to read, though he did see it change slightly as Asa came in behind him. If she had any specific thoughts on them she didn't say them. In fact, she didn't say anything even as Stefan shut the door behind them and stood awkwardly in front of his guests.

"Well," he said eventually. "Tea?"

Hana laughed. "Stef, you dope," she said, finally pushing off the wall and making her way toward them. "Make the tea, I'll handle the talking."

Stefan gave a bit of indignant bluster at being called a dope but did as he was told, fading into a different room to leave them alone.

Asa watched him before turning back to the others. "I hope you don't want privacy," they said, gesturing to the other room. "I can help with the tea."

"No," Hana replied. "It's best if we're not left completely alone." She paused, and Kennet watched as she made no secret of examining Asa. "What are you? A performer of some kind?"

"A musician," Asa replied, gesturing to their vihuela.

"You're not from here, are you?"

"I'm from Lucien. Been here for about a year."

Hana nodded slowly. Her eyebrows quirked at the mention of their home country, and she immediately remarked on it. "I don't know why anyone would leave Lucien for Bladland," she muttered. "The weather here is awful."

"I haven't been here for a bad winter yet. I expect that'll be what sours me to it. So far everything's been lovely," Asa said.

"You speak Bladstongue well, too." She sounded intrigued. "Do you speak Anjeonese?"

"My grandmother was Anjeonese, I know a bit."

"Wonderful. Then you can translate when I inevitably lose my temper with this one." She gestured to Kennet, then turned her back on them both sharply, moving again into the back of the room by the fire. Kennet took that as his cue to follow, and Asa trailed behind them. Asa sat cross-legged on the floor, pulling their instrument in front of them and leaning on it as Kennet took the same place on the bench as he had the night before. Hana, likewise, leaned on the back wall, and crossed her arms.

"So, what do you need to know?" Kennet broke the silence, laying his hands on his knees.

"Well, let's start from the very beginning," Hana replied.

"You were hired by a lord because his daughter was poisoned, is that correct?"

Kennet nodded.

"So what did this poison do to her? What do you have so far?"

Kennet laid out the details as he remembered them. The soup, the mushrooms, the fits, the herbalist he'd met in Ornhult. The mention of a sun-cap brought a frown to Hana's face, but she nodded. To Kennet's relief she seemed to immediately have recognized it. He delicately left out Asa's part in everything, especially seeing how they tensed up at his first mention of them. When he brought up the breakdown that Torger had in the bar, Hana shifted her weight from one foot to the other, seeming to consider something. She didn't say exactly what. She was polite enough to refrain from interrupting Kennet until he brought up Stefan's terrible job from the night before.

"You both made fools of yourself, no need to bring that up again."

"No, don't stop him, this is so much more interesting than I was led to believe," Asa butted in, and Hana looked at them again, blinking slowly like a cat considering a mouse.

"You've been traveling with him through all of this? Why?"

"Companionship and boredom," Asa replied simply.

"His companionship?" Hana snorted. "I've been his traveling companion before. It's not much better than going it alone—maybe even worse."

"Hey now," Kennet broke in, "let's stay focused, can we?"

"Right." Hana nodded. "All right, I think I know what we need."

"Just from that?" Asa was impressed and sat up straighter in interest.

"Well, I have a few ideas," Hana clarified. "You did well in gathering what you did, and I believe I have additional insight that might . . . prove useful." Her gaze flicked to Kennet for a moment. It seemed like she was trying to get at something, though he couldn't imagine what. Had she dealt with this poison before? What had she seen that he had missed?

Stefan reentered the room presently, holding a mug in each hand. "I can only carry two at a time," he said, and then Kennet saw the boy James behind him, with a third mug of tea carried carefully in both hands with intense effort made not to spill. As Stefan handed a mug each to Hana and Kennet, James made a beeline to Asa, and presented them with the tea with pride in his smile.

"For me? Thank you, kind sir." Asa accepted the tea and made a show of blowing on it to cool it down before taking a timid sip. "Ah! Delicious. Did you make this?"

James shook his head shyly and pointed at his father, who ran a hand through his tangled hair. "Ah, James, but you helped," Stefan said, then added to Asa, "He put the leaves in the pot."

"That's the most important part!" Asa said to James with gravity in their tone. "You did very well."

"Thank you," James said bashfully, rocking back and forth on his feet for a moment before he pointed at Asa's vihuela. "Do you play that?"

Asa made an exaggerated scoff at his question. "Do you think I carry it around just for fun? Come now." They set the tea aside on the floor carefully and positioned themself to play, striking up a lighthearted tune to the boy's delight.

Hana watched this display for a moment, then turned to the two men with her, dropping her voice to a near whisper. "You two," she said, "with me."

Stefan and Kennet didn't argue. They left Asa and the boy alone as Hana led them to the kitchen and pulled a curtain door closed behind them.

"I don't want to worry your friend," Hana said to Kennet,

"but I think there's more going on here than you're getting at."

"Hana, I missed all of that," Stefan broke in. "What are you talking about?"

"We're talking about a child! The daughter of a lord. It's the most despicable thing I can think to do, and I don't know a single person who would do it. What are you leaving out?"

Kennet scratched at the stubble on his chin, considering whether to tell her about Hagen's lineage or not. While it was important to his investigation, he didn't see why it should matter to Hana. However, he had paused too long. Hana was on to him.

"You're leaving something out," she repeated with more conviction this time. "If you don't tell me, you can count me out of this. We have James to think of. I'm not getting involved if I don't know the full scope."

She had a point there. He was asking a lot of her already, and it was unfair to keep key information from her, even if it wasn't strictly necessary. So, he let out a sigh. "You remember the rumors of how the king had disowned his son?"

"Oh gods," Stefan exhaled, immediately putting two and two together. "You're working for the bloody prince."

Hana was silent at this revelation. She scowled and put a hand to her temple in deep thought.

"He doesn't want this information out there, of course; he's been trying to keep out of everything. It seems he wasn't disowned after all, but left of his own volition. Didn't want to be prince anymore, I suppose," Kennet continued.

"Didn't want to be prince!" Stefan repeated in awe. "If only it were that easy for all of us, eh?"

Kennet hummed in agreement, watching Hana's expression carefully. "Does that clear things up for you, Hana?"

"Somewhat," she replied. "It certainly makes more sense why someone would even dare to do something like this."

"Makes finding the culprit a sight harder, too, doesn't it?" said Stefan.

"I'm not worried about that right now," Kennet said.

"You should be." Hana shook her head. "After how panicked that man was—the herbalist you mentioned—it seems like whoever this is might be particularly powerful."

"Or they're just trying to be frightening. They're a coward. They went after a helpless young girl," Kennet pointed out.

"They're certainly that, too," Hana muttered. "Well, you're right. At least for now, we needn't focus on all that. We just need to get the girl healed. And I can do it—I'll just need the afternoon to gather the supplies I need. We can set off as soon as I'm done."

"We?" Stefan and Kennet asked in unison.

"Not you, Stef," Hana said tiredly. "I just mean that I'll be going with them, of course."

"You will?" Kennet echoed, still confused.

"The antidote for a sun-cap's effects has a very specific dosage that needs to be administered at intervals over a period of time. And not that I don't trust you, Peders, but . . ." She shrugged. "I'd feel better if I did it myself. So—" She threw open the door to the kitchen. "Shoo, out of my house. Come back later, and we'll leave."

"Can't we help you gather supplies at all? Time is of the essence, of course," Kennet said, and Hana considered his offer.

"Yes, actually." She nodded. "Good for you, make yourself useful. I'll write you a list."

∽

"Can you read this, Stefan?" Kennet held the list that Hana had written out to the retired Hawk, who squinted.

"Mate, I can hardly read at all anymore," he said, "much less Hana's chicken scratch."

Kennet clicked his tongue and held the paper out farther from himself, trying to decipher it until he felt a tug at his coat and looked down to see James staring up at him with big brown eyes.

"I can try to read it," the child said.

"Oh, by all means, then." Kennet handed the list down to the boy, and watched as he slowly looked it over.

"One . . . bundle . . . of . . . garlic," James said, then beamed up at his father and Kennet.

"Gods. I forgot Hana's been teaching him to read," Stefan said with a little surprise.

"Do you think he's ruining his chances, learning to read with her handwriting? Would he be able to read something actually legible?" Kennet wondered.

"I'll need to look into that."

"Where's Asa?" James asked, losing interest in the list as he handed it back to Kennet.

"I don't know, but they should still be in the shop. Why don't you go find them for me? Maybe they got lost in the herbs."

James giggled at that and wandered off to find Kennet's friend, leaving the two men alone in front of several hanging dried goods. They each sorted through them, searching for garlic through ropes of dried peppers, neither man facing each other. For a few minutes, they stood in relative silence.

Then, Stefan spoke.

"I know what you did," he said. His tone was no longer cheerful.

Kennet's heart dropped. "Hana told you?"

"I heard it through the grapevine long before I heard it from her. I told myself then if you ever showed your face to the Hawks again, I'd come out of retirement just to help them take you down."

That wasn't good. What was he getting at? Was he going to try and fight him here, in the busy shop? Was this a threat? Kennet bit his tongue, letting the man continue as he began to speak again.

"But the Hawks are gone now. I'm a father—the only thing the boy's got. Hana's wonderful, of course, but if James were to lose one of us, I'd rather it not be me. So you're off the hook." A cold glare caught Kennet from the corner of Stefan's eye. "For now."

Kennet felt himself breathe easier. He wanted to lighten the mood somehow, to joke, to say something about how he wasn't even sure that was a fight Stefan could win—which he truly believed. Before he could so much as come up with a way to phrase it, Stefan said something that stole every joke from Kennet's lips.

"I was friends with Isak too, you know."

There was immense sadness in Stefan's voice as he continued to avoid eye contact with Kennet.

"We never worked together, you and I. Everything I know about you, I heard from Isak. Hana never spoke about much outside of work, so it all came from him. He loved you. Truly, he did. You know that, don't you?"

Kennet knew that. God, if he didn't know that. His chest ached at the memories that were beginning to surface. "Stefan—"

"Sir Peders," Stefan stopped him. "Save it for someone who truly cares. Hana, perhaps. I think you ought to know that if it weren't for *why* you're here, I'd kill you. I'd let Hana kill you. I'd help her kill you. You wouldn't have left our house last night. We talked about it, of course. She acts like she's the tough one of the two of us, but she had to convince *me* to hear you out. I wanted to lure you in and end it there."

The gravity of everything hit Kennet suddenly. He'd known Hana didn't want to talk to him, but this? Well, it made sense. In fact, it was what he had expected from her from the beginning. But after everything had happened—after Isak—he'd waited for months for just that, for an end. He'd breached conduct so hugely, he'd thought it was only a matter of time until they came after him. Then months had crawled by, and . . . nothing. Even after he resumed work, continued to use the same name, almost daring them to come after him. Nothing.

He wondered why. What had happened to the Hawks?

But he knew he couldn't ask. He felt like he was pushing it even by being here, now. No, he *knew* he was pushing it.

Just like he knew that if they had killed him, he would have deserved it.

He felt like he was in danger, a feeling he hadn't experienced in years. He wanted to get out. Stefan's gaze was still on him, chilling, though the man was no longer speaking. Was he waiting for Kennet to say something? Should he say something?

"She wanted to hear me out?" was all he could manage.

"She figured you either wanted to die, coming to her like this, or you were in some kind of trouble. She even thought, just for a second, that maybe you had come to clear your name. Then I reminded her that you didn't even bother to hide it, coming back into that keep alongside the very men who took Isak's—"

"Stop." Kennet stepped back, feeling himself start to shake again. "I know what I did, Stefan."

"We all know what you did, that's my point." Stefan's voice was tense with pain and anger. "What we don't know is why. And why you have the *gall*"—he spat the word as he rounded on Kennet, finally facing him—"to come here and ask for help."

"Marna—"

"That child would be dead if Hana hadn't stopped my hand," Stefan snapped. "You could have killed her by coming here."

Kennet wished the floor would swallow him up. "Why are you telling me this?" he asked. Any stoicism was gone. He felt . . . small.

"I just thought you should remember your place, Sir Peders." The anger didn't leave Stefan's tone, though he drew himself up straighter, and brushed his hair out of his face. "I may let you speak to my boy, I may let you stay in my home. And Hana—well, she's her own person. If she wants to make the foolish choice to travel with you, so be it. But don't think, not for a moment, that I don't know what you really are."

Stefan knew what he really was. And Kennet knew Stefan was right, before he even said it.

"A monster."

"I found them!" The cheerful voice of James cut through the tension like a hot knife through butter, though the pit in Kennet's stomach didn't leave. The child held Asa's gloved hand in his own as he dragged them toward Stefan and Kennet, the latter of whom broke out into a smile that felt so very, very fake.

"Thank you! Where were they?" he said, shocked to hear no tremor in his voice.

"In the herbs like you said."

"There's just so *many* of them," Asa said with mock breathlessness, "it's so confusing. But I think I got what we need." They held up a bundle of dried grey leaves triumphantly.

"That looks like hell-weed to me," Stefan confirmed with an equally disingenuous smile. "Good job, you two. Let's buy our goods and get back to Hana. It's time we got you on the road."

∼

KENNET WAS OVERCOME with relief as they rode away from Grankoping, with Asa and Hana alongside him. Hana's horse was finer than either Starling or Emilio, and she clearly outclassed all of them even in looks alone. She rode at the front for a while, sitting tall in her saddle, while Kennet and Asa took up the rear.

This only lasted for a little while, though, until the silence apparently became unbearable for Asa, and they gave Kennet a concerned look. He shrugged at them. What was there to say? Or at least, what was there to say in front of Hana?

Asa shrugged back. Then, with a little click of their tongue and a snap of their reins, they urged Emilio up toward where Hana was riding.

"Sorry, Miss Oh," they said, coming up beside her, "I didn't get to properly introduce myself earlier."

"That's true," Hana agreed. "I didn't think I'd be traveling with you both so I didn't think to bring it up."

"But here we are, traveling together! So—Asa of the Isles, at your service as much as you require me to be, for the duration."

"I'd introduce myself, but you seem to already know my name. What all has Peders told you about me?" Hana asked. Kennet wondered if he was detecting curiosity or amusement in her voice—it was always so hard to tell.

"Just that the two of you used to work together, and that it didn't end well."

"That's one way to put it," Hana said. Yes, she was definitely at least slightly amused by this. "It's not something I like to talk about."

"Nor does he, from what I've learned," Asa confirmed.

"Then let's not talk about it. Let's talk about you. Are you really enjoying all this?"

Asa glanced over their shoulder at Kennet. Their expression told him they were considering telling her about their real reason for coming—their influence—but they seemed to be asking for his permission. He shook his head at them, an indicator that he thought that might not be the best idea. They turned back to Hana without missing a beat.

"As much as I can be," they said. "It's hard to enjoy anything with a little girl to worry about."

Hana nodded seriously at that. "Well, I'll do my best to take that off your mind," she said. "The poison the girl was given won't likely kill her before we get back, at this rate. Likely it would take months. It's a slow burner, and needs several doses to be effective. I'm guessing there's an insider agent in the keep. We know our poisoner isn't opposed to using others for their dirty work."

"Her dirty work," Asa interrupted, and Hana furrowed her brow.

"Her?"

"That's what the herbalist said. Said it was a 'she.'"

Hana only considered this for a moment before continuing, but Kennet could tell that something about that had shaken her when she flicked her eyes in his direction as she started to speak again. "Anyway, she's not opposed to using others. So a small dose of this poison every once in a while—initially a larger dose in her food, now likely in her water, since I understand her father won't leave her side. The poison is distilled from a mushroom, as you two had suspected. A powder can be made from the mushrooms if they're dried, but it's much less potent. I'm guessing that's what they're feeding her now, to keep her in this state of sleep, until eventually she wastes away. While she's certainly in danger, if what you've told me is true, I believe we'll be able to see her recover with some time to spare."

Kennet felt his shoulders lose tension, and his jaw unclenched as the meaning of her words sank in. It struck him how very, very right he had been to come to her. Even if she hated him, even if Stefan wanted him dead—and rightfully so—nobody else would have known all this, or said all of it so succinctly and with such confidence.

This all seemed to be occurring to Asa in sync with his own thoughts, as they let out a low whistle. "I can see why we came straight to you," they said, and Hana chuckled softly, the first laughter Kennet had heard from her in years.

"I'm glad you did," she said.

That was surprising to hear. Did she mean it? She rarely said things she didn't mean.

Hope blossomed in his chest. Was there a chance, then, for him to redeem himself to her? He hadn't thought it possible, but if he could . . .

He couldn't let himself believe it, as much as he wanted to. And god, how he wanted to. Some part of him knew that if she could find him good again, it could be true. Really, actually true. Not the delusions of guilt, but the soft glimmer of a new, better person.

The person he wished he had always been.

CHAPTER 8

THE JOURNEY BACK

If there was one thing Kennet was certain of, it was that he would have been absolutely miserable if he'd never asked Asa to come along.

It wasn't that Hana refused to speak to him now, but he could tell that every time she did, it was only out of necessity. So there was Asa, who could speak to both of them frequently. Asa, who could clear the air of discomfort with a reassuring smile—though these smiles always carried some measure of concern.

This concern came to a head the first night of their journey, after Hana had retreated to her tent. As Kennet made his last check on Starling, he heard a soft cough behind him, the bard announcing their presence. When he turned, Asa raised their hand in greeting.

"You've been quiet recently," they said, and when Kennet didn't reply immediately, they prompted further. "Is everything all right?"

"I'm doing about as well as can be expected," Kennet said, running a hand down Starling's neck.

"And how well is that?"

Kennet sighed. "I'm just glad we're going to be able to help Marna after all."

"I'm not asking about Marna, Sir Peders." They came around in front of the horse and leaned on the tree that Kennet had tied her to. "I'm relieved as well, of course, but you've been acting like an entirely different person since we gained our new companion. I feel as though I've barely heard you say a word, and certainly not a happy one."

Kennet had nothing to say to that. He looked up at the branches of the fir tree that towered over him. The stars peeked through the gaps in the needles, the only light in the absence of the new moon. He felt Starling nudge him. Did the horse also sense his discomfort? He stroked her neck again.

Asa was still watching him. He could sense it. "I don't want to pry," they said slowly. "It's really none of my business."

"As true as that is, I do feel bad if this is making you uncomfortable."

"No, I'm always comfortable!" Asa laughed. "Even in others' discomfort. That's when a performer thrives, you know. It's our job to lighten the mood."

They paused, and Kennet finally looked back down to see that they were tugging at their gloves.

"Do you need me?" they asked. The earnestness in their voice struck Kennet like a blow to the chest. He was lost for words for several seconds, struggling to think of some way to respond that wouldn't sound desperate.

"I . . ." He still couldn't, he still didn't know how. Luckily, they didn't let him finish.

"Give me your hand," they said, and one glove slipped off. They held their bare hand out to him, and he only hesitated briefly before placing his palm against theirs.

It was nothing like it had been the first time. It was warm, like the first sip of a hot drink spreading from his chest to the tips of his fingers. It wasn't happiness, not like he had expected them to give him. It was just . . . calm. They gave him calm, and they gave him comfort, a balm for the rawness his heart had felt over the past three days. Just as with the first time their hands had touched, he felt tears spring to his eyes, but these weren't tears of anger or fear. They were of relief. Tears that came with the lifting of a weight off his chest, and the realization that they wouldn't even allow him to feel guilty for letting that weight go.

He didn't feel like he was burdening them by asking for this. In fact, it wasn't what he would have asked for at all. He would have asked for numbness. But what he felt, he realized, was what they wanted him to feel. And that, in of itself, brought something he hadn't expected at all.

A shuddering breath came with the realization that they were looking at him, intensely, as he stared at their fingers that had entwined with his. He met their gaze, and smiled.

"Thank you," he said, and as they examined his face, they seemed satisfied with their work.

"Happy to help," they said, and Kennet felt a soft squeeze as they drew away. He almost didn't want to let go.

But the calm feeling stayed once their hands had parted. Asa pulled their glove back on and paused, looking as though they might want to say more, but rather than make any further statements they made their way back to their tent.

It was so confusing—the feelings they had given him were so pleasant, and calm, and he didn't feel anything negative coming to darken their presence. Nevertheless, there was something more there than just what they had given him. A stirring in the area between his chest and his stomach, a fluttering like anxiety but sweeter. He hadn't felt that in some time.

The little remarks here and there that caught him off guard were one thing. The stumbling in his words was a symptom of his lack of clever wit, or the result of the objective fact that Asa was attractive and he had always been bad at talking to attractive people.

This on the other hand was different, and it was unmistakable.

It was desire.

As he fell asleep that night, it was desire that overwhelmed him.

∼

KENNET WOKE up to hear Asa's voice ringing brightly from outside the tent. Though he couldn't make out what they were talking about, he could tell they were passionate about it. He sat up and realized he felt remarkably rested, perhaps the most rested he'd felt since before this journey started. For a moment he wondered why before he remembered the last conversation he'd had with Asa, and his heart skipped a beat again.

"That's enough of that," he scolded himself. With a groggy rub at his eyes to get the last of the sleep away from them, he stuck his head outside the tent and took in the day before him.

Asa and Hana were sitting around the remains of the last night's campfire, chatting with remarkable amiability. Asa was doing most of the talking, as usual, with their vihuela lending a soft musical background to whatever conversation they were having. Neither of them saw Kennet at first, so he took a moment to discern what they were discussing.

"See, I told Stefan that," Hana was saying presently, braiding her hair as she talked, "but he doesn't see the point of learning other languages."

"If my parents had taught me Anjeonese when I was younger, I wouldn't be so nervous to speak it now. I've always sort of resented that nobody took the time to teach me, and I never traveled far enough south to be tossed in headfirst like

I was with Bladstongue. Which, of course, is exactly how it would be for James. It's not like he's going to make it out to Anjeon any time soon."

"No, but that's exactly the thing that Stefan has a problem with. If James isn't ever going to go overseas, why would he need to know the language?"

Asa considered that. "You know what it is? He's afraid you and James are going to talk about him in front of him, without him ever knowing it."

Hana snorted and tied off the braid with a thin green ribbon. "Oh, he's certainly terrified of that. He already hates that James and I made up a game he can't play with us."

"Why can't he?"

"He can't see very well, but James and I have a game we play where we see what's the farthest away we can hang a sign and still read it. It might be in bad taste, honestly. But to be fair, I started it to test James's eyesight periodically, and he thought it was a game."

"Oh no!" Asa laughed, then paused, seeming to notice Kennet for the first time. "Good morning, Sir Peders!"

Hana took a moment, but eventually focused on Kennet as well, giving him a short nod. Kennet nodded back and finally pulled himself all the way out of his tent and to his feet. "Good morning, Asa," he said.

"Ready to head out?" Hana asked.

"I've only just woken up," Kennet protested.

"And very late, I might add. Not a moment to spare," Hana said.

"You said it wasn't as urgent as we had treated it."

"That doesn't mean that we should waste time. That girl will be in pain every moment we spend on the road, so whether it's strictly necessary or not, we should still move quickly."

Kennet had to concede that point, and he tried not to be annoyed with his own sluggishness as he pulled his boots on and laced them up. In no time at all, the group had packed their things and was back on the road.

They made for the most efficient path, passing through Ornhult without stopping. As they rode, Hana was the most talkative Kennet had ever seen her, pointing out plants and animals to Asa along the way. Every once in a while, the two would slip into Anjeonese, a language that Kennet was completely unfamiliar with. Asa seemed to speak in a sort of mix of this and Isla, snapping their fingers when they couldn't remember a word in Anjeonese, until finally giving up and saying the Isla equivalent instead, to which Hana usually nodded in understanding.

Feeling completely lost, Kennet resigned himself to thinking about nothing in particular. Starling was confused by the unfamiliar noises coming from his traveling companions, and her ears swiveled curiously as she walked. Kennet wondered if she knew they were speaking a different language —how smart were horses, he wondered? He had thought about it often, especially with Starling. Did she know she was disobeying when she was being stubborn? Or was she just acting on animal instincts, with no real regard for him at all?

He thought she probably knew exactly what she was doing. There were incidents he could recall that were far too specific to be done by accident.

"Kennet?"

Kennet snapped out of his train of thought when he realized Hana had been talking to him. "Sorry, I didn't hear a word of that."

"I said, should we try to find a place to stop tonight?" Hana said. "I don't really want to camp again, and there are a few small towns that are mostly on the way."

"I'm not really familiar with the area," Kennet admitted, "but I would also rather not camp again, if we can help it."

"Good. At this next fork, then, we'll take a left."

Kennet nodded. Traveling with Hana was certainly

bringing back familiar feelings. She'd always been much more organized than him, thinking ahead and remembering which town was where, and what was in each one. The only towns Kennet was familiar with were ones where he had spent most of his life.

It was a double-edged sword, of course. When there wasn't a strict deadline to reach, Hana's organization could be insufferable. There were countless times he could think of where they had been traveling at their own leisure and she had planned every moment, every meal, down to the minute. It had made their friendship outside of work very difficult— that, among other things.

Perhaps they'd always been destined to have this kind of tense relationship.

He watched how effortless Asa was with her and it almost made him jealous. Even though he knew he was nothing like them, he wondered if he could be. If he could be friendly and draw people in the way they did. The closest he ever got was with Gerrit and Britta at Hagen's keep, and that had all been for the investigation's sake.

Well, but hadn't he been friendly to Asa? He'd drawn *them* in, hadn't he?

No, wait. That was likely the other way around.

"Kennet?"

Dammit, he'd missed something again. "Yes?"

Asa was the one addressing him this time, with a smile, and they didn't seem bothered to repeat themself. "Hana was asking how we met, and I've been talking long enough. Why don't you tell it?"

Feeling a bit put on the spot, Kennet cleared his throat to buy himself some time. "Aren't you the better storyteller?" he asked.

"I've never heard you tell a story, so I suppose we don't know for sure. And for another thing, I'm quite interested to hear everything from your point of view. I feel that from mine, it was mostly boring."

What did that say about Kennet? He had thought their meeting anything *but* boring, but he supposed that to them, they simply met a stranger in a bar, then ran into the same stranger a few days later in a different town. Truly, he had a more interesting story to tell than that.

"Well," he started, slowly, riding up alongside them to the point where the three took up the entire width of the road, "I had gone to a tavern in Osternas to gather some information from one of Lord Hagen's manservants. There wasn't a free table, so we sat with Asa. The bard playing was . . ."

"Awful," Asa interrupted.

"Right," Kennet agreed. "Not very good. And my companion challenged Asa to do better, and they took that challenge to heart. They walked up to the stage and slapped the man across the face."

Hana raised her eyebrows just a fraction. "Was he that bad?" she asked.

"That bad," Asa confirmed seriously.

"He backed down immediately, and they delivered one of the best performances I had seen in ages. When I ran into them again in Ornhult it felt like fate," Kennet said. "They were traveling the same direction as me, so I invited them to tag along. Safer to travel in groups, anyway."

"And then when I heard about the girl, well, it's just not something I can let conclude without me," Asa added.

"That's understandable, I suppose," Hana said.

Kennet became acutely aware that without the added context of Asa's strange abilities, it really did seem like the bard was just taking pity on him. But Hana didn't wear on that point any further, simply considering the tale in silence as they rode. He glanced over to see if her face betrayed anything of what she was feeling and was surprised to see that she was looking back at him. When she didn't drop his gaze as he looked, he immediately looked back at the road, feeling heat rising in his cheeks.

"What about you and Stefan? You used to work together—you thought to go to them immediately?" He tried to continue the conversation.

"You don't want to hear about Stefan and me," she responded flatly. "I'm sure there are details in that story you'd rather I not bring up."

Asa looked from Hana to Kennet. "Is this about the thing that went badly again?" they asked with innocence that Kennet knew they were faking.

"It certainly is," Hana replied. "I really do mean to let Kennet tell you that one himself," she added, "but if he keeps trying to make conversation I just might overstep his boundaries."

"Sorry," Kennet muttered quickly and pulled back from the group again. He heard Asa say something in Anjeonese, and Hana shrugged, before the bard drew back as well to ride beside him.

"I can't emphasize how little I care about what happened between the two of you," Asa said, "and I mean that in the most polite way possible."

"Thank you, Asa." Kennet sighed.

"You're both lovely people."

"Hana certainly is lovely," Kennet replied.

"Enough of that!" Asa said, and he heard hurt in their voice. They dropped their tone low and said confidentially, "I know it might be easy to forget since we can't talk freely about it at the moment, but I didn't come along for no reason. You and I—we're a team for now, and Miss Oh being here doesn't change that I'm here for you. I'm taking that seriously."

"I know," he said, but he had to admit that it felt good to hear it from them.

"You might know logically, but I can tell she makes you

feel like shit." They paused and glanced at Hana before hushing their tone even further. "Remember what we talked about on our way to Grankoping? How I knew what you were when I joined you? How I left my home because people thought they knew me, but all they knew was who I used to be? I care, Kennet, about the man I met who's working tirelessly to save this girl. Whatever happened before that, it's neither here nor there to me. So please, be that person for me?"

He made the mistake of looking down into their eyes when they said that, and his heart began to flutter again. They had no idea what they were saying, no idea what they were asking for, because they had no idea who he had been. And he played off that, let them believe he was something he wasn't. And yet, the fact that they believed in him . . . they weren't naive, like they said, they had to have some idea of what he was capable of. And here they were, in spite of that. So the least he could do was try.

"I'll try," he said, perhaps more gruffly than he meant to, as he tried to hide what he was feeling.

"That's all I ask, really," Asa said. "That, and that you help me write a grand victory song about all this when we're done."

Kennet felt a smile growing at that remark, and he let himself laugh. "You don't want me to write a song."

"No, I don't. I want you to *help*. And by help, I mean I want you to listen to what I've already written and tell me how good it is."

"Ah, I see. Well, I'm sure that will come very easily to me."

"It had better! Otherwise, what am I keeping you around for?"

∽

The small town they landed in was nothing special. It reminded Kennet of his hometown, the hometown he had been so desperate to leave. If they had been close enough to the coast to be overtaken by flocks of seabirds squawking, then he would have felt even more at home. As it was, things were already too close for comfort.

The inn was equally small, equally unimpressive. When Hana asked for three rooms, the innkeeper gave her a confused look.

"We only got three rooms, so that's gonna cost ya," he said.

"How many beds have they each got?" Kennet interjected.

"Two in two of 'em, one in one."

Kennet glanced at Asa, who shrugged. "We'll take two rooms," he said. "One in one, two in the other."

The innkeeper shrugged, and took the coin that Kennet and Hana slid him with no particular fondness. Kennet figured they didn't get many travelers, but he had always hated how one could open an establishment to feed and house others, and then be surprised when people came in to be fed and housed.

"So! Rooms." Kennet turned to Hana and Asa. "Do you . . .?"

"Oh, I had assumed that it would be us in one, and Hana in the other," Asa said casually. Kennet couldn't fathom why the way they said it made his chest tighten.

"That makes the most sense to me," Hana replied in agreement.

Then it was settled. They didn't dwell further in the entrance, with Hana bidding them a curt goodnight before retreating to the smaller room.

"Which bed do you want?" Asa asked as they entered the room that they and Kennet had been directed to. The two beds were on opposite sides of the small space, with one under a window while the other rested against a bare wooden wall.

"I've really got no preference."

"Then you get the window. I think there's a draft," they teased, and set their things by the end of the other bed.

There was idle conversation between the two as they got ready to sleep. Asa recounted most of what they had talked about with Hana—it turned out to have been mostly questions about hometowns, about politics, about local wildlife. Some also, Asa admitted, had been about food.

"I mean absolutely no offense to Bladlanders," they said presently, "but your food is hardly anything special. Mostly meat and potatoes and gravies. Some good soups, I'll give you that much, but if there's one thing I miss about Lucien it's the spices."

"I feel like I can't argue, only because I don't know what I'm missing," Kennet replied as he fluffed the pillow for his bed. The room was sparsely furnished and the blankets looked as though they had been hand-knit. It was hardly fine living, but it seemed comfortable enough. He looked toward Asa. They were sitting on their own bed, watching him, as though they had been waiting to speak until he was finished.

"Are you feeling better than you were last night?" they asked.

Kennet considered the question. He did feel better, certainly, though not by any means spectacular. "I feel fine," he said noncommittally.

"Do you want anything to help you sleep?"

He almost said no. He almost told them it wouldn't make much of a difference either way, until it occurred to him that after they arrived in Osternas, it was likely they would part ways. In their wake, would he not want to have savored every moment of peace they could offer him?

So he nodded. "If it's not too much trouble."

"Not at all." They patted the bed next to them, beckoning

him to sit. As soon as he had joined them, they held out their hand again, and once again he put his own over theirs.

The feeling of calm was back, as intoxicating as it had been before as the stress of the day melted away. He took a deep breath and let it out in a sigh, closing his eyes as he exhaled. It felt like it took less time to sink in than it had the night before. They gave him the same little squeeze of their hand before they drew away.

"I feel like I haven't been as useful as I promised to be on this trip," they said, half-jokingly.

In his newly calm state, Kennet couldn't even bring himself to entertain the nonsense buried in that statement. "You can't possibly be serious," he said, and they laughed.

"Don't get me wrong, I do feel like helping you any way I can is important. I just feel like I should have been able to help Hana be less of a pain in the ass."

Kennet chuckled at that. "You think that's what she's being? She has a right to be a pain in the ass, you know. We're dragging her all the way to the coast, and I'm sure she has things she'd rather be doing."

"Well, less of a pain to be around, I guess. I feel like I could get her to loosen up if I wanted." They kicked their feet against the bedframe absentmindedly. "But I also feel like that would be crossing a line."

"If she wasn't a pain to be around, she wouldn't be Hana," Kennet said, and he hoped to Gethin that the walls were thick enough that she couldn't hear them right now. "And either way, you're doing more than enough just by doing what you're doing."

"And so are you," Asa replied with feeling. "We're both doing enough. Marna will be okay, and I just keep telling myself that's what matters at the end of the day."

"Seeing her and her father reunite will make me feel a great deal better," Kennet agreed.

"Oh, that poor man," Asa sighed. "Gods, we're going to

undo all the hard work we just did to make you feel calm. Go, go to sleep. The sooner we do, the sooner all these good things will be a reality."

Kennet let them give him a little shove to get him off their bed, and made his way back across the room, collapsing onto his own bed with little decorum. Glancing out the admittedly drafty window, he could see a few stars, and the sliver of the moon as it began to grow in its cycle again. He was glad that he could do exactly as Asa asked, and even more glad that this sleep would likely be the last one he had to take before all this hard work would be made worth it.

CHAPTER 9

DISTILLATION AND CLARIFICATION

Osternas had never been such a welcoming sight.

Kennet rode at the front of the group, as the representative. He knew that Hagen would have men waiting to watch them enter town, and sure enough, the moment they approached the keep the gates were opened for them without hesitation. Their horses were whisked to the lord's stables, and they were whisked into the keep itself, where they were met by none other than Gerrit.

"Sir Peders! And friends." Gerrit gave a bow to Hana and Asa as well.

"Master Gerrit." Kennet bowed back and smiled. "I suppose Lord Hagen has been waiting for us."

"Anxiously, yes." Gerrit nodded. "He wants to see you and your friends immediately, but he's been . . . well, he's not been well." Gerrit dropped any formal pretenses, beginning to fidget. "He hasn't bathed since you left and I swear to god he hasn't slept half as much as he should in that time, either."

"Poor man," Asa repeated their sentiment from the night before under their breath.

"He's gone to freshen up before meeting with you, and bids you to meet him in Marna's room."

"Yes, that will do," Hana interrupted the conversation. This startled Gerrit, who blinked at her with little recognition. "I need to see her as soon as possible, to assess her condition. Lead us there immediately."

Gerrit glanced from Hana to Kennet, waiting for an explanation, but no explanation came. Kennet simply nodded, acknowledging Hana's request as being his own. With that confirmation, the manservant relented. He gestured for them to follow him and began to lead them down the main hall of the keep.

When they arrived at Marna's room, Kennet was unsurprised to see Britta sitting by her side in Hagen's absence. She had her legs crossed, pulled up onto the chair with her, and was watching the girl intently with a sorrowful look on her face. When Kennet and company entered, she looked up in surprise.

"Sir Peders," she said, then quickly stuttered out a protest as Hana pushed through the group to the bedside, pulling a waterskin from her belt. "Hey, you can't be in here—"

"She's with me, Britta, I've brought her to help," Kennet reassured the cook, who hadn't made much of a move to stop Hana anyway—likely she could tell just by looking at Hana that she couldn't be stopped.

Hana bent over the girl's body and tipped her waterskin to Marna's lips as she propped her head up with her free hand. As the girl swallowed, Hana jerked her head toward the bedside table. "Peders, the cup," she said.

Britta and Gerrit were visibly uncomfortable to see Kennet ordered around, but Kennet was already moving, doing as he was told without so much as a second thought. He held the cup carefully in his hand and tilted it to look in as he held it up to the dimming sunlight from the girl's window. The water seemed perfectly clear. If there was any powder in it, he assumed it was very little. Or perhaps he just didn't know what to look for.

Hana remained at the girl's bedside after she had finished helping her drink. She checked her pulse, and rested the back of her hand on Marna's forehead, until she nodded firmly and addressed Kennet without looking up. "This is exactly as you described it."

Of course it is, why would I lie? Kennet kept his annoyance to himself, nodding solemnly instead. "So your estimation was right, and we've plenty of time?"

"Yes, at least enough that I don't feel like we're wasting any by talking right now," Hana replied.

"Very good."

"Why are there so many people in there? Move, please." The "please" seemed to be an afterthought as Lord Hagen joined the group, shoving his way past Asa and Gerrit who had taken up station near the door. The lord stopped next to Kennet and Hana, sparing a quick glance at the water in Kennet's hand before settling on the strange woman who was crouched over his daughter. "Who is this?"

"This is Hana Oh. She's a friend of mine," Kennet replied. "She knows how to cure your daughter."

"Lord Hagen." Hana pulled herself up off the bed and held her hand out to the man. Hagen stood gobsmacked for a second, and Kennet noted that though the man looked a good deal worse than he had when they had left him, he at least looked clean. His hand was steady as it shook Hana's, and a smile broke over his face.

"Wonderful," he said, with deep relief in his voice. "Oh, wonderful. What do you need? What can I do to help? How soon can you have it done?"

Hana had to pry her hand out of the man's grateful grip. "I'll need some sort of a heat source—a stove, a hearth—and some pots or similar vessels to boil the antidote in. Lead me to your kitchen, and that will be enough."

"Excellent. Yes, that can be done." Hagen nodded. "Britta, will you take Sir Peders and his friend to the kitchens?"

"Yes, my lord." Britta gave a small bow, then gestured to the door, leaving with the expectation that they would follow. As Hana and Kennet exited, Asa caught Kennet's arm. They held him back for just a moment.

"I suppose they won't want me to stick around," they said. "I'll have Gerrit show me out and meet you at the tavern later?"

"Sorry," Kennet said sheepishly, and Asa shrugged.

"I'm not needed at the moment. Go, don't worry about me. I'll see you when this is taken care of."

"Indeed you will," Kennet replied. "I still have a lot to say to you."

Asa started to grin at that and seemed to have a cheeky response, but Kennet found himself being dragged away from the conversation by a harsh cough from Hana. She had clearly had enough, so Kennet left the bard behind and turned his attention to the pressing matters that awaited him in the kitchen.

∽

Britta seemed eager to help the two hire-swords, showing them around the kitchen with a frantic sincerity, then standing stiffly when she had finished. "I'll, er, leave you to it, then," she said, and Kennet could see stars in her eyes as she watched Hana stand in the kitchen, taking it all in slowly.

"That would be best," was all Hana said in reply, and Britta gave a little squeak before bowing and scrambling to make her way out.

Kennet set down the cup of water by Hana near the stove, and looked toward the door after the cook. "I'll—" he began to say that he would leave too, but was immediately cut off.

"Not you," she said. "I need to talk to you."

He had been afraid of that.

"All right." He didn't attempt to argue, walking toward the

countertop in the center of the kitchen and pulling out a stool to sit on. He felt his stomach churn, like when he had been a child and had been told he was in trouble, but not what for. As he waited for the conversation to begin in full, Hana took her bag off from around her chest and set it down on the counter. She took out the contents one by one and laid them out in front of Kennet.

"Chop some of these. Might as well keep you busy while we talk," she said as she slid him a bundle of root vegetables he didn't recognize. Kennet pulled a knife from the block of wood that sat next to him on the countertop and got to it. "Finer than that, please," Hana corrected him, then watched until she was satisfied with his work, and returned to organizing her ingredients.

He wondered if she was going to speak again, or if she was enjoying holding him in suspense. He decided not to give her that power. "What is this about, Hana?"

Hana said nothing, untying the bundle of grey leaves that Stefan had identified as hell-weed and laying them out flat. She stood back on her heels, mulled over the spread in front of her, and then spoke matter-of-factly. "That Asa. They're very sweet, don't you think?"

What? Was that really what she wanted to speak to him about? "They're excellent company," he acknowledged slowly, wondering where she was going with this.

"They're spoiled on the likes of you," she said.

"I know."

"Then why are you involving them? Don't you think it's selfish of you to ask them to put themself in danger?"

Kennet's brow knit together. He paused in his chopping to scrape the diced root into a pile before starting on the next one. "They're not in danger."

"Anyone who chooses to associate themself with you is in danger."

"You're here," Kennet pointed out.

"That's different. I know better."

Kennet chose not to make the eye contact that she clearly wanted him to make, and instead focused on the task she had set him to. "They wanted to come along."

"Don't say that again." She began to pull the hell-weed's leaves off its stem one by one. "I know it's bull."

He grimaced but refused to elaborate. There was no need to mention Asa's abilities. If he did so just to clear his own name, that would truly make him as selfish as Hana was accusing him of being.

"It's because of what they can do—the emotions they can manipulate."

Kennet's head finally snapped up at that, and Hana watched his expression a moment before giving a soft scoff and returning her attention to the leaves. Kennet couldn't hide the surprise in his voice. "They told you?" he asked.

"Yes. It seems your company has made them too trustful, or my friendship with you made them trust me too easily. Either way, I believe they shouldn't have disclosed it, but it does make a few things make more sense. You're using them."

Hana's words cut deep—because they were true. He didn't feel guilty for it; they had asked to be useful. However, Hana clearly saw this as a grave overstep. "It's not as though I'm not offering anything in return, you know," he said.

"A share of the reward? Generous," Hana chuckled softly. "I can almost understand why you're doing it. They're intriguing." She paused, then added, "Extremely so."

"I have a few theories on all of that," Kennet said.

"Me too, of course. My immediate thought was that we may be in the presence of the newest prophet of Gethin."

"They don't like Gethin very much."

Hana hummed in consideration at that and carefully piled up the hell-weed on top of a thin sheet of cheesecloth. "Did they say why?"

"Not a fan of the church, I suppose."

"Can't argue with that. I suppose that's ruled out, then."

"Right. But I think we're on the right track with that idea—perhaps a different god?"

"Perhaps," Hana agreed. She pulled the corners of the cheesecloth to its center, creating a bag that held the hellweed within it, and tied it off with twine. "How would you ever know which, though?"

Kennet shifted in his seat, wondering if he should say what he was thinking. He'd been considering it for a while, but he hadn't decided if it would be the right way to go about it—there was somewhere they could go. Or at least, someone who could tell them where to start looking. "I was thinking of taking them to Lange."

This admission earned a new bout of silence from Hana before she pointed out something that had already occurred to him. "Have you told them Lange is a former member of the Order of Gethin?"

He hadn't. He hadn't even brought Lange up to them yet, and it was partially because of that exact fact. "Former." Kennet stressed the word. "But he doesn't identify with them anymore."

"Still worships Gethin, though," Hana said. "Don't lie to them about it. I agree that he's certainly the best option the two of you have, if you're intent on pursuing it. I'm half tempted to join you. I'll admit, I'm more curious about this than I've been about anything in years."

"I'm very anxious to pursue it," Kennet said, careful not to accidentally invite her along.

"Well, I'll have to ask them to visit me once you figure it out."

He noted that she was equally careful not to invite him back to her house.

For another long while, they were silent. Kennet finished chopping the roots, and Hana took them from him without a single word, scraping them into a mortar and adding a pile of dark purple berries. It seemed like this might be a good opportunity for Kennet to make his escape. He began to slide off the stool, but was stopped when Hana started talking again.

"I know where Lange is. Perhaps you should let me take them there, after the girl is healed."

Kennet felt something tangling inside him—annoyance, frustration, jealousy—and turned back to her with a tinge of darkness over his expression. "Why would I do that?" he demanded.

"I can see the way you act around them, Kennet. You're going to become obsessed with them, and may I remind you what happened to the last man you loved?"

"And?" The tangling grew worse, and Kennet knew he was about to say everything he had wanted to say since the first night they were reunited. "What about it, Hana? What's so irredeemable about causing the death of one man—that man, specifically? You've killed countless. Why do you deserve a happy life, a family, and peace, but I don't?"

Hana clearly had been waiting for this, because she retorted without hesitation. "The men I killed were strangers. You betrayed your family."

"We stripped so many of their fathers, brothers, sisters—lovers and mothers—why is it only different when the family was yours?" Kennet rose in his seat, standing over the counter with heaving breaths as his heart pounded, and his voice raised. "If I hadn't done what I did, someone else would have, and they wouldn't feel bad about it the way that I do—the way I always have! You can hate me as much as you want for what I've done, Hana, but it will never be as much as I hate myself." He seethed. His hair hung in his eyes, and he felt like he was gasping for air.

Hana looked like she wanted to say more, and he didn't want to hear it. He couldn't bear to hear it. Instead, he shoved the stool back under the counter, tugged at the collar of his coat to straighten it, and turned on his heel. There was no call after him—he knew his words had fallen flat in front of her. But *he* felt better . . . didn't he?

As he stormed through the hallway of the keep, he didn't do much to take stock of his emotional state. He knew there was a courtyard, and waited until he had reached it to let himself stop and take a breath. The space was empty, thank god, apart from the trees and flowers that were so well-tended. He collapsed onto one of the stone benches on the border of the yard and buried his hands in his hair.

He was so tired of feeling this way, of ending every conversation feeling like an outcast. The end of this job couldn't come soon enough. Though he knew that Hana had truly been the only one who could help, she wasn't alone in wishing that it could have been anyone else.

The silence of the courtyard was reassuring. Surrounded by it, he tried to calm himself, to remind himself of how he had felt under Asa's influence. He had indulged in their touch enough that he missed it, but not so much that he had forgotten how to regulate himself. In fact, it helped give him something to center on. He felt the anger melt away as he took deep breaths. The sentiment of his outrage remained: the feeling that he was being unfairly judged. It wasn't as though he didn't feel he'd done anything wrong, and truthfully he did think she had a right to be mad, but to judge his relationship with Asa?

He wasn't tearing them down. No matter what Hana tried to imply, he felt at least secure in that. There was plenty of room for him to have new relationships—no matter how unworthy he felt of them, he deeply resented the idea that he might somehow harm them. He would never. He couldn't.

The man who had been capable of that had died the same day he killed his lover.

"I don't want to do it," Hagen said, still sitting by his daughter's bedside, but with a remarkably more relaxed air to him. He hadn't stopped fretting, of course, though now it was over something new—whether or not he had to fire the entirety of his staff at the keep. As Kennet stood by his side, he watched the lord drag a hand down his face, then rest his chin in that hand. "I really hate making decisions like this, you know."

"Unfortunately, it's a decision that must be made," Kennet replied. After taking some time to rest in the courtyard, he had remembered an important factor: there was still a suspect at large within the keep itself. Whether or not the mastermind would ever be found, there was no option to ignore the inside man. It wasn't safe.

"I know." Hagen slumped back in his chair, and Kennet fought the urge to lay a comforting hand on the man's shoulder. It simply wouldn't be appropriate to do so, so he clenched a fist behind his back and cleared his throat.

"If it helps, I can be by your side through the whole thing," he offered. "It will certainly stand as a symbol of the gravity of the situation."

"Oh, would you?" Hagen sighed languidly. "I do appreciate it, I feel like I must be a terribly weak leader if someone would dare to poison my own child right under my nose."

"I don't think that's true. One rather . . . expects more of humanity as a whole, I think, than to expect someone to poison a child."

"Consider me jaded," Hagen muttered.

"I didn't think I could be any more than I already am, but I find myself unable to ignore this particular instance," Kennet sympathized. "Would you like me to gather the staff?"

"Let's wait until after Marna is out of the weeds," Hagen replied. "I would rather worry about one thing at a time."

"Understood, my lord."

There was a wry chuckle from the lord, and he looked up

at Kennet with an odd glimmer in his dark eyes. "You know, I'm really very lucky to have you. I almost hired someone else, but I didn't even know where to start. The desperation drove me somewhere I never thought it would—you're really the only person I can tell this, but I reached out to my father for recommendations. Do you know what he told me?"

Kennet suspected he knew, but it wasn't really something a person would say unless they were bragging. "What's that, Your Highness?"

Hagen caught onto the change in the way Kennet was addressing him and shook his head with a tired smile. "He told me I wouldn't find a finer man for the job than you, Kennet Peders. You've worked for him in the past, have you not?"

"I *have* been knighted," Kennet pointed out. "But I've not worked particularly closely with him. Been hired by his men to carry out some delicate jobs. Hana has, too."

"If it's fit for a king, then it's fit for my Marna, I suppose," Hagen said. "It's funny, I never thought I'd speak to him again after how we left things, my father and I, but it was unexpectedly pleasant. Perhaps I was too quick to judge him."

Kennet shrugged, unsure of how to address a relationship as tested as that of a father and his son, especially when the father and son happened to be royalty. "Judgment often comes too quickly and too strong," he said slowly, and Hagen nodded in agreement.

"I wish you weren't so good at your job, or I'd hire you to be my advisor."

"I absolutely despise politics, Your Highness."

"Stop calling me that. Someone's bound to hear."

"Yes, my lord."

CHAPTER 10

FAR FROM OVER

It had been nearly a full day since Hana administered the first dose of her antidote.

There had been no immediate effect, but after a sleepless night of Hana waking up to give a dose every few hours, Marna's condition had improved rapidly. As the sun began to set on the second day, the long-awaited moment arrived. Marna opened her eyes.

Eyes as brown as her father's stared up at Hagen, and Kennet felt his breath catch as he realized he was beholding the moment he had worked so hard to achieve. He wished Asa could be there to see it too, but he understood why they weren't. He did his best to mark down every detail in his mind to relay to them later. The way that Hagen's face contorted to hold back tears, an effort that ultimately failed. The way Marna called out to him when she realized he was there, and reached out, wiping the tear from her father's cheek which just caused more to follow.

He cradled her body in his arms, whispered to her that she was all right. That he would never let anything like this happen to her again. She held him back, and began to cry too. Kennet felt like he shouldn't be in the room.

But Hagen insisted that Kennet stay. Kennet and Hana, who crossed her arms and beamed at the father and daughter, rightfully proud of her good work.

Kennet glanced over at her, wondering what exactly she was thinking. The two had hardly spoken a word to each other since their fight in the kitchen, but as they stood overlooking the touching scene before them, he was startled to feel her hand on his shoulder.

"We did good," she said.

She'd said this to him before, after much less heartwarming moments. It was the mark of a job well done, usually only given when there had been no mistakes made. He hadn't expected to ever hear it again, much less now, but it brought the same swell of pride when he heard it.

"We should leave them alone," she added.

"Right, of course."

"Thank you both," Hagen said without looking away from his daughter. "You'll . . . come back later, won't you? In a few days. We'll have a celebration, a feast."

Kennet bit his tongue not to mention the staff issue. He knew that Hagen would likely remember it himself once he came down from his emotional high, so there was no reason to bring it up now. He gave a shallow, polite bow. "As you wish, my lord," he said, and he and Hana left the room.

Gerrit stood outside the door at his usual post, and as they left, he turned around for a moment to catch a glance at the goings-on beyond. The smile that crept over his face was all Kennet needed to see for his mind to be put at ease concerning the boy—he hadn't wanted to believe that Gerrit could possibly be behind the poisoning, but there was no way of knowing for sure. It was unfortunate, and it was part of what he and Hagen had discussed the night before—that there was plenty of time for any number of people to have encountered both the soup and the water before they made it to Marna's bedside.

Hana had confirmed the water's contamination status, testing it with a counteractive agent of some kind before she administered the antidote. It had confirmed both her suspicions about the water, and the identity of the poison itself, which she had wanted to be sure of before going forward.

Things were all coming together exactly as expected. Kennet felt like he was finally able to relax.

"You did it, Sir Peders!" Gerrit said, his smile not fading.

"Care to join us for a celebratory drink, Master Gerrit?"

"Who's us?" Hana protested mildly.

"Hana, say what you will about me, but I know you've never been one to turn down free ale," Kennet scoffed, and Hana gave a shrug of surrender.

"Do you think that would be all right?" Gerrit asked, glancing back at the room again.

"Ask. If it isn't all right, then it's no matter."

Of course it was all right. After what Kennet had done, he could have likely dismissed the entire staff for the day if he wanted to, and nobody would have dared to argue. With Gerrit in tow, they made their way back into town, to the tavern where Kennet had spent that first fateful night.

When they entered, Kennet immediately recognized the melody that was sailing over the ambient noise of the patrons. He felt almost embarrassed by the way he knew his expression must have changed when he heard them. That embarrassment wasn't enough to stop him from swiveling around to face the stage, though, and he broke into a full smile when he saw Asa standing there.

They were playing the song they had sung him on their travels, and they saw him as he saw them, giving a bow in his direction with a wide grin. He could see the charming gap between their front teeth even from the distance he and his companions stood from the stage.

"They really are good, aren't they?" Hana remarked, and

Kennet realized this was the first time she was hearing them play in their full element.

"Extremely," Kennet agreed.

"You'll have to buy them a drink, too," she said, pushing past his starstruck stance to get to the bar. At her statement, he snapped out of his trance and joined her as she walked.

"What, I'm allowed to buy them things now? Won't I ruin them?" He risked a teasing remark and was rewarded with a wicked glare.

"I'm in a good mood, Peders, don't ruin it by reminding me of our last conversation," she said.

"You're right. Sorry."

"We'll talk about that later," she added, letting him know he wouldn't be getting away from all of that easily. "I wasn't finished when you ran out. There's something that needs to be discussed, but it can wait until the celebrations are over."

"Thank you," Kennet said meaningfully. He felt that he could weather whatever it was she still had to say to him, because when she was done, it was likely she would leave, and he could process things without a fresh barrage of accusations every time he turned his head.

He watched as she leaned against the bar—he had expected her to change back into her old, more familiar garb upon leaving Grankoping for this job, but she had stuck to the forest greens and beiges in her dress. No dark colors, no gloom except for the expression on her face. She even kept her sleeves rolled up as she had when they were in her home, completely unashamed now of the scars that she used to hide religiously.

Maybe it didn't matter if she forgave him or not. Maybe it didn't matter if she got to move on, and he didn't. It honestly made his heart soar to see her even slightly happier than he had left her. Whether or not they deserved happiness didn't matter. He was glad to see it, either way.

Gerrit hung back near Kennet, and he could see that the

young manservant was as fixated on the bard as Kennet himself had been seconds ago. He followed Gerrit's line of sight to the stage again and saw that Asa was finishing their song. When the music had entirely died down, they turned toward him, and struck up a new one that this time he felt for sure was for him. It was odd, the pride he felt swell. The feeling that though everyone in the audience felt that this song was for them, he knew—he knew it was for him.

He knew that the wink thrown in his direction was actually intended to be meant for him alone.

And he knew that no matter who in the crowd was enchanted by their singing, none of them would be invited to have the conversations he had with them. None of them would know Asa like he did.

He gave the slightest incline of his head in their direction, and watched them react with a flourish, accepting his acknowledgment as their cue to return their attention to the rest of the crowd. They were singing in Isla, and Kennet wondered if this was just another song about food, or if there was more meaning to their choice this time.

"Do you speak Isla?" Kennet wondered as he slid up next to Hana at the bar.

"Wondering about the bard's song?" Hana answered his question with one of her own.

"Of course."

"I don't speak much Isla, but I know this song." Hana sighed. "Pay for my drink and I might tell you what it's about."

"I was already going to pay for your drink," Kennet said with amusement, but he did as he was told, hailing the bartender and ordering a round of ale for the four people he felt responsible for. When the ale was delivered, Hana kept her end of her bargain.

"It's a folk song," she said. "About a dangerous part of town, and a woman who goes walking through it. She gets attacked by robbers, and a strange man swoops in from the rooftops to save her. They fall in love, he dies by the sword of the son of one of the robbers he had killed to save her. Very romantic, very intense. Typical Lucien ballad."

"Sounds interesting," Kennet remarked, and Hana shrugged.

"I like a Lucien song now and again. I admit, it's odd to hear one in a Bladland tavern. Feels like two things that shouldn't go together." She took a sip of her ale and considered it with surprise. "This is good."

"Do you just expect everything to be awful these days?"

"No, but it wouldn't surprise me, not with how things have trended."

Kennet knew she was talking about him. He tried not to dignify the jab, replying, "You said you were in a good mood."

"I am," she snorted, then added, "I'm sorry. I'll tone it down for the night."

Gerrit, who had been quiet this whole time, suddenly blurted out, "Where are the scars from?"

Kennet could have killed the boy.

However, shockingly Hana didn't seem bothered by the question. She turned to Gerrit and pulled her sleeves back a little farther to reveal darker, deeper scars. Kennet had never seen these. They were like dents digging into her flesh, thick and leathery. He felt the urge to look away, but she held her arms out to show them more clearly.

"You're young," she observed of Gerrit. "Have you heard of the flesh-eating plague?"

Gerrit shook his head, lost for words.

"There was a serious disease that swept the entire coast—my country, Asa's, others," Hana said, like she was telling a ghost story. "It decimated entire nations. It left orphans, cost people limbs and livelihoods. I left with only a patch this size, on my wrist"—she made a circle with her fingers about the size of a coin—"and by the time we made landfall in Bladland, it had spread. I had to be quarantined for the voyage. Sat in the brig with nothing to keep me entertained. Almost went mad."

Kennet had never heard this part. Maybe he should have asked more questions when they had been closer—or maybe living with a child had strengthened her tolerance for this kind of conversation.

"Holy Death," Gerrit breathed, "but you made it alive?"

"And without spreading anything to the rest of the passengers. I'm lucky," she said. "Well, more than lucky. There was a woman on board who was skilled in healing. She taught me about the powders and the herbs that were in the powders to dry the plague out on my skin and stop it from spreading," Hana said. "Without her, I would have certainly wasted away on that ship."

There was a reverent silence left in the wake of Hana's story, as Gerrit sat with eyes wide, looking at her scars with new understanding. He scratched his own arms absentmindedly, and Kennet saw the ghost of a smirk on Hana's face. She had enjoyed scaring the boy. Of course she had. He wondered if her story had been entirely true, or if she had exaggerated some of it, though he didn't know what parts he would have identified as fake. It all sounded horribly, awfully real.

Kennet almost sighed audibly with relief when Asa came to join them.

"Good evening, my friends!" They noticed the looks on everyone's faces. "What have I missed?"

"Not much," Kennet replied. "Hana was just telling us a story."

"Ooh, I do love stories. Too bad I missed it." They didn't seem to hold any actual regret, and accepted the ale that Hana held out to them with a smile. "I assume the fact that you're all here means we have an update on dear Marna, and the fact that we're all drinking means it's good news?"

"Correct and correct. She's well and reunited with her father."

Asa held up their drink. "Wonderful! To Marna, then!"

"To Marna!" The other three echoed Asa's toast, and when they did, Kennet saw that the entire tavern had turned their eyes on their group. There was a hush, and then suddenly, a cheer.

"To Marna!" The roar of the crowd met Kennet's ears. He'd forgotten that they'd been waiting as anxiously as he had, that this news was a relief to an entire community.

Strangers began to filter their way up to Kennet at the bar, clapping hands on his shoulder, and offering to buy him drinks. They shied away from Hana for the most part, but a few offered the same to her. While Kennet declined many of the offers, Hana accepted everything. He wondered how many of them she would actually drink. When the drinks started coming her way, though, she passed every other one off to Gerrit, who hadn't had a single offer of his own. She tried the same for Asa, but they declined, saying they needed to keep at least a bit sober if they were to continue performing.

Eventually the bartender came over to let them know that as far as she was concerned, they could drink their fill. By the time things had come to that, Gerrit and Kennet were already at their limit. Hana, however, simply lifted her mug in thanks and took another swig.

The excitement died down after a while, leaving an ambient buzz of positivity that hummed through the tavern until long into the night.

It was nice to feel like a hero, and Kennet marveled at the sensation, swirling the last of his latest drink in his mug absentmindedly. It was something he could get used to, but a reward this great would necessitate some equally high stakes, and he wasn't anxious to have to deal with that again. He decided to simply revel in the glow for now.

"How's our lord?"

Kennet looked up to see that Asa had sat back down next to him again. They'd been flitting back and forth around the bar, playing off and on, but it seemed that now they were settling. "He's well," Kennet replied. "Holding a grand feast at some point, said to tell you that you're invited."

"Lovely! Feasts are always wonderful," Asa said. "But he'd better not be expecting me to play."

"Oh? You wouldn't, if he asked? Not even for such a grand occasion?"

Asa considered what he had said, cocking their head and stroking their chin in apparent deep thought. "Well," they said with a grin, "not for free."

∼

THE KEEP itself was the site of the celebration. The staff buzzed about with equal parts excitement and stress, with many casting anxious glances at Kennet as they worked. Kennet knew why—but they didn't need to worry anymore. The danger was past, none of their jobs were on the line now. If they knew the truth of the matter, they would be thanking him, because Hagen alone wouldn't have gotten the same results.

When Hagen had gathered the staff to fire them, he had done so with incisiveness. He hadn't told them why he was summoning them. Rather, he let them wallow in anxiety at Kennet's suggestion, and when they all stood before him, Kennet was there behind the throne and the lord in it. He had been mostly silent except to lean down and whisper in Hagen's ear every now and again. That hushed conversation had been sustained for only a few moments before Hagen had loudly proclaimed that he knew, without a shadow of a doubt, that one of them had been involved in Marna's poisoning.

That was all it had taken. Immediately, the man Kennet

knew to be Gerrit's immediate superior had peeled away from the group, his hands clasped in pleading. He'd said he regretted it immediately—this could not be true, since he had continued to poison Marna even after she had fallen ill.

Kennet had been surprised by Hagen's reaction. The lord had been furious. He hadn't shown it, not to the staff, but as Kennet stood near him he could see it where they couldn't. The way Hagen began to tense, the way his fist wrapped around the armrest of the throne and gripped it with enough strength that Kennet could swear he heard the wood straining. He was surprised too, then, to hear the punishment.

Banishment. It was almost tame, Kennet thought, but Hagen had a reputation for being merciful for a reason. He calmly explained that he would be sending notice to the other lords of the area immediately, and that the man would no longer be welcome anywhere in Bladland. Though the servant had been visibly upset, he seemed to realize that he was getting off lucky.

Even with this mercy, the attitude in the keep had shifted noticeably.

Not toward Hagen. Most seemed to understand his actions and not hold them against him, which meant Kennet's presence had been effective. They were afraid of *him*, not their lord. Balance had been maintained, even restored, under his hand.

Gerrit, of course, had not been affected at all. Even as he'd been before Hagen and Kennet, the boy hadn't flinched, possibly because of the hangover he had been suffering at the time. As such, he was the only one who now dared to treat Kennet with any familiarity. Even Britta seemed to be avoiding him, though she had become quite smitten with Hana.

That was fine. He didn't need to be loved, anyway; that was something he knew very well about himself. At the very least he didn't need to be loved by *many*. Just by some. Maybe just by one, in particular.

"Ah, it seems I've arrived too early." Asa of the Isles stepped into the hall to be met by the same scene Kennet had been watching for the past half an hour—people bustling about, making last-minute preparations.

"That's fine, more time to talk before things get loud," Kennet replied, and they shrugged in agreement.

They hadn't brought the vihuela after all. Apparently they were sticking to their previous statement when it came to performing at this celebration—a celebration that they considered to be, in no small part, thrown in their honor. That made sense to Kennet. They should not be working. On today, of all days, they should be rejoicing.

Still, Kennet would miss their music.

He thought about that when the feast actually started, and a full band began to play. They were skilled and played the songs he would expect them to play, but it was that expectation that made them fall flat for Kennet. Not that it truly mattered either way, since he could hardly hear the music at all over the chatter that rang throughout the keep.

All sorts of people were milling about, but mostly nobles from surrounding areas, some of whom Kennet recognized from their dress. He could even pick out one or two that he had worked with before. He thought about approaching them to catch up before he realized that they likely wouldn't want to admit to associating with him. It would be slightly incriminating to do so.

He chuckled at that realization when he made it and shook his head. Asa had gone off to get something for both of them to drink, which left him fully unattended for the first time in a few hours. He felt a little overwhelmed. Hana was nowhere to be seen, and Gerrit had only come by to say a polite hello before being swept off with a few of his peers.

Kennet sometimes wished he could, even just for a night,

be on that level. He had been, once, when he was much younger, and at the time he had loathed his station. Now, he fit in with neither the common folk nor the nobility. Not that he truly wanted to—even his fleeting wishes were washed away quickly by the pride he felt being above it all.

He was taken aback, then, when someone eventually dared to approach him.

A woman with dark hair and eyes, wearing deep reds and golds, stepped up next to him with a warm smile. He recognized her immediately.

"My lady, Alva Sundstrom," he said, bowing deeply.

"Sir Kennet Peders." She didn't bow back, but allowed him to kiss her hand lightly, and smiled when he did. "I heard you were behind all this."

"In a way," Kennet replied.

"And Hana Oh, too," Lady Sundstrom added. "I ran into her earlier."

So she is here, Kennet remarked inwardly, but only nodded in response.

"I wouldn't have hired you," Sundstrom said.

Kennet knew she wouldn't have. He was the reason her marriage had ended—even though it had ended in her favor, with her managing to maintain her claim to her husband's land. Even with her coming out on top, it was a testy subject. "Of course not," Kennet said with a politely teasing smile, and she exhaled sharply through her nose.

"I would have been wrong, too," she admitted. "You managed something many of us feared impossible."

"Well, I'm glad nobody told *me* it was impossible," Kennet replied, and she laughed again, more clearly this time.

"As am I. That girl is simply darling. Would have liked one of my own, you know."

Why does everyone always feel the need to remind me that I ruined their life, as if I don't already know? "There's still time for that."

"Oh, are you offering?" She eyed him as she took a sip of dark wine from a glass that was balanced delicately in her thin fingers.

"Unfortunately not." Kennet managed to keep his words clear in spite of the way she was looking at him.

"Pity. Then you're spoken for?"

Kennet opened his mouth to say that he wasn't, but now was the moment his words chose to stumble. He clapped his mouth shut before any sound could come out, and Lady Sundstrom noticed.

"I see," was all she said, and she took another sip of her wine. "I'm happy for you, you know. With everything you've been through, I never would have thought you'd be able to find work again, much less something like this."

"It's been hard," Kennet admitted, "but with time, I think I've managed to recover."

"It helps that not all of us find your disgrace to be a fitting punishment for your actions. Many of us know the truth—you're not a disgrace, you're just good at your job."

Ah, the opposite of Hana. It made him ache that the only people to have any lingering respect for him were people who hadn't the slightest idea of what he'd been through. "I can be both, I think," he said slowly, and she tittered another laugh. This one felt more malicious than the others.

"Oh, I'm sure you can," she said.

Kennet was about to ask her what she meant by that, or at the very least he was going to try and make some kind of remark to recover from it, when Gerrit approached with a loud cough to interrupt.

"Master Gerrit," Kennet said, surprised at his forwardness in the presence of the lady.

"Sir Peders." Something seemed off. Where earlier Gerrit had been flush with ale and enjoyment, now he almost stuttered out Kennet's name. "My lord desires your presence. Immediately."

Kennet and Lady Sundstrom exchanged a glance. She raised her eyebrows, and gestured toward Gerrit. "You've been summoned. Don't dally on my account."

"Of course." Kennet gave her another bow. "Apologies, m'lady."

"None needed, Sir Peders. It was nice to talk to you again."

Kennet followed Gerrit away from the crowd, toward the back of the great hall. The crowd was thick enough that Kennet couldn't see Hagen right away, so he referred to Gerrit in order to gauge the amount of stress he should be feeling. "Everything all right, Master Gerrit?"

"No, sir," Gerrit said, through gritted teeth.

"Care to elaborate?"

"No, sir."

"That bad, is it?"

"Yes, sir."

That was encouraging. Kennet didn't pester the boy further, allowing himself to be led through the crowd. Nobody parted for them, leaving them to weave behind the backs of people who had congregated in small groups to talk and eat merrily. Finally, they stepped into view of the dais at the back of the great hall, and Kennet saw Hagen seated in his throne overlooking the celebration. The lord's expression, however, was anything but jovial.

Hana stood on one of the steps and nodded curtly to Kennet as he approached. When he got to the bottom step, Kennet kneeled out of reflex, and curiously, Hagen didn't stop him.

"Rise," the lord muttered darkly. He didn't make eye contact with Kennet as he stood. "Come here, Sir Peders, I've some things to say that are for your ears alone."

Kennet glanced at Gerrit, who also seemed to be trying to look anywhere but at Kennet. As Kennet ascended the steps to Hagen's side, Gerrit clicked his heels together and dismissed himself with speed Kennet had only seen previously from the boy when he had been offered free food.

"Is it Marna?" Kennet asked immediately when he was near enough to Hagen to speak in hushed tones.

"Gods, no." Hagen seemed to suddenly realize the implication of his mood. "No, she's fine. Look, she's there, fit as can be expected." He gestured to the bottom of the dais steps where Marna was sitting at a table within view, chatting with some children her age. There were servants on either side of her—she would be well-guarded tonight. Kennet felt a weight lifted off his shoulders.

"You had me worried."

"My apologies, that wasn't my intent."

"Then what was?"

The cloud that had been briefly lifted from Hagen's countenance returned almost immediately. "I've been thinking. I spoke to Miss Oh about this already, but things have developed in a way that I find . . . unsatisfactory."

Hana had drifted up the stairs as well, and was now standing directly next to Kennet at the throne. Kennet felt almost sick to his stomach. "What do you mean?"

"The threat on my daughter's life was much closer than I had initially thought. There were more people working on it than I had expected. The man in Ornhult that you spoke to. My own servant. It's unacceptable."

Kennet nodded in understanding. He was still unsure of where this was going.

"I've been too sick with worry to think clearly," Hagen continued, sighing and leaning his head on a fist as his elbow rested on the throne. "Every moment of every day, only thinking of how scared I was to lose my daughter. But now that she's well, I find myself preoccupied by a new thought."

"A new thought, my lord?" Kennet hesitated, but he was starting to piece things together.

"Punishment." Hagen's soft voice was taut with emotion.

"I cannot, as a leader and a father, sit idle while the person who almost killed my innocent child still walks free. And furthermore, I won't feel safe until I know that it has been taken care of."

Kennet felt a chill in the air at the lord's words. He didn't speak, waiting for what he knew was coming next.

"I am not finished with you, Sir Peders," Hagen said.

"I am at your service, my lord," Kennet replied.

"It would be foolish of me to try and find someone new to take over where you have already done so much. The details would be lost, and I know for certain that you are more than capable. So I charge you: find the person who would wish my daughter dead. And find out why, who they're working for, anything you can."

"And then, my lord?"

Hagen finally looked up at Kennet. There was a flash of something unrecognizable in those dark, royal eyes. "And then kill them, Sir Peders."

So it was like that. Kennet was resigned to this new direction, bowing his head farther. "As you wish, my lord." If it weren't for the fact that Hagen was right—that his daughter was still in danger—Kennet might have dared to refuse. But the point had been made. As long as there were those alive who had dared to harm Marna, she was not safe.

"Do you need anything more from me?" Hagen added, sitting up straighter in the throne. "I hope I need not assure you that your reward will be great."

"I have many reasons to accept this job, and only one of them is monetary," Kennet replied, and saw a ghost of a smile on the lord's face.

"That pleases me to hear, if I'm honest. I had hoped, of course, but I wouldn't have judged you if it were only the money you were interested in."

"Nor do I need anything more from you right now, my lord. I find that this is more an extension of my current assignment than anything else." Kennet gave a bow that felt too stiff. "I will not leave town before speaking with you though, in case you've thought of anything more."

"Good. Then I'll not keep you from your celebration—or myself from mine. This is a weight off my mind, Sir Peders, I hadn't felt able to truly enjoy the night before now."

"It's a night worth enjoying, Lord Hagen. I hope you're able to relax."

"Thank you. You're dismissed," Hagen said, and gave a gentle wave of his hand that told Kennet he was being asked to leave.

So he did, turning and making his way away from the dais, and down the steps. He almost missed the sound of footsteps coming after him, but before he could make it back into the fray, was stopped by the sound of his own name.

"Kennet." Hana was walking after him with strong, urgent strides. "We have to talk."

"About?"

"This assignment."

"Don't worry, I wasn't going to ask you along. I've bothered you enough."

"Not about that." Hana was irritated, visibly irritated, which was new. Kennet stopped walking and gave her a puzzled look.

"Then what?"

She glanced around the room. "Privacy," she hissed, and motioned for him to follow.

They made their way out of the great hall itself, out the door, and into the courtyard that Kennet had found solace in just a few days ago. She stopped as soon as they were out of earshot of the crowd, halting so abruptly that Kennet kept going a few steps without her before he noticed.

"What's going on, Hana, you seem—"

"It's Maryska."

Kennet's blood ran ice cold. He felt like he had been paralyzed by those two words, like he would never be able to move again. He wasn't even able to reply to Hana, instead just looking at her with his mouth hanging agape like a fish's.

"You hadn't brought her up before now, so I have to assume you hadn't figured it out yet," Hana continued without waiting for him to acknowledge her. "But it has to be her. A woman—we know this from the herbalist—one who knows poisons. One who would poison a child."

"Maryska would poison a child?" Kennet echoed. It didn't seem like her, he thought, but Hana's expression told him there was something here that he didn't know yet.

"She would," she said flatly. "The Maryska you know is dead. I bet you wish you'd finished the job now, don't you?"

Kennet flinched at her words, his head spinning. "What?"

"Oh, did you think you *had* killed her? Is that why you didn't even think to suspect her? Is her being alive at all a surprise to you? If that's the case, I'm even more impressed that you dared to show your face to me in the first place."

"Hana, no! No, god no!" Kennet interrupted her. He held up his hands, trying to think of the way to say what he wanted to say. "I never intended for Maryska to die. That was the whole reason—I mean, it's the reason that I did what I did, even though I knew—" The words weren't coming out right. He had never known how to explain why he had done what he had done, which was why he had never tried.

"Maryska said you poisoned her," Hana said slowly. There was a little bit of doubt seeping into her tone, which was a good sign for Kennet. "She said it felt like you were rubbing it in that you could."

"I poisoned her to keep her immobile, so she wouldn't try to fight them and she wouldn't get hurt," Kennet said, rubbing his temples. "I knew she was alive, but I thought she would go back to you. That's why I didn't kill her. One of them had to die, just one, that was the deal. And for a moment I did consider choosing her! I did!"

Hana was noticeably confused now. "Then why didn't you?"

Kennet's hands, held up in surrender, dropped to his sides as he admitted, "Because of you. One of us was going to lose one of them, and I don't think I could have lived my whole life lying to Isak about how his sister had died. In my heart I'd already lost him, so I thought I could at least spare you that same loss." He sighed bitterly. "It was misguided, but I thought maybe I could minimize the damage. Clearly all I did was make things worse."

Hana's eyebrows furrowed, then relaxed, as she seemed caught between two trains of thought. "You let her live because . . .?"

"Because I knew the two of you were in love. The whole ride out, she wouldn't stop talking about you. She told me . . ." He paused, feeling bile rise in his throat at the memories of that day. "She told me she was worried about the fact that you didn't know Bladland's customs for marriage, because she wanted to ask you to marry her. And she was afraid . . . she was afraid you wouldn't understand . . ."

Hana's stony facade finally slipped completely, and Kennet felt a slap flash across his cheek. He stopped talking, but absorbed the sharp pain without flinching further.

"You ruined us," she said. "I don't care what you meant to do, or what you thought you were sparing us. You *ruined* us. Every one of us, including yourself."

"I know," Kennet whispered.

"And now . . . god, now I have to hunt her down myself, for poisoning a hell-blessed child. A *child*, Kennet. You not only became this despicable creature I don't even want to look at, you made *her* into one as well."

"I know," he repeated, then realized what she had said. "Wait, hunt her down yourself? What should I tell Hagen?"

"Nothing. I've already let him know I might travel with you, and what you've told me changes nothing." She straightened up, taking a deep but shaky breath. "This is our responsibility. Yours, primarily, but mine as well."

"You don't have to—"

"I know." It was her turn to say those words, and she said them sharply. "But without me, it will take you ages to find her. You're obviously the last person she wants to see."

"And with you . . .?"

Hana deliberated for a moment before she sighed with resignation. "I know where she is," she said.

"You could just tell me, you know. Go home to Stefan and James, leave this messy business to me. I don't want to hurt you more than I already have."

"No, I couldn't," Hana replied. "What if Maryska manages to kill you, and I'm not there to see it? I'd never forgive myself for missing that."

Kennet didn't know how to respond to that, but he didn't have to think of anything, as Hana rolled her eyes at his baffled expression.

"I'm joking," she said, "obviously."

It didn't feel that obvious to him.

"I'll be glad for any help I can get," he said, unsure of what else to say, unsure of how to even address the myriad of emotions that he was currently stuffing down with each breath.

"Then you'd best ask your friend Asa to come along, too," Hana said. "We'll need all the levity they can provide."

∽

THE FEAST WAS WINDING DOWN, and most of the nobility were making their way out of the main hall. Kennet noted that he should likely be leaving soon, too. Though the new assignment wasn't under the same kind of time constraints as the last, he knew that Hana would want to be home sooner rather than later, so they would leave within the week.

He was just thinking of how to politely make his way back up to the dais to say goodbye before leaving when a brightly clothed figure caught his eye. Asa approached with a smile, though the expression was quizzical on their face.

"Why has Hana told me that I'm to pack my things and be ready to leave in the morning?"

"God, did she really?" Kennet groaned. "I was hoping to get to you first."

"She didn't tell me anything else, absolutely no details, if that helps," Asa said. "So I can easily pretend that you're telling me for the first time."

"You don't have to come," Kennet began with a clarification, "but Hana and I have been asked by Lord Hagen to track down the person responsible for the attempt on Marna's life."

"Ah! Sounds dangerous."

"It . . . might be," Kennet admitted. Especially if Maryska was involved, and even more so if Maryska was angry—and she would be. "So I'd like to stress again: you don't have to come."

"Hana seems to think she'll kill you before you reach your destination if I don't come."

"That's possible," Kennet said, and Asa laughed.

"Well then, I'm coming. This might surprise you to learn, Sir Peders, but I rather like you alive."

"I'm unsurprised, but I *am* flattered," Kennet replied with a sigh. Then, something new occurred to him, and he brightened immediately. "I meant to tell you! After all this is finally squared away, or at least once we've exhausted our current lead, I have something I'd like to do with you."

Asa raised their eyebrows and opened their mouth to make a snide remark, so Kennet cut them off before they could.

"There's a religious expert I know, I think he could help us figure out your . . . er, condition." He stumbled over the last part of the sentence, realizing he shouldn't be too open as long as they were still technically in public.

"Oh, very interesting!" Asa said. "I can't say I expected you to continue taking an interest in that."

"I've not been able to stop thinking about it," Kennet said honestly, not adding that he hadn't been able to stop thinking about them in general. "Hana said I should warn you, though —he's a former worshiper of Gethin."

The bard made a face at that. "Well, that's not the end of the world," they said slowly, "if it's 'former'. And if he might help."

"Then it's settled. We'll make our way there at the earliest convenience." He smiled with satisfaction. "I think you'll like Lange."

"If he's half as sunny as the other people you've introduced me to," Asa said, "I'm sure I will."

END OF PART 1

PART II: THE ASSASSIN

CHAPTER 1

ASA ATTEMPTS TO DETERMINE WHAT COUNTS AS AN "ADVENTURE"

There had never been much of a plan when it came to this journey.

There had never been a through-line, a goal, anything of the sort, and that had always been fine. Asa had always figured that by the time they really needed a plan, the way forward would already be obvious, and so far that had been true—down to the point that now, they had more of a plan than they had ever had in their life.

Of course, most of it had been handed to them by a frightening-looking man in a dark coat with a shady past. But that was part of the fun, wasn't it?

If anyone could have told the Asa from just five years ago that this is where they would be at this point, they knew it would have been nearly impossible for them to believe it. As far as they were concerned, that meant they had succeeded. And on top of all that, they had saved the life of a young girl! Well, they hadn't actually done all that much to help with that. Kennet Peders had assured them that their help was integral, especially now that they were trying to hunt down the culprit, but they couldn't help but feel that they hadn't contributed much at all.

Maybe that hadn't been the point, though. Maybe the interrogations, the intrigue, that wasn't what he really had needed them for.

He was a strange one, that man. Asa had met many people on their travels, and most of them were very average, which was kind of the point. But Peders . . . Asa wanted to know more about him. There was something there worth knowing. They were sure of it.

"You've been quiet," Peders said, riding up alongside them. They had all been riding single-file for some time now, since the road was narrow, and they weren't far from a few major towns. But now that the road was widening and the distance between them and civilization was growing, it would be easier to chat.

"I've not really had anything to say." Asa shrugged, speaking honestly. They had to look up at Peders. Even when they were standing this was the case, but Emilio was so much shorter than Peders' horse, Starling.

"Then you've been thinking this whole time?" Peders asked, and Asa snorted.

"I didn't say that. Truthfully there's not been a thing happening, I was mostly just looking at the scenery."

"It's all the same stuff we saw before." Peders batted a branch out of his face as Starling strayed a bit off the path to try and nibble at a fern. "And it's all hot and sticky," he added. "At least the evenings are nice."

Asa was amused by how much the heat annoyed Peders. He had already complained twice about having to shed his coat, which Hana and Asa had both teased him for. The teasing was better-natured than it had been on the previous leg of their journey. Still tense, of course. Undoubtedly tense. But that was why Asa was here in the first place, as they understood it. To be a buffer.

They'd never had to be a buffer before. It felt nice to be wanted for their personality, and their company, but it came with a good bit of pressure. Especially when the history between these two seemed so . . . burdened. Oh, how they longed to be nosey, but they had a bad feeling that would get them nowhere. On top of that it might also completely ruin the goodwill they had right now.

"What about you?" Asa turned the conversation around, smiling up at Peders. In the midday lighting, his hair sparkled where the sun hit the bits of grey that were sprinkled through it. It was pretty in a way. They often came close to mentioning it, but they were afraid he would think they were teasing him again.

He looked down and noticed they were watching him, and quickly looked away. He did that often. It was amusing. "What about me?" he asked.

"What have you been thinking about?"

Peders was quiet at that. He looked up toward the sun above them, then back down at Asa. "The scenery, I suppose."

"Good, then neither of us have been thinking at all. That leaves it all to Hana."

"As usual," Hana piped from the front of the group.

Asa liked Hana. It wasn't the deep sort of liking, and it wasn't complicated. They just enjoyed being around her. They hadn't expected to—she was intimidating. Where Peders appeared frightening but got easier to be around the longer they talked to him, Hana had been intimidating to look at, and more intimidating to talk to. While Asa was sure that she meant to be that intimidating, they had quickly learned that they didn't mind it. Especially since she seemed to like Asa, too.

"What are you thinking about, Hana?" Peders ventured.

There was an incredibly long pause from the leader of the pack, until finally, resentfully, she replied, "The scenery."

Asa couldn't hide their smile at her admission, and they saw that Peders was doing his best to try and hide his own. So they were all completely void of any introspection, unless one of them was lying. Which, of course, they had to be. Despite the way the tone had lightened, Asa was sure that Peders, at least, was always thinking. Constantly.

He never seemed to show it, of course. Hana either. She was better at hiding it, with her constant air of annoyance. And when she was relaxed, she was cheerful. The emotion that she hid was joy, buried under a surprisingly thin layer of irritability. Peders, on the other hand . . .

They had heard him crying.

It had been on one of the nights on their journey, the night that he had found Hana Oh and Stefan Bergstrom without Asa. They had been unable to sleep and stayed up working on a song, one they were certain would be a masterpiece if they ever managed to finish it. They'd heard his footfall up the stairs, and the creak of his door.

Then, alarmingly soon after all that, they'd heard his sobs.

They hated to think about it, even now as they rode alongside him, because they knew it was likely those same emotions were tumbling just under his well-composed surface. But it stuck in their mind, the shaking, shuddering noise they'd heard through the thin walls. They'd wanted to go and see him that night, to offer what they had eventually given him—peace, and a good night's sleep. It seemed rude, though, to barge in on a man crying like that.

Besides that, they thought he'd likely rather die than know that they had heard.

So they had kept it to themself, only approaching him when the moment had seemed right.

That had gone much better.

Even with all that said, none of that necessarily meant that he wanted to talk about it. In fact, it seemed to be quite the opposite. Well, that was the cost of traveling with someone so interesting. They got to see interesting things at the cost of never talking to anybody about anything meaningful.

There was still no conversation as they traveled, until they reached a point where Hana called them to a halt.

"We should keep going until sunfall," she said, "but I'm starving. Let's take a moment to eat."

"Gladly," Asa agreed enthusiastically. "And to stretch."

"Indeed."

The trio dismounted, and as Hana rifled through her saddlebags for food, Asa approached their first companion and friend.

"Sir Peders," they said, slipping up beside him with a few soft pats to alert Starling to their presence. "Now that we're alone—"

"Are we hiding from Hana?" Peders interrupted, and glanced at her over his horse's back.

"A little," Asa admitted. They didn't want to, but he behaved so differently around her, and it was annoying. They wanted the Peders they had first met, and he only seemed to be around when the two of them were alone.

"Let's do a better job of it then, shall we?" He gave Starling a pat goodbye, then gestured to move farther away from the horses. Hana noticed them moving off, and seemed resigned to their antics. She didn't give them so much as a shrug.

As soon as they were suitably out of earshot, Peders turned to Asa with a smile. "Right, you were saying?"

"I was saying," Asa said, "now that we're alone, truly, I was wondering if I might ask: should I be worried about Hana poisoning you or killing you in your sleep? The way she asked me along has me worried."

Peders realized immediately that they were trying to lighten the mood, and he laughed his hearty laugh. "God, I hope not," he said, "but do keep an eye on her for me."

"Gladly." Asa nodded.

"Did you just pull me aside because you wanted to chat?"

"Perhaps." They shrugged. "I need a break from the tension, you know. I asked both of you what you were thinking about, and you both lied to me."

Peders' expression darkened at that, and he cast a look aside at the ground, putting a hand over his mouth. Asa had learned he did this when he was trying not to betray his true feelings on a situation. He did a terrible job of it. "I suppose I did," he muttered, a bit sheepishly.

"So, what was it?"

"Asa, my friend, has it occurred to you that I lied because I didn't want to talk about it?"

"Perhaps," Asa repeated, giving their best disarming smile, "but perhaps it was just because of Hana."

"Or perhaps both."

"Well, as always, I won't make you tell me."

"As always, I thank you." There was silence from the man for a moment, before he sighed. "I promise you I won't keep everything from you forever, you know."

"I hope not. How am I meant to write a grand epic about our adventures if I don't know half the story?"

Peders snorted. "Is that what this is? An adventure?"

Well. That was a question. "What else would it be?"

"A job."

"A job for a hire-sword is most certainly an adventure to the common man. And I've been tasked to record such things."

"Tasked by who?"

"Myself," Asa said, and they hoped he would laugh. He did.

"Of course, of course," Peders said. "I don't feel like this has been an adventure worth writing about, though."

"What? Come now. We have the brave hero—you." They gestured to him. "The innocent maiden who needed to be saved. The noble king."

"King?" Peders cocked an eyebrow.

"Prince," Asa clarified.

"Lord," Peders corrected. "Don't go writing about that, he'll have me hunt you down next."

"Oh, of course." Asa nodded seriously.

"But I'm a hero, am I?"

"In this story, yes." Asa wasn't naive. Nor did they desire to boost Peders' ego needlessly. Truthfully, they had no doubt that whatever had happened between him and Hana, it had been entirely Peders' fault, and it had been awful. Even Peders seemed aware of that, so there was no need to pretend otherwise.

"I'll take it." Peders nodded in thanks. "Well, hopefully this next part will be well worth writing about."

"I'd argue that we should hope it won't be," Asa replied. "If it goes smoothly, it'll make for a poor song, but good luck for us."

"Either way, you'll come out on top."

"As I usually do."

Peders chuckled softly and shook his head. He pulled his hair out from where it had settled under his shirt collar, tossing it over his shoulder and casting another glance back at Hana and the horses. "Well, that's enough of that. If we linger much longer, she might get the wrong idea."

Asa loved it when he said things like that. He never meant it the way it sounded, but it always gave them the opportunity to pretend that they thought he did. And then he would blush. "The wrong idea? And what might that be?"

There was the blush. "That we're conspiring to murder her in her sleep?" He recovered smoothly enough, and Asa pursed their lips in consideration.

"Is that not what we've been doing?"

"Nevertheless, we don't want her to catch on."

Asa laughed and gestured for him to lead the way back. Hana, who had been blatantly watching them talk the entire time, barely acknowledged their approach. She remounted her horse and waited for them to do the same.

"All right. Let's try to make it to Ornhult before sunfall," she said, checking the sun in the sky. "I think we'll be able to do that just fine."

"Ah, then we can say hello to that poor bastard Torger, let him know everything turned out all right," Asa suggested.

Peders nodded. "No thanks to him, I'm afraid," he said. Then he sighed and admitted, "Not that I blame the man, but still."

"We managed just fine with what we had," Asa said comfortingly.

"If we'd gotten just a bit more, we wouldn't have had to bother Hana."

Asa looked over to Hana at that. She raised an eyebrow. "I wager he told you everything he knew. If he'd known an antidote, what would it have done for him to keep it to himself? So you would've come to me either way. And anyway, if you hadn't, you wouldn't know where to go next," she said.

Truly, everything had happened in its own way, just as she said. And from where Asa was sitting, they were far from unhappy with how events had transpired.

"I would have figured it out eventually," Peders protested as they began to ride again, and Hana tilted her head as she considered his point.

"Probably," she agreed eventually, "and wouldn't you have been in for a nasty surprise then?"

Kennet grunted at that. Asa looked between their two companions, but they had fallen silent once again. More of that "thing" that "happened," of course. It was beginning to get annoying how often they insisted on bringing it up with no intention to clarify anything to Asa at all. If they wanted to argue so badly, then they should have said so, and Asa would have stayed behind in Osternas.

Would they have?

Well, no, probably not. That was another thing—Osternas was fine, but it was dreadfully boring. Of all the towns and cities they'd visited in Bladland so far, only Grankoping had really interested them. And from what Asa understood, they wouldn't be making their way back that direction until this debacle was entirely taken care of. They could have gone back there without the hire-swords, of course, on their own, but enduring days of lonely travel seemed just as bad as what they were going through right now.

Besides that, now they were going to visit another new, exciting place on this trip.

Hagertrask was the name of the town. Another mouthful for Asa's uninclined tongue, as most of the city names were. But it was tit for tat. Hearing Peders try to say the word vihuela tickled them every time.

"This city is by the same lake as Grankoping, isn't it?" Asa tried to change the subject, and it worked immediately.

"It is, though it's a bit farther around," Peders replied. "There's a small strip of land if we want to take a more direct route, sort of splitting it into two lakes."

"There *are* two lakes," Hana corrected him. "It's just because of the stories that all the Bladlanders think of it as a single one."

"Stories?" Asa perked up, and looked at Peders expectantly.

"Yes, Kennet, tell us about the lake snake. It'll be fun." Hana only sounded half-sarcastic this time, looking over her shoulder briefly at her companions. "Tell us why what are obviously two lakes are really just one big lake."

This was clearly yet another sore subject, but at least this one seemed a bit more lighthearted. Asa counted it as a victory, prompting Peders to start talking with a pointed raise of their eyebrows and a wave of their hand. "Please—the snake! The lake! Tell us!"

"God, if you insist." Peders laughed as he surrendered to their requests. "It's pretty simple, honestly. Back in the time of the gods, there were some pretty interesting creatures that walked Bladland. Or, slithered, I guess."

"A giant snake?" Asa guessed.

"A giant snake," Peders confirmed. "One lived in the lake, a creation that was a collaboration between Gethin and Sten, the god of Stone."

"Sten?" Asa thought hard. They were familiar with the god of Stone by another name, but they couldn't quite remember what it was.

"Seok," Hana interjected, and Asa gave a hum of understanding.

"Ah, of course."

"Seok is what he prefers to be called, you know. It was our people he lived among, during the time of the gods," Hana added.

"That's not really relevant."

"I just think it's important to note that Seok likely never even set foot in Bladland during the time of the gods."

"Why wouldn't he have?" Peders reached up to rub at his right temple in annoyance.

"Can we continue?" Asa prompted. "I don't think it matters."

Hana was quiet for a moment, before muttering almost with embarrassment, "Sorry."

"Anyway, Sten and Gethin worked together to create this giant snake, grey as stone and with skin as strong as iron. For a long time, it coexisted with humans, only eating a couple here and there according to myth."

"How well-behaved," Asa remarked.

Peders laughed. "Honestly. If I were a giant snake, you wouldn't be able to stop me from nabbing a fisherman for a snack every now and again."

"So how does a snake split a lake, then?"

"Well, I'm getting to it. The story is, humans were growing tired of having to travel all the way around the lake, or make the journey by boat—a voyage that was made even more dangerous by the snake in question. So, one clever man devised a plan to shorten the trip. He lured the snake out of the water with an offering of cattle, and when the snake tried to attack, its teeth sank deep into the soft earth and it got stuck. It writhed for a while, destroying some towns and creating great cliffs on the northern side of the lake, but eventually it stretched out long and lay still, dead."

"And they used its body as a bridge?"

"Precisely. And we still do, to this day."

"And that's why they don't even bother to name the second lake," Hana said. "It's all just Lake Ormsten."

"They named the lake after the serpent?" Asa noticed the distinction and had to laugh a little. "Isn't that a bit cruel?"

"I'd never really thought of that, but yes, it does seem cruel, doesn't it?" Peders acknowledged. "But one could think of it as paying tribute."

"If I die in a terrible way like that, I hope the person who kills me names the place I died Asa-death or something like that," Asa said. "Are there songs about the lake?"

"A few. Your typical epics, none of them catchy enough for me to remember how they go," Peders said. "Hoping to corner the market on lake snake ballads?"

"No, too much work. But maybe I could improve on one of the existing ones."

The air was suitably lightened by the story, despite Hana's continued protests about how unnecessary the entire thing was. Inwardly, Asa agreed that it was likely just two separate lakes, but they found the story entertaining. Not to mention, they were sure Peders knew the truth, too. But stories and myth had a way of pervading, and it didn't make the man stupid to refer to the lake as one instead of two. It just meant that he had grown up calling it one lake, and that everyone he knew called it one lake. Why would he change that, just based on Hana's complaining?

Not to mention, it was a fun story. They were looking forward to seeing this "snake" themself, on the way to Hagertrask. They'd never seen a giant snake before.

⁓

Ornhult was the same as it had been before, though quieter. Unsurprising since they were coming in at a far earlier time than Asa had arrived the last time they'd passed through. They remembered it fondly—walking into the tavern, seeing the familiar face of Kennet Peders, and then recognizing the frustration on that face as he talked intensely with a wide-faced man.

A lovely evening.

They went to the same inn as before, the Wilting Dove, and Peders explained the location's significance as they walked.

"I met Asa here, and the herbalist that we mentioned. He seems to have been a regular here, so we can chat with him again. Maybe get more information."

"You mentioned he was terrified of her," Hana muttered to herself. "Perhaps I can make him more terrified of me, and he'll crack."

"Awful," Peders remarked on her attitude in Asa's direction.

The bard just laughed. "You didn't think it was so awful when I laid hands on him."

"I didn't know you were going to do that!" Peders said defensively.

"But you told me it helped, and you asked me along on the basis of that incident, so clearly you appreciated it," Asa pointed out.

"Damn you, let me have the moral high ground for a moment, won't you?"

The teasing tone only lasted until he had opened the door to the inn. Immediately, the look on the bartender's face struck Asa as odd. There was a flash of recognition, then the previously kind face took on an expression of horror and anger.

"You," he said. The empty inn became eerily silent as Peders paused just beyond the threshold.

Peders looked just as confused as Asa felt. "Me?" he repeated, and the bartender pointed to the door with emphasis.

"Get out."

"Wh—? What? Why?" Peders glanced at Hana and Asa, who shook their heads in equal bafflement. "Has something happened?"

"You wouldn't even know." The bartender seemed unsurprised by this, though his annoyance only grew. "Of course you wouldn't. Your type never do. You blaze through small towns, places where folks have honest lives; you bring your big business with you—and then you have no consideration for what happens afterward."

"What are you talking about?" Peders said, but there was the beginning of realization creeping into his voice. Asa looked from Peders to the bartender, hoping that this realization would be made clear to them soon, as well.

As soon as it was, they regretted ever wondering.

"Your business. We don't want any of it. It got Torger killed."

Peders' eyes widened, and even Hana's composure slipped for a moment as she glanced toward Asa in shock. "Killed?" she asked. "By whom?"

"We don't know. They found his body by the edge of the woods—strangled, and his mouth stuffed with some of his own inventory."

Hana looked up sharply at the bartender. "What exactly was it? An herb?"

"Why should I tell you?"

"We're after what I assume to be the same person who killed him," Hana said, and despite the man's warnings, she stepped farther into the room. "So tell me, or let his death be in vain."

"His death will always be in vain. If it weren't for this nosey bastard, he wouldn't have died at all. He was nervous from the moment you left, whispering about how she was coming for him. He didn't have a happy moment from your departure to his untimely death."

Asa flinched at that. Could that have been their fault? No . . . no. Their influence never lingered that long. The anxiety they gave him would have worn off within an hour of their visit, if that. But the idea left a bad taste in their mouth, and they found themself looking at the situation with new eyes.

Hana was still advancing on the bar, like a big cat stalking her prey.

"I'll make this easy for you," she said slowly. "I'll ask you a question, you say yes or no. If you stay silent, then I'll have to get dirty, and neither of us want that, do we?"

"What are you going to do? Kill me?" The bartender seemed unimpressed. "Threats like that are unbecoming of someone who claims to be on the path of avenging an innocent life."

"Not so innocent. He's complicit in the near-murder of a young child," Hana replied. "And I wouldn't kill you. I wouldn't even maim you. My target is more . . . collateral."

She pulled a knife from her hip, and casually threw it with deadly accuracy, shattering a bottle of mead that had been sitting behind him on a counter. The liquid spilled over the edge of the countertop and onto the wooden floor—sprigs of rosemary and lavender floated on it like tiny boats over a waterfall. A sputter of indignation broke from the lips of the bartender, and while he seemed to be rethinking his position, his attitude did not break.

"That was the last of my lavender!" he said. "You people are animals."

Hana pulled another knife from her belt.

"What are your questions?" He said this more meekly, his eyes locked onto the knife.

"In the dead man's mouth, was it a mushroom?"

The bartender nodded, then remembered what she had said would come with silence. "Yes," he answered firmly.

"Was it a mushroom of warm orange, with yellow gills under the cap?"

"I didn't see it myself."

"Surely you heard accounts?"

"Yes."

"And was it as I said?"

". . . yes."

That was apparently all Hana had needed to hear. She sheathed her knife again and gestured behind the bar. "Hand me my other knife, please."

"After what you just did?"

"The knife," she repeated.

He finally relented, retrieving the knife that had destroyed his mead and handing it to her. With a nod of thanks, Hana spun on her heel and walked past Peders and Asa through the door without a word. The latter exchanged a worried glance, but followed. The bartender was left behind in his empty bar speechless and with one less bottle of mead. Strangely, Asa almost felt worse about the mead than the death of Torger. Almost. If he had known he was poisoning a child, they likely wouldn't have felt bad for him at all, but as they recalled he'd not had any idea at the time.

The danger of the situation was beginning to dawn on them as they met Hana at the edge of the road. She was pouring some water out of her waterskin to clean her knife of mead. As she wiped the blade off on her tunic and sheathed it, she looked at Asa. Noting the look on their face, her own expression softened.

"Did I frighten you?" she asked.

"No," Asa replied, "I just haven't ever known someone who got killed before."

"You knew this Torger fellow?"

"Not quite. I only saw him the night Sir Peders interrogated him, and I touched him for that brief second. But still —I saw him, I touched him, he was real and I knew him. And now he's dead. Because of us."

Peders cleared his throat. "Not because of us," he clarified. "And certainly not because of you, Asa."

"Are you certain?" Asa turned on Peders, trying to make sense of what he was saying. "You said so yourself, if I hadn't touched him, he wouldn't have told you about her. She might not have killed him."

"Or she always would have," Peders replied. His tone was soothing, and he held out a hand to them. "If she was following old Hawk protocol, she was likely tying up loose ends."

Asa looked to Hana for confirmation, and she shrugged. "That's what we were taught," she said, "though some of us have our own methods. Bribery, blackmail. Death isn't always the answer, but Maryska hasn't exactly been open to other solutions as of late."

"Assuming this is Maryska," Peders added, "which we aren't sure of. It could be someone even more malicious."

Hana's expression told Asa that Peders was in denial. "This town is between her and the child, is it not? A small town, one fitting her needs."

". . . yes." Peders frowned. "But Maryska was never fond of asking for outside help."

"She also hasn't worked alone in years. She was used to

working with me—she would know the effects we needed, the poison that would provide it. I would know where to find that poison. Without me, she only had half the equation. The herbalist would have provided the other half."

Confronted with this information, Peders fell silent. His frown had only deepened as Hana spoke. "Hmm." He grunted. Whether she had gotten through to him or not, it seemed he was still choosing to live in the possibility that she was wrong. Hana huffed and turned back to Asa, returning to the subject of their concerns.

"Likely she came through, checked in with him and realized he'd been talking, and then killed him. That's what the mushrooms were for—they're the same kind that they used to poison Marna, so it was her way of telling us that she knows he talked."

"Then we *did* play a part."

Hana looked from Peders to Asa, and then sighed. "I won't lie to you, Asa. Peders is trying to soften the blow, but yes. It's possible that if he hadn't spoken to you both, she wouldn't have killed him."

That was crushing. Asa felt something like a stomachache mixed with a heartache, and they blinked to try and clear it. They heard Peders sigh, and he laid a hand on their shoulder. They almost shook him off—but what good would that do?

"It's never our fault when someone decides to kill someone else," he said slowly, as though he was trying to convince himself as much as them. "We didn't kill him. She didn't *need* to kill him because of us. It's just another reason we need to find her and stop her before she can go any further."

What he was saying was true, and they knew it was true. It didn't help, though. Maybe it would help later when they could think straight, and they could logically address all of this. *If* they could get to that point.

But that wasn't what they needed to tell Peders right now.

He had enough on his mind, enough to feel guilty about, or so it seemed. They would be able to handle this on their own with some time, best to make out like they had already done that.

"I suppose you're right," they said as they attempted to compose themself. "Sorry," they added, though they didn't know what they were sorry for.

"Don't be," Hana interjected, "not for this. You were trying to save a child. Whether or not that led to Torger's death, Kennet's right—as much as I hate to admit it. The only one responsible for killing is the killer. Though in this case"—she gave a forlorn look toward the inn—"the killer is also responsible for us having to spend a night on the road."

God, and now they had to camp, too.

Things were getting worse and worse.

CHAPTER 2

A PHILOSOPHY REINFORCED, THE DEDICATION TO IT CHALLENGED

The lake sparkled in the early morning light, a sight that Kennet couldn't quite appreciate with the state he was in. He hadn't been able to calm his nerves since leaving Ornhult, and over the day and night that had passed since then, he was beginning to accept that those nerves were there to stay. This was awful for two reasons—the first was obvious: he needed to be calm or his nerves would be very much justified when they made a bad situation worse later on. And the second reason was that he was completely missing out on enjoying Asa's reaction to the snake they had been so excited to see.

"These stones . . ." They had noticed the most interesting part first, pulling Emilio's reins and bringing the mule to a halt at the pass's entrance, where the two halves of the lake began to diverge and the "snake" revealed itself. "I've never seen anything like this."

The stones in question were definitely interesting. Kennet supposed the novelty had worn off on him at some point, since he'd known about them since childhood. But it was true, he'd never seen anything like them anywhere else. They were interlocking, shaped like hexagons of varying heights, stretching like stair steps down into the water. The center of the pass, which could fit four horses abreast, was covered with soft dirt and then paved over with cobblestones much more friendly to a horse's hooves.

"They're like scales." Asa picked up on the significance of their odd shape almost immediately.

Their enthusiasm seemed to have rubbed off on Hana, whose disdain for the myth was quickly melting away—or at least, it was beginning to fade just a bit. "I suppose it's unusual," she admitted, "and to imagine that they're the scales of a giant snake . . . it makes some sense."

Kennet was only half-listening, and he could tell that Starling had sensed what he had been trying so hard to contain. She shifted from foot to foot, absorbing his nervousness and letting it out in her own horsey fashion. He tried to soothe her, rubbing her neck gently, but it didn't seem to do much good. He was sure that the impending trip through the pass wasn't helping—she had never much liked water.

Hana noticed this, and her appreciation of the scenery halted abruptly. "We should keep moving," she said, looking at Asa. "Perhaps on the way back you can sit and let the snake inspire you."

"Ah, but I'm sure that spending too much time dwelling on one landmark will keep me from finding another equally interesting one." Asa shifted the vihuela on their back in preparation for their return to riding. "The longer we dally, the less of this world I get to see before I die."

Kennet couldn't decide whether he found that line of thinking comforting, or if it just added to his ever-present anxiety.

"Off we go, then," Hana said, and took the lead.

Starling took each step carefully, clearly not enjoying this trip any more than Kennet enjoyed the thought of what was waiting for them at the end of it. Her ears swiveled around erratically, caught between the noise of the water and the other hooves on the cobblestones. Kennet spoke softly to her. "That's all right, girl."

"Emilio doesn't like it either," Asa piped up from behind them. "He's going very slowly."

"We'll wait for you on the other side," Hana called back. "He's a workmule, I assume he's just like you—never seen anything like this before."

"I'll take this time to get inspired like you suggested, then."

When Kennet looked over his shoulder at the path behind them, he was surprised to see how far back the bard had been left trailing. At the pace they were going, it was possible they would be left far behind the others. Kennet pulled back on Starling's reins to slow her, and watched as Hana looked back at them and went through the same line of thought. However, when she slowed her horse, she slowed it to the point where she dropped back, coming to rest side by side with Kennet, riding in step alongside him.

This wasn't good. It meant she wanted to talk.

She opened, as she often did, by stating the obvious. "You're nervous."

"And you aren't?"

She paused. Without a change of expression, she replied, "You have significantly more to be nervous about."

That was undoubtedly true. But it didn't change the fact that she was hardly going into this unscathed, and though her reasons to be nervous were different, and significantly less than his . . . they were still there. "Have you seen her?" he asked, hesitantly. "Since everything happened?"

"No. Well, wait, that's not true. I saw her directly after it happened—you said you hoped she would come to me after what you did, and that's precisely what happened. But she wasn't in any state to have constructive conversation. She stayed with me for only three days, and every one of those days was torture. On the third . . . I lost her. She left in the middle of the night, and I didn't notice until the next morning. I tracked her here." She paused. "That's why I went to Grankoping—to Stefan. Because it was close enough to Hagertrask that I could . . ."

She trailed off, and Kennet saw that she was chewing on her bottom lip. There were no tears in her eyes, but it was clear that it wasn't for a lack of emotion. "So you could check on her?" He gave a gentle prompt.

"Yes," she said. "I know it's wrong. If she wanted to leave everything behind and start over—I understand that. I do. It's part of why I'm so angry at you, you know, even as I'm starting to understand your side of things. You really thought that by letting her live, you were sparing me some pain, and— Well, and I believed the same thing! I believed that I was lucky she had survived, because it meant that even though our lives had fallen apart, we still had each other."

Strangely, this admission did soothe Kennet somewhat. Though there was no world in which things would have gone exactly as he had planned, at least he wasn't the only one who had been delusional enough to believe it.

"She doesn't know that you know where she is?" he asked.

"I don't know," Hana admitted. "I haven't exactly been subtle. Sometimes I think she knows very well—I can't help myself, you know. Sometimes I go and I watch her as she walks around town, just to get a glimpse of her. I never go near her house; I don't want to invade her privacy like that. But I miss her, Kennet."

The silence that sat between them after that was as painful as the nervousness had been a moment ago. Finally, he ventured, "You know, you really don't have to come. This isn't your problem."

"If it is her, then it's my problem," Hana replied. "And I'll tell you why—I should have gone to her. If I'd known she was capable of this, that she had sunk so low as to poison a young girl and kill the only loose ends so callously, I would have gone to her. I should have chased her down, told her I still loved her, and that what happened wasn't her fault." She was talking more than she usually did, and the words seemed to be tumbling out of their own accord. She stopped to catch her breath and arrange her thoughts. "It's like what you told Asa in Ornhult. What happened to her was nobody's fault other than yours."

There was the guilt again. He turned away, feeling like he'd rather die than continue to face her. "I know."

"I know you know. But she might not. And now I can't save her—I can't absolve her of any blame, if this was all her doing. All I've done is contribute to what she's become, by not being there for her."

He wanted to call out that she was being hypocritical yet again. How was it nobody's fault but his that he destroyed their family, but it was Hana's fault somehow that Maryska had potentially gone out of her way to poison a child? There were plenty of people out there who had lost loved ones, and most of those people didn't decide to poison children to cope. But Hana was already closing off again.

"Besides that," she said, her voice regaining its stony tone, "if I let you go alone it's very possible you'll make a mess of it. So if you and I are going to take responsibility—as I said, it's both of ours—then I want to make sure it's done right."

Kennet nodded, accepting her judgment this time with grace. It was surprising how much less it stung when she was being honest with him. There was a lot more he wanted to say in response but he didn't want to push his luck with her.

She rode next to him in silence for a bit longer, before deciding she had said her piece. Without so much as a second glance in his direction, she took the lead again, leaving him to sit with what she had said.

He did feel glad that she had come with them, especially knowing how things had left off. If Maryska had been responsible, then Kennet approaching her alone would have led to disaster, inevitably. As it was . . .

Well, disaster was still imminent. He hoped that Hana had some kind of real plan, because he certainly didn't. Every time he played the scenario out in his head it ended in blood —even if Maryska wasn't the one who had poisoned Marna. Whose blood? His, usually.

There was more to it, as well. What if she wasn't guilty? Then all this pain, these memories that were resurfacing—it would be for nothing. There would be no purpose to what he was putting Hana through, or what the two of them were about to put Maryska through. She had already been through so much by his hand, how could he justify doing more just on a hunch?

And yet, that was what was so worrying. Because Hana wouldn't do what she was doing if it were just a hunch.

The way she had asked questions in Ornhult had been so self-assured. The way she had approached him at Hagen's keep had been so upfront. It seemed like she had already made up her mind and now there was no other possibility, not one. She hadn't just assumed the worst, she was sure of it.

And when she said it, he knew he should agree with her. Her logic made sense, when she said it aloud. If it were Maryska, Ornhult would have been the last stop on the way from Hagertrask to Osternas. It would have been her last chance to get the herbs she needed, so finding Torger would go from being a happy coincidence to just . . . making sense. Of course she would have asked a local. It would have saved time. She wasn't above working with whoever was convenient, never had been—but in the past, she'd been above killing them after the job was done.

The sick feeling was back.

And if Hana was right, which she was so sure that she was, then the words that she had spoken that night echoed in his head: that he had turned Maryska into a monster. And god, what kind of monster had he created? Someone who would poison a child? The Maryska he knew never would have done that.

If he had created that, he would have to look upon it . . . to see what she had become, what he had made her, the kind of person who would do things that no amount of money could have ever tempted him to do.

His stomach churned, and he couldn't hold it together any longer. He stopped Starling abruptly, barely managing to call out a "whoa" as his voice faltered and he nearly stumbled as he tried to dismount. Kennet rushed to the side of the road as the bard looked on first inquisitively and then with concern.

They hadn't eaten much between Ornhult and the pass, but that didn't stop his stomach from expelling every bite he had taken since then as he crouched at the edge of the lake. He sat there for a moment, heaving breaths as he recovered from the action—he didn't feel better, either, wiping a bit of lingering vomit from his lower lip and groaning in annoyance. Was he going to be like this for the rest of the trip? How hard could it be to get a hold of himself? Hadn't he used to do stuff *far* more dangerous than this all the time?

He felt weak, and there was nothing he wanted more than to stop feeling that way. He could ask Asa for help but . . . no, that seemed cheap. The feelings were there for a reason. He deserved them. And furthermore, to ask Asa for their help in front of Hana would negate any goodwill their conversation had earned him. She would go back to thinking of him as a coward who had run for so long, and now that he couldn't run anymore, couldn't even face the consequences of his actions with grace.

Graceless was certainly the word for how he felt right now.

He stood up, shaking a bit from the effort of throwing up. Asa hadn't moved from their spot in the road, though Hana had finally noticed their pause and stopped herself. As Kennet walked toward Starling, she pawed restlessly at the ground.

"Are you all right, Sir Peders?" Asa asked. They tugged at one of their gloves, holding the reins in one hand, and tilted their head. It took the little effort he could spare not to melt at their concern.

"Better now!" he lied, trying to sound bright as he remounted his horse. "Must have eaten something rotten."

Hana didn't comment, but he thought he spied some amount of similar concern in her eyes for once. If it weren't for their talk, he might have interpreted the expression as judgment—and there still could be judgment, of course. She had plenty to judge him for. It was ridiculous that a man who was capable of causing so much harm would be in a state like this. Surely if he had the balls to do what he had done, he had the balls to face the consequences.

Ah, but he was a coward. In fact, he had been the whole time.

He'd just been better at hiding it back then.

∽

THEY LEFT their horses in the town itself, in a stable that was closer to the cliffside than Kennet would have liked. But Hana insisted, and the stablemaster knew her by name, so he supposed that it had to be safe. Or at least, it was as safe as any spot in Hagertrask. As they had ridden up to the city, Kennet had instantly become equal parts exhilarated and terrified by the structure of the buildings, with so many perched as close to the edge of the cliffs as they could get away with. Some of them even had balconies that jutted over the edge, and Kennet could imagine standing on one, peering over the edge and watching the waves of the lake crash into the cliff walls below. Somehow, the thrill of the imaginary act of danger helped to distract from the much more real threat at hand.

From the top of the cliff, though, the city seemed far more normal than it had on their approach. Narrow roads wound through several-storied buildings, and people went about their lives. Kennet began to make his way into the city itself, but was stopped by Hana's hand on his shoulder.

"No," she said, and gestured to a small dirt path leading away from the stable, away from the city. "This way."

So they began to walk in the opposite direction that Kennet had expected, through rolling grassy hills that bordered the cliffs. The grass was dry and golden, and it moved like waves as they exited the protective barrier of the city's buildings and the wind picked up greatly. There were a few houses that they passed as they walked, and as they neared each, Kennet expected Hana to stop and declare that they had reached their destination. He felt his chest tighten with anticipation as they passed each one, only to be strung along as they walked even farther, until the houses were so far apart that he couldn't see the next one past the hills.

"Couldn't we have brought the horses?" he asked. It was a non-issue but it was all he could think about. They were prolonging the inevitable and with each passing moment he felt that his ability to handle this in a rational and clear-headed manner was slipping.

"No, she has no place to keep them," Hana replied. "Besides that, I don't want her to see us coming."

Ah, so she did have a plan.

"So we're sneaking up on her?" Asa chimed in, apparently finally done holding their tongue.

"Not quite. Though I will want to go up alone at first. I think it would be best, I mean. If she didn't see Kennet."

Not only did she have a plan, but the plan was to spare Kennet the exact moment he had been afraid of—him, standing on her doorstep, with no way to warn her or prepare her for what she was about to see. Guilty or not, she didn't deserve that. He was glad Hana planned to ease her into it.

"This is a delicate situation," Hana continued. "So I'll take it from here."

Kennet nodded, then gestured for Asa to fall back with him. They did so readily, giving Hana a good few feet to walk ahead of them, and as they did Asa ventured to ask a question that had clearly been weighing on them for some time. "So . . . what should I expect, exactly?"

Right, they were likely as anxious as he was, or at least very confused. He had kept them in the dark—not without reason, of course, but it would still do them no good to be completely unprepared. He didn't want to tell them anything, of course. But there was no avoiding it anymore, not at this point. So he prepared to be honest.

"I don't know," he said. "This person . . . I want you to hang back a bit, even farther out of view than I am. I don't know how she'll react to seeing us." He paused and corrected himself. "To seeing me."

"I have no idea what your past with this woman is, but I take it that she might get violent?"

"Well, I . . ." Here he went, he had to say it sooner or later. "Last time she saw me, she thought I was trying to kill her."

Asa's eyes widened. "Oh."

Kennet pursed his lips, unsure of what to say further.

"But you weren't trying to kill her, were you?"

Strictly speaking, he hadn't been. It wasn't like what he *had* been doing had been much better, but that was more honesty than he was prepared to share at the moment. So he didn't lie, but he didn't expand on anything either. "No," he said slowly.

"That's good." Asa seemed satisfied by the answer. "Beyond the killing thing, what's she like? If this doesn't go the absolute worst way it could, what should I expect? I only ask because it might've been nice to get a warning about Hana."

Kennet wished that he could react to their attempt to lighten the mood the way that they wanted him to, but in the absence of the ability to laugh, he answered with honesty. "She's . . . sharp. Very sharp. Incisive. She and Hana were a nightmare together, ruthless and efficient. That being said, she's easier to talk to than Hana—she has a mean streak, but it's always meant in love."

He remembered sitting around the fire, the same way he had with Asa, and the way that the atmosphere had rippled back then. The jokes they had told, the way Hana's laugh had sounded—he could hardly even imagine her laughing now.

Asa leaned forward to get a better look at his face from where they were standing next to him. Slowly, they examined him, until finally they said, "It sounds like you knew her well."

"I did."

"I hope there's a chance, at least, that you'll be able to explain yourself."

There was no chance of that. In fact, anything he had to say would likely make things worse.

He didn't want to tell them that, though. He truly, really didn't. Not now, not ever if he could get away with it. If he could manage not to tell them, if they could part ways never knowing the truth about him, that would be best.

And yet . . .

He also didn't want to part ways with them at all.

Well, he'd cross that bridge when he got to it. For now, the half-truth would have to do.

Hana had stopped walking. The path that they were on was about to round the edge of another hill, and Kennet knew that they had gotten as far as they were going to get with denial. He looked to Hana and saw she showed none of the discomfort she had to be feeling. Just determination.

"I'll go ahead from here," she said. "Keep yourself hidden

from view from the threshold, but do keep an eye out. If anything goes wrong, I might need backup."

It was a familiar speech, but he was used to receiving it with Maryska by his side, not opposing each other. Kennet clenched his teeth, and nodded. "Of course."

"And Asa, please run if you feel any danger. Don't try to save us."

The impact of that statement was not lost on Asa, and their eyes widened. For once, they seemed lost for words, simply nodding vigorously in response.

Satisfied with that, Hana turned sharply and made her way around the corner.

Kennet followed her only a short way, until he saw the house in the distance. It wasn't as far as he would have liked, nestled at the base of another hill. It was small, made of stone and plaster with a thatched roof. Smoke drifted lazily from the chimney, leaving no doubt in his mind that Maryska was home. Any chance that they wouldn't have to deal with this immediately evaporated.

Hana was stoic and graceful as she walked down the thin dirt path, and Kennet watched her let her hands trail through the long grass on either side of her. Even from the distance they stood, he could see her chest inflate with a deep breath, which she held for a moment before she let it out. She reached the threshold of Maryska's house, and stopped. She stood there, resolute, and suddenly Kennet wondered if this was a trap. Had she lied to him, lured him here so that she and Maryska could kill him?

God, the way his mind wandered in fear. Of course that wasn't the case. Insane to consider, even.

But even so, the wild possibility lingered in his mind.

Then it vanished in a second.

Hana knocked on the door while he was agonizing over all this, and in his spiral he almost didn't see her at first. He almost missed the exact moment he had been worrying about for the entire journey, watching her step out into the sunlight. But the moment she came into view, he felt reality crash down on him again.

There she was. The same as he had left her. The same white-blonde hair, the same pale skin that was barely differentiated from it. She wore simple, practical clothing that looked too loose—just as with Hana, this was the most striking thing to him. It was the lack of the uniform that they had all worn, the uniform that designated them as dangerous. Nothing about her seemed dangerous now. She stood stunned, still, in her doorway. It looked like Hana was talking. Then Maryska replied. He could hear their voices, but not what they were saying. They weren't far from him, a stone's throw away really, but the wind was too strong. He wished he knew what they were talking about.

He got his wish immediately, in the worst way possible. The first word he recognized came from Maryska—it was his name.

Both women turned toward Kennet. Instinctively, he pushed Asa farther behind him. He prepared to tell them to run, fearing the worst—and the worst seemed to be happening, as Maryska pushed by Hana, and began to run toward them. He couldn't find the words to react. In any other situation, he would have run, or shouted, or drew his sword. But his palm only twitched in the direction of his weapon, frozen in fear for the first time in his life.

Maybe it wasn't fear. Maybe it was the belief that whatever happened next, he deserved it.

Whatever happened next—but it was the only thing he truly believed he didn't deserve.

Rather than burying a knife in his chest, Maryska threw her arms around him. He heard his name from her again, in a tone that hadn't even crossed his mind to expect.

Joy.

"Kennet!" she cried as she embraced him, and he stood, still unmoving.

"Maryska," he breathed. His own voice sounded shocking to him—like it was coming from miles away. He wondered if he would faint.

"I never thought I'd see you again." She held him close, and tight, and spoke into his ear. "Gods, I really thought I'd never see you again."

There was no response he could possibly come up with for that. So he didn't, gingerly putting a hand on her back as she held him, and trying to process it all. He tried to figure out how he felt—how she felt. Was she happy to see him? Really, truly? Why?

"And you brought a friend!" She had noticed Asa. "And Hana." She pulled back finally, scanning his face with clear blue eyes. "Something's wrong, isn't it?"

On top of everything—the sight of her, her reaction, the fact that her words were contradicting their very purpose in visiting her—it finally came together in a giant symphony. Her eyes were too familiar. Her hair, up close, shining in the sunlight. Gods, even the way she smelled.

She was just like him. Like Isak.

He felt like some cosmic trick was being played on him. With all his strength, he willed himself to become numb.

There was no peace in this. Nothing like what he could have asked from Asa. Just the desperate numbness of a man who needed to function long enough to get answers. "Something is very wrong," he replied, slowly, finally addressing what Maryska had been saying.

"It must be"—she nodded seriously—"for you to come to me. I can't imagine what it took you to get to that point—oh, but honestly." She seemed to suddenly realize where they were, standing in the middle of a field on the hillside. "Let's go inside."

∼

The little hillside cottage was intensely cozy inside, with a warm fire crackling cheerfully in the hearth and a few chairs set up in front of it. Hana sat in one of these chairs, her hands folded in her lap. Ever composed, right now there was maybe a hint of bewilderment in her posture and expression, but overall she seemed shockingly calm. Kennet hoped he looked half so calm himself as he stood in front of the fire stiffly, while Maryska sat adjacent to Hana, and both of them waited for him to explain why they were all there.

"I'm sorry," Kennet said, when he could bear the silence no longer. His gaze flicked to Asa, who sat farther back into the room that functioned both as a sitting area and a kitchen. They widened their eyes at him, and grimaced exaggeratedly. No help at all, but why would they know how to handle this any better than he did? Somehow, that still made him feel better. "I can't go on without addressing how uncomfortable this is," he admitted.

Maryska let out a long sigh full of emotion. "Oh, thank god," she said. "I agree, but you seemed so serious when you got here, I thought maybe someone else had died."

Kennet shook his head. "No, nothing like that," he said.

"Good! Good. You had me worried! Then please, say what you want to say."

"You're a good deal more . . . chipper than I thought you'd be." Kennet struggled to find the word for it, and she blinked at him and pursed her lips in thought.

"I am," she agreed, "probably. I don't know how chipper you thought I'd be. But given how we parted ways last, probably not at all."

"No, not at all."

"That's understandable on both our parts, I think. You did kill my brother, after all."

Kennet saw Asa stiffen out of the corner of his eye, and

though he hated seeing it, he forced himself to ignore them. "I did do that." So there it was, out in the open. No ignoring it, no dancing around it any longer.

"I can't imagine that was easy for you," Maryska said slowly, and Kennet furrowed his brow. When she noticed his expression she scrambled to finish her thought. "Oh, of course it wasn't easy for me! Of course not. And it wasn't easy for me to come to terms with the fact that I should've died then, too, but that's me. You, though. What must it have taken to make that decision, to spend that whole journey with us knowing you were leading us into a trap? What must that have done to you?"

What had it done to him? A lot, but that was besides the point. What had it done to *her*? This wasn't at all what something like that *should* do to a person. She shouldn't be able to forgive him—but he was getting ahead of himself, she hadn't forgiven him at all. She'd only asked him a question.

"It ruined me," Kennet replied. His answer startled him. He wanted to demand why she was acting this way. Why she wasn't angry with him. But this was the first time anyone had bothered to ask him that question, so he felt compelled to answer it.

"Of course it did." She seemed genuinely sympathetic. Her face fell, and he saw sorrow in her eyes.

"But let me—please, I need to tell you this—but you were never meant to die. They were only there to kill one of you. I only needed you to be knocked out so you wouldn't try to get involved."

At this admission, there was a flash of something more familiar over Maryska's face, slicing through the sympathy and sorrow. Kennet couldn't put his finger on what exactly the emotion was. It didn't show itself in her next words. "Well!" she said, surprised, and looked away into the fire. She stayed that way for a moment, and Kennet looked toward Hana for help. There was no help to be found.

"Well?" he ventured to ask, hesitantly.

"Well!" she repeated. Then she turned to face him again. "Well. Honestly, that *is* a relief."

Thank god. "I wish I could have told you sooner."

"You really couldn't have, though," Maryska admitted. "If you had even come a year ago, you probably wouldn't have made it two paces from me, much less spoken a word in my direction."

That sounded more correct. "So what's changed?" Kennet finally asked the question. Once it was out in the open, he felt the knot in his stomach tighten again. "What's different now than a year ago?"

There was a long silence again at that. Maryska focused on the fire once more, and her face scrunched up, her nose wrinkling. It was an expression he was familiar with from both her and her brother—he had always called it their "thinking face." It had always been endearing to him, especially when Isak would do it. He'd always had something stupid to say after, stupid yet somehow profound in its simplicity.

Kennet quickly looked down at the floor. Anywhere but her face. He examined the patterned rug that lay under his feet and continued to scrutinize it until she answered him.

"It's not that anything's changed since then, not that profoundly," she said pensively. "It's more that things have been changing ever since we parted ways. It's been a process. I think I've just . . . I probably could have stood to get even further in the process before you got here, but this might be good." She considered the statement, then nodded. "Yes, this will be good."

"A process?" Kennet prompted.

"Oh, yes. You see, I had a revelation not too long ago, Ken." She adjusted her seated position, drawing herself up straighter and looking him in the eye with a tilted head. "I feel like I'm almost being a complete hypocrite."

Kennet threw a look at Hana. If the situation had been appropriate, his expression would have said "I told you so," but under current circumstances it only showed shock. Maryska didn't seem to notice this, and so continued.

"I mean, I've done exactly what you did. The exact same thing—you remember, right? I think you were there for that one. The Weissler job."

He had been there for that one. It hadn't been pretty, but the circumstances had been fairly similar to his and Maryska's situation. "I remember that," he said. He glanced at Asa again. They were on the edge of the wooden chair they'd taken up station on, listening intently. He wished he hadn't brought them.

"That was nothing to me. Honestly, genuinely. I barely thought about it after we did it—not until everything happened between you and me. Then suddenly I realized . . . that what I was feeling—everyone we had ever worked with, everyone who knew someone we killed, they felt the same thing I was feeling." Maryska leaned back in her chair. "It really put everything into perspective."

"Did it? But didn't it make a difference that—"

"That it was you?" she interrupted him, and considered his point. "Well, I thought that too, but then the more I thought about it—I'm hardly as innocent as the people we got hired to kill. So of course it's going to be a little more complicated. Did it hurt more? I have to assume so. But most people haven't put themselves in the position where they personally know men who would be able to kill them and their family like that. I kept the company of wolves—I was a wolf myself."

Kennet risked a peek at Hana. This revealed more than he had feared it would. Rather than watching him as she had been this entire time, Hana had chosen to stare into the fire too now, deep in thought. "So you think, then, that . . . ?" He turned his attention back to Maryska.

"Kennet. Have I really got the right to be mad?" She smiled at him. "Don't I deserve a little sadness in my life? Isn't it unfortunate that you and I managed to run around, living life, loving and smiling and being free when we took that freedom away from so many others? We ruined too many lives to stay angry when our own were finally ruined."

He agreed, didn't he? Hadn't he raised this exact point? Why did the arguments, which should have been even more compelling coming from her than from him, ring so hollow in his ears?

She was still smiling, though. "Don't you remember how horrible we both were? Really, I mean, we really do deserve it. I didn't even get it that bad—you left me completely intact, no petty slicing up my face to leave me a reminder of the events. That's an exception for us, don't you think? Sometimes death was the least of their worries when they were dealing with us."

Now, she wasn't going to go into all that, was she? Not in front of—

"Remember that time we carved a man's nose off his face? He wasn't even unconscious—well, he wasn't when we started. To be fair to him, though, I probably would have passed out the moment I saw the knife coming at my face."

Kennet noticed Asa turn to him sharply, but he couldn't bring himself to look at them directly. "Yes, I remember that."

"You know he's still alive, right? We just left him like that, walking around without a nose. I'm sure he'd rather be alive than dead, but—no, actually, I'm not sure of that."

She was purposefully using verbiage that obscured which of them had actually done the deed. She kept saying "we." He wondered if she was doing it intentionally, because of Asa—that even though he had been deliberate in his effort not to look back at them, trying to draw attention away from them, she was leading them to believe that he had done all of these things. If he believed she was thinking how she used to, like the old Maryska, then he would think she knew that was the last thing he wanted.

But . . . he had to stop. He had to stop thinking the worst. Nothing else in this entire conversation would suggest that motivation. She was probably saying "we" just because she truly didn't remember which of them had done it. At this point, he was beginning to doubt that he remembered events correctly either.

Maryska was still smiling. She had been for a while now, and it almost seemed like she was remembering their old exploits with the same fondness she would recall her childhood. He had to stop himself from shuddering in disgust. It had become increasingly often these days that he would have moments of overwhelming regret for every step of the path his life had taken—and now was one of those times.

It was Hana who eventually broke the uncomfortable silence. "We didn't come here to discuss the past," she said tersely.

Kennet couldn't help but wonder how Hana was feeling at the moment. He couldn't imagine it was good. Maryska hadn't so much as thrown her a second look since they arrived at the cottage. It had been him that Maryska had thrown herself into a hug with, it had been him she had directed all her conversation to. She wasn't ignoring Hana completely—she acknowledged Hana when words were spoken—but still, it was hardly the reunion he would have expected. It made him uneasy.

"Oh, right. You came for a reason, of course. I doubt that you would make your way here without some kind of terrible thing to motivate it. It can't have been easy for you to make that decision," Maryska stressed again, looking at Kennet as she said it.

"It wasn't, but it was . . . urgent," Kennet replied, and he took a moment to recenter himself. He still didn't allow his eyes to wander to the bard in the back of the room, instead choosing to look up at the ceiling, focusing on the planks as he tried to get his thoughts straight. "There was an attempt on someone's life, and I was hired to look into it."

"I've never known you to care about someone's life so much that you'd put yourself through this much turmoil to get to the bottom of it," Maryska said, and for the first time in the conversation, he had no doubt that there was a sliver of her past self in the comment. It was snide. She was unimpressed.

"It was a child," Kennet said, a bit defensively. He watched her expression as he said it—and saw nothing but shock.

That settled it, in his opinion. They had come all this way, stirred up all of this . . . for nothing.

Then why did he still feel so on edge?

What a silly question. Even if she hadn't poisoned a child —and he was immeasurably glad she hadn't—there was still nothing pleasant about this situation.

Even as he was thinking this, Kennet saw Maryska's expression change, screwing up into her thinking face again. "Then . . . if you came here about that . . ." She looked up at him, understanding settling into place. "You can't have possibly thought that I did it."

"You did just describe striking a man's nose from his face," Asa had the surprising audacity to pipe from the background, "with shockingly little regret, I might add."

"Oh, yes, well. That's different," Maryska replied, barely acknowledging the stranger in her house even as she addressed them directly.

Asa was looking directly at Kennet as Maryska said that, and Kennet forced himself to look back. They made a face at him, one that told him that they didn't at all see how it was different. He felt a scoff-like chuckle of disbelief leave him involuntarily at the absurdity of the back-and-forth, and he saw a similarly bemused look in their eyes as well. He didn't look forward to the questions it would inevitably come with later, but perhaps they'd been telling the truth when they said they'd already taken into account how awful his past must have been.

"It did seem a bit like your work." Kennet brought the conversation back to the point at hand. "Poison, I mean. But I can see now that we were wrong."

"I hope you can!" Maryska shook her head. "Gods—is the child all right, at least?"

"She's fine," Hana interrupted before Kennet could answer. "Kennet came to me about it, and I was able to set her straight within a day."

"That's a relief to hear. What twists and turns this visit has taken on, I swear."

"We're sorry to spring it on you like this. I promise we wouldn't have come if we didn't have to," Kennet broke in.

"I'm sure you wouldn't have."

Kennet hardly knew what else to say. There was nothing else—it all seemed settled, even things he had never thought *could* be settled. He took a step back, toward the fire, and cleared his throat. "But it seems we came for nothing, after all."

"Not for nothing," Maryska said soothingly. "This is more than I ever could have hoped for between us. I really thought I would have to live the rest of my life without having this conversation."

"Me too," Kennet replied. He hesitated, then added, "But I'm glad we had it."

Maryska's dream-like smile took up its place on her face again. He saw it once more—the same smile on a different face in his mind's eye. He forced himself to forget it as best he could.

"I'm glad we did, too."

CHAPTER 3

ASA OF THE ISLES MAKES A FRIEND

"She didn't so much as look at me!"

This had been going on since they reached Hagertrask properly, and Asa couldn't help but sympathize with Hana's frustration as they sat at a back corner table in a busy tavern. Initially, none of them had quite known what to do—to continue on, to part ways, to try and brainstorm further. In the end it had been Asa's suggestion to go back into town and take the night to make a decision. While that had stalled the inevitable, as soon as they'd all had a moment to think, things had fallen apart.

"It makes no sense." Peders was in agreement with Hana, for once in the time that Asa had known them. Two people who Asa had trusted to know all the answers now sat without any answers at all, united in a near-complete loss for words.

"I haven't seen her in nearly three years. When she left, even then she told me she loved me every day. She left me a note to tell me she didn't want to hurt me. Then silence, for years, and now—what? Nothing? She sees me and the first thing she does is look to you?" Hana's hand wrapped around the handle of her third mug of ale.

This was the most Asa had heard her speak that wasn't in Anjeonese, and the most distressed they'd seen her, hands down. It left them useless in this situation, except that they were the only one who seemed lucid enough to keep the ale flowing. As they noticed the level in their companion's cups lowering, they grabbed the arm of a passing waiter, and ordered another round.

"It was like you didn't even exist," Peders muttered. "None of it makes sense."

"I'm a fool." Hana gritted her teeth and knocked back the rest of her ale. "I want to go back—but would it even do any good? Would she ignore me if you weren't there?"

"Do you really want to know?" Asa finally broke in, gently. They couldn't stand to hear her spiral any more. "Would the answer really satisfy you, either way?"

Hana was quiet for a moment. "I think the real problem is that I already know the answer. She forgot about me the moment she left, didn't she? The only person on her mind since then was you, Kennet."

For the first time since they'd gotten to the tavern, the entire group at the table fell completely silent. They sat with the statement, and nobody moved to remark on it even as the waiter returned and set three new mugs of ale on the table. Asa thanked them—that was the only word spoken, for several minutes.

"I almost would have rather she was guilty," Peders said, then immediately looked as though he regretted saying it.

"No, you wouldn't," Hana replied, but she didn't seem shocked by the statement. "This is the best outcome for you."

"Not for both of us, though."

"It wouldn't have been better for me if she'd greeted me with an embrace but then turned out to be guilty. I should be grateful—I should be happy just to see her alive, and well, and innocent." Hana stared into her ale. "But I'm not."

Asa sat up straighter in their chair, and leaned forward. "Hana—"

She looked up at them with her eyes, keeping her head downturned. Asa paused at the fact that there were tears welling up there. They glanced at Peders for any kind of guidance—he only shook his head mournfully.

"What?" Hana demanded that they finish their thought, and Asa sighed.

"Do you want me to . . ." They gestured to their gloves, which they had laid out on the table. "You don't have to feel this way. I can help."

Hana glanced toward Peders as well, with a similar look of hesitation. Once more, he only really reacted with ambivalence, though perhaps a bit more encouragement in the way that he gestured from her to Asa. Did she think she needed his permission?

The sigh that Hana let out was long and heavy, but she nodded once before the hesitation came back. "How does it . . . feel?"

What a question. Since nobody had known about their ability to influence, nobody had asked them questions like that. They had made a rule when they left Lucien—they were going to be more careful, both in how they used their influence and who they told. And then they'd met Sir Peders, and all of that had evaporated at once. Of course, they were a good deal more conservative with their use of the influence than they had been in Lucien, all the same—the gloves were an entirely new addition to their wardrobe, an attempt to be more mindful of others.

Despite this care, they hadn't bothered to ask Sir Peders what it was like, or how it had felt. The first person they *could* ask, and they hadn't.

Better late than never.

They turned to Peders and repeated Hana's question.

"How does it feel, Sir Peders?"

Peders raised his eyebrows as the ball was thrown to him, and he sat back in his chair. Asa was already feeling relief. Even if Hana didn't accept their help, the change in topic had considerably lessened the tension. Peders seemed to feel the same way, and he took a moment to sip his ale before he answered them. "It feels . . . natural. I suppose that's partially because I've always known to expect it happening, but it's always felt as though I'm feeling things for myself. If I didn't know it was going to happen, I wonder if I would feel the same—"

Sensing an opportunity, Asa reached across the table and rested their hand on his. They willed, as they always did, a specific emotion. In their heart, they tried to feel it. That's how it had always worked, ever since the beginning. They had to feel it themself to channel it, though they never felt it as deeply as the other person would receive it. Anger had been hard—they were rarely angry. But this time, they picked something easier for them. Joy. Laughter.

Peders snorted the moment that their skin touched his, and he broke into a wide smile. Where he had been leaning back, resting an arm on the table, now he leaned forward as he was overcome by laughter. They loved the sound of it, always, since the first time they had heard it. Hearty and warm and deep. It was a relief to hear it again, especially after how tense the last few days had been. They hoped he would appreciate it.

The emotion would only last moments after they touched him unless it took hold, and he started to feel it genuinely. Often, this would be the case. It was hard to stop feeling something once the feeling had started. They drew away, and almost immediately the laughter died down.

But the joy stayed to some extent, and he cast them an amused look. "Oh, I see," he said, laughter still in his voice.

"Do you want to change your description?"

"No, I don't," Peders said, leaning back again. "No, that

still felt natural. Only, for a moment I didn't know what I thought was so funny."

"And now?"

"Oh, I think it's *very* funny how you did that."

Hana was watching the two of them as they talked, Asa realized. Where the incident seemed to have genuinely cheered Peders up, a shadow had fallen across their companion's face. They were losing her.

"Does that answer your question, Hana?" Asa brought it back to her, and while she didn't look particularly impressed, it seemed like she was still interested.

"It does," she replied. She reached a hand out toward Asa. "I have to say, I've been curious about this since you described it to me."

"I'm happy to satisfy any curiosity," Asa said, though this was only true to the two people sitting in front of them.

Two things occurred to them—firstly, how odd it was that the two people they trusted most in the entire country were, by their own admission, some of the least trustworthy. And secondly, they realized that because of the first part, they had assumed that their role during this journey would be more . . . sinister. They had anticipated more interrogations, more underhandedness. Instead, every time they had been called upon, it had been for this—to help the least trustworthy people they knew feel perhaps a little better about themselves. Some might challenge whether or not they deserved that level of comfort or peace.

Asa, though, honestly couldn't care either way.

They held an emotion in their heart for Hana. When they'd done something similar for Peders, it had been serenity. The most calming calm, the most peaceful peace. For Hana, they didn't know if she'd be content with that. The hurt she was feeling was certainly just as hurtful, just as complex, but they didn't want to shut it down completely. For Peders, they'd just wanted him to stop hurting.

For Hana . . .

They didn't know what to call what they gave her at first. They felt sympathy for her pain, and her anger, and her loneliness. Then, they remembered Stefan. They remembered James.

When they finally found a name for what they were going to give her, they called it hope.

Hana's hand rested in Asa's, and Asa watched her eyes as they gave her this bittersweet feeling. They didn't know if it was what she wanted, or if it would help, but it was all they had to give her.

She seemed to be inspecting Asa's face. They didn't flinch or look away as she did, and they sat with their hands clasped together with the noise of the tavern around them almost fading away with the focus they were giving to the things they were both feeling.

"Hana . . .?" Asa finally prompted. Hana frowned. She still didn't speak, but she pulled her hand back. She raised her mug to her lips. One sip. Pause. Another sip.

"I see," was all she said when she eventually spoke.

"Did I do all right?" Asa was confused. They had never gotten this kind of response before. They wondered if they had done something terribly wrong—or worse, if it just hadn't worked at all. Had they held her hand for too long? Had she started to feel anxious as they became anxious to see her reaction?

"You are . . . extraordinary." She spoke in Anjeonese, as though the words she wanted to say just weren't there in Bladstongue. "I don't think there's any other way to describe you."

Asa felt pride swell. They smiled. "I'm only doing my best," they replied, and finally Hana smiled too.

When she spoke again it was in Bladstongue, purposefully to loop Peders back into the conversation. "Lange is going to get a kick out of you."

"This Gethinist I've heard so little about?" Asa said, perking up at the mention of the mysterious figure. "I've always found they don't like me very much. The feeling is mutual, of course."

"I think he'll be different. I've never liked Gethinists much myself, but Lange . . . well, you'll see," she said with a knowing smile.

"I can't wait to meet him."

"And you won't have to, not much longer, at least," Peders broke in. "I thought we could head straight there."

Asa blinked in surprise. "What about Hagen? What about the job?"

Peders brushed that concern aside with a wave of his hand. "Never mind that. We've hit a dead end—I can't do much more with Torger dead."

"What about the servant at the keep?"

"I questioned him—nothing. He didn't do the initial poisoning, just kept dosing the girl in her water. Apparently he never even met his employer—just got a series of notes and the powder to use. He didn't even know it was a woman."

Then that was that. "You can really just put it aside and go gallivanting across the countryside with me?"

"It's not exactly gallivanting. Simple there-and-back trip. We go to Lange, he tells us what he thinks is going on with you, and then we . . ." Peders paused, and Asa watched as his expression shifted between several emotions in a second.

They knew why, almost immediately. It was because the end of that visit would spell the end of their partnership. Once they had met his friend there would be no reason for them to continue traveling together. With Hana gone, and their leads exhausted . . . that would be it.

It was sad, of course. Undoubtedly so. But they'd known it was coming sooner or later, and rather than fight it, they stated it outright. "We part ways," they said.

"Right, you go on doing your bard-ly duties, and I get into

my least favorite part of my job—the part where I have no idea what I'm doing and actually have to investigate."

"Sounds boring," Asa teased.

"It is," Peders agreed.

"You've been around for easily the most interesting job we've been on together—maybe ever," Hana said. "Usually it's a lot more frustrating. You got lucky quite a bit—but it seems that luck's finally run out."

"Seems so," Peders said.

"And so has our time together." Hana stretched, pushing back the ale, apparently finally done with her drinking spree. "Tomorrow I'll go back to Grankoping. I'm sure Stef has been worried sick, I was supposed to go straight back."

"Do you want company?" Peders volunteered. "That is, if you aren't sick of me yet. It's on our way, after all."

Hana quirked an eyebrow. "I've been sick of you this entire time, Kennet."

"Ah." Peders sounded embarrassed, but Hana wasn't finished.

"But in light of the . . . revelations we've had today, I think I could stand you a little longer, if only to keep from being left alone with my thoughts," she said. As she spoke, she stood up and faced the table with finality. "We'll leave tomorrow. It's not far—but I'll be glad to have you both."

As Hana left, Peders shot Asa a look that was full of shock.

"What did you do to her?" he asked, half-jokingly. "That was you, right? That wasn't genuine?"

"Nothing I gave her would have done that," Asa replied with a shake of their head. "Perhaps she's just warming back up to you."

"Impossible," Peders said, but then he conceded, "I suppose if Maryska isn't angry at me, Hana has nothing more to hold onto."

"Things seem to have only gotten more complicated with that visit," Asa observed.

"That's putting things lightly," Peders agreed. He looked out over the tavern for a moment, seemingly deep in thought, before he added, "I feel as though I should be relieved, you know. Everything has gone . . . better, I suppose, than I ever could have hoped for. But I don't."

Asa considered him at that, and when he didn't continue, they prompted, "Do you think that's because you don't think you deserve it?"

"Damn you, be a little less correct for once," Peders said. "But, no, not exactly. It's because I *know* I don't deserve it. It's funny—the way Maryska talked about it is exactly the same as I did to myself, for years, to justify what I'd done. It's the same things I told Hana when she was angry at me. But when Maryska was saying them, I couldn't believe them. Maybe I never really did."

Asa hummed in understanding, propping up their chin on their hand. They already knew he had never truly believed himself justified—whatever he had done, he only seemed all right with it when he wasn't thinking about it at all. But whatever it took to get him to a place where he could ignore his past and live in the present . . . it hadn't been real acceptance. What was interesting was that it seemed like this was the first time *he* was acknowledging that. They wished they could help, but without knowing exactly what had happened, they were nothing more than a listening ear.

They were done asking for an explanation, though. It seemed like the big picture was simply one they would never get to see.

And with what they'd been able to glean so far, they weren't sure they ever wanted to see it.

"There's nothing to do about it now," they said in an attempt to be practical. Peders sighed.

"That's certainly true. Which is why!" He slapped his

hands on his knees and made a move to stand, prompting Asa to do the same. "We won't do anything about it. We'll drop Hana off, and it'll be no more about me, about poison, about dead men—it'll be all about you, my friend, and honestly that's far more preferable to me."

"And me!" Asa agreed cheerfully. "You know how much I love to talk about myself."

"And I love to listen."

There was a moment there. As they both stood next to the table, and that statement lingered in the air, Asa felt energy crackle for a split second. Was there something to that, something more than the usual teasing? Was there some undue warmth?

Their heart raced at the idea. They'd thought about it before, once or twice, when he'd said something similarly charged.

But hadn't it been like this since day one? The man was a flirt, even if he didn't know it.

No, that was nothing.

Asa forced themself to grin. "Wonderful, because I'm not going to stop either way," they said, and gave a small bow of farewell. "Well, I am going to stop for now, anyway. Briefly. Only because it's so late."

"Ah, naturally." Peders bowed back. "I'll see you in the morning, then?"

"See you in the morning, Sir Peders. Sleep well."

∼

Asa never went straight to bed. They were incapable of it—it was worse when they shared a room with someone else and couldn't wind down in their preferred way. But tonight they were alone, which gave them license to do their nightly ritual as they wanted.

Cross-legged on their bed, they strummed at their

vihuela, a melody that they had crafted long before any lyrics had occurred to them. It was a well-written structure, perhaps one of their best, which was why it had gone so long without a proper story to accompany it. They were afraid to sully it with subpar lyricism. But now . . .

They plucked at the strings, deep in thought, with a small notebook set in front of them with the beginnings of a ballad written out in Bladstongue. They wanted this to be good, and though they didn't want to share it until it was done, it was becoming clear that they'd have to get a second opinion sooner or later. And unfortunately, that opinion was likely going to have to come from the person the song was written for.

That was why his words at the end of their conversation had given them so much pause. Because if it was more than just a quirk, more than just the friendly flirting they were used to from him, then it meant that sharing this song with him would be risky. They didn't want him to take it the wrong way.

But what was the wrong way? How did they mean for him to take it?

They knew the implication. Writing a song about someone was rarely a platonic thing. And truthfully, they weren't even sure if it was platonic in this case, either. But that was just the thing—they weren't sure.

And as long as they weren't sure, it was risky to share it with him. It might bring questions they didn't have answers to.

They were running out of time, though. Would they rather be asked those questions than he never hear it at all?

Well, there were at least a couple days to figure that out. And it wasn't quite in a state to be shared yet, anyway.

They strummed at their instrument again.

What did it matter either way? It wasn't like there was a future there. That's why the flirting from Peders had to be just friendly, because what would it mean if it wasn't? Where could he possibly think it would go?

They scoffed at themself. He probably wasn't even thinking about it as hard as they were, this man who could give them pause so casually. And besides that, it was precisely because there was no future between them that this song was so important. It was a memento of the most interesting friendship either of them had ever had, no matter how short-lived that friendship had been.

A new line of lyrics occurred to them with that thought, and they leaned over their vihuela to pick up their notebook and scribble down their thoughts. With that, inspiration had struck them and the previous line of thought went almost completely washed away by a flood of ideas. Softly, under their breath, they sang a few bars and nodded in satisfaction.

Meant in friendship or otherwise, this song would be worth sharing.

～

IF ASA WERE EVER to settle down in one place again, it would have to be in Grankoping. There had been a market like this where they had grown up. Just like this, yet different in every way. They loved the feeling of it being just like home but nothing like home. The attitudes were different, mostly. In Lucien when you walked through a market, it was noisy, and it was a friendly kind of noise. People would shove their wares in your face, but not in an attempt to make you buy them—just to get you to try them. They knew their work spoke for itself, and if you just tried it, you'd be a customer for life.

It was like that here, too, but it was quiet. The stall owners knew that their work would speak for itself, and so they didn't speak almost at all. The nature of their product was all they needed. There were already crowds of loyal customers around most stalls, Asa noticed, and it intrigued them. Even without constant advertisement, there was an alluring element to the way they handled things, the soft implication that they were missing out, missing out on something that all these people clearly knew. Asa wanted to be in on the secret.

Sadly there was no time for that today. Perhaps after they dropped Hana off at her house, then Asa could convince Peders to come back and they could do some shopping. Buy some food for the road, maybe.

"Oh look." Hana had been leading the way as they walked through the city streets, but now she paused. "It's Stef."

Stefan Bergstrom was standing at a stall, a meat stall with slabs of beef carefully laid on large blocks of ice. Asa would likely have looked right over his head if Hana hadn't directed their attention to him. They were by no means a tall person themself, but Stefan was still a good deal shorter than them, and only a few inches taller than his son who stood next to him. James was watching his father examine cuts of meat with a look of intense seriousness on his childish face, like he was part of the purchasing decision. It was the child who noticed their approach, and he lit up when he saw them and tugged at his father's sleeve.

"Pa!" he cried out happily. "It's Auntie!"

When Stefan looked over at the approaching group, Asa waved. He seemed surprised to see them but a smile quickly took over his face as he and Hana met eyes. When they all reached his side, he greeted Hana with a quick hug before turning back to the stall.

"I'm glad you're back," he said. "You can help us pick out the cut for tonight."

"Oh, can I?" Hana looked over the meat, and pointed to one at the far back, one that Stefan could not reach. "What about that one?"

He looked at her, and raised an eyebrow. "Asshole," he said, and James gasped.

"Pa." The boy scolded his father for his language. Stefan just smiled.

"Don't worry Stef, I'll get it for you. No need to get short with me," Hana continued. Her deadpan method of delivery only added to Stefan's growing annoyance as his upper lip curled in a teasingly mocking sneer. Hana only responded with a calm smile, trading some coin with the vendor to acquire the beef in question wrapped in brown paper and tied with twine.

The good-natured teasing ended only when Stefan broke the façade with a laugh and gave his friend a playful slap on the back. "Welcome back," he said, and James let out a little sigh of relief that the moment of tension between his two adults was over.

"Thank you," Hana said.

"You were gone a good deal longer than we were expecting," Stefan added with a bit of concern in his voice. "We were starting to worry."

"No need, we just stayed for some celebrations since the job went so well," Hana replied. Asa was unsurprised that she wasn't divulging the little side trip they had taken. Likely there was nothing good that could come of it.

"Well! That's good to hear. The girl's all well, then?"

"As well as can be." Hana nodded. Stefan seemed satisfied with that, and gestured for the group to move away from the stall to make room for others.

"That's it for errands, more or less," he said. "Let's go home."

He hadn't acknowledged Hana's tagalongs, though he did smile at Asa before they turned to walk back toward the house. James, on the other hand, immediately directed his attention to Asa. As they walked, they slowed a bit to allow for his short legs to keep up. He smiled up at them and showed them the bag he was carrying—there were a few loaves of bread in it, loaves that were very fresh. The smell made Asa's mouth water.

"Those smell delicious," they told the boy, and he nodded eagerly.

"Pa says you should always have bread to mop up any sauce on your plate, and this is the best type of bread for it."

"He's right, it looks like it has a nice thick crust."

James made a face, apparently disagreeing with Asa. "Too much crust hurts my teeth," he grumbled.

"Mine too," Asa admitted with a bit of amusement, "but that's why you let it soften in the sauce."

James nodded reverently in agreement. Then, it seemed like something occurred to him and he struck up a new line of conversation. "You helped the little girl who was sick, didn't you?"

It tickled Asa to hear James refer to the lord's daughter as a "little girl" when he couldn't have been much older than her. Nevertheless, they nodded to affirm his statement. "I did."

"Did you find out why someone would want to do that?" There was a bit of hesitation in the boy's voice.

"Are you afraid someone's going to poison you, James?" Asa asked, and he nodded. "Oh, dear, no. Nobody would do that to you."

"But Pa said that she didn't do anything wrong. So they did it for no reason—and then it *could* happen to me."

"Nobody does terrible things like that for *no* reason," Asa replied soothingly. "We just haven't found out what the reason is yet, but I'm sure there is one." They didn't mention the lord's true birthright, or any of that. It seemed too heavy for the boy's heart, and beyond that, it wasn't their story to tell—as much as they wanted to tell it.

"Well, when you find out, maybe come back and tell me."

"If I find out, I'll do that. But I'm not going to work on that job anymore—that's all up to Sir Peders."

James glanced toward Peders at that. Their companion had clearly been listening in on the entire conversation, and when James looked in his direction, he was caught looking back. He averted his eyes and pretended not to be eavesdropping. James pulled Asa down to his height just as they reached the door to the house, holding the bard back a few steps with him.

"Pa doesn't like Sir Peders very much," he said in hushed tones.

Asa knew that. But they didn't like that Stefan had told James about it. Asa had noticed that Peders cared very much what people thought of him, and the child was no exception. But again—none of their business. "I know that," they whispered back.

"But you do like him, don't you?"

Ah, right. Of course. "Yes, I do."

"Very much?"

Asa wished that children weren't so forthright. "Yes."

"Why?"

Damn, he'd got them. They looked over to Peders, who had been watching them again. Again, he looked away. They chuckled softly. "I like spending time with him. He's funny."

James leaned around Asa to get a better look at Peders. They could see in his eyes that he was unimpressed by this explanation. "Really?"

"Yes, really." Asa snorted at the boy's disbelief.

"What else?"

Did they have to do this here? Hana and the boy's father had gone inside, and it was clear that Peders was waiting for them to be finished talking before he followed, though he was standing a respectful distance away. Asa returned their attention to James. "He's interesting."

James looked confused. "No he isn't. He's just a man."

Asa had to hold back a full-blown bark of laughter at that. "An interesting man," they said. "I think so anyway. He has a lot of scars, and you know, each scar comes with a story."

"My pa has a lot of scars too," James said slowly, as though he was beginning to understand.

"And you ask him about them, don't you?"

"Sometimes. He doesn't like to talk about them."

"Doesn't that make you want to know even more?"

That made it click, it seemed, and James nodded. "I guess I would want to know more if I saw Sir Peders on the road. If I didn't know what Pa thought about him."

"Exactly."

This satisfied James, and he let go of Asa's sleeve to let them stand back up again. As they did, they saw Peders was still watching them, and when they acknowledged him he made a quizzical face. They shrugged and shook their head—private conversation. He shrugged back. Into the house they went.

Hana and Stefan could be heard talking in the kitchen, and James made his way in after them to deliver the bread. With the boy gone, Peders turned to Asa.

"What was that all about?"

"Just curious about Marna's health," Asa replied.

"Ah, I see. That explains why you both kept looking over at me and making sure I couldn't hear what you were talking about—because I don't know what happened to Marna." He crossed his arms, but he was clearly more curious than cross.

"That's exactly it." Asa didn't bite at his bait, and he clicked his tongue, annoyed.

"Fine, don't tell me, then."

"I won't."

The two stood in that disagreement for only a moment before Peders' expression softened. "How are you doing?" he asked.

"It's been a long few days," they replied honestly. "I'm glad it's over, at least for me."

"And Maryska . . . that whole thing. You're all right, after all that?"

He was probably afraid that what they had heard had changed how they felt about him. And to be fair, it had a little. But not as much as it probably should have. In the first few days after meeting Sir Peders, Asa's mind had run wild with theories about his past. They had thought of the people he may have killed, the things he may have done that were worse than murder. They had wondered whether or not there had been a line he wouldn't cross. They had wondered whether or not that would matter, as long as there was no danger of him crossing that line with them.

Nothing they had heard had been worse than what they had imagined he was capable of.

"The nose story did unsettle me a bit," they admitted, and Peders cringed.

"It was a bit much, wasn't it? I wish I remembered why we'd done that."

"You mean to tell me not only did you cut a man's nose off, but you don't remember *why?*"

"I've done a lot of things, Asa, I can't be expected to remember all of them—"

"Can you two discuss that at another time?"

Hana Oh had practically materialized by Peders' side as they spoke, her presence stern and scolding.

"Sorry, Hana."

"Yes, sorry, Hana."

"James might hear," Hana elaborated, though they had both immediately picked up on that being the issue. "And I don't need to hear about *that* for the next three months."

"Sorry, Hana."

The two exchanged a conspiratorial glance as Hana tried to scowl at both of them at the same time. As they held each other's gaze for a moment, Asa saw Peders' eyes sparkle with quiet mirth and they wondered if their own face showed the same. They realized that the two of them were a pair—a team—friends, even. Not just two strangers traveling together for convenience, anymore.

Their first real friend since they'd left home was a man who had cut another man's nose off.

What a story they would have to tell, if they ever went back.

CHAPTER 4

A BALLAD FOR A BASTARD

IT SEEMED LIKE THE WORST OF IT WAS BEHIND HIM.

That was a relief. He wasn't sure how much more his heart could have taken. It had all happened in such quick succession he could hardly decipher the beginning from the end. One moment he had accepted a job from a lord, the next he was face to face with the last person on the continent that he had wanted to see. And now it was over. Now he could stop being Kennet Peders, assassin and murderer, and go back to being Kennet Peders, Man of Mystery.

Kennet Peders, friend of Asa of the Isles.

Kennet Peders—perhaps a good man, buried under all that.

It had taken a few days, but his outlook on the conversation with Maryska had slowly shifted. Whereas in the moment it had felt unsettling, unfortunate, and even unbelievable, in hindsight it was almost a relief. He no longer thought of her name and felt cold, unbridled terror. Now he just felt . . . sad. But a normal kind of sadness. A sadness he could learn from.

The only thing he couldn't overlook from that day was how she had handled Hana—that is to say, how she hadn't handled Hana at all. How was it that she could stand to face her brother's murderer, but not the woman she had at one point wanted to marry? Was one really less emotionally taxing than the other?

Perhaps they'd just been too much to handle at the same time, and in her distress she'd picked one to address at random—and it had been him.

Either way, he felt horrible for Hana—and grateful that Asa had been there to help her through it.

Asa. Finally, he could focus on them solely. He'd been waiting for that this whole time—and though his continued employment with Hagen would be present in the back of his mind, there was no reason to dwell on it for now. Not when he could be dwelling on them, instead.

He was excited for what their conversation with Lange might yield. Lange, who had devoted so much of his life to the study of folk tales, to the study of the time of the gods. Even without considering Asa, he was excited to see the man again. Someone who actually liked him—someone he could tell about everything that had happened, who knew everyone involved but was removed enough that he could put it into context.

"You're sure the Gethinism thing won't come up too much?" Asa wondered as they rode, back into their routine of taking the countryside by the reins, just the two of them.

"No, no, he's hardly a Gethinist anymore. I promise you—the moment you lay eyes on him, you'll stop worrying," Kennet assured them.

They gave a nervous chuckle. "You're that confident about it, are you?"

"I promise you, Lange is . . . I think he's the type of person you'll like."

"There are a lot of types of people I like," Asa observed. "More than there are types I don't."

"That definitely seems to be true," Kennet agreed, "from what I've seen."

They fell quiet again, but it wasn't an uncomfortable kind of silence. Kennet had missed silence he could just sit with, without feeling like he should be saying something to defend himself or make himself easier to be with.

Though even being around Hana had become easier over the last night they had spent with her. They had even stayed at her house—they hadn't meant to, and Stefan hadn't seemed thrilled about it, but as Kennet and Hana had started drinking, every other person in the house had slowly turned in for the night until even Asa was asleep on the rug in front of the fire. Kennet and Hana hadn't had the heart to wake them to take them back to an inn.

Their conversation had been everything—sad, and happy, and warm, and reflective. They had talked about old memories and hope for the future. And when the future was in question, Hana had turned her eyes to the bard.

There had been a knowing look in her eye. But she hadn't been rude about it this time. Instead, she'd been . . .

Well. She'd given him her blessing, more or less.

"You've gotten attached to them, haven't you?" she'd said.

That was all she had to say. He hadn't really known how to answer, but she hadn't waited.

"They care about you, too," she'd continued. "They never told me as much, but the way that they talked about you to me . . . the way they're always worried about you. I can tell they thought I was being unfair to you."

"You weren't," Kennet had been quick to reply, and she'd sighed.

"No. But of course they would think I was."

That was the silence that had been comfortable. A silence where he hadn't felt the need to interrupt her, nor had he dreaded what was coming next.

"I was wrong," she'd completed her thought with an air of

finality, "about the two of you. I thought you would corrupt them, but . . . I don't think they're that easily corruptible. Naive, of course. But only a little, and only in a way I hope they never grow out of—they shouldn't have to. The things that hardened us are things we never should have had to see, even if we chose to do so. In the end that was our mistake—it was what made you think what you were doing was right, and what made me think that we were victims. And we are—but we're also in the wrong."

Those words were the ones that had stuck with Kennet, after all was said and done. Not the screaming, or the slaps, or the accusations. The negative had bounced around in his skull day by day for the past three years. The positive was like a light that broke through the cracks in the tightly packed shadows, and finally allowed him a moment to consider that maybe, just maybe, he did deserve the same happiness that Hana had found.

Not that he needed her approval to find it, but the fact that she was willing to give him some . . . it meant something.

"What are you thinking about this time, Sir Peders?" Asa's voice brought him back to the present. "The scenery?" they teased.

"No," he answered honestly. "Just thinking about Hana, and how much she and I have both changed."

Asa considered that, and nodded slowly. "Do you ever think about what it would be like if you met the same person at a different time?"

An interesting question. Were they referring to the two of them? "Do you mean us?" He decided not to let it go unsaid.

"Yes."

"I do think about it sometimes," he admitted. "Only because if I had seen you back then—I wouldn't have talked to you, I don't think."

"Oh? Would you have thought me too frivolous? Were you too dark at the time?" they asked, raising an eyebrow.

"Well, no. I've always been me, Asa, it's hard to bury the idiot I am under any level of darkness. I would have thought the same thing I thought about you when we met."

"Which was?" they prompted.

He glanced away, trying to collect his thoughts, because he couldn't be honest. Was he supposed to tell them that he'd thought they were beautiful? That he'd initially sat with them just because there was nowhere else to sit, but that he'd quickly become entranced over only a single night? That he'd wanted to see more of them, though he'd thought that was unlikely?

Why shouldn't he tell them, though?

That was a thought that bore some weight to it, something that needed more thinking on. It wasn't the sort of thing he could decide to do the moment it occurred to him, as much as he wanted to. He'd have to think it over. For now, he made a mild attempt at deception instead.

"I would have thought that you were a bard, and a good one. I would have noticed you weren't from Bladland, and that would have intrigued me, but that would have been all. I wouldn't have gone out of my way to speak to you."

"Too haughty?"

"Again, I was as humble then as I am now." Kennet was amused by what their perception of his past must be. "No, I would have been too busy. And probably surrounded by people who *were* too haughty. Hana, and Maryska."

And Isak.

That was the one thing he hadn't quite recovered from, despite the relief he was experiencing. Though he didn't think he'd ever recover from Isak. He probably didn't want to.

"That's understandable, I suppose." Asa didn't seem to notice that his face had fallen, focusing on the road in front of them. "Honestly, if either of us would have been too proud to talk to the other, it likely would have been me."

This surprised him, allowing a welcome distraction from the thoughts that were starting to creep up on him again. "Really?" he said in genuine disbelief.

"I was a royal pain, even just before I came here. I think it was a defense of some kind—not that that would excuse anything, but seeing who I am now, I like it so much more. I wonder why I was ever like that."

Kennet knew what they meant, though all he could do to show that was give a hum of agreement before they continued.

"I was prideful, and I refused to be reliable. People thought I was this good little child, and when I grew older, when I began to be able to do the things that I can do, I tried to become something new. And they wouldn't let me. And suddenly, nothing felt right. Nobody felt like they knew me, even though they all said that they did. Nowhere felt like home. And if nowhere felt like home, what was the point in staying? I felt terrible before I left, though. I made promises I never intended to keep. I told people I loved them when I didn't mean it."

They fell silent, and when Kennet looked down at them, he saw there was a thoughtful scowl on their face.

"Sometimes I think people only meet at the exact time they were meant to," he said softly, and the scowl melted in an instant.

"I think so too," they agreed. "And even if there are dozens of people I should have met and loved but was too awful to back then—I think it may all have been worth it to be here, and do the things that you and I have done."

Warmth spread over Kennet when they said that, and he felt a ridiculously giddy smile take up residence on his face. "Really?" he asked.

"Oh, absolutely. Aside from the whole 'young child being in danger' part. I could have done without that."

"Right, of course."

There was a lot to be said for the passage of time, he thought to himself as they fell back into comfortable silence. Even if it was hard to imagine Asa as awful when all they had been since he had met them was kind and caring.

There were likely people like Hana in their life, though, people who would be all too happy to hold them to the standards of their past. He counted them both lucky that they were far away from that kind of person. The Asa he knew now seemed to consider themself the best version, and that was the only version that really mattered to him.

∽

THE NIGHT WAS BEAUTIFUL. A little chilly for Kennet's taste, but that's what blankets were for. As he set his things aside in his tent, took off his boots, and leaned back on his heels as he kneeled on the ground, he let himself be calm. He could hear the crackling fire behind him, and over it, a melody from Asa. They must have finished getting ready before him. He took a moment to listen to them play, and realized this song was a new one—or at least, new to him. He wagered there was likely a litany of songs they knew that he'd never heard before.

It was nice. The only reason he continued to wonder if it was completely new—not just to him, but in general—was the inclusion of some more western stylings. He decided to get closer, to hear it better. He steeled himself and grabbed the thick wool blanket from on top of his bedroll, taking it with him as he stepped out into the chill of the night.

Asa was also wrapped in a blanket, though theirs was loosely draped around their shoulders while Kennet held his close. They looked up as he exited his tent, halting in their strumming.

"Don't stop," Kennet said as he came to sit next to them. He considered taking a seat on the same log they were using as a bench, but something stopped him—as though if he were too close to them, they would see his face flush and hear his heart race. He pulled a different log, swiveling it to sit near them but not next to them in front of the fire.

"I wasn't planning on stopping," they said as he sat. "I was actually going to start over."

They didn't resume playing right away, though. Instead, they waited until he was properly settled. When he turned to them, they were watching him intently.

"Are you listening?" they asked, poising their hand over the strings.

"I'm all ears," he replied.

"Good."

He wondered what was so different about this, but they didn't elaborate at all, or warn him of what was coming next. They just began to play.

> If you were to gather round,
> And ask me to tell you a tale
> I'd sit and ponder for a time
> I'd tell you many things in rhyme

> But if you asked me for a story
> Of death, disaster, fear and glory,
> There's only one story I'd tell
> And you're in luck, for I know it well

> The town was small (as many are)
> The lord was kind (as many aren't)
> His daughter lay ill in her bed
> Quite sick, quite ill, and soon to be dead

. . .

So call upon a hawk
On wings as dark as night
Call upon the night itself
And see if it can set things right

The man was strange and frightening
He walked with the walk of a wolf
But his heart was strong and steady
Quite strong, quite steady, and oh he was ready

The hawk rode into town
On wings as dark as night
Hands that hurt now poised to heal
To see if he could set things right

The lord's daughter clung onto life
She thrashed and struggled in her bed
Her brow was wet with slick hot sweat
Quite ill, quite sick, but still not dead yet

The hawk declared it poison
And swept back out of town
He would find the wretched soul
That tried to strike the poor girl down

. . .

The hawk sought out a widow first
A woman wise in herbs and cures
She had no fondness in her heart
No love for him, no, not on her part

He made his motives clear
The widow took his word
They flew back fast as they could
To save the girl, to find a cure

The cure was found, the girl was saved
But who, they asked, had done the deed
The hawk would never let them go
And so he took pursuit once more

He found a track that led
Into a twisted woods
There he found another hawk
This one like him, but not as good

"But what is good, and who decides?"
This hawk asked when their eyes had met
"For you and I both work a job,
To save, to hurt, to give, or to rob.

. . .

"When they call upon a hawk,
With wings as dark as night,
They might well call Death himself
We both know this, so must we fight?

"Act like a hero, if you like,
And pray to god your honor holds
But you and I both know the truth,
You'd have done this job too for the right sum of gold."

Then hawks clashed steel on steel
And blood was shed by both
Neither one would walk away
Yes both of them were slain that day.

So here's the question that I ask
Of you and also yours
With both men dead, is the world better off?
Was the good hawk's work then all for naught?
I haven't the answer, I may never know.
So I'll ask you this before I go
Yes, here's a question for you, instead:
If a killer turns hero then dies,
Is it the hero or killer who's dead?

They spoke the last line with weight and pondering, and when they fell silent, he finally found the strength to look at them. His heart fluttered, and his breath caught in his throat. They had said that they would be writing a song about all of this, but he hadn't expected it so soon, he hadn't expected to get to hear it. The privilege of seeing himself through their eyes—the moment he had realized that's what it was, he had felt lightheaded. He forced himself to calm down now, to take deep breaths, to focus on the way that they were looking at him.

They were waiting for him to say something. What could he possibly say?

"Well?" they demanded when they could wait no longer, leaning forward. "Come on, don't leave me with silence. Did you hate it that much?"

"Hate it? No, no! That was—that was very good."

"Are you sure? I can change it, if you like. I can keep the melody and make it about something else. It doesn't have to be about you, I just—"

"Oh, it's about me, is it?" Kennet tried to tease, but he felt like he might lift off the ground from how light his heart was. "I wasn't sure, since nobody has described me as 'walking with the walk of a wolf' before."

They laughed, but the laughter was hesitant. "Too much?" they asked.

"Asa, no. No. I'm incredibly flattered."

They didn't seem completely satisfied, though they took his approval with a nod. "Good. You should be, I've never written a song about anyone I know before."

"I've never had a song written about me before," Kennet replied. They gave in to that, smiled again, a smile that felt genuine.

"You haven't yet, really," they said. "It's not anywhere near finished—I made up the ending entirely, of course, but if I find out how things really end, then I'll rewrite it."

"I think the ending is perfect as it is. I'm sure reality won't be nearly as poetic or satisfying."

"I suppose I should hope it isn't—I'd rather you didn't die."

"I'd rather I didn't die too!" Kennet said, and they laughed, beginning to play again. It was the same tune but slightly different, and this time they didn't sing, just focusing on trying different embellishments.

Kennet felt like he had run a mile. Breaths were coming with considerably more effort than they should, and he didn't need to wonder why. It had been like this with Isak, too.

Stop thinking about Isak.

That was the main thing holding him back right now, how all he had to compare this to was Isak. He shouldn't, though, should he? Isak had been different. There had been different risks—courting within the Hawks was frowned upon, and there was already an established relationship within their even more tight-knit group. Maryska and Hana had beat them to it. Not to mention, if Isak had rejected him, then things would have been even worse than if he hadn't. Luckily, all that worry had been for nothing, since it had been Isak who approached him first, before Kennet had been able to properly work up the guts.

The risk was significantly less with Asa. Or at least, it was different.

The pros were far greater. If they felt the same way, he already knew it would be effortless. He had felt that way since day one—he had always felt like he was meant to be with them, in some way, even if it was only for a short while. That feeling had only grown.

And the cons, if they were to feel differently?

As much as he hated to even consider that, the cons were far less pressing than they had been with Isak. With Isak, they would have still had to work together. He would have still been friends with Isak's sister and her lover. But with

Asa, if he embarrassed himself now, he would be done with it in a few days. They'd leave, he'd be devastated for a short while, and then one day they'd be a bittersweet memory and he'd never have to think of them again if he didn't want to.

Though, he was sure he'd always want to.

So shouldn't he wait? Shouldn't he wait until after Lange, until the last moment, and minimize the time for things to be awkward?

His heart wouldn't let his mind speak logic.

"Asa," he said their name without meaning to, and his heart leapt when they responded by looking in his direction.

"Hmm?" They didn't stop playing but slowed a bit, facing him with a quizzical expression. Just meeting their gaze made his stomach churn again.

"I've wanted to talk to you for some time about something, and since our journey is nearing a close, I . . . feel it would be silly to wait any longer."

"Well, I agree—if there's anything you want to talk to me about you should certainly do it now because if this Lange actually knows anything about the things that I can do, I'm going to become insufferable after we meet him, and I might not even be able to say goodbye properly."

Kennet gave a soft snort at that, but their attitude did nothing to spare his shaking hands as he clasped them together and leaned forward. As he did, what he didn't see was that their eyes rested on those shaking hands, and the way that his chest heaved with each breath, and the way that he wouldn't look at them. He didn't see that their eyes widened—and though he did note a faltering in the notes they were playing, he didn't make anything of it as he continued.

"I think . . . I think I don't want to say goodbye." He let himself phrase it abstractly at first, but as he started to speak, the words began to spill out, sharpening and clarifying the image that was in his mind's eye. "I don't think I ever do, rather. And I don't . . . well, I don't see why we should have to."

Asa was silent. So silent, in fact, that even their hands failed to make a sound. They watched him, waiting for him to say more, and so he kept going.

"I've grown very fond of you," he said, slowly, trying to find a way to say it that fully conveyed how he felt for them, "and I can't imagine being . . . this fond . . . of anyone else. I would like it if we could keep traveling together, for as long as you'll have me. If you'll have me."

There was no room for misinterpretation there—at least he hoped there wasn't. He hoped it was clear that his intention was more than friendship, more than just companionship. But there was no quick answer. Certainly no enthusiastic yes. The silence was sickening, and he felt himself sinking into the ground at their lack of response.

And when they did respond, it was no better.

"Sir Peders . . ." They were trying to get him to look at them, but he refused. "Kennet—I . . . I assure you, I'm also hesitant to part ways. This time we've spent together—I make no secret of how these have been some of the best days of my short life, but . . ."

There it was. Kennet felt a bitter smile replace his nervous frown. "But," he repeated.

There was no real need to say more. So Asa didn't, instead letting the silence say what they couldn't. When they did speak again, it was only a soft "I'm sorry."

The sorrow he heard in their apology broke his heart. "Oh, Asa—no, no, don't be sorry." He looked up finally, forcing himself to meet their eyes again. "You can't help what you feel, it's not your fault at all. I was . . . I simply . . . Well, I wouldn't have forgiven myself if I hadn't at least tried."

They seemed relieved by this statement. All the same, they didn't speak again for a moment, letting the crackling fire fill the space between their words and his reaction. He felt silly immediately, embarrassed. He wanted to apologize to them, to take it back and have never said it. He wanted to never speak to them again.

No, that wasn't true. He could get over this. He had to.

"Maybe we should turn in," he suggested weakly, desperate to escape the conversation for good.

"Please, let's not," Asa said. "I don't want to leave it on that note. I don't want you to fall asleep thinking about this."

He didn't want to either, but that was probably inescapable at this point. However, he agreed with the greater issue. "I hope you have a good topic to switch to, because I haven't," he said, letting every emotion that was still bubbling up in him out through a long sigh.

"Hmm." They started to play their vihuela again, trying to kick off their thought process. "Would you like to hear a story from when I lived in Lucien?"

That was exactly the kind of thing he needed to take his mind off of everything. "I would, yes."

"Right, wonderful. So, I grew up in this city called Figaroa. It's huge, the biggest city in the country—or at least, I'm pretty sure it is. The point is, there's a lot going on there, enough people that you're unlikely to see someone more than once unless you're actively trying to. But, I lived near this building where the Guild of Architects met up every few weeks, so I saw a lot of them all the time. You think of architects, you probably think stuffy, number-obsessed types, but these people weren't. Generally, they were a pretty good time."

Kennet had never met an architect before but most academic types were usually standoffish around him. He'd only ever met any in Guldfjord, and those academics had been in service of the king, which made them even worse. He found it hard to imagine enjoying spending time with academics of any kind, but as Asa continued on, it started to get easier.

"They were often so tired from work by the time I got to

them that they were looking for any kind of fun. And the fun an architect can get up to is . . . unusual. They've got the skills and even the tools to wreak a special kind of havoc if they want to." A wicked smile flashed across their face, and they struck up a jaunty tune that evoked an atmosphere of mischief. "One night, I went over to the guild just to see what they were up to, and found them in the middle of one such scheme. It was simple—they had two structures, just made of wood, and a crossbar, and with them they could lift any conceivable weight. All they needed was a target."

They cast a glance at Kennet, to see if he was interested. He was—very much, though he wasn't completely free of the uncomfortable feelings he'd brought upon himself. He gestured for them to carry on.

"I provided them exactly the thing. There was a fountain —just inside the gates of the Church of Gethin. The gates are pretty much just for show, with iron bars that are wide enough for any average person to fit through. So, a couple of us would slip in, and open the gates as quietly as possible. And so we did. The priests were none the wiser. The statue on top of the fountain—it's of the founder of the church, Angelica Figaroa. I think she's one of those prophets you talk about. She looks very pretty, by her statue, but unfortunately for the church she was also very small. The statue was heavy, but light enough and low enough to the ground that it fit our needs."

Asa changed up their playing to match the narrative again, a slow suspenseful tune, and they kept going. "I went with them, mostly just to watch since I wouldn't be any physical help. They even insisted since the fountain had been my idea. In the dead of the night we crept in, dressed in all black. We even painted the wood of their mechanism black so it would blend in better with the night sky and we were less likely to be caught. Two of us slipped in just as planned, and opened the gates. It was so much easier than we ever expected, honestly. They set up the structure, hooked it up to the statue. Lifted it up—and then, while it was in the air, a couple of them spun it, ever so slowly, to face the other direction. And then . . . they set it down again."

Kennet raised an eyebrow, holding back laughter. "They turned it around? That's all?"

"A harmless prank! We only wanted some fun, not destruction. We had to be so careful, too, about finding out their reaction to it. It would have been too suspicious for the entire Guild of Architects to hang around the church, so that's where I came in again. They sent me to watch and report back, a fitting task since I am, by trade, a storyteller." They snickered to themself. "I'm most pleased to announce that it took them a full day to even notice that it was wrong at all. One of the novices actually noticed it first. I heard her squeak when she realized, and she ran inside, and within minutes the whole courtyard was filled with priests like little birds, all squawking about the statue. It took them a full team of men and *scaffolding* to do what we had done in a single night with only the small crew we had."

"And did they ever figure out who had done it?"

"Well, who else would they suspect? The only people who knew how to do what we'd done were the architects, so there was no real question. But they had no proof, and we'd really done no harm other than waste their time. So we never faced any consequences—and even if the guild had, there was no connection to me personally. It was the perfect crime, as far as I was concerned. I got all the fun, and didn't have to do any of the work or anything!"

That got an actual laugh out of Kennet. "Not to mention you got to poke fun at your number one nemesis."

"Ah yes, the church. My mortal enemy."

"Is that really just a feeling you have?" he asked, remembering how little he really knew about their vendetta against Gethinism.

They paused, and shrugged. "How much do you know about the Church of Gethin?"

"Not much at all. It doesn't have much of a presence around here, not the way it does out east."

"In the east, Gethinism isn't just a religion, it's a monolith. It's a government. I've heard that Lucien's church is far more forgiving than Byvar's—not that that's saying much. They serve the god of Life and Death, but you could have fooled me about the life part. They're greedy. Deeply greedy. During the plague, they traded cures for coin, when nobody had coin to spare. They didn't share the formulas for their cures—no, that would mean less coin for them. So the people of the south, Hana's people, wasted away. The people of the north had to rely on their own, even worse priesthood. And we—well, Luciens are broadly a decently rich people. That is to say, the rich were the ones who survived. We did better than anybody else, certainly, but everyone I know back home lost at least one person to the plague."

That made more sense. Kennet shook his head with a bit of melancholy. Was that the god he was associated with? But before he could get wrapped up in that train of thought, Asa cut it off.

"That's the church, though. I agree that . . . well, in theory, the Creed of Gethin makes sense. To live and die with the purpose of leading a fulfilling life and helping others to lead fulfilling lives—I think that's an admirable creed to keep."

Kennet smiled at that. "I always thought so, too," he said.

"I think you're keeping it well," Asa told him, "and I know you will continue, even after we part ways—I thank you for following it, honestly. Even if I'm not a fan of the god or his followers, I can confidently say that if there was a way to do Gethinism correctly, you would be doing it."

"Because you're an expert on such things?"

It sounded a tad more combative than he meant it to—or

at least, they reacted as if it sounded that way. They recoiled, just slightly, like he was accusing them of some kind of immorality. There was no sense in that reaction—and even they seemed to realize that, laughing at their own unusual response.

"I suppose I know more than you about it, since you've never even seen a proper church before."

"That's true enough," he conceded, and paused to yawn. Asa noticed and sighed, casting a glance at the dying fire.

"Well, are you feeling better after that story?" they asked.

"I think I am," he said. "Thank you."

They gave a little bow of their head and began to stand. "Then I'll let you get some sleep—and try to get some myself. I'm so excited about this visit and what it might bring I can hardly stand it."

"If you're too tired to travel tomorrow I'll just sling your unconscious body over Emilio and we'll carry on like that."

"That sounds awful."

"Then try and get some sleep so we don't have to resort to it."

They laughed and surrendered to his badgering. With one hand gripping the blanket that was hanging around their shoulders and the other holding their instrument, they ducked into their tent and disappeared from view.

And Kennet Peders was alone again.

He didn't linger long by the fire, eventually standing and shuffling over to Starling and Emilio. He'd go to bed shortly, of course, but first he would seek a bit of consolation from his stubborn horse. She seemed as happy to see him as she ever was, while Emilio greeted him with much more emotion, nuzzling Kennet with his big, square head.

"Hello, old boy," Kennet mumbled, giving the mule a scratch between the eyes. "You sweet thing. You know, I'll miss you too."

He stood in the quiet, absorbing the moment while he

continued to pet the mule. It was nice, and he felt the disappointment and any lingering embarrassment subsiding.

Emilio jerked his head back and his ears swiveled suddenly. Kennet squinted. In the dying firelight, it was hard to determine why the mule was reacting the way he was.

"What's wrong, Emilio? Was that too much?" he wondered aloud.

A familiar voice answered him.

"I suppose I've been found."

Maryska stepped into view from behind an outcrop of rocks. Her hair almost glowed white in the remaining firelight, and her eyes flashed with an unreadable emotion. Kennet stood frozen. He watched her, with no impulse, no reaction. He couldn't get past the pure confusion that came over him, stammering it out in words that took too long to find.

"How—how did—"

"I followed you from Hagertrask. And I did a good job, too. You didn't even notice! Usually you're so very diligent about that sort of thing—though I suppose you were a bit distracted this time." She looked meaningfully toward Asa's tent.

Realization started to dawn over Kennet. "Why now?" he demanded.

"And not back at the house? Oh, that's easy." She stepped closer to him, and his hand went instinctively to his waist—only for him to remember, too late, that he had left his sword and all his other weapons in his tent. "I needed to get you alone."

"Alone," he repeated. She was so much more present, now, speaking with so much more clarity than she had been at the house. That had all been an act, then? If that was the case, then did that mean—

"Without . . ." She frowned, and when she spoke again, she sounded almost wounded. "Why did you have to bring her, Kennet? Why'd you drag her into this? I had it all planned out: you'd show up, I'd kill you, I'd finally be able to move on with my life. But she—there was no world in which I thought—I never thought you'd have the guts to go to her."

"To Hana." Kennet said her name, and the moment he did, he saw that flash of emotion again. It had to be anger. Hatred. Sadness. Loss.

He barely got to comprehend it before she moved, quicker than he could track, and he felt a dull thud on the side of his head. As he collapsed to the ground, quickly losing consciousness, the last thing he heard was the panicked whinnying of the horse and the mule. The last thing he thought of was Asa—

And how he was going to end up hurting them, after all.

CHAPTER 5

ASA GETS THEIR ANSWERS

As soon as Asa entered their tent, it hit them all at once what they had said and done. And they felt like hitting themself—after all that, exactly what they had been afraid of had happened. And they'd reacted just like they'd hoped they wouldn't.

He'd liked the song, so that was a benefit. But everything else had been disastrous. The worst-case scenario.

And the worst part was, they hadn't meant it.

Now that they'd said it out loud, and told him outright that they didn't see a future with him, they knew that they didn't mean it in the slightest. Why should they? What reason was there to say no?

And even more than that, what wasn't there to gain if they had said yes?

Regret bore heavy on them as they carefully laid their vihuela and gloves on the ground and pulled their silk scarf from their bag of things. They began to wrap their hair up, as they did every night, taking the time to think over their actions. He hadn't been reading into anything incorrectly, not really. That was the problem—Kennet Peders had every right to think that he could ask them that question, and even think that they might answer positively.

They'd known—*they'd known*—that opening up to him about that song would likely get this response. They'd known he would likely think it was a confession of their own, or at least an admission to caring for him. And didn't they care for him? So what was the problem here?

Why had they said no?

They hadn't meant it.

They tied off their scarf and sat cross-legged, scowling subconsciously as they continued to stew in their emotions.

Well, they could take it back, couldn't they?

Would he accept that, if they did? They didn't see why he wouldn't but they imagined the embarrassment. They could imagine going back to him and having him reply with "no, you were right," leaving them as stranded as they had just left him. They cringed.

But he had taken that risk, and it was only fair that now they do the same. It was also far less of a risk, since they already knew that there was some level of feelings there.

They wished it hadn't taken a gut-reaction reply for their true heart on the matter to surface, but perhaps it was better late than never. And at least he hadn't waited until the last minute. He had given them time to think everything over, and that's all they'd really needed—to be confronted with it, and have a moment to think.

And the idea of traveling with him—even if it wasn't forever, there was something to the idea of being that partnership in sincerity. The idea of being bonded in a way that made them both feel lucky to be together. It awakened an ache in their heart that they had to acknowledge and try to fulfill.

That settled it. They'd go to him.

He hadn't felt the need to wait any longer, why would they?

They could hear the horses whinnying. Someone was out there with them, which meant he was still awake. Perfect.

Taking one last, deep breath, they rose to their feet and crouched as they exited their tent.

"Kennet, I wanted to—" They started to speak as they came into view of the dying fire, then stopped in their tracks.

A woman stood over Peders' prone body, a stone in her hand, blonde hair falling over her face and obscuring it from Asa's view. Nonetheless, they knew who it had to be. It was Maryska, the woman they had visited. Asa's mind raced, trying to put the pieces together, but they couldn't quite add everything up before they felt compelled to act. They had to run, they had to—that's what Peders had told them to do if she got violent.

She lifted her head slowly, dangerously, like a snake. As she did, she pushed her hair back from her face, driving her fingers deep through the strands, then pulling them out like threads of spider silk. The action revealed her eyes—wild with exhilaration and locked onto Asa's. She was smiling wide, the dying firelight giving the expression an eerie effect, and Asa felt as though their legs had turned to jelly underneath them. They still tried to run, or find the motivation to.

They felt a sharp pain in their neck. They'd hardly noticed her move, but she had quickly raised a small tube to her lips and shot a puff of air through it. A dart was embedded in their neck, and they knew immediately that there would be no running.

They tried anyway.

They turned and began to sprint as fast as they could through the woods. The woman didn't give chase—not immediately. Asa could hear no footsteps behind them, though honestly they couldn't hear much over their own heartbeat. As they ran they dug their fingertips into their neck, ripping the dart from their flesh and throwing it onto the ground behind them. It was no good, of course. Their vision was starting to blur.

Was there somewhere to hide? To pass out in peace, where she couldn't find them?

They couldn't think clearly. They stopped in their tracks —part of them knew it was a mistake to do so, but that part was fading fast. So fast, in fact, that it was quickly gone along with whatever part of them had thought it was a good idea to hide. And the part of them that knew how to stand.

The ground rushed up at them. Soft pine needles cushioned their fall, and though it helped somewhat, they still landed hard as their legs crumpled beneath them. They waited for their vision to fade along with their reason, but it didn't. Neither did their wakefulness. They tried to move, to scream, to cry out for help, but try as they might they weren't able to. Awake, but paralyzed, they had no choice but to lie in the dirt until a pair of boots finally stepped into view among the trees.

"You're smarter than I was," said Maryska as she crouched down in front of Asa. "I didn't even bother to run."

She didn't wait for an answer she knew wouldn't come. Instead, she circled out of view again, and Asa felt two strong hands wrap around their legs. The pine needles shifted under them, going up their shirt and pulling off the scarf from around their head as they were dragged across the forest floor, back the way they came.

Their heart sank as they realized they hadn't run far at all. Maryska stopped dragging them only a short while later, leaving their body lying on the ground at the edge of the fire. She threw a couple logs onto the dying flame, and it flared up briefly.

"Are you comfortable?" she asked, not looking toward them as they could barely move their eyes to follow her movement. "I know you can't answer," she added after a moment of silence, "but I do want to be a good host. After all, it's going to be a long night. No need for you to suffer any more than necessary." Now she looked down toward them, and Asa saw a calmer but still unnerving smile.

They wanted to respond, to be sharp, to be witty. But their tongue was stiff in their mouth, dry like wool. Her smile grew at their helplessness.

"I have nothing against you, of course," she said. She turned her attention to the fire again, then looked over to her side. Asa couldn't see what lay in the direction she was looking, but they assumed it was Sir Peders, by the way her expression changed. She gave a dark sigh and faced Asa once more, resuming her smiling. "You just have an unfortunate taste in men."

~

For what seemed like hours, Asa lay motionless at the woman's mercy. She had barely even looked at them since laying them in front of the fire, which was now back to its full potential. It roared away and gracefully lent them a bit of warmth as they lay on the cold ground.

They weren't able to turn their head, even after hours, so they weren't able to see what Maryska had been doing. They'd heard her singing, off and on, mostly to herself. Every once in a while she'd make a remark to Sir Peders' unconscious form, about him, about their past, or about their circumstances.

Asa was still having a hard time forming coherent thoughts. All they knew was that they were paralyzed, and they were in danger—and so was Sir Peders, even more so.

Eventually, Maryska returned to their limited field of vision. She was dressed differently than she had been back at the house, abandoning the softer-looking farmhouse clothing style for something much more fitting, at least to Asa's assumptions. She looked more comfortable, and moved more confidently. It made it even clearer that the farmhouse conversation had all been an act.

She was clothed head to toe in black, in a similar style to Sir Peders' usual outfit, only without an undershirt under the leather vest. Bracers capped off each of her arms at the wrist, emphasizing biceps that had been unnoticeable under the simple tunic she had been wearing before. This was a force to be reckoned with, and she no longer cared who knew.

The same threatening air was present in her eyes when she knelt in front of Asa again.

"Sorry to leave you waiting," she said soothingly, "but I had to make sure you'd be able to see everything all right. I wasn't allowed that courtesy, but you know, this is all about doing things the right way. He was sloppy with it, but I've always been more of an artist than he was."

Asa wanted to ask what she was talking about. She knew that, and grinned at the confusion that must have been apparent on their face.

"Let's get you a better view," she said, and put a hand under each of their arms, pulling them around the fire to the other side of it, and propping them up against the log they had been sitting on mere hours before. As she did, their head lolled to one side, but they were still able to see what she had brought them over to see. And when they registered what they were looking at, they felt sick to their stomach.

A small wooden frame had been haphazardly lashed together, between two small trees, and Kennet Peders was strapped to it. He hung by his arms, which were outstretched over the crossbar, with ropes binding his wrists to it. His legs dangled but were able to touch the ground, bound together and leaving a trail in the dirt where he had clearly been dragged from where she had found him to where she had set up this whole display. He was still unconscious, for the moment, but groaned a little as he seemed to be waking again.

"Got a good look?" Maryska asked, her head ducking down in front of the scene she had laid out for them. She scanned their face. "I hope so. Don't want you to miss a single thing."

Asa deeply wanted to scream. To hit her, to get up and run to Peders and address the still-dripping wound on the left side of his head, the blood intermingling with the streaks of grey in his hair that almost glittered in the firelight.

But they still sat motionless. How long would this last? Would they still be stuck, long after Peders was dead? Would they survive that long?

Maryska didn't supply any answers. Not immediately, anyway, as she seemed satisfied with her work and stood up straight again. She walked away from them, toward Peders, stopping when she stood only a few paces from him. With one last glance at Asa, her smile faded.

"Good," she said, "let's get on with the show."

She slapped Peders across the face, hard.

The strike brought him awake immediately, as he had already been close, and he cried out when he was able to register what had happened. Asa's heart broke as they saw his head whip around, trying to determine where he was. When he realized he was bound, he strained against the ropes.

"Maryska," he growled, slumping again when he had confirmation that there would be no slipping from his bindings.

"Hello again, Ken." Maryska swayed from one side to the other, slightly, as she looked at him. He looked past her, and his eyes settled on Asa. They saw rage come over him almost immediately.

"What did you do to them?" he demanded. "They're not part of this, please. Don't hurt them."

"Oh, look at you." Though Asa couldn't see Maryska's face, they could hear the sarcastic pout in her voice. "Caring about whether or not someone else gets hurt. Is that what you did with me? Is that why you poisoned me? You said it was to keep me from getting hurt, but was that really it? Or did you just know I'd be able to stop you?"

Peders scowled, looking away. "I didn't want to hurt you," he said. "I promise. I never wanted to hurt you."

"Of course not. That's why you poisoned me, with a poison you asked me for. You said to make something that would immobilize a person, so I did. Because what are friends for, if not to help each other out? And the poison I made does exactly what you wanted it to. Shuts the body down—as you can see, of course." She gestured to Asa. "But when I made it, there was one thing I didn't take into account, because—well, god help me, because I hadn't considered it'd be used to keep me still while my brother was murdered!"

There was no response from Peders. He refused to look at her.

"Do you know what that thing was, Ken?"

"No," he finally answered her, and she laughed.

"I forgot to make it a sedative!" Her voice broke. "I forgot —I forgot, and did I ever pay for it. Because, Ken, *I saw the whole thing.*"

She paused for a moment, letting the phrase hang in the air. Asa watched as it settled in for Peders exactly what that meant—and though they didn't know the details themselves, they could glean from what they had heard. They knew what it had to mean to her.

"Maryska—"

"I watched every moment, I couldn't help it. For a moment, I thought he was going to get away—you couldn't get the poison into him the way you did with me, so he fought back. But you helped them bring him down. And I had to watch the whole thing. I couldn't look away, or close my eyes, or anything. I had to watch as they came down on him, as they held him down, and ran him through. You had tears in your eyes, I think. Were those genuine? Were they because you 'had' to do it?"

"I did have to . . ." He paused, then hung his head in shame, his shoulders sagging and causing the wood frame to creak with the movement. "I thought I had to," he muttered.

"Watching him die was one thing." She didn't ask him to elaborate on his answer, starting to pace back and forth in front of him with an idle calm to her movements, as if this were just a casual conversation between old friends. "That was bad enough, but remember what they said? So casually, too, they said, 'Well we don't need the whole thing, do we?' And then! They cut. Off. His. Head."

Asa's stomach turned, and they watched Peders' face contort in the pain of the memory.

"At least you had the luxury of looking away. I had to watch every second as they cut through my brother's neck like they were butchering so much meat."

Peders retched. Maryska laughed, reveling in his discomfort.

"I know you really loved him. I guess that's the only thing that stopped me for so long, knowing that you loved him so much. And he loved you. I told myself you must have been truly desperate. But then, if that was the case, why him? Why not me? There was a clear choice there. Answer that one for me, Ken. Why not me?"

"Hana." When he said her name, Maryska's entire posture changed. She looked over toward Asa, and they were surprised to see some mourning in her expression.

"Hana," she repeated. "Always putting your friends first, even at the cost of Isak's life, is that it? Is that why you went back to her? This was all for her, was it?"

"For both of you," Peders broke in. "I wouldn't have been able to look Isak in the eye if you'd died. I was going to lose him either way, I saw . . . I saw no reason why you and Hana would have to go through that same loss, if I was going to lose all of you—I thought—"

"Oh, so selfless," she sneered as she whipped back around to face him. "And that worked out so well for us, didn't it?"

"I was naive to think it would."

"That's an understatement." She took his chin between her thumb and forefinger, lifting his head so he was forced to look her in the eye. "You tore me apart; even though you spared my body, my heart was left desolate. Whether or not you meant for me to see it, meant for me to be hurt—I am hurt, Kennet. No amount of good intentions or repentance can ever account for all that you did to me."

There was an indescribable amount of anguish in his voice when he answered. "I would never claim that."

"But you want forgiveness, don't you?"

Silence. Then, slowly, "No . . . No, I don't."

This was the first thing he'd said that seemed to genuinely catch her off guard. She cocked her head, and Asa wondered how she would react, until she let go of his face and stepped back with a scoff. "Of course not. Always a martyr. Luckily, I've come to offer you something much better than forgiveness."

She waited for Peders to respond, as much as he appeared that he desperately didn't want to. When he sat quiet for too long, she answered the question he left unasked.

"I'm talking about justice, Ken," she said. Asa saw that her hand was tracing over her waist, toward a sheath on her hip. "You've become such a fan of justice since we last talked—you even joined the church of Life and Death." She pulled a knife out of her belt and considered the blade in her hand, holding it up to shine in the firelight. "They have such funny little sayings they use to define justice. There's the creed, of course, but I'm thinking of another one. What is it? 'An eye for an eye'?"

The moment the words had left her lips, she lashed out,

striking quickly with a slashing motion across the right side of Peders' face. Asa felt a scream within their heart, one that was matched by Kennet out loud as blood began to stream down his face, but they could make no sound of their own. His cries of pain subsided into a whimper as he wrestled against his restraints again, clearly desperate to cup a hand over the bloody mess where his right eye used to be.

Maryska clicked her tongue, examining her work closely as she twirled the knife in her hand. Beads of blood flicked off with the movement—a few drops landed at Asa's feet, and a few splattered across the side of Peders' face that had been previously left unstained. He barely flinched as the liquid hit his cheek, hanging limply in his restraints as his shoulders heaved with breath. Maryska didn't seem certain she was satisfied with her work, though, and reached out to lift up his bloodied eyelid and inspect the eye underneath. Peders cried out again at her touch. She cut him off by covering his mouth, barely missing wounding him a second time as the knife that she held slipped from her grasp and dropped to the forest floor.

"Ah, damn," she muttered, and bent to pick it up. She wiped it off on her pant leg and considered it again before saying, "Not really sanitary, but it's not going to matter to you in a moment. You know, I've been thinking about this for a long time. Of course I have been—who in my position wouldn't fantasize about revenge? But I really thought it would stay a fantasy, and nothing more, forever."

Peders was in no state to continue conversation with her. Maryska didn't seem to mind, however, continuing on as though he had asked her to.

"But then, you know a funny thing? I got approached by a very rich client to do an . . . almost unthinkable job. He wanted me to poison a child. Now, of course, I'm not a monster. There's no amount of money he could have offered that would have made me willing to do such a terrible thing.

But he didn't offer me money, no. He offered me whatever I wanted—and I wanted your head."

Asa realized suddenly that they were about to get a confession—useless as that confession would be to them, they thought, as they were sure they'd both be dead before the sun rose. But at least they would die with this one question answered.

"It would have been too easy to ask for that, though. I didn't want someone who didn't know you to have the pleasure of killing you. That seemed so impersonal. So I came up with a plan—a pretty good one, I think. That was always the big problem with you, Ken, you never thought enough to have a plan. If you had, maybe you would have come to me or Hana about your issue instead of resorting to leading your own lover to his death."

She grinned when he winced at her words.

"The plan was easy. The little girl would get sick. Her father, a lord, would be desperate for a cure and he would look to hire an expert. Luckily, he would have a trusted source to help him find one. My client. His father."

If Asa's eyes could have widened in shock, they would have. Maybe they did. They didn't know how much control they had over their body anymore.

"The king." Maryska said it so matter-of-factly that it sounded completely wrong. "That was the whole point of the thing, of course. To get the prince to come back home, or at least get him started. And if I was able to do that, then I got my end of the deal—the king would recommend that his poor, grieving son hire the Great Kennet Peders, the only man for the job. And when you started looking into it, I wouldn't even have to hunt you down, you would come straight to me. And you did." Her glee at how everything had worked out was evident.

"The king?" Peders repeated, his voice weak but as shocked as Asa felt.

"Yes, the king. Is that what you're focused on? Royal infighting has always been below you, what's different about this? The little girl? She's fine, isn't she? You did your job—I knew you would, I even made it easy for you where I didn't have to. Probably could've done without that homey fellow from that little village, but you know, I wanted to leave a *bit* of a trail."

Torger. He hadn't needed to be involved at all. That was her idea of doing them a favor—involving a man who would otherwise have lived many years more. It occurred to Asa that she very well might have intended to kill him from the start. But much like she hadn't given his life much pause in her planning, she didn't do so now, either, continuing with hardly a moment to breathe.

"So the girl was never really in danger as far as I was concerned. The only thing I didn't plan on was Hana, but that worked out fine. Completely fine. It worked out in my favor, even, because I got to meet you—Asa of the Isles." She turned to Asa now, smiling widely again. "And ah, how my plan fell into place."

"What are you talking about? What have they got to do with it?" Peders demanded. Some energy was returning to his voice, along with desperate panic as he watched Maryska's focus shift to the bard.

"Oh, everything, Kennet," she said. "They brought it all together. Because now, not only do I get to cut your head off just like they did with my dear brother, but I have an audience just like you did, too! The same captive audience, just waiting to be destroyed."

Horror lit up in Peders' remaining eye. With renewed strength, he struggled again against the ropes that bound him. Asa felt the same rush of terror in their own veins and tried desperately to move. Anything—to blink, to shut their eyes. Ideally, to stand and fight her. To lay their hands on her

—that was all they would have to do, if they could so much as lift their hands to touch her.

With great effort, they tried to move—

Their head slumped over onto their chest, too heavy for them to hold it up on their own.

Their small action was met with silence. Then, a frustrated scream tore from Maryska, and they heard her bootfall as she thundered toward their body.

"NO!" she shouted. "No, you MAY NOT look away. You'll suffer like I did. You'll WATCH. WATCH!" she commanded, and her hand shot out to pull their head up by the hair.

As she did this, her palm brushed Asa's forehead.

That was it.

In a flash, Asa willed their emotions to flood into hers. Like a hot kettle pouring into a cup, they flooded her with fear, the same fear that they were feeling, the same helplessness. They willed her to freeze.

And like that hot kettle pouring water into a cup is liable to cause a splash, a spill, liable to overflow—

Her emotions flooded back into them.

It had never happened like this before. They had never felt—never seen—what they were feeling and seeing now. They felt her anger, raging and white hot, built up over years and years, finally ready to be unleashed only for Asa to stop it in its tracks. And then, as she started to feel the fear that they were feeding her, they felt that fear too.

And with that fear, they saw something entirely new.

They saw a dark night, much like the night they were living now, with firelight. The air was cold and blue. They saw their breath in front of them as their head lay limply on frozen ground—and beyond puffs of that, they saw four men.

One was held by two, and the fourth stood off to the side. His back was to Asa, but the color of his hair, the posture, the scars and calluses on his hands as they were clasped behind his back were all intensely famil-

iar. He was breathing heavily, and his hair was loose and tangled, with a patch of it missing. They could see a lock of the same color caught in between the fingers of the pale-haired man who was being restrained.

They felt immense anger, and fear of course, but also disgust. Betrayal, betrayal so deep that it was as though they were watching their own brother held down, turned over by their own friend's hand. They only hoped to never experience these emotions in earnest, but this was bad enough as it was, and it was matched only by the feeling of helplessness that they had grown to become too familiar with over the night.

"Go on then," one of the strange men shouted, his grip tightening on the shoulder of his captive. The other was silent, but he joined his companion as they forced the blond man to his knees. "Finish it."

The man with his back to Asa froze. "Me?"

"Either that or you help hold him while one of us does it."

The man's hands clenched into fists behind his back. He hesitated.

"Do it, man!" bellowed the stranger.

There was no way out of it. The man with his back to Asa drew his sword, and stepped up to the one on his knees. There was still hesitation—along with hatred in the pale blue eyes of the restrained man, hatred that didn't leave his eyes as the two stared each other down. Asa's heart was in their throat. He wasn't actually going to do it?

He hadn't yet. Asa watched as his grip tightened on his sword, and it seemed perhaps he might have been about to move, but before he could there was another shout.

"ENOUGH!" The thug had lost his patience, and released his grip on his captive, moving quickly as he grabbed the other man's sword and used it to finish the job.

There were details Asa wouldn't have noticed if they had been there. There were things that stuck out to them that only did because they weren't seeing through their own eyes. The way his eyes widened when the sword plunged into his belly. The way blood sprouted up through lips that had once smiled, laughed, and loved, then dribbled down his chin as he coughed and sputtered. The way that his beautiful, kind blue eyes went cold and clammy almost immediately, like he *passed out from the pain before life fully left him. The way it all took so long, too long, to happen. Perhaps even longer in their mind.*

They felt like crying, like sobbing and screaming, but they couldn't. Someone else was crying, though—the man who hadn't been able to finish what he'd started. Tears had formed in his eyes and they felt even more angry to see them, angry that he could cry when they couldn't.

"All right," said the one who had killed him, "let's wrap this up. No need to drag the whole thing back with us, eh?"

"Must you?" begged the crying man.

"I might not have if you'd just killed him when I asked, but now we have to make up for the time you wasted." He grabbed the dead man's head by the hair, holding it still as he dragged the blade of the sword across the neck—

Asa felt themself, in the present, scream. Finally they were able to scream, and the sound was raw, and louder than they knew they were capable of. They realized their target was beginning to pull away from them, and felt a rush as they knew they couldn't let her. They had to bring her down completely, and they had to do it now. With their newfound strength, they forced their arms to work. They grabbed her head between their hands, burying their fingers in her blond hair, pressing their palms to her cheeks. The flood of emotions didn't wane—despite their terror, they only gave her more. And she screamed back. The feedback grew stronger.

The memory changed. They were still lying on the ground, in the same position, but all the men were gone. The only thing that was left was a body, too close to them for comfort. It was facing away from them. At least they were spared a view of the aftermath. Their stomach still churned, and they knew they'd been lying there, staring at it, for hours. They still could not move.

The crunching of boots on frosty ground broke through the eerie silence. They didn't see him, but they could hear his voice as he referred, surprisingly, to them.

"I suppose I should at least take him with me. Bury him. Have it over and done with, and I'll never have to see either of you again," he said. They watched as he stepped around them and crouched down to take the body's wrists in his hands. Asa could see that while the tears had stopped flowing, they left stains like rivers carving through dirt and blood on his face. His expression was set resolutely.

"Don't touch him!" they wanted to scream. "Don't take him from me!"

But they still could not make a sound.

Finally, they broke free. They felt no more, only relief and lingering terror as they blinked, and were finally conscious of what they were seeing. Their hands still grasped Maryska's head between them, but she was no longer screaming. Neither of them were. Asa was panting with effort, with exhaustion and with the realization of what they had just done. Maryska . . .

Maryska reeled backward. Asa could see tears streaking down her cheeks as she tried to get to her feet, and stumbled, then collapsed—unconscious.

They had done it, they realized, though they could scarcely believe it.

They had saved them both.

They had won.

CHAPTER 6

THE INEVITABLE

Kennet sat as still as he could, allowing the bard to cup his face in their hand, separated from their touch by the leather of their gloves. They had insisted on putting them back on before touching him in any way—it seemed that whatever had happened with Maryska, they weren't eager to repeat it.

With their free hand, Asa gently dabbed at Kennet's right eye with a wet rag. He had asked them to assess the damage, but by the expression on their face and the fact that he couldn't even see darkness on that side, he figured there would be no recovering from the attack.

"What's the outlook?" He attempted to sound cheerful, unsure of what else to do.

They pulled back with a frustrated sigh. "It's not good. I've . . . well, I've never seen anyone lose an eye before, but I'm fairly certain this is what that looks like."

Kennet clicked his tongue. "Damn," he muttered. He tried to remind himself that he was lucky to be alive, that he could have lost far worse, but it still stung deeply to be wounded like this.

The eye was only the most urgent item that needed to be

addressed. His head had been swimming every second since Asa had cut him down—he was forcing himself to stay calm, though. Address what he had to address, by order of importance.

The first thing had been obvious. His wounds, and there were a couple, were in immediate need of attention. Asa had even insisted that they wouldn't talk about anything else until they had taken care of that. Unfortunately, with their gentle help, the easy part was over. Now they had to move on to the next pressing issue.

Asa said it before he could. "The king, huh?"

The king, indeed. Everything else that had come up was to be expected, more or less, but the answer to their questions regarding Hagen had blindsided Kennet as much as the knife to his eye had. It was a bold scheme from the king—to manipulate his son into resuming their relationship by putting his own granddaughter in danger. While Maryska had even said she was sure that the child was safe, he wondered if the king had bothered to make sure of that. Regardless, it seemed that despite her attempts to show herself an impartial party, Maryska wasn't completely divorced from her morals after all.

With all that said, it was disappointing to have Hana's theory confirmed for certain.

This came with a few realizations. For one thing, Kennet felt a twinge of guilt. If he hadn't been responsible for Maryska's decline, then Marna would never have suffered in the first place. If he had only—

Asa was looking at him, concerned, watching his face as it was undoubtedly darkened by his thoughts.

"What's the matter?" they asked, tucking their index finger under his chin and gently raising it to face them fully. Their touch was comforting, and he was reminded of their exchange in Ornhult, and what he had told them then. It was equally applicable now—even if Maryska's hurt was his fault, her actions were not.

She alone was responsible.

Which brought them back to the matter at hand.

"We need to figure out what to do with her," Kennet said, gesturing to where Maryska lay on the ground, bound at the wrists and ankles, and unconscious. She had been completely still since Asa did . . . whatever they had done.

"Eventually we will," Asa agreed, glancing over to her when he motioned in her direction. They seemed reluctant to look at her for more than a few seconds.

It was his turn to examine them, before saying, gently, "Do you want to talk about it?"

They shook their head, then slowly began to nod. "I think we should. But you're hurt—and we're both tired. If you don't want to talk now, I understand."

"I want to make sure you're safe before we do anything else," Kennet replied emphatically, and they sighed. They glanced down at their hands, dropping them into their lap before turning toward the fire. It was still crackling away from when Maryska had renewed it. Had that really only been a few moments ago?

How quickly everything had happened.

Asa watched the fire silently, and Kennet wondered if they wanted him to ask something. A stabbing pain shot through his eye, and he winced audibly. Immediately they were fussing over him again.

"Let's bandage that first, then we'll talk," they said.

They retrieved bandages from Kennet's saddlebag at his direction, and then sat next to him again. As they brushed his hair out of his face to clear a place to wrap the bandage, he found himself having to resist the urge to lean into their touch. He longed for that comfort, but they had made themself clear. This was no time to push boundaries.

Even as he was thinking this to himself, Asa began to

speak. "I wanted to tell you . . . It's hard to phrase it, but now more than ever I need you to know . . . I changed my mind. Well, I guess the truth is more that I finally made it up." They were avoiding his gaze, focusing on their work as they wrapped the bandage around his head.

In spite of his exhaustion and pain, Kennet's heartbeat fluttered. "In . . . in regards to what?" he asked hesitantly, hoping desperately that he wasn't jumping to conclusions.

"In regards to us," they replied. "Our . . . standing with each other."

His heart's reaction must have shown on his face, because they smiled.

"I care for you very deeply, Sir Peders. Kennet." They said his name softly. "I meant to tell you even before you were in danger, but that solidified it for me. I don't know if it was seeing you like that, or the poison, or . . . well, it doesn't matter, but it brought something out of me, and I'm not sure what it was." Their face fell, and Kennet frowned.

"It looked . . . painful. For both of you."

"It was."

There was another moment of silence as they tucked the end of the bandage into itself. After they examined their handiwork and nodded in satisfaction with it, they turned to face the fire again. Kennet watched them out of the corner of his good eye before facing them fully. They seemed lost in thought—until slowly they started to lean toward him, and he felt their head rest against his shoulder.

"It was like . . . it was like her feelings leaked back into me, when I touched her. I felt angry—so, so angry, and I never want to feel like that again."

Kennet sat frozen, unsure of what to do until he remembered how to move again and untucked his arm from under them. He wrapped it around their shoulder, pulled them closer, and held them next to him. With this movement, they leaned in farther, and he let out a breath of relief that he had done the right thing. "That sounds horrific," he said with feeling. They shook their head, their curls rubbing against his shirt as they did.

"That wasn't even the worst of it," they said. "It was . . ." They paused. He couldn't see their expression but he was sure that they were thinking hard. "I'm not going to hide it from you, Kennet—I saw everything. Everything that she saw that night, everything she was talking about."

As if his heart could take anymore, it now sank as deep as it could. Before he could protest, or explain, or apologize, they kept going.

"And then I saw more—I saw his body, lying not far from me. It seemed like she had been staring at it, unable to look away for . . . ages."

That would have to be correct. It had taken Kennet at least an hour to collect himself after everything had happened, at least an hour to consider his next steps, and that entire time Maryska had been lying only feet away from Isak's corpse. He felt immensely sorry for her, realizing the position she had been in.

He felt even sorrier for Asa, who'd had to experience the same thing.

It registered that they were waiting for him to speak and he scrambled to find his words. "Yes. His name was Isak," he said. They still didn't speak further. He grimaced. "I . . ." What could he say? That he had loved Isak? He had, but now hardly seemed the time to lead into the story like that. "It's a very long story."

They sat up straight now, shaking his arm off and turning to face him. They did that thing they often did—flicking their gaze over his face, taking in every inch of it, like they were trying to stare into his soul. When they spoke, their voice was firm. "I need to hear it," they said. "I need to know what you did, and why. The whole thing. In your own words."

Of course. He had known when he decided to be honest

about his feelings for them that he would eventually have to be honest about everything else, too. And he knew they deserved it, and he knew that there was no hiding it. So he forced himself to begin speaking.

"Hana and I used to work together alongside two others—a brother and sister, Isak and Maryska. The four of us were the most tight-knit ingroup within the Hawks. We worked so well it was frightening. A force to be reckoned with—and of course, when you work so closely together, things start to . . . well, look at you and me, for example."

They settled in a little more, no longer sitting at attention as they listened, and when he said that they snorted in acknowledgment. "Of course," they agreed.

"So, Hana and Maryska . . . and me and Isak. Everyone who saw us knew it was going to end badly—they told us as much, but we didn't listen. I don't think even the people who warned us could have foreseen *how* badly it was going to end, though." If he had a coin for every time he wished he had taken that advice and spared them all the pain, he'd be rich. "Everything went wonderfully, for a time. Until one job—we were hired to take out a fairly high profile target, and when it came down to it, really only one of us needed to make the final move. We all worked together to plan it, to set it up, but in the end. . . Maryska was the one who finished it. It had been a tricky one, but we'd executed it almost perfectly."

He paused for a moment before continuing, furrowing his brow as he tried to remember the exact details of what had happened next. It had been so long ago, but most of it was as clear as if he was remembering what he'd had for lunch that day. "We didn't even think about that job for months, until one day, I got a missive from a very important client. A lord, from a large city, farther north. Next to the king, this man was perhaps the most powerful man in the country. I was thrilled to be summoned by name, personally, to his presence. I went without questioning it."

The crackling fire filled a pause in his story, and he glanced at Maryska again. He hoped that she was really unconscious this time and wouldn't have to hear him recount the details. "It was, ah . . . it was a trap." He scoffed at his own past stupidity. "As it turned out, that high profile target had been the lord's lover. Nobody had known about the two's romantic entanglements, so nobody had known that killing them would raise any issues. But it had. And rather than just take it up with whoever had hired us, he was going one further. He wanted the head of whoever had taken his lover's life. And he knew that, although it hadn't been me, I'd been involved, and I was close to them. And I would be able to help him get what he wanted."

Kennet wondered how he should present what had happened next. "I wish I could say he had threatened my life," he said, "but he didn't. He just said that if I said yes, he would trust me, and kill who I told him to kill. If I said no, he would choose indiscriminately. In my pride, and in my foolishness, I thought I could . . . I could at least control the outcome. I thought I could make it the best-case scenario for everyone involved, so I invited Maryska and Isak out for a mysterious 'job.' I promised I would explain on the way. I had planned it carefully—Maryska had made me a poison that would paralyze, believing it was for the job when really it was for them. The question was, which one of them would make it out alive?"

"The truth was that Maryska had been the one to end the target's life, so the revenge rightfully should have been directed at her, but something was holding me back. It was Hana—I said this a while ago to Hana, and then to Maryska just now, but truly that's what it came down to. I knew that it was going to tear us apart no matter what, but the question was not about who would die, it was about who would survive. There would be me. And if I left Isak alive, there was really no option to stay with him, not knowing what I had done to his sister—even if he never found out, I couldn't have lived with that. So no matter what, I was going to lose him, and I would break Hana's heart too if I chose Maryska, but if I left her alive . . ." he trailed off, staring at the unconscious body of his friend-turned-enemy once more. "Clearly it didn't work out that way."

"I see why you thought to do it," Asa said, but Kennet couldn't accept that.

"I've told myself the same thing every day, that anyone would see why I'd done it, but Asa—I've lied to myself." He felt tears welling up in his good eye, and he did nothing to stop them. "I watched them kill him—I *let* them kill him, right in front of me—not because it was logical or the right thing to do, or because it would spare anyone pain. I did it because I was prideful—because I thought I knew what was best. Because I thought I had it under control, and I didn't—I should have told them what was going on. Perhaps we could have gone into hiding, or we could have—" He hiccuped, feeling sobs come faster than he could let them out. He raised his eye to the bard's, scanning them frantically for answers. "Help me, Asa."

Their eyes widened and they recoiled just the tiniest bit. "But . . ." They hesitated. "What if—"

"What if what?" he demanded, his voice cracking in desperation. "Never mind any of that. I don't care if what you did to her happens to me, I can't bear to feel this way anymore. I can't bear to hate myself one more second. Three years I've lived like this, and it never does anything. Never means anything—never changes. I can't do it, I can't. Please," he repeated himself, reaching out to them, "help me."

As he reached out toward them, he saw that they were reaching back. They must have removed their gloves while he was talking because as their fingertips brushed his cheeks they were bare. And immediately, he felt relief.

Relief so strong it only made the tears fall harder as he began to comprehend what he was feeling.

Would they ever do what he asked and make him feel numb? It seemed like they never would, because even in this pathetic state, they made him feel more than he ever could have asked for.

He felt *loved*.

That was the only way to describe it. His heart swelled, and the hand that he had outstretched toward them pulled back, resting on their wrist as they pressed their palm against his cheek. He felt loved, and in feeling it, he knew it was a love with no bounds or conditions. How could it have conditions, if they were giving him this after everything he had told them? After everything they had seen for themself?

It felt like forgiveness—not just from them, who he had put in danger, but from the world. Permission, maybe. Permission to forgive himself.

As he felt all this, he saw their eyes in warm firelight, full of the same thing they were giving to him. Caring. Even love.

They stroked his cheek softly, once with the back of their hand, tucking his hair out of his face before they started to draw away. Their skin had parted with his, and even his own hand was only touching the fabric of their shirt at their wrist. There was no more influence from them, and they hesitated.

"May I . . . May I kiss you?" they asked. Their voice was tight, as though they were terrified he would say no. Now that he was able to feel more than what they had given him, he felt his chest swell with a new rush of emotion.

"Please," he responded, and that was all it took.

Their lips crashed into his—they were warm, and soft, and everything he hadn't allowed himself to long for. His hand ran down their arm from their wrist to their shoulder, wrapping around their back and pulling them in closer as their own hand brushed against his cheek again, then tangled in his hair.

There was no question, once their lips met, that Asa was as elated as he was. In fact, it was almost overwhelming as he felt their elation and it overflowed back into them, like an infinite spring of passion that only grew in strength the longer they embraced. When they finally drew away, and they reentered reality together, Kennet felt like a man stepping out into the cold of an early winter's morning. He sucked in a sharp breath and pulled back. Their hand rested over his shoulder, dangling behind his back, and he still held them even as they leaned back a bit.

"Are you all right?" they asked. Even after all that, there was still concern in their voice.

"I'm much better," he replied sincerely.

"Good," they said, and leaned in to kiss him again.

∽

THE RIDE back to Grankoping was painfully long. They had decided against sleep, since neither of them felt safe sleeping while Maryska was still with them. Instead, they loaded her onto Emilio's back, and the two mounted Starling together to head back toward the town.

They would leave her there, in Grankoping's custody, and go back to Osternas to deliver the bad news. Then, Hagen could decide what to do with her from there. There was no world in which Kennet wanted to take her with them all the way back, and they weren't really equipped for that at this point. So, letting the authorities take care of it would likely be the best-case scenario for everyone.

He was looking forward to being done with it all, though he didn't particularly want to have to be the one to deliver the news to Hagen about his father. Luckily, he had a good few days' ride to figure out how to do that properly.

"We should go to Hana again," Kennet said presently, glancing over his shoulder to see Asa's face much closer than he had expected it to be. They were behind him on Starling's back with one arm wrapped around his waist, and though he'd known they'd be there it still startled him a bit to see them so close.

"Oh?" they seemed confused, but not for long. "Ah, I suppose we should let her know about everything that's happened."

"I would hate for her to hear it from someone else." He nodded and gave a quick look farther back behind them before facing the road again. Emilio trailed obediently behind them, and Kennet figured they'd pretty quickly find out if Maryska came to. It had been a while, but she was breathing and she had a heartbeat. Honestly as far as he was concerned, she could stay passed out until she was safely contained in a prison cell. That way he didn't have to look her in the eye ever again.

"What do you think will happen to her?" Asa asked, noting his glance back toward the mule and their prisoner.

"I don't know. That's up to Lord Hagen," Kennet answered.

"I suppose that makes sense."

"He said he wanted her dead, but that was in a moment of passion. Part of me is . . . doubtful that he'll follow through," Kennet added. "But stranger things have happened."

"I would be surprised if he did." Asa sounded like they hoped the lord would hold himself back, though Kennet couldn't imagine why.

He did realize, though, that if they were willing to give him grace it was possible that they had the same leniency for Maryska. Even if he was special to Asa, they weren't a hypocrite, not the way that he and his friends were. They really seemed to see the best in people—or at least, to see potential, to believe that there was something worth saving.

If they didn't believe that, he would be dead. So of course

he couldn't resent them for having that same sympathy for Maryska.

If he was honest with himself—and he had decided to be —he felt the same way that they did.

He still felt responsible for her behavior, of course. He probably always would. And with that in mind, for her to die at his hand felt . . . wrong. It wasn't his move to make. So, he would give that decision over to Hagen, and if Hagen wanted her dead, he was perhaps the only person in the world who had that right.

They arrived in Grankoping in the evening, having made it a good ways from the city before they were ambushed. Their first stop was to a guardpost, where Kennet very quickly described the situation to the men who were working.

One of the heavily armed guards stepped forward— though all of them wore green and brown gambesons, this one wore considerably more heraldry and a hat with a green plume curling out of it. He listened to Kennet for a while, then sent one of the other guards to relay the message to the local lord.

"We'll keep her here for you, of course," he said. His voice was rough, and deep. "We've heard all about Lord Hagen's misfortune—personally I think death's too good for the dog who done it."

Kennet cringed a bit, but nodded, and said, "Will you send word ahead to Lord Hagen? We mean to spend the night here to recover before we head back to Osternas."

"Of course, Sir . . .?"

"Sir Kennet Peders."

With that squared away, Kennet and Asa left the guardhouse and made their way back into the city itself. The stablehand was the first one to really react to Kennet's face— it was her third time seeing him in the past few weeks, and he looked . . . distinctly less healthy.

"Sir!" she gasped upon seeing him, eyes wide. "What happened?"

"Ah, job went a bit rough, I'm afraid." He tried to smile at her reassuringly. He knew that beyond the bloody bandage that covered the wound that used to be his right eye, he was also covered in dirt and soot, and so was Asa. They looked like death—and felt it, too.

"I can see that!" the stablehand said with feeling. "I can recommend a wonderful doctor, if you're in need of one."

"That won't be necessary. I have a friend in the city who can help."

As they left their mounts at the stables and walked through the city, Kennet felt like all eyes were on them. Asa, who had been trailing just behind him, quietly slipped up next to him and suddenly his fingers were entwined with theirs. They were still wearing their gloves, but even without their influence, their presence calmed him greatly.

They walked in silence, until they came for a final time to Stefan Bergstrom's door.

James was the one who answered, and his jaw dropped. He seemed unable to speak until the voice of his father interrupted his stunned silence.

"Who's there, boy?"

"It's—it's Asa and Sir Peders, Pa, they're hurt!"

There was a loud clattering. Stefan and Hana both appeared at the door in unison, equally clumsy in their approach as they stopped abruptly behind the boy. Stefan looked past Kennet to Asa, scanning them quickly to assess any wounds on their part. Only when he was satisfied that they were mostly unscathed did he turn his attention to Kennet, with a bit of an unimpressed scowl.

Hana, on the other hand, gave James a gentle shove and stepped up to Kennet with shock, concern and confusion all intermingling in her eyes. She stood still in front of him equally as stunned as James had just been until finally she managed to put words to the question that had no doubt been in her mind from the moment she heard his name.

"Was it her?" she asked.

Kennet nodded morosely, and her expression clouded. Anger and sadness fought for control as she backed up, leaning on the doorframe and burying her face in her hands. Every feeling she must have been bottling up finally let itself out in a muffled scream into her palms coupled with a few stifled sobs. Stefan patted her arm comfortingly and motioned for James to go inside. Though the boy was reluctant to miss an explanation for all this, he did as he was told without question.

They weren't invited inside, not at first. Stefan stepped out into the quiet street the house was located on and closed the door behind him. He took Hana's arms in his hands and looked up at her face through her fingers. At his touch, she lowered her arms slowly—she hadn't cried, not really, but there were angry tears in her eyes and she pushed her hair out of her face with a sniff.

"Did you kill her?" she asked, turning her tear-filled eyes to Kennet. It wasn't an accusation. If anything, it was said with reluctance, like she knew that if he had it would have only been done out of necessity.

"No," he replied. "She's in custody now. The guards said they'd turn her over to Hagen as soon as we're able to debrief him."

Hana nodded at that, understanding immediately. "That's as it should be," she said, straightening her posture to compose herself and wiping both eyes. She squinted a little at Kennet, and seemed to be looking over his wounds now that she had gotten past what they meant. "She really did a number on you, didn't she?"

"And she would've done more," Kennet said, and he heard Asa clear their throat behind him. When he looked back at them, they shook their head. Hana noticed the gesture but said nothing, waiting for Kennet to continue his explanation. "We got lucky."

"You'll tell me about it one day," she said. "Did she just nick you there? That's a lot of blood." She gestured to his eye.

Kennet's shoulders sagged. "Ah, no. She took it—the eye, I mean. I can't see a damn thing, and it hurts like hell." He felt frustration starting to creep into his voice—he had been holding it back for one reason or another the entire day, but now all those reasons were gone. Exhaustion finally began to overtake him.

Hana and Stefan exchanged a look. The latter sighed, and shrugged, then turned and went back inside.

"Come around the back," Hana said, apparently taking her friend's reaction to mean that she was allowed to have them in. "I'll take you in through the kitchen. We'll take care of that wound, get you cleaned up, give you a moment to get into clean clothes. Stefan won't likely want you to stay the night, but we can at least set you straight."

"Thank you. That's more than you have to do."

Hana smiled wryly. "I know," she said, and started to make her way back into the house. "Meet you in the kitchen." She managed to slip the direction in just before the door closed behind her.

∽

THE SALVE that Hana had used on Kennet's wounds stung, but she said that meant it was working. He sat on a wooden chair in the kitchen, with Asa leaning on the counter across from him. The room was long and narrow, mostly a pantry with a single counter on one side and a very small table on the other. As Asa looked up at the ceiling they were met with a face full of dangling, dried herbs. They took a deep breath through their nose—Kennet thought it must smell amazing.

He couldn't make out any scents past the powerful-smelling salve.

Hana had run off to fetch something from another room, leaving Kennet and Asa alone again. The bard had already changed—they had been wearing their bedclothes since the moment Maryska ambushed until now. They seemed more themself in their costume again, looking just as they had the day he had met them—except now there were dark bags under their eyes instead of bright eyeliner.

"I'm glad it's not infected," they said. "It looked pretty bad when I was cleaning it."

"She says it's *very* bad," Kennet muttered. Hana had delivered most of the bad news when Asa wasn't in the room. As he had expected, he had completely lost his right eye—the knife had gouged into it deep, leaving him sightless. Though it hadn't been infected, Hana had been very thorough in her treatment, and it had hurt very much every step of the way. At one point, he thought he might have passed out.

"At least we're alive," Asa attempted to brighten the circumstances, but their expression fell a little when they saw his. "It's very unfortunate though."

"Very."

"What's another scar, at the end of the day?" Hana entered into the room and the conversation simultaneously, holding a few things in her hands. One was a fresh bandage, the other a dark patch of fabric that had been carefully stitched together with straps on each side. She held the bandage up first. "This is for now. You're still leaking blood a bit, on both sides of your head, so you'll need to change the bandages fairly often. Keep them clean, reapply the salve before bed and then in the morning. Asa, can you help him with that?"

Asa nodded, yawning as they did. Hana's brow furrowed in sympathy but she continued to talk.

"This"—she held up what Kennet now recognized to be

an eyepatch—"is for later. You're free to refuse it, of course, but the wound is going to look pretty ugly for a while, even after it's started to heal."

"What do you think, Asa? I think perhaps you get a little bit of a say in my looks." Kennet turned to his companion and caught them in the middle of another yawn. They laughed lightly through the end of it, and shrugged.

"Eyepatches are attractive, I think," they said. "I'll have to add that into the song, though."

Hana gave each of them a knowing look, but again refrained from commenting on anything beyond a smile. "Eyepatch it is, then," she said. "You can always change your mind later, but we've had this one lying around for a while. Stefan made it for a 'disguise' and he was insistent that to make the disguise convincing he had to make it properly, so it should serve you well."

"He's all right with you giving me this?" Kennet asked, remembering his last and only real conversation with the man. Hana shrugged.

"He didn't say anything when he gave it to me, but I think as far as he's concerned, he's satisfied that you're no longer getting off easy. Even if he thinks it should've been your life."

Kennet snorted. "How kind of him."

"And on top of that, his hospitality seemingly knows no bounds tonight—I think it's because he saw how Asa was about to fall over, but he relented on his house rules. You're allowed to get some sleep here before you leave."

Asa sighed with relief, slumping a bit as tension released itself from their shoulders. "Thank god," they muttered.

"I'll get you some blankets and things; you can stay in front of the fire," Hana said, handing the eyepatch to Kennet and the bandages to Asa. "Get him wrapped up. By the time you're done I'll be ready for you."

And with that, she was gone. Asa looked at the eyepatch

in Kennet's hands and he saw a smile slowly grow on their face. "What's so funny?" he asked.

"I was thinking about how I always wonder where each of your scars come from, and now there's one that I know—one I was there for, and it's the most interesting one. People are going to see you on the street and think, 'I wonder how that man lost his eye,' and I'll be the only one who knows."

Kennet chuckled at that. He had always enjoyed exactly what they were talking about—the imposing effect that his scars gave him, even if a lot of them came with painful memories. The eyepatch would certainly lend to that as well, he agreed, and he couldn't help but share their sentiment. "Our little secret," he said.

"Not so little," they retorted as they began to bandage his wounds again, "it's your whole goddamn eye!"

CHAPTER 7

ASA SINGS A SONG

Asa stood on a stage, in front of a crowd, and they felt complete.

Osternas had consistently been a great crowd, ever since their first night onstage when they had taken the room by force. They hadn't needed to repeat that action since, having proven their capability and won the favor of one of the staff in particular. They always had a place in this tavern, and they always felt welcome.

Tonight was no different. Kennet Peders sat at the bar, watching them onstage. He had wanted to go straight to the keep, but without the imminent threat on his daughter's safety, the lord was now less easy to reach. They had arrived too late to earn an audience with Hagen, and they'd been told to return in the morning. That was fine by Asa, who didn't even want to be present for the conversation that was going to have to take place. They really didn't want to, but Peders said that they had to. They'd been there for the whole thing, after all.

There was no use thinking about that.

They had to think about the stage, and the crowd, and the song.

When they played the first chords of their opening song, a cheer broke out in the audience. They recognized this one, and it was a favorite. A good one to start out with. It would set the tone.

As they began to pick up the pace with their playing, they rocked onto their back foot. When they knew the crowd was enjoying their playing it made it easier to play—it made the music all-encompassing, unhindered by the social and business pressures of needing to please the audience. And in turn, it made the audience's experience more enjoyable too. The best situation possible.

Even more so with everything that had been going on.

But that was just how it was with music. They had always felt most at home when they were playing, since they were young. Nobody in their family had quite understood it but their parents had encouraged it, at least. It had always been a safe space, a place to get their feelings out without it affecting anyone else. And while that had been true even before they'd been able to directly influence the emotions of others, it had gotten even more important after the fact. When it came down to it, they often found themself presented with a choice. They could either lash out, hurt someone, create more of a problem than fix one . . . or they could put that energy somewhere more productive.

It was an easy choice.

Like now, for instance. They had no idea how to communicate what they were feeling and they certainly didn't want anybody else to feel it. There was confusion from what their influence had done when they touched Maryska. There was elation over finding someone who they cared for as fully as he cared about them. There was lingering fear from having been lying, helpless, unable to move—that was a feeling they thought they'd never be able to forget. And all those emotions mixed together to create something not quite positive, not quite negative, and that came out in their music unhindered by such rudimentary concepts as "good" or "bad."

The energy was pure. Neither positive nor negative, it flowed freely from their fingertips onto the strings, and then out into the crowd. They could make all of this into something productive. They could make it *them*.

And they didn't have to use confusing, unfamiliar influence to do so.

The song they were playing was entirely instrumental, a perfect warmup for exactly that reason. The lack of lyrics played into it being a fan favorite, since their classical Lucien playstyle could be appreciated without any lyrics to confuse it.

As they slowed their playing and finished the song, there was a scattering of applause. Asa glanced over to where Peders was sitting and saw him smiling—a smile that somehow got bigger when they looked at him, despite it being very wide to begin with. They smiled back and on impulse blew him a kiss.

Someone in the crowd whistled, and the rest laughed as they looked back to see—who's the lucky bastard that earned that kiss?

A man at the bar clapped his hand on Peders' shoulder, giving him a rough shake of congratulations, and Peders laughed at the attention. He gave a small joking bow as the heads turned. When the crowd was satisfied that the target of the bard's affection deserved it, they turned back to their own business, and Asa turned back to their songs.

They wished that their song was finished, the one that they had written for him. But now the story it told had taken another turn, and it perhaps needed another rewrite. So instead, they began a song that they knew was ready for a crowd like this—especially one that had seen them play before.

It was the "Painter's Muse," the one they'd sung for

Peders so long ago. Hopefully he hadn't been lying to spare their feelings at the time, and it was properly ready for a crowd this size that spoke the language they'd translated it into.

They hoped to the heavens that it was ready, but launched into it without another second to doubt themself.

The crowd responded well almost immediately. They were curious—usually Asa stuck with either simple Bladland drinking songs or their more complicated Lucien ballads, but this was neither. This one melded both, and they seemed excited to hear it.

As Asa sang, they remembered the melancholy way that this song often affected them. They'd never known why, but it was the opposite of the way that they felt about their influence. One was a tune without lyrics, the other was passion without motivation. When they sang the lyrics to Peders, they'd held it back a bit, trying to focus on pronunciation. In Isla, they'd always let loose. The second to last verse, that one hit the hardest. They played it best and sang it loudest, and it ripped from their chest with fervor every time. Something lingered within them, though it had never made sense. There was nothing to that song that related to them. It wasn't born from any personal experience, and yet . . .

It happened this time, too. Now that they were finally confident in their Bladstongue, they got to the second to last verse, and felt that same swelling in their heart. When they sang, they belted, and whoever hadn't been listening before fell quiet now. Conversations were silenced with the first line, and stayed that way as Asa powered through the rest.

"Between the two of us I found myself suddenly alone—" Their voice almost broke with the feeling behind it. Caught up in the moment, they didn't think twice. Perhaps it was all that had happened to them finally working its way out. Perhaps it was something completely different. Maybe it was fear of being left behind, like in the song. Was it because of

Peders? But why would they be afraid he would leave them? Hadn't they always been the one doing the leaving?

As the verse ended, they brought their voice back down, letting it tremble a bit in the final verse as the passion gave way to sweet, soft sorrow and acceptance. They always liked to end this song on that note. When they sang the last word, they felt it hang in the air for several seconds.

Then, applause.

They breathed a sigh of relief. Sometimes it was a risk to get that emotional onstage, but it seemed to have paid off in this case. Not to mention, they felt a lot better, for whatever reason. They seemed to have needed it—even if they hadn't known that. Instinctively, they looked back over to Peders. He was clapping, perhaps louder than everyone else. They gave a flourishing bow.

When they stood up, and looked at him again, he held their gaze.

"Are you okay?" he mouthed.

They nodded, once, with confidence.

That satisfied him. He smiled.

While their nod had been honest, it was strange—they felt tired. No, that wasn't that strange. They had been through a lot recently. They wanted very much to surrender the stage, to go down to him, and sit and drink for a while. But that part of them was warring with the part that wanted to play another, happier song to recover the mood before they left the crowd hanging. And the latter part was the only one of the two that was getting cheers. And money. And they very much liked both of those things.

So they looked away from Peders and toward the crowd, and began to play again.

∼

ASA ABSOLUTELY ADORED GERRIT DIENSTER.

It was the kind of fondness they would've had for a brother, if they'd ever had a brother. Seeing his messy straw-blond hair and genuine smile always made them feel a little bit brighter, no matter what mood they were in. And it seemed like he shared that feeling, as his face lit up when they entered the keep one last time.

"Sir Peders! Asa!" he said, nearly dropping the basket of onions he'd been carrying toward the kitchens when he saw them.

"Master Gerrit!" Peders replied with equal enthusiasm. "Please, don't stop on our account, Britta's likely waiting on those onions."

"She's had me carting vegetables for the past hour," Gerrit huffed, shifting the weight of the basket from one arm to the other. "I'm fed up with it."

"Take her those onions and tell her I asked for you to take me to Hagen personally," Peders suggested. Gerrit gave a little bow of appreciation.

"Yes, sir!"

As the manservant scuttled off toward the stairs, Peders looked around the keep and let out a sigh. Then his brow furrowed. "He didn't even mention the eyepatch," he said. He sounded disappointed.

Asa snorted. "I think he didn't even notice, darling." They paused, feeling their cheeks flush as they used the pet name they had only called him internally up until now. "Oh—I'm sorry, is that all right?" They looked to see his reaction, and saw that his own face had reddened with blush.

He covered his mouth and looked to the side, the same old gesture, the same old Kennet Peders. "It's fine," he muttered. Clearly, it was more than fine.

They snickered to themself at his reaction as he continued to avoid their gaze, probably trying to get his face back to a normal color before Gerrit returned. Luckily, when the manservant reappeared, he proved Asa correct by stopping in his tracks and staring at Peders in a most uncultured way.

"What happened to your face?" he asked, and Asa laughed out loud.

"Thank you for asking, Master Gerrit." Peders' delivery was monotone and Gerrit stammered as he tried to save the interaction. Before he could make it any worse, Peders joined Asa's laughter. "We ran into some trouble on the road."

"I'll say!" Gerrit said. "Well, I suppose that means you have a lot to tell Lord Hagen. I'd better not keep you waiting any longer."

Without waiting to make sure that they were following, he began to walk farther into the keep. Asa let Peders go in front of them. They trailed behind, absentmindedly looking around the hallways as they walked. They were going a different way than they had in the past. They'd only ever gone to Marna's room before, but Marna was better now. Hagen almost certainly had a different place in mind for this conversation.

Sure enough, Gerrit veered sharply into a hallway to the right after a moment of walking, leading them down to a great double-doored room with a large table in the center of it. Asa wondered if it was some kind of meeting room—there was a map in the center of the table, and several chairs surrounding it, though Hagen wasn't sitting. He stood behind the table and acknowledged their approach with a nod.

When he didn't look like he was about to cry, Hagen cut a much more intimidating figure, standing up straight with his chest puffed out. Back at the beginning of this journey when Asa had first learned Hagen was the prince of this land they had scarcely believed it. He had seemed weak, and scared, and sad. But now, seeing him stand at the head of this great table, waiting for their presence with an air of decorum, they believed it.

Which made what they were going to have to tell him that much more difficult.

Lord Hagen didn't smile at them when he saw them this time. He waited until they were in the room with him, then looked to Gerrit first.

"Thank you, Gerrit, you're dismissed. Please close the door for us."

Gerrit gave a bow, and with an encouraging smile directed to Asa, he ducked back out of the room. The doors shut behind him with a loud creak and a thud.

The first words Hagen spoke to them were relieving. They were of concern. "Good god, Sir Peders, what's happened to you?" he asked. The intensity of his expression faded a tad as he scanned Peders' face—the eyepatch did a poor job of obscuring the still-red wound that had healed a good deal, but not completely.

"I'm fine, my lord," Peders said with a soft smile to try and reassure him.

The two spoke fondly to each other. It was clear that though Hagen was giving the orders, it wasn't because he didn't think of the other man as his equal. In fact, if Asa hadn't secured their relationship with Peders before this meeting, they might have felt a little jealous at the warmth in Peders' voice or the way that Hagen looked like wanted to fret more but was only held back by the more pressing questions at hand.

"Very well. I'm sure I should hear the whole thing in order. Give me your update," Hagen said.

"Well, it's good and it's bad," Peders said.

"Start with the good," Hagen said. "I'm not sure I can take much more of the bad without something good first."

"Right. Well, we found out who was responsible for Marna's illness. It was a woman named Maryska Lindahl. She was an old companion of mine, one I knew closely—hence the . . . particular level of intensity to my injuries." Peders motioned to his eye, and Hagen clicked his tongue.

"Quite a coincidence," he said. "But I suppose there are only so many in your line of work to be found, it's bound to happen now and again."

Peders pursed his lips. "Not quite," he said. He paused—as much as Asa felt the pause was excellent for dramatic effect, they knew that he was most likely trying to figure out how to say what he needed to say next. "It seems like her involvement was directly contingent on you being convinced to hire me. Which leads me to the bad news."

"To hire you?" Hagen had no idea what Peders was about to tell him. He scowled in thought, trying to think of what could be meant by that. "But you were recommended to me by—" His eyes widened.

"By the king." Peders said it so that Hagen wouldn't have to. "I'm sorry, Your Highness, but your father was the one behind your daughter's poisoning."

"That doesn't make sense—" he started to protest, but his scowl darkened as he began to think over the details. "No—so you're saying that my father knew this would make me desperate enough to reconnect with him? That he hoped I would come to him, knowing I've never dipped my toes into the darker parts of his life, and then . . . what? He'd recommend you to me as part of his bargain with this Maryska?"

"Yes, that was the deal. Maryska drove you to him, and you drove me to her. Gold was never the cost, nor the reward."

"How did you find this out?" Hagen asked, snapping his head up to meet Peders' and Asa's eyes as he looked back from one to the other for explanation. "Perhaps she was lying to you, trying to start a war—because this could start a war, you know."

Peders cringed at that. "I highly doubt she was lying, Your Highness, given that she was moments away from a very easy attempt on my life. She was telling me simply for her own gratification."

Denial no longer an option, devastation washed over Hagen's face. "I suppose that there's no question, then." Then he paused, and a new question occurred to him. "However did you make it away?"

"That was Asa's doing." Peders gestured to the bard, who gave an awkward smile.

"She didn't expect me to play any part at all, honestly, I just caught her by surprise. But I can back up what Sir Peders is saying. She explicitly said that the king was behind all of this, and that he did it to get your attention," they confirmed.

Hagen stood tensely. He stepped away from the table, and wandered toward one of the grand windows that were stained orange and green, casting colorful light into the room as much as it shaded them from outside eyes. There he stopped, and stood silently for a while. "I'm glad you're both safe," he said finally.

"As much as we are sorry that we have to be the bearers of this news," Peders replied.

"What did you do with her?"

"We surrendered her to Grankoping's authorities. They'll turn her over to you the moment you say the word."

There was more silence. Then, Hagen turned to Peders and said with desperation, "Now what do I do?"

This question seemed to catch Peders off guard. He looked at Asa for suggestions, but they had none. "My lord?" he asked, confused.

"It's my father, which means this was just the beginning. If he finds out that *I* found out—and he will, since I suppose word will get out soon enough now that Lindahl has been captured—then he'll get worse. He knows where I am. He knows that I know that. What will he do? What can I do to stop him?"

"You mentioned war," Peders said slowly, though it was

clear he didn't want to give the suggestion any more weight than it had already been given.

"I did. I know many were devastated to learn that Marna was sick. Many would take my side if they knew what had happened—if you were to back me up, back up my word. Some would call me a liar, but not enough to stop me from getting the numbers to . . . but it's the last thing I want to do . . . but what else is there?"

Asa could think of one more thing. They didn't know if they dared to interrupt, but if it was between being a bit rude and failing to stop a war before it started, they'd be a bit rude.

"You could disappear," they said.

Peders' and Hagen's heads both snapped to look toward Asa, and they felt their heart skip a beat at the attention they had drawn to themself. "What do you mean by that?" Hagen asked slowly.

"Give up your station," Asa elaborated, "take Marna, and go somewhere your father will never look for you. Don't tell anyone you're going to do it—not your servants, not a replacement. Just go."

"But where would we go?" Hagen demanded. "Nobody recognizes me as a prince, but most high society would recognize me as a lord. And Marna—I can't lead her away from civilization, the wilderness would not treat her well, especially when she's still recovering from her illness."

Peders had been watching Asa since they began to speak. They knew that their reaction was coming from a place of instinct—a place that had led them to so easily abandon their own family and friends and come to a new country all alone. They knew it was something that others couldn't do as simply, but still, surely the effort it would take would be better than war? Surely it would be better than the danger Marna and Hagen would both face otherwise if the king had already been so willing to go this far for the sake of manipulating his son?

They looked to Peders for support and for a moment, they wondered if they had completely overstepped. Maybe they were so out of line that he had no choice but to let them down on this one.

He dropped his gaze, letting it travel over the map on the table.

"They're right," he said, "and I know where you can go."

Hagen's shocked expression only intensified now as he looked to Peders. "If you have a good idea then I'm open to it," he said, seeming to trust the word of the hire-sword far more than that of the bard. Not that they blamed him—they'd hoped that Peders would weigh in for that exact reason.

"Go to Grankoping, assume a new identity there. It's a huge city, full of people to get lost in. More than that, you won't be alone. I know a family—old friends of mine, though these are ones you can trust. You've already met Hana; it's her family, her and another old member of the Hawks. They have a boy about Marna's age. She would have someone to show her around, someone to keep her company right away."

He was sending them to Stefan and Hana? Asa nodded slowly as they thought over his suggestion. They weren't sure that their friends would appreciate what Peders was doing, but they knew that at the very least they'd want to see this through. If nothing else they'd be able to help the prince and his daughter get situated and safe.

"Do you think Miss Oh would do that?" Hagen seemed doubtful. "I don't think she liked us very much."

"She likes you. And even if she didn't, she'd do right by you and Marna. She knows you have no other option—or at least, no *good* other option."

Hagen pressed a knuckle to his lips in thought. It was a lot, Asa knew, but it seemed like he was opening up to the idea. "How long do you think I have to make a decision, Sir Peders?"

Peders considered the question carefully before answering. "Not long. A few days, at most. And I must stress Asa's point—if you do decide to do this, tell nobody you are doing it. Tell nobody where you are going."

"What will happen to my people?" The new stress occurred to Hagen quickly.

"Let the lord of the surrounding lands take care of it. They will, too—I know you're no stranger to a lord dying without an heir. At least one has taken place while you've been in power here."

Hagen was more reluctant about that than anything else, but he was clearly not thinking straight. He leaned on the windowsill and stared at the ground.

"I know this is hard, Your Highness," Peders attempted to console the lord, "but you know what you have to do. And if I may be so bold—I firmly trust you to do what you believe is right."

That seemed to get through to Hagen, and he smiled sadly. "Thank you, Sir Peders. I wish I had the faith in myself that you do."

"If you want me to, I can send word to Hana to expect a guest, a friend of mine."

"I think you should do that, yes." His voice strengthened with resolve as he nodded, talking himself into it. "I'll take a few days to prepare and pack—and then we'll be gone."

It was a hard decision to make, Asa was sure, but with that it was made. They hadn't expected Hagen to listen because unlike Asa, Hagen had duties. He had responsibilities, and people who relied on him. Things would certainly settle over time like Peders had said, but the process would likely be far from smooth for the people of Osternas who had so loved their lord. The idea of leaving them helpless, alone, confused and in need of guidance sent a pang through Asa's heart, even though they knew it had to be the best option.

It was such a specific situation, and so damning. The

empty space left behind to be filled by someone who couldn't possibly fill it—the idea was captivating to Asa, but they couldn't fathom why they'd be so fixated on it. If they thought too hard, they felt confused, and a little bit sick.

The fuzzy feeling lifted from their mind with the realization—this was exactly the sort of thing that would make for a *fantastic* song.

Perhaps one day, when such a song wouldn't put Marna and Hagen in any kind of danger anymore, they would write it.

~

"WE'RE DONE!" Peders shouted the moment they stood outside earshot of the keep. He threw his arms up as he said it, then turned and pulled Asa into an embrace, lifting them in a hug and spinning them around with him. He laughed, a laugh full of relief, before setting them back down again. "Thank god, we're done."

Asa laughed too, feeling equally relieved. They had finally done all they could—finally, they were free.

"A job well done?" they asked. Kennet grimaced.

"I don't know about that," he said, "but a job done, well or not, is better than a job failed. Hana always said that."

"It's a good saying."

The town was before them, and the keep behind them, as they stood on a bridge over a small river that separated the two. They could see the gates locked behind them, and they hoped that they would never see the inside of them again. It was done, like Peders had said, and all they felt was relief. Things may be unsure for Hagen and Marna, but they were better than they had been when Asa had arrived. Whatever happened to them now, it would have nothing to do with Asa.

They could breathe easy again.

"So," they said, planting their hands on their hips. "Did you still want to go to Lange?"

"My dear Asa," Peders said, "after what happened with Maryska, I think it's more necessary now than ever."

Asa grew quiet at that. Even they weren't sure what exactly had happened that night—or why, or if it could happen again. When they had kissed Peders, the feelings had been positive, but those feelings had also been so strong they weren't sure if it had been the same kind of situation. They tugged at the edges of their gloves, pulling them on tighter, and Peders noticed the gesture. He took their shoulders in his hands and looked into their eyes, full of concern.

"He can help you," Peders said. "I'm sure of it."

"I hope so," Asa replied, trying to smile, to be excited about the visit the way they had been before, "because if he doesn't I'm not sure what I'll do with myself."

"You'll stay with me. And you'll be the same brilliant musician and wonderful friend you've been to me since we met. No matter what happened with Maryska, no matter what happens next—I am here for you. That will never change."

That brought a genuine smile to their face, and they couldn't help themself but reach out and cup his cheek in their hands, gently pressing their palm against him and slipping their fingers into his hair. Despite their desire to kiss him again, they forced themself to hold back. They would certainly be doing that again, but not now. Not with the memory of Maryska's terror living near the forefront of their mind like it was.

"Thank you," they said instead. "I . . . I need that, I think, right now."

"There's no shame in needing people, Asa."

Wasn't there? They had never needed people before. They'd always been the one who was needed. But they'd never felt like those who needed them were a burden—even Hana and Peders, whose needs had been so much greater than any Asa had encountered before. They had liked being needed. They wanted to be needed, and yet to need—that was something new.

Something they were going to have to get used to.

But there was no time like the present, no person like Kennet Peders.

"I know," they said, and let him hug them again.

In his warm embrace, they felt ready to do things they had never thought they would do. They felt ready to find themself, the reason they had come here in the first place. Tomorrow, they would begin that search in earnest. And unlike when they had originally come to Bladland, they wouldn't have to do it alone.

END OF PART 2

PART III: ASA

A LETTER TO LUCIEN

My dear parents,

By the time this letter reaches you, it will have been well over a year since I left you. I suppose you must have been going mad with worry—you haven't had any clue whether I was alive or dead, or even where I had gone. It's unfair, in hindsight, what I've put you through. But I have good news. I am alive. And I am well.

I'm in Bladland! You can read that over again if you like, but your eyes do not deceive you. I shipped myself across the entire western sea and to the farthest shore. It's cold here, and grey as all hell. The people have less class as a whole, and the food is bland.

I have never been happier.

You see, I had to leave. I was dying there, even with the sun and the good food. It wasn't your fault, even though I couldn't tell you what I was feeling. It was hard—I did try to tell you, I'm sure you'll remember, but for all my wordsmithing I never really figured out a way to tell you in a way that would make sense. I'm sorry for that. If I could have thought of a way to say it that I hadn't already tried before, I would have. But I feel like I truly did everything I could, used every combination of words I had, and yet I wasn't getting through to you.

So I left without another word, not one. And I won't apologize for that.

I will apologize, of course, that I haven't contacted you between then and now. In truth I hadn't really thought about it. A year passes so quickly when you're constantly experiencing new things, and I was too wrapped up in all that—so busy trying to forget my life in Figaroa that I also forgot about you. I really am sorry for that. But I am writing to you now, as soon as I found it within myself.

Ah, what to say now, now that I've gotten the hard part out of the way.

Let me tell you a bit about my time here! I spent the first few months with this lovely family, the Lars family. They were so kind and they helped me practice my Bladstongue before I ventured farther. I purchased a mule, Emilio, and off I went to find more of the adventure I was craving. It didn't take me long to find it, either. I stopped in this city called Osternas and it was there that I found the thing I'm most excited to tell you about—the reason I'm writing, really.

I met this man. Mother, you'll be worried upon reading that. You know how I've fared with men in the past. And I would be lying if I said this man was special, or different in any way. In all honesty, I think the only thing that's changed is me. I was more open to it, this time—it still took me at least one foible but I managed to be honest with myself, and with him. His name is Kennet Peders, and he's kind, and thoughtful, and a little bit anxious—but mostly, he's so easy to be around. Truly, I feel comfort I haven't felt in years just by being around him.

It sounds too romantic when I put it like that, but am I not a bard?

Anyhow. Kennet Peders. To tell the story of what brought us together would baffle you, worry you, and you might even find it unbelievable. I'll keep it simple and say that we were brought together to help a sick young girl, and we managed to do just that. The girl was very nearly dead when I first met her, but she's doing much better now. It was a lot of hard work, and a lot of traveling, but I met a few fun people along the way! There was a woman named Hana—terri-

fying, but I think Father would like her. She was very practical. And then there was a man named Stefan—very short and very angry. We didn't spend much time with him but I think it would've been fun to. Maybe he would've been a better sport if he were a bit less sober.

But we are done with all that now, which is why I am writing to you. Things have settled down and I feel at ease for the first time in a long time, since before I even left Lucien. And we continue forward. Kennet says that there is a possibility he knows somebody who can help determine the source of my influence. I told him about it, of course, and that was the first thing he said—that he wanted to help me find out why.

Remember how you never cared why?

I'm sorry, I'm getting angry. There's no room for that here. I love you both, and I'm excited to find out what's happening. I hope that when I have something definitive to show you, we can all three sleep easy knowing who I am, what I am, and why I am this way.

Please tell the cats I say hello, and that I miss them.

Your child,

Asa

CHAPTER 1

THE SINGER AND THE STORYTELLER

The area where Kennet's friend Lange lived was home to some of the most gorgeous scenery that Asa had seen in Bladland so far. They had seen a lot—the thick woods heavy with underbrush, the rolling hills with no tree cover to speak of, the lake and the cliffs that bordered it—and every time they had thought the same thing. Perhaps they were just easily impressed, but was that a bad thing? It meant that they were always happy with their place in life, especially if that place happened to be new and exciting.

This new and exciting thing may have been to some people just another forest, but to Asa there was definitely more to it than that. Whereas many of the forests they'd been in so far had been coated with ferns and thickets, this one was littered with large boulders, almost more boulders than trees. They were round, covered in moss, and sat both in impossibly upright positions and also tilted to the side, leaning against each other to form natural structures that the road wound around and through at random.

At one point, the road went directly through a split in one of these boulders, and Asa found themself wondering how such a split had come to be. They imagined a massive stoneworker towering above the trees, bringing down a chisel to rest on the boulder that was easily twice the height of Asa even as they sat on Emilio. The stoneworker would crack the stone in two with an equally massive mallet, and then grateful humans would put a road in the crevice left behind.

"We're almost there." Kennet's voice interrupted their fanciful thinking. He adjusted his eyepatch—he did this often, almost constantly, clearly still not comfortable with the strange cloth on his face.

"You don't have to wear that thing, you know."

"No, no, we decided I would back in Grankoping."

"That was so arbitrary. If you don't like it, you don't have to wear it."

There was silence from their companion for a moment before the honest answer came out. "The wound looks rather awful, though, doesn't it?"

It did; they couldn't lie to him about that. "It does. But it's just you and me out here. We haven't seen another soul in days. If the patch makes you uncomfortable, please don't wear it—at least not when we're alone. I already know well and good what's under there."

Kennet fidgeted with the reins, then sighed and removed the eyepatch. The wound had healed a great deal on their journey, thanks to constant care and attention from the both of them. Nevertheless, it still wasn't pretty to look at—but like Asa had said, they were well aware of that. There was really no use in covering it up.

"I'm just going to have to put it back on in a moment anyway," he said, but he seemed relieved not to be wearing it for the time being. "We really are very close. Look—" He gestured, and Asa saw he was pointing to the edge of the forest. They were coming out of the thicker tree cover to a more grassy knoll, and as they entered the clearing, Asa could immediately see the house that must belong to the man they were there to see.

It had a lovely red roof, that's what Asa noticed first. Then they took in the rest—that it was a stone tower of pale white and cream-colored blocks that shone orange in the setting sun as they approached it. The tower had a smaller, wooden room that branched out from it, and near that wooden structure was a whole mess of vegetation that Asa could see had been tended carefully. They wondered if the bushes they were seeing yielded useful produce—berries, or the like—but their thoughts were interrupted by the first signs of the land's sole inhabitant.

A clear, sharp ringing of an ax hitting wood breached the ambient sound of the forest, reaching Asa's ears as they tilted their head to try and identify the sound. It was rhythmic, and even just from the noise they could feel a power coming from it. They began to get restless from the excitement that had been growing over the past few days—every new thing they saw only intrigued them more.

Before they could wonder much longer, they had begun their approach to the house, and cleared the bushes that had been obscuring their view.

A man stood around the side of the wooden portion of the building, at the base of a stump, setting up a small log to chop before picking up an ax. He considered the log for a moment, then swung the ax up over his head and brought it down cleanly with a loud *THUD*. His hair, which was long, curly, and impossibly red, flopped in his face as he did this. As he turned to wipe it out of his eyes, he caught a glimpse of his new visitors, and he stopped still in surprise.

Asa's expression must have been equally shocked as they gave themself a moment to truly take in their biggest chance at answers. Despite them having nearly no expectations, he managed to exceed all of them. Since he had clearly not been expecting guests—and why would he? They hadn't warned him—he was not dressed to entertain. In fact, despite the rapidly cooling weather, he was hardly dressed at all. He only wore a sturdy pair of boots and a simple skirt of thick brown material that came down just past his knees. No shirt—which drew attention to the second thing.

Kennet had described the man as being an expert of religion, and an ex-Gethinist. They'd known many scholars, so the only thing they'd really expected of this man was for him to have the typical physique of a scholar, or at the very least, to be out of shape. Now that they saw where he was living and the fact that he seemed to maintain it entirely on his own, they weren't surprised that he didn't meet that expectation. His muscle structure was not particularly defined but there was a great deal of strength apparent in his build. The last thing that Asa caught a glimpse of as he fully turned to face them was a spattering of dark plague scars across his back, like streaks of paint flicked off the brush of a skilled painter.

Between the hair, the lack of shirt, the scars, and the powerful build, Asa found themself uncharacteristically speechless.

"Kennet Peders?" Lange broke the silence with incredulity, and Kennet responded with a sheepish smile.

"Hello, Lange."

There was another pause as Lange seemed simultaneously too stunned to speak and in the midst of trying to say several things at once, before he blinked hard as if to reset his thoughts. When he'd done that, he smiled wide, an almost wicked expression when enhanced by his wild red hair and thick, sharply arched eyebrows. "Hell and death, you've been through a bit since I've seen you last! Is that an eye you're missing? God, that's awful. Let me have a look."

"That's fine, I've been taking good care of it—"

It was too late to deter the man, though, and he stepped up beside Starling and took her reins from Kennet's hand, gesturing for him to dismount. Unsure what else to do, Kennet obeyed, and Asa followed suit. They rarely felt overwhelmed by new people—they thought of themself as friendly, very easy to get along with, but this was bordering on too much even for them.

Lange, still holding Starling's reins, looked carefully over Kennet's face. From up on Emilio, Asa had been under the impression that the man was fairly short—not as short as Stefan Bergstrom, but certainly not tall. Now that they were on the ground, however, they saw that he was taller than them, if not almost as tall as Kennet. He didn't have to stretch up at all to examine the man's wounds, and as he did so, he clicked his tongue in annoyance.

"Hmm. Yes, I've seen worse."

"Really?" Kennet wondered aloud.

"Sure," Lange replied with a noncommittal shrug. It was only now that he seemed to notice Asa. "You brought someone with you this time? Very different from the company you usually keep. Much brighter. What are you, an actor?"

"A bard, actually," Asa replied. They pulled their vihuela around their body on its strap to prove it.

"Well! How about that. Just as bad, in my opinion. Or good, depending on your opinion of bards."

"Or of actors," Asa pointed out, and Lange laughed.

"Oh, I like them," Lange said to Kennet. Kennet gave Asa a look that said *See what I meant?* before returning his attention to their host.

"They're actually why I've come to visit. You see, we—"

Lange looked so unimpressed it stopped Kennet's explanation in its tracks. "Always business with you," he said. "I haven't seen you in years, and it's business again. You always need something from me. Have you ever thought that maybe I have things going on and I can't just be interrupted by a washed-up old murderer like yourself whenever you happen to feel like gracing me with your presence?"

Asa was shocked by Lange's words, and suddenly

wondered if they'd made a horrible mistake in coming here, but Kennet seemed utterly unperturbed.

"We both know you have nothing going on," he said flatly.

There was a moment where the two men stared at each other intensely. Asa felt like they should do something, especially since they weren't convinced that Kennet could beat this man in a fight. Just when they were beginning to calculate the distance to the nearest town should Kennet need even *more* medical attention, the tension was broken by a loud bark of laughter from Lange.

"Even so!" Lange said, and he picked up the ax one more time to lodge it into the stump before collecting the wood he had just chopped. "It's been too long since I've seen you for us to jump into business. Let's at least catch up first—please, take your horses around the back, get them some water and all that. I'm going to freshen up, then we can sit inside and have some food—some drink! Doesn't that sound better than business?"

Kennet looked to Asa for approval of that plan, and they shrugged. "We aren't exactly in a hurry," they pointed out, and Lange's grin only grew.

"Perfect. You and I are going to get along well, my friend."

Just as with Kennet, when Lange referred to Asa as "friend" in passing, they felt there was something deeper there—like he really meant it. And just like with Kennet, Asa was equally intrigued by him as he was about them.

∽

ASA SAT cross-legged on the floor in the central room of Lange's tower home, on a thick bearskin rug. They ran their hands through the fur absentmindedly as their eyes took in the full scope of the room around them, then the additional floors that stretched upward. The wooden room that was built almost as an afterthought was Lange's personal quarters, they'd learned, since he'd not entered through the same door that they had and as far as they could tell that was the only exterior door at all.

Beyond that, there were no other rooms—just the one that they sat in, a circular room that was split in two with a fire on one side with a few wooden chairs set up around it, and a table on the other side behind them. It was open, yet cozy, and Lange seemed to see little need to keep it very tidy. The mess was organized enough, with clear categories to the piles of things that sat on different tables and countertops on the dining side of the room. Near the door that Asa and Kennet had entered through there hung a robe-like garment, and a round woven mat—Asa wondered what they were for. It seemed like they went together, since they were the only things on the rack by the door.

Once they had finished fully taking in the room around them, they turned their eyes upward. The sun had set since they'd come in, and with the only remaining light coming from a few candles and the fire in the hearth, Asa strained to make out anything above them. They knew that the tower had to have more rooms going farther up, but all they could see was a dark void. Not even a wooden roof to the room they were in—just some railings that framed a small shelf of a ceiling between them and the darkness. They could see a ladder attached to one of the walls not far from them, leading up through a hole in the narrow strip of ceiling, and they desperately wanted to climb it and find out what lay beyond.

They held themself back, though. It was getting late, and they knew they'd get a chance to look at it tomorrow. Still, it was hard to wait.

When they turned to look at Kennet, who sat behind them in one of the wooden chairs, they saw that he was smiling at their excitement.

"It's a lot, isn't it?"

"Just as you promised," they agreed. "Do you know what

that is?" They pointed to the odd robe and wicker mat hanging by the door and Kennet hummed with interest.

"He didn't have that last time I was here," he said, "looks a bit creepy, doesn't it?"

"A bit. What do you think the mat is for?"

"A mat? I thought it was a half-formed basket." Kennet squinted his eye to try and get a better look, but he was interrupted by their host as he joined them.

"It's my beekeeper's uniform." Lange closed the door to his room behind him, and gestured to the costume in question. He was wearing a shirt now, although only technically. A wrinkled, flowing white poet's shirt was draped over his body but it hung so loosely he might as well have been wrapped in a blanket. "I made it myself. It's all to protect me from getting stung. The 'mat' as you're calling it is a mask, keeps the bees out of my face."

Asa's curiosity only deepened with this new information. "But how do you see?"

"Quite easily, actually. Here, catch." Lange stepped over to where the outfit was hanging and pulled the mask off its hook. With a light snap of his wrist, he sent the disk of woven branches whizzing toward them, and they snatched it out of the air before it could sail over their head. When they held it up to their face, they could see that although the gaps in the weaving weren't big enough to allow a bee through, it was easy to see through when held close to the eyes.

"Interesting," they muttered, mostly to themself, adjusting how they held the mask to mimic how they thought it must be worn. They swiveled their head to look at Kennet, who snorted with amusement.

"I was right," he said, "it's uncomfortable to look at. You look faceless."

"What would you do if you saw a man in those robes with this face come up to you in the night?" Asa prompted.

"Attack them on reflex, probably," Kennet replied.

"So much for changing your ways," Lange teased. He rolled up the sleeves on his shirt as he came around the backs of the chairs to sit in one next to Kennet.

"I said reflex," Kennet protested, and Lange snorted.

"Excuses, excuses," he said. Before their back-and-forth could continue, however, he turned to Asa as though suddenly remembering he hadn't ever met them before. "Kennet's friend! Friend of mine, of course, but Kennet Peders has so few friends I think we'd better acknowledge that first. What's your name?"

"I'm Asa of the Isles. And I'll have you know, I've met a good many people who would consider themselves friends of Sir Peders," Asa replied defensively.

Lange raised an eyebrow. "Then he really must have changed like he said he would. Not only does he have friends, but one of them is from the Isles! I haven't met a Lucien citizen since I was . . . what. . .?" He furrowed his brow, creating a dark shadow over his eyes. "Fifty?"

"Fifty?" Asa echoed. "How old are you?" The moment they said it, they knew they were being rude, but Lange didn't seem to mind.

"Oh, I've lost track. At least sixty," he replied.

"You don't look it." Asa tried to make up for lost ground but it wasn't entirely insincere. They never would have guessed from his looks.

"It's the hair. And the clean living." Lange grinned. "But yes, it's been years since I've been to the Isles. It's the first place I went after I left the church, and I've never visited the same place twice. No time—too many new places to go. At least, there was at the time."

"I'm sorry." Asa stopped him before he could start an entirely new conversation without them. They cast a concerned look toward Kennet, but before they let their assumptions run away from them, they decided to clarify. "Did you say 'left the church'?"

"Exited the Order, I guess, if we want to get formal about it," Lange confirmed, and Asa gave Kennet a shocked and slightly annoyed glare.

"A priest?" They addressed Lange, but they didn't turn back to him right away, as though as long as they weren't looking at him he'd be something different.

"Yes." Lange was audibly amused. "Are you okay, friend Asa?"

"Oh, yes." They gave him another look-over, trying to process the new information. They had seen priests before. They knew what priests looked like—at least in Lucien. Lange clearly was Byvaran, by his accent alone, but the church up there wasn't that different. They would wear the same black and white robes, have the same strict no-nonsense attitude. If anything, as they had explained to Kennet not long ago, the Byvaran priests had all the same qualities of the Lucien priests . . . except worse.

This man was not monochromatic, nor did he seem opposed to nonsense. No, he almost seemed to be the complete opposite, with the ill-fitting clothes and messy home. They would have been angry about this revelation if the anger wasn't so quickly overwhelmed by an entirely new wave of intrigue.

"You're quite different from any priest I've ever met," Asa said, and Lange grinned.

"I'll take that as a compliment. Now you've asked me a question or two, and I've answered, so it's my turn to ask something of you. Something new. You're a bard, I know that. You're Lucien, but I could have told that much from your accent. Here's one, then—I could ask you why you've come to me, or to Bladland, for that matter but I feel that's too obvious—and it'll likely get us into all that business talk I wanted to save for tomorrow. Maybe . . ." He tapped his chin, leaning back in his chair to consider his options. "Ah! Tell me what happened to Kennet's eye."

Asa was taken a bit off guard. "That's not even a question about me," they pointed out.

"Perhaps not. But you were there for the event, weren't you?"

"Yes," Asa admitted.

"And you're a bard, are you not?"

"I am."

"Then you'll be able to tell it much better than he would. I've heard him try to tell important stories like that before—he gets very emotional."

"Hey now," Kennet said, mostly muttering the protest to himself more than expecting it to actually stop the insults from flowing.

"The last time I saw this man, he was in even worse shape than he is now, if you can believe it."

"I can," Asa said solemnly. They didn't know the full story, but they knew that Kennet said he had converted to Gethinism as a way to process what had happened between him and Maryska and Isak. That would place his last meeting with Lange freshly after that incident, and with how Kennet had been affected just by those feelings resurfacing, they knew it must have been even worse directly afterward.

"He didn't speak to me for nearly two weeks. I found him in the woods, actually, at the foothills of the mountains. He was an absolute wreck, never seen a man so desolate. Do you remember that, Kennet?"

"Like it was yesterday," Kennet appeared to be trying to sound cheerful, but Asa worried that this discussion wouldn't be good for him. He had been trying so hard to get past all of that. They reached up toward him, and put their hand on his knee, giving it a soft squeeze of reassurance. The action got a soft smile from him, and when he continued, his voice was stronger. "Those were the lowest days of my life."

"And you hadn't even lost an eye back then." Lange did back off a bit as he observed Asa's movements. He turned his attention back to them, and Kennet relaxed noticeably as he was released from scrutiny. "So, the eye. Tell me about it."

"Right, hold on." They stood up with one final pat on Kennet's knee and fetched their vihuela from where they had propped it against one of the inner walls. As they walked back toward the fire, they tested out a few notes, tuning before they began to speak. "If I'm going to tell this, I'm going to do it properly."

○─

"'An eye for an eye,' she said, and struck like a coiled snake, faster than lightning. I almost heard Kennet's cry before I could even register her movements," Asa said, leaning in for emphasis. Lange was locked onto them, like a child with how entranced he was by the story. For the first time since they had begun, he stopped them from continuing, raising a hand as though he was asking for permission to speak. "Yes?"

"That's wrong, you know," he said. He broke his eye contact with Asa, looking toward Kennet when he said it. "An eye for an eye. The correct phrase is actually 'by the eye, for the eye.' It's about justice like she said, but it's about how retribution is useless. Retribution looks to the eye like a fulfillment of justice, but that's all it is—for appearances alone. The heart is less easily satisfied, which leads to the second half, 'by the heart, for the heart.' It means that true justice comes from healing, through community. But like many scriptures of Gethinism, it's been . . . twisted. The original meaning, entirely lost." He grimaced.

"Even by the correct definition, I think it works about as well as she intended it," Kennet muttered. Lange shrugged.

"The intent remains, yes. I suppose with the kind of work I've dedicated myself to, I find misinterpretations more annoying than most would."

"Your line of work?" Asa completely forgot about the story they had been telling, and it seemed like Lange did too, much to Kennet's apparent relief. "What's that?"

"I'm a storyteller. A story-keeper, too. I've made it my business to travel to as many different cultures as I can and cobble together every story they'll let me hear. I've gotten so many—of the time of gods, of eras long forgotten. Stories of men, women and others who may or may not have been real, but whose impact is as real as you and I." Lange stood as he spoke and began to walk toward his room. Asa watched, curious, but didn't stop him from leaving, sure that he would return soon enough.

Exactly as they expected, he reappeared shortly with something in his hands. He held it up for them to see—an instrument they were familiar with, one made of different lengths of hollow reeds lashed together. They lit up when they saw it.

"Ah, a reed flute!" they exclaimed.

"You're familiar, then?"

"My grandfather played one. I think the island he was from might have originated it—he's the only person in my whole family other than myself that I ever saw play music."

Lange nodded, slightly impressed though in Asa's opinion it was entirely unimpressive. They loved music, and the instrument was local to Lucien. Of course they knew what it was.

"Do you play with other people?" The storyteller picked up a new line of questioning as he resumed his seat.

"I can. Did you want to play? I thought we were talking about stories."

"We are." Lange flashed an impish grin. "But you and I both know—some stories are told. Others are sung."

They couldn't hold back their own smile when they saw his, and at his prompting, the two began to work to tune the vihuela to be able to play along with the flute. Asa occasionally glanced over at Kennet while they worked. Their partner seemed almost half-asleep while the two of them were swept up in their conversation. His head was propped up on his hand, and when they looked over at him he would give them a sweet, sleepy smile of encouragement, but offer nothing more. Eventually, Lange noticed this too.

"Don't fall asleep on us, Sir Peders!" he scolded. "We're going to need to borrow your voice."

This snapped him fully awake almost immediately. "What?" he asked, slightly panicked.

"You know the Woodsman and the Swan, don't you?"

"Gods. I do, but—"

"Well, I won't be able to sing it with this," Lange waved the flute for emphasis. "And they don't know the words. So please, I need you to sing. I'll interpret the story afterward, but the song itself must be sung, and you're the one to do it."

Kennet looked to Asa for help—they didn't want to offer any, though. Truthfully, the title of the song intrigued them, along with the chance to play with a group of friends. They hadn't had that chance in years. And beyond that, there was another new experience attached to it—the chance to hear Kennet sing.

"I didn't know you could sing," they said innocently, and he groaned.

"I . . . I'm not *good*," he protested.

"I don't need you to be good, I just need you to know the words," Lange interrupted before Asa could encourage Kennet.

"I should've lied about knowing it," Kennet grumbled.

"I would've known you were lying," Lange replied cheerfully. "Now come on! We'll get the music started, and you can join us."

"But—"

"Please?" Asa ventured, allowing a little bit of a pout to their tone, and they watched Kennet's expression melt. It tickled them—they'd always known they had this kind of way with him, but they'd never felt comfortable using it before, not when they were just friends. It had felt manipulative. But in situations like this, it was not only harmless but also fun.

"All right," Kennet relented. Asa clapped their hands together in delight before returning their attention to their instrument.

"I'll give you a key and a rhythm, you just follow me, all right?" Lange instructed Asa, and they nodded. "It's a fairly simple folk song. I don't think you'll have trouble keeping up, but tap to let me know if you do."

"I will."

With that, Lange played a single note, which Asa echoed on their own instrument. One, two, three, four—one, two, three, four again and they began to play together. Lange hadn't been lying—with them playing mostly just a few chords, the entire progression repeated with minor variations. When it seemed like Asa had gotten comfortable with it, to the point where they had begun to add some harmonies to the pattern Lange had set, the storyteller turned to Kennet and pointed a free hand in his direction.

Kennet hesitated. He looked to Asa and they wondered if he would give up, so they gave him the warmest smile they could muster. Quickly, he averted his eye. Perhaps it was too much to expect him to sing and look them in the eye at the same time—but he picked singing, after all, because he grounded himself by staring at the fire and began to sing.

His voice was so clear it was startling. Asa was used to his speaking voice, which was soft, and rough, but warm. His singing, by comparison, was clear like a bird singing out over running water. Each word was so carefully pronounced, and each note was held with only the slightest tremor. They were familiar with Bladland folk songs—many of the melodies could be complicated, with trilling note changes in the middle of words, and this seemed to be no different. But

Kennet took each line without hesitation, and Asa's playing almost faltered as they found themself lost in his singing.

Laughter danced in Lange's eyes as he continued to play and gestured with his head, bidding them to pay attention to the lyrics.

At first Asa had been confused as to why a folk song would need any kind of interpretation, but as they attempted to follow the story through the words, they found that it hardly made any sense to them. There was a woodsman and a swan, as the title promised, but a lot of the song repeated words they had never heard before—names of places, they wondered? Eventually, they gave up on making sense of it on their own and took note of just the larger plot details. The woodsman met a swan in a beautiful grove, she offered to give him wealth if he would simply leave one tree standing. For some reason, one that Asa was not sure of, he accepted her offer at first but eventually turned to felling the tree anyway.

The song ended with the swan dying of grief as the falling tree crushed her nest full of eggs, and Asa felt their heart sink a bit at the tragedy of it. When the song faded out, they turned to Lange for his promised interpretation.

"So! This story is a very old one," Lange said, sitting up straighter and setting aside his flute. "It tells the story of a man who is greedy, and makes a deal with an unknown entity for eventual wealth, but there's a catch that he doesn't know yet. Some versions of the story say that it's Gethin, but I think those are later versions that just filled the entity in with the most well-known god. I don't think it was Gethin at all."

"What do you think it is?"

Lange shrugged. "The way that it acts through the song, it doesn't match any of the gods I've read about, so perhaps it's a new one none of us have heard of. Anyway, this deal is brought to fruition when he's told by a swan that he can cut down any tree in her grove except one. As he fells each tree, he finds gold in their trunks, gems and such. As he continues, he is told by this entity that surely the reason that she doesn't want him to cut down the last one is because it holds the greatest wealth within it. He tries three times to resist the whisperings of this entity, but eventually gives in. When he fells the final tree, there is no gold, or gems. It's just a normal tree—but it does crush the swan's nest. When the swan dies of grief, so too does the forest."

"Terribly sad," Asa observed, "but also intriguing."

"Isn't it? It's one of my favorites. I always love a story that doesn't have an easy ending, or an easy explanation."

"I can't say that I always agree, but I can see why you'd think that."

Lange smiled broadly at their approval, and then said to Kennet, "Wonderful singing, Sir Peders. Thank you for humoring us."

Kennet sighed. "Thank you," he said, "but please don't ask me to do it again."

◞

IT FELT nice to be held. They hadn't been in so long, they'd completely forgotten what it felt like. Now, with Kennet's arms around them, they wondered why they had been so afraid of this, so afraid to let themself have this. Perhaps they'd never know why. The fear was completely irrational—so much so that they almost laughed at themself for it.

They could hear Kennet breathing, and thought to themself that he was very much still awake, just by the pattern of his breaths. They couldn't blame him—as comfortable as the floor was with the fluffy rug they had to cushion themselves, it was still a rug. They decided to take advantage of the moment that they had alone together, and spoke softly.

"You lied to me," they said cheekily, and they felt a soft puff of air go over their head as he scoffed in disbelief.

"How's that?" he said back, equally soft.

"You said you weren't a good singer."

"I'm not."

"You most certainly are. It made the story all the more interesting—perhaps I'll have you sing onstage with me one day."

"No, no, don't do that." He squeezed them tighter as he protested, and they laughed lightly.

"You're really depriving the world of a wonderful sound, but that's all right. I'm more than happy to keep it all to myself," they said, and with some slight effort they managed to roll over to face him, pressing their forehead to his. He pressed back gently before pulling away just a bit with a sigh.

"I'm happy to sing for you again, if you ask me to," he replied. "I'd do it in a heartbeat. In fact, I'd do almost anything for you."

"Except sing in public."

"Except that."

They both laughed at that, and Kennet pulled Asa into a kiss. It was a lovely moment, and when they parted, Asa breathed in deep and smiled with contentment.

"Thank you for bringing me here."

"Like I said, anything for you. I hope that we find some answers tomorrow."

"I do too," Asa said slowly, hesitating just enough that Kennet caught the pause immediately and latched onto it.

"Is something wrong?"

"I'm just . . . as excited as I am, what if there are no answers? What if I explain everything to Lange, and he has no ideas? What will I do then?"

Kennet was quiet for a while. It was an echoing of their distress when they had first set off on this journey, only now they had more words to put to the fear. He pulled them closer to him and pressed them against his chest, and when he spoke again, they felt his voice buzz against their skull as they heard it. "Then we'll go somewhere else," he said. "We'll go to the ends of the earth, if that's what you want to do. Or we'll give up and do something else. But I don't think it will come to that. Lange may seem . . . overwhelming to say the least, but he's the most knowledgeable person I could possibly think to go to. If he doesn't have the answer, he'll at least be able to give us new questions."

That was more reassuring than Asa was expecting it to be. Even still, and even as they told Kennet that it made them feel better, they didn't feel any more calm. It dawned on them that they might not feel calm at all again until this visit was completely over and done with.

At any rate, they certainly weren't going to sleep much that night. Their thoughts were far too loud.

CHAPTER 2

DEMONSTRATIONS OF KNOWLEDGE AND POWER

Asa eventually nodded off, late into the night, but their slumber was short and they woke up quickly. They didn't even bother to try and fall asleep again, knowing it would be useless. Instead they lay still and looked up at the rest of the tower, taking in the heights they'd been unable to make out the night before.

From where they were lying they could see it clearly—book shelves stretched up floor after floor, until they stopped when the conical roof started to take shape with exposed beams and a window that was held open by a chain. They could see that every few shelves, a new floor would start, each circular balcony connected by a ladder. It made them want nothing more than to climb up and look around. And why shouldn't they? Lange hadn't come out of his room, but as long as they didn't touch anything, they didn't see a problem with looking around a little.

They had wriggled out of Kennet's embrace at some point during their sleep, leaving them free to move about without disturbing him. Still, they were cautious as they got to their feet, stepping carefully on the wooden floorboards that still creaked softly under their weight despite the care they were taking. Eventually they had made their way to the base of the ladder. After a pause to re-secure the scarf around their head, just to be safe, they started to climb.

As they peeked over the edge of the hole in the second floor, they saw that the books were not just contained to the shelves. They were stacked on a small desk that sat in a gap between the shelves, as well as on the floor next to it. They pulled themself up through the hole fully, and immediately went to the railing to look down at the room below.

Kennet still was lying as they had left him, curled up in front of the fire. They could hear him snoring softly from where they stood, causing them to smile warmly. The rest of the room's setup looked a good deal less cluttered from above, and even less so compared to the way that the second floor was laid out. They stepped back from the railing again and turned their attention to the books on the shelves.

Most of them were bound in leather, some with titles engraved in their spines and gilded in gold. Asa saw that a few of the titles were in Isla, though the stories they claimed to hold were familiar to them. Things like *Stories of the Isles, Vol. 1* and so forth, grouped together neatly despite the apparent chaos of the library. However, the amount written in Isla were largely outnumbered by volumes titled in Northspeak, a language that Asa had never bothered to learn. They'd never ventured very far north, and most of the people they met from Byvar had learned the language of the Isles to do business more effectively since Lucien commerce was so important. While they had some Anjeonese heritage and therefore a reason to learn its language and connect with it, Byvar . . . Byvar had been as foreign to them as Bladland.

They realized that none of the books on this level were labeled in Bladstongue, and wondered if those volumes were being kept farther up. It was tempting to explore farther, but going higher wasn't overwhelmingly appealing. There was something different about heights that were man-made—the cliffs in Hagertrask had barely bothered them, but already the second floor of the tower was making them nervous as they imagined the floor giving way beneath them.

So they descended back to the ground floor, and decided they'd ask Lange to give them a tour later.

For now, they picked up their vihuela. They desperately wanted to play—to revisit the song from the night before, and learn it better, to try and remember the words. However, they didn't want to wake Kennet. He hadn't woken in the midst of their little expedition to the second floor, and it seemed like he needed the rest. They looked over to the single, circular window on the first floor. The weather looked nice enough, so they decided to take their noise outside.

There was a slight nip to the early morning air. Nothing Asa couldn't handle, though. Their playing would join the bright singing of the woodland birds. They walked a bit away from the house, past the block where Lange had been chopping wood when they'd met him, and found a small cluster of mossy boulders that they decided would work well as a place to settle. They could still see the house from where they sat, facing toward it should anyone come to fetch them.

The dampness of the morning dew on the moss threatened to soak through the seat of their pants as they sat, but they ignored it in favor of trying to remember the song. They went for the melody that Lange had played, mimicking the breathiness of the reed flute with light and delicate plucking. They would have to get this down satisfactorily before they attempted to sing along with it, and as they continued to experiment, they realized it might be more difficult than they had initially assumed. With a small amount of chagrin, they gave up on the experiment, at least for the moment. Perhaps it would help if they warmed up first with a song they already knew well.

Rather than repeat their same mistakes over and over again, their fingers changed their motion, and they began to play something familiar—an old lullaby, one of the first songs they had really enjoyed playing when they were first learning. It was their go-to song when they were bored or just wanted to remind themself what it was like to play flawlessly. The key was different, since they didn't want to bother tuning away from where they had played along with Lange's flute in case he wanted to play again later, but it was easy to transpose and they quickly relaxed again.

Not long after they had gotten comfortable, their solitude was interrupted by the creaking of an opening door. Lange stepped out of the wooden structure with a book under his arm, and paused when he saw Asa. He seemed surprised, which in turn caused Asa to stop playing, and the two stared at each other for a moment.

"Am I in your way?" Asa asked when they realized what the problem might be. "I can go inside if you want—"

"Oh, no! No, not at all. Sorry, not used to guests. You're fine right where you are as long as you don't mind a little company."

"Of course not."

Lange came over to the clump of rocks and sat down next to them on one of the smaller boulders, placing himself a bit below them. He crossed his legs, and set the book down in front of him—it was a massive thing, and when he opened it the pages flopped open dramatically. Asa gave a sidelong glance at the writings—they were in Northspeak.

What a shame.

They started to play again, leaving the lullaby behind in favor of some more complicated Lucien classical playing. Their focus, however, was broken now and they found themself stumbling over notes. This was embarrassing—Lange was enough of a musician that they were certain he could tell that they were making mistakes. No use continuing, then. If they weren't going to be able to play well, they might as well not play at all.

"What are you reading?" they asked, since they couldn't read it themself.

Lange looked up at the sound of their voice, and they realized that maybe it had been rude to interrupt and he wanted to read in silence. It was too late now, though; they had already asked. Luckily for them he didn't seem bothered at all, instead smiling widely at their question. "It's a history of southern Anjeonese stonework," he said cheerfully.

"Oh." That was decidedly less interesting than they'd wanted to hear.

"Not as exciting as you were hoping it would be?" Lange snorted as he picked up on their disappointment.

"Not really, no." Asa was honest, furthering Lange's amusement.

"It's more interesting than you think. There's a lot of tradition built into stonework for the Anjeonese. Some say they were taught how to shape stone by the god of Stone himself."

Asa's eyes widened at that. "I've heard some people say that the god of Stone lived in Anjeon during the time of the gods."

"And so it's said. Hard to know for sure when we can't ask him ourselves"—Lange chuckled—"but most accounts agree —if he lived anywhere during his time among men, he lived in Anjeon."

"You study the gods, then?"

Lange shrugged. "Among other things. Mostly, I record everything that I can, any history that I find interesting or useful."

"What made you decide to do that? What makes a man leave the priesthood and devote his life to many gods, instead of just one?" Asa pried, finding the concept more and more romantic the more they heard about it.

"What made you decide to leave Lucien? To visit an old man who lives alone in a hut with nothing but books? What makes a young person like yourself attach themself to a man who's spent his entire life making himself unlovable? What makes you love him?" Lange countered their question with so many of his own in rapid succession that it made their head swim.

"I— Well, it's not quite like that—"

"Of course not. No, that's too many assumptions on my part." Lange sighed. He flipped the page of his book, and Asa wondered if that had been his way of shutting down the conversation, but he kept talking. "Perhaps I'm asking the wrong questions. How about we go back to what I mentioned last night—back to the business at hand, I suppose. What brings you and Kennet Peders to my home? He hasn't visited me in years, and when I last saw him he was in disarray. And now, this visit is hardly just a friendly get-together. It's about you, he said. So . . . what about you?"

Finally, he was giving them permission to begin. "Kennet thinks I might be a prophet."

This revelation was enough to make Lange abandon his book entirely. He looked up at them, raising one eyebrow in its high arch as he focused on their face. "A prophet?" he repeated. His tone was full of intrigue.

"Yes."

"Why's that? Can you do something unusual? Do you have abilities beyond the natural?"

He asked so many questions. They knew it was part of his profession, and they knew that he was trying to help, but it still overwhelmed them. Strangely, the result was that they were lost for words. "I can."

"What can you do?"

They struggled, as they always did, for a way to explain it that he would understand. "When I touch people, I can change their emotional state."

"Is it an incidental change? Or can you control it?"

"I can control it."

"Is it instantaneous?"

The word he used in Bladstongue was one they were unfamiliar with. "What's that?"

"Does it happen instantly?" he clarified patiently. His attention had been squarely focused on them since the conversation had properly started, and his unblinking attentiveness was a bit unnerving. Nevertheless, they answered him.

"Yes."

"Can you show me?"

It was the same question that Kennet had asked them, back then. And just like then, they hesitated. "No," they said, after deliberating.

"Oh? Why not?"

"The last time I did it to someone intentionally, something happened that was entirely new. It was uncomfortable and I'd rather not go through that again."

"I'm sorry to hear that." There was certainly sympathy in his voice, but it was largely overshadowed by continued curiosity. "Can you be more specific?"

Asa grimaced and began to pluck repeatedly at one of the strings of their vihuela to help them think. "I didn't finish my story of how Kennet lost an eye, but it was then. Maryska came toward me, and when she touched me, I tried to make her afraid. And it worked, but something more happened. I started to see a memory—I think it had to be because it was a time where she felt afraid. It was horrible. I hated every moment of it."

They were afraid he'd ask them to recount the memory they'd experienced, but instead, he seemed more focused on his original goal of getting them to give him a demonstration. "It was a fearful memory?"

"Yes."

"The bad memory came from a bad emotion. So as long as you don't make me feel some bad emotion—I won't give you a bad memory. Does that seem right?"

That made sense. They weren't eager to experience all that over again, be it positive or negative, but with his reassurance they agreed that it was more important to find out the truth rather than preserve their comfort. So they nodded. "I guess that's true."

"Here, then." He held up a hand toward them.

With no more excuses, they relented, and reached down to him. As they did, they picked an emotion. Joy was hard, since he was clearly already feeling that just from the prospect of what he was about to experience. They had to pick something good, but something distinct. Right before their hands met, Asa settled on longing. As they drew from their own feelings of homesickness and longing for the past, and their hands met, it happened again.

But just as he had said it would be, it was better this time. The memory was soft. They were sitting in a room of white stone, near an elaborate arched window. It was a cushioned bench seat that allowed the person sitting in it to look out over a courtyard with beautiful flowers, and they could smell lilacs. When they looked down, they saw that they were holding a stone mug full of hot tea, the scent of which intermingled with the lilacs and created a warm feeling that spread over their whole body. There was a stack of books next to them, all bound in black leather, labeled in silver. They had a distinct feeling that they were in no rush. It was early morning on a spring day, and they had all the time in the world to read and relax. They would talk to friends in the afternoon. They would sleep in a plush bed in the evening.

This time when the memory ended, they didn't feel relieved—they were almost sad it was over. As they drew away, Lange looked toward them expectantly.

"Did you get anything?" he said.

"I was sitting at a window, with a lot of books and a cup of tea. It seemed like a comfortable memory."

A smile tugged at the corner of his thin lips. "That was the temple in Byvar," he said. "I was the master of archives, a high priest, so I had a whole personal study that overlooked the courtyard." A deep sigh followed his words, full of the longing that Asa had given him. "It was . . . It was almost like a prison sometimes. Others . . ."

"It seemed nicer than I ever imagined the inside of a church could be," Asa said.

Lange snorted. "Not a fan of the church, are you?"

"Not particularly."

"Can't say I blame you. In fact, I wholeheartedly agree."

With how pleasant his memory of the church had been and how clearly he had longed for that moment, Asa was surprised to hear the fervor in his voice as he disowned it. But before they could get sidetracked by their interest in him again, they forced themself back to the more pressing topic. "But, with all that—do you think I'm a prophet?"

Lange thought it over, running a hand through his long, curly red hair and tugging at his scalp as if trying to stimulate thought. "Hmm. I don't know."

Asa's heart sank when he said it. There it was, their worst fear—that this man would be no help after all, that he would be like everyone else who had seen all of this. Stumped. Another dead end. As they began to stew in this apparent hopelessness, they were interrupted by Lange continuing his thought.

"You certainly are capable of something a prophet would be capable of, but that's not the whole story. I'd have to ask a few more questions, get some more information."

More questions. They could do that, they could answer more questions. Hope flared back up again and they sat up straighter with a firm nod. "I'll answer as well as I'm able," they said eagerly.

"I hope I'm not tiring you out. I know this is a lot, and it's very early."

There was no way Asa was going to slow the momentum they were gaining. "It's no bother," they reassured him. "I love to talk about myself."

That got another chuckle out of him before he launched back into the questioning. "This one might seem obvious so I'm sorry for asking, but I need to know for sure—have you ever met a god?"

Asa shook their head.

"I see." He leaned back on his wrists and stretched, looking up at the sky. "That's what I was afraid of."

"What do you mean?"

He ignored them completely, barging on with the rest of whatever line of thought their last answer had sent him down. "Did this happen suddenly? Do you remember when you first realized you could do it, was it monumental?"

That was an easy answer, even one they could elaborate on. "No, I don't. It happened slowly. I think I might have done it a few times by accident before I realized what was happening. Maybe I've even been doing it my whole life and I just didn't know it. I try not to think about it—there's too many more questions that would raise, and I don't want the answers to them."

Lange nodded seriously, still looking at the sky. Then he sat forward again and leaned his elbows on his knees. "Then, with that, I think I can answer you—no, I don't believe you're a prophet."

Asa felt their whole face scrunch up at his answer. It wasn't a dead end, not exactly. But it wasn't a solution either, and it certainly wasn't satisfying, especially since they had no idea what made him so sure that their one theory was wrong. "Why not?" they asked.

He tilted his head from side to side in deliberation before

he clarified. "Unless you're some whole new kind of prophet, that's not how prophets work. Never before."

"What makes you so sure?" They didn't want to sound combative, so they quickly backtracked. "It's not that I don't believe you, it's just that I want to understand fully. This is the closest I've ever come to something that made sense, and you're dismissing it so cleanly . . . I would just like to know why."

That gave him pause. He considered their words, then began to stand, taking his book up with him. "Follow me," he said, and started to walk toward the house, leaving Asa to scramble after him.

∽

The fourth floor of the tower was exactly as terrifying as Asa had thought it would be, but having Lange there with them helped ease their nerves somewhat. He was even higher up than they were, on another ladder that allowed him to scale the front of one of the shelves to access the tome he was looking for. Since Kennet was still resting, the two kept their voices down, but the excitement was clearly shared by the two of them as he shuffled through the books at his eye level, muttering to himself before he snapped his fingers in satisfaction and looked back down to the bard.

"Here," said Lange, holding out a book that was thin and bound in simple brown leather. They took it from him, and waited for him to descend and continue the conversation he had so abruptly stopped by coming inside. He led them to a desk that was identical to the one they had seen on the second floor, and pulled the chair out. "You can sit on the books, it's all right," he added, gesturing to a stack of very heavy-looking volumes that was roughly the height of a chair.

Asa didn't feel right about sitting on books, but did as they were told, and curiously opened the book they'd been handed to the first page. Written in Northspeak was a short phrase they didn't know, and then a name: Kristoff Lange.

"You wrote this?" they asked.

"Recorded it," he replied, holding out his hand for them to give the book back to him. When they'd done so, he began to flip through it as he talked. "It's one of my many collections of oral histories passed down from generation to generation, stories that may have never been written down by anybody else before me. This specific volume is from the islands off the coast of Lucien—there's a story in here that I think will help me explain myself."

"About prophets?"

"About *a* prophet. Singular."

"I didn't think Gethin had a prophet from the Isles. The only prophet from Lucien I can think of was Angelica Figaroa, and she was from the mainland."

"When did I say it was a prophet of Gethin?"

That got Asa's attention. Kennet had mentioned prophets of other gods, but they'd never heard those stories themself, just the vague concept of it being possible. They leaned in, and Lange smiled at their renewed interest. "Go on," Asa prompted.

Lange cleared his throat, looking down at the page before him, but when he started to speak his tone was so conversational that Asa couldn't tell if he was reading or simply using the page as a jumping off point for a summary. "There is an island so small that it isn't on any map—nor is it visible from the mainland, but if you journey to the westernmost shore of the westernmost island, you can see it as well as you'll ever be able. According to those who live on the nearest larger island, nobody dares to visit it, and the reason why—a creature made of plants. I asked where the creature came from, and nobody had a solid answer, but there were a few ideas. As I continued to travel around the Isles, I would bring up the creature each time, and everyone was familiar with the story—though accounts varied. Eventually, I caught on to a recurring theory."

"That it was a prophet," Asa guessed, and Lange nodded.

"Indeed—a prophet of the god of plants. They call him Verdor. I'm familiar with him as Cobb, but the story doesn't change based on what we call him. The story goes thusly—the island was being visited often, its resources were being over-harvested, and the plants were being mistreated. This angered Cobb, and he decided to take measures into his own hands. Gethin had set a pattern with his prophets, making one every now and again when he felt it right. It's thought that this gave Cobb an idea—to create a prophet of his own."

With everything they had been told so far, that struck Asa as strange. "I never heard of a prophet of Cobb before. That's the sort of thing people base entire religions on, isn't it? Why isn't there a church of Cobb?"

"Well, this is where the monster comes in. Cobb found a man—nobody knows much about who he was before it all happened, but perhaps that doesn't matter—and he touched the man. A prophet is one touched by a god, and so this man became a prophet. But while Gethin's prophets had gained mysterious abilities, abilities that were usually very useful, when Cobb touched this man something much worse happened. The man was transformed—plants grew out of his skin, and his body was warped with wood and bark. He became a horrible twisted creature made of flesh and leaves. The creature disappeared into the jungle of the island, never to be seen again, except in glimpses by those brave enough to get close to the island's shore. Despite things not going to plan, Cobb ultimately got his way—after he created his prophet, nobody was able to visit the island and come back alive."

Asa's eyes had tripled in size over the length of the tale, and they forced themselves to remember to blink. They considered what Lange was telling them—it was horrific, of course, but what did it mean for Asa? They couldn't make any connections that made sense, so they held up their hands in helpless confusion. "I don't understand."

Lange was happy to elaborate, shutting the book again as he spoke. "If you were a prophet of Gethin, you would know it. He would never make a prophet without making it clear that's what was happening, because he always makes them with specific purposes in mind. So it can't be him. And the only account of prophets that we have from other gods demonstrates that in the unlikely event a different god had touched you, the results would be far less predictable."

This was distressing news. Their only lead had turned out to be useless. They furrowed their brow, and bit their lip, trying to process the information—all they found was frustration. "What other options are there?" they asked.

"I don't know. But I don't think prophethood is the answer."

"It could be, though, couldn't it? I mean, that's only one god. And aren't there many more than just Gethin and Cobb? Perhaps there's another god that could do what's been done to me?"

Lange considered this, hemming and hawing to himself. As before, when something occurred to him, he didn't bother to tell Asa about it. Instead he stood and began to wander off toward the bookshelves, and Asa found themself almost left behind again. As they caught up to him, they listened to his mutterings with rapt, stressed interest.

"Cobb is definitely a no," he was saying, "but it does seem that the power of the prophet would indicate the god they were created by. So let's be logical. Not Cobb, no, emotions have nothing to do with plants. Nor do they stone, nor time. What's left, who's left?"

"I don't know. I've only ever heard of Stone, and Life and Death before today. I didn't even know about Cobb."

"Most don't. They know one or two, but not every god

made themself known to every culture. I only know all of these because I went out of my way to look. And yet, there are even more. No, not too many more. Just two more." He stopped, and sharply turned to face the shelves, crossing his arms as he looked upward toward the books. "Yes, two more, but one of them . . ."

"Yes?" They egged him on, but he had fallen persistently silent for once.

"I suppose it could be her," he muttered to himself. "It fits her better than anyone else. And to touch a human without them knowing—it wouldn't be out of the question, not if you take her domain into account."

"Who?" Asa demanded, looking from him to the shelf, following his gaze and desperately trying to make the connection he had clearly made.

"Yes, if it's anyone, it has to be her," he said, still to himself, then snapped his attention away from the shelf and back to Asa. "I think I have a theory. It's still unlikely but it's less of a long shot than I'd originally thought."

It was so hard to hold back the annoyance they were starting to feel at his confusing way of talking, at the questions and the muttering. In fact, it was all they could do to just repeat themself, and hope his answer would be satisfying for once. "Who is it, Lange?"

"Essaim." He said the name like they would recognize it.

"Who is *that*?" Asa couldn't hide the exasperation in their voice anymore.

Lange blinked, then continued a bit apologetically. "Right, I'm sorry." He turned to face them fully. "I think it might be Essaim. The god of the sun, the god of insects, the god of fire."

"None of that sounds like me."

"No, but it's what all of those things have in common— her greater domain, that's what interests me."

"And what would that be?"

Lange grinned wickedly, revealing that some of his roundabout presentations had been intentional to string them along. Before they could get properly angry at him, though, he had finished his little pageant with one word. It came out menacingly, both due to his tone and the implication that came with it.

"Chaos."

CHAPTER 3

CHAOS

THERE WERE MANY WORDS ASA WOULD USE TO DESCRIBE themself. In fact, it was rare that they had a hard time coming up with descriptions, let alone for the one thing they knew better than anything else. Perhaps, at some point, the word "chaos" would have passed across their mind.

Beyond that, it even *seemed* right. Just the word, anyway. They had no real reaction to her name—maybe curiosity, but the same could be said of any of the gods at this point.

Gathered in the floor level of the tower, Lange sat on the rug with several stacks of books on the floor around him. It had taken a good amount of time to gather all the transcripts he'd wanted, and it would have taken them even longer to get them all down safely if Lange hadn't thought of that long ago. They had been able to lower all the books down via a pulley system that Lange had installed in the roof attached to a wooden tub large enough to hold any book in his library.

Kennet was awake now as well, and he was terribly lost.

"I didn't even know there was a god of Chaos," he said, leaning to one side in his chair as he watched Asa pull one of the books off the top of a stack.

"There are many gods you don't know about," Lange

replied, likely in an attempt to console him, but it still came off as condescending. "Bladlanders have many stories about the time of the gods, but specifics have been lost to the ages. Honestly, that much isn't even unique to Bladland. I like to think that I'm the only one with the big picture—and it took me half my life to put it together."

"That's a bit bold, don't you think?" Kennet said with an eyebrow raised, looking toward Asa with amusement. They snorted in agreement, and Lange looked annoyed at their lack of trust.

"Yes, I suppose you're right. There are likely gods that even I don't know about. But I do have the big picture—bigger a picture than anyone else, at least," he clarified. "Especially when it comes to Chaos—and Order, for that matter, because you aren't going to see one without the other."

"That does make sense." Asa nodded. "Are they enemies?"

"Quite the opposite," Lange replied cheerfully. "Which is lucky for us, since much more has been recorded about Order than Chaos—Helice, she's called."

Asa considered that. That name, of all things, rang a bell. "I thought that was the god of mathematics or something."

Lange's grin widened. "Now, why would you know that?" he asked in such a way that Asa wondered if they had said something wrong, even though there was a sparkle in his eye.

"I lived near an architect's guild. They had a shrine with the word 'helice' on it, though I always thought that was more superstitious than anything by the way they treated it. They always put all sorts of odd stuff on that shrine when they had a big project coming up—their models and designs, for one, but also snail shells, or the curled sprouts of ferns. Anything spiraled, actually."

"That's one of her symbols, the spiral. And you're right—she is the god of mathematics. And of the sea. They say that she arranged the night sky with purpose, so that sailors could use the stars to navigate."

"They both have a lot of symbols, don't they? You said Essaim had insects and fire alongside the sun," Asa wondered.

Lange nodded. "Most of these attributions weren't initially to Essaim or Helice—they were individual symbols of what people believed to be individual gods. I more or less just connected the dots. The Isles mentioned a god of insects, the north mentioned a god of fire, and slowly I started to piece together that everyone was talking about the same god. On her own, Essaim didn't make much sense. What did all those things have in common? But then, when I held her up next to Helice, everything became clear."

"Chaos and Order."

"Sun and moon. Swarm and spiral."

"Complete opposites." Asa furrowed their brow. "But you said they're often together?"

"Of course they are," Lange said, and he pulled one book down, flipping through the pages. "They're in love."

Asa's eyes widened. "Oh!" They felt an ache in their heart at the idea of such an odd couple, followed by a thrill of inspiration. "The sun and the moon—in love! How romantic!"

"Isn't it? Everything I gathered on the two of them together was *terribly* romantic. In fact, I think you'll start to put two and two together on your own." Lange gave Asa an expectant look.

They thought about it, and slowly began to come up with the sort of thing they thought he meant. "Is that why wedding ceremonies begin at sundown?"

"In Lucien, yes, that's exactly why. A remnant from the time of the gods."

"And why silver and gold are gifts for lovers—the sun and the moon?" they continued, and he nodded excitedly.

"Here's one you may not realize. When you sweeten a gift

of food for your potential lover, what are you meant to use, in Lucien?" Lange asked.

"Honey," Asa replied readily, "but what does that have to do with . . .?"

"Another symbol. An insect—the bee, that travels in swarms. But where do bees live, friend Asa?" He didn't wait for them to answer. "In a hive. One of the most structurally sound creations in nature. So together—swarm, and structure—chaos and order—and therefore, romance."

"This is all very interesting," Kennet interrupted, leaning forward, "and I think you'll be pleased to know I'm very confused. But what does it have to do with Asa? Do you think that one of these gods is responsible for the way that you are?"

"Lange thinks that Essaim may have made me her prophet." Asa affirmed his suspicions.

"As what? As a joke?" Kennet looked concerned. "I thought the whole point of the time of the gods being over was that the gods stopped meddling in human affairs, and we stopped meddling in theirs."

"That is true," Lange admitted, "but the time of the gods had a beginning and an end. Perhaps that's also true of our time without them."

Asa and Kennet made eye contact again, and Kennet pursed his lips. Asa shook their head. The exact message the two were sending each other wasn't clear, but the general attitude was felt mutually—neither of them were overly fond of being the epicenter for a new time of gods. Kennet took this concern and voiced it first, before Asa could even fully process the implications.

"But this god hasn't been seen since back then. In fact, you're not even entirely sure of her realm, or her activity. You made it all up from your notes," he accused, and Lange rolled his eyes as he pulled down two more books and laid all three out in front of him.

"No," he said, "I'm right. You can doubt me if you like, but it's not as vague as it sounds. If you had all the information that I have, you'd agree with me."

He opened each of the three books to different pages. Each manuscript had an illustration in them—and though each illustration was in a different style, clearly drawn by different people, it didn't change the fact that each drawing was definitely depicting the same thing.

On one side of each page was a woman with fiery hair—not fiery in the same sense that Lange's hair was, as the drawings were done in black and white and the color was impossible to discern. It was drawn as flames that sprouted in radial spokes from her head, like the sun's rays. There was little more to her features, but what was there looked sharp and angular. On the other side of the page was the opposite—a woman composed of softer curved lines, with dark skin. Most notable about this second woman was one simple addition that was consistent across all three drawings of her—a third eye, in the center of her forehead.

Beyond that, each image varied a bit. In one, the sun's hair draped down her back, while in the other it was quite short. Two of the drawings of the moon gave her hair that looked wispy, like thick fog being blown over the ocean's surface, but the third showed her with fluffy and billowing hair like a thundercloud.

Despite these differences, Asa needed no further convincing.

And even more than that, they were entranced.

"They're beautiful," Asa said, standing from where they had been sitting in one of the wooden chairs and coming closer to Lange to get a better look at the pages. They felt like they were looking at pictures of old friends, friends that they had never met. The feeling was indescribable—they knew it wasn't just the gods' beauty, but that was all they could think to ascribe it to at the moment. "If one of them visited me and that's why I'm able to do all this, I wish she would've made herself known. I would have loved to see them in person."

"You may get your chance," Lange said.

"What was that?" Kennet sat up straighter. "What do you mean?"

"I mean, right now this is only a theory. The only theory we have, of course, but it's still just an idea. However . . . there's a chance you could confirm it."

"How?" Asa had heard the stress in Kennet's voice but they found only excitement in their own. Unfortunately, before Lange could speak again, Kennet held up his hand to stop the storyteller in his tracks.

"Asa," he said softly. "Do you mind if we talk?"

Asa looked from Lange to Kennet, and for a second they almost said no. But when they looked at Kennet and saw deep concern written in his expression, they relented.

"All right," they said. "Sorry Lange," they added as an afterthought, and he shrugged.

"Gives me time to gather the information that I need. I'll be here when you get back." He gestured to the door. "Go check on your horses or something."

Asa smiled gratefully at their new friend before turning to Kennet and following him as he stood up and stepped out into the sun.

∼

"HOW ARE YOU FEELING ABOUT THIS?" Kennet only asked the question when they had made it to their mounts' sides in Lange's surprisingly well-built-and-stocked stables, leaning on the side of the stall that Starling was tied up in. Emilio's head was barely visible over the fence between the two stalls, but he was doing well otherwise, so Asa left him alone to join Kennet and Starling.

"I was about to ask you the same thing. You seem unhappy with how things are going, but I'm not sure why."

Kennet shrugged. He ran a hand through his hair, which hung loose down his back instead of in the ponytail he usually kept it in. His hand got caught halfway through in tangles, and he tugged once in annoyance before letting out a frustrated sigh.

"I suppose I'm starting to wonder if he hasn't gotten a bit carried away with this," he said. "It seems both like the easy answer and also too terrifying to even consider. I hadn't dared to dream that gods like this, ones I've never heard of—powerful gods of realms like chaos and order—could be getting involved in humanity again."

Asa nodded along with him. If he had been anyone else, they would have considered this an attempt to give up on them, but they knew he was approaching this from a place of real concern and a good deal of fear. As he had the right to! If what Lange was proposing was even close to true, it was much bigger than just them—why would a god make them a prophet? Why would a god get involved in humanity? What would the outcome be? Of course that sounded scary to Kennet. In fact, it should certainly sound scary to them, too. But it didn't. And that, too, was curious, maybe more than anything else.

"You said he was the one with the best knowledge on this kind of thing," Asa said.

"I did," Kennet admitted, "and he is, but he's hardly unbiased. It almost feels like he's eager to jump on the first sign he's seen of the old gods being active in his life, and that sign is you."

"That was the point, though, wasn't it? That there are gods that have been inactive for eras, or so we thought—and it might be one of them?"

"But *Chaos*, Asa! I don't know what I expected, but it

wasn't that. It wasn't something like the god of the damned sun!"

"I know that! I know that it's big, and it's frightening, and I understand all of those feelings but I also don't feel them—it doesn't feel that way at all to me, it just feels . . ." They struggled for a word, gesturing with their hands to try and conjure it up. "It feels *right*."

As soon as they said it, they knew there was more to it than that. Kennet didn't contradict them, instead leaning forward. "Right?" he asked.

"I feel like . . . so many things feel familiar, Kennet. They have, for as long as I can remember. The way my influence feels, just on the tip of my tongue, like one day everything will come together and I'll know for sure. And this, more than anything, has felt that way. It's so hard to find words for, but when I saw them—I *know* them, Kennet." They paused, and they felt more sure for having said it. "Why do I know them? That's what's frightening—think of these powerful, terrifying gods. And then think . . . think of being *sure* that you know who they are."

"I thought you said you'd never met a god?" Kennet said slowly, edging closer to them and holding out a hand for them to hold. They drew away from him with a shrug. They weren't wearing their gloves, and they certainly didn't want him to feel what they were feeling at the moment.

"I've never seen either of them before in my life. I'm as sure of that as I am that I know them. I know it doesn't make sense, but I also know, without a doubt, that Lange is on to something. I'm not sure if he's right, but even if he isn't, even if Essaim didn't make me a prophet . . . I'm certain, down to my core, that she has the answers I need."

There was a long silence after they had said that. Kennet moved his outstretched hand to their back, resting it there as the two let the conversation hang in the air. When Asa could stay silent no longer, they tried to clarify everything one more time.

"I haven't ever felt this way before. I'm sorry that it's so confusing for both of us—but don't you think it would be better to know for sure than just live the rest of our lives guessing?"

They meant the question earnestly. Part of them thought that if he said no, if he wanted to live in ignorance, they would give up on their pursuit then and there. The thought of it felt like relief. They would go back to being a bard, to wearing their gloves, to vowing not to use this gift ever again. They could just be Asa of the Isles, not the prophet of anyone, living with Kennet Peders. The two could be normal, perfectly average people together.

But he didn't say no. "You're right," he said instead. "You're absolutely right. I'm sorry—this is exactly what I signed up for, no matter how big the god, nor how confusing the feelings."

"Nevertheless, if it's too much—"

"Never." He cut them off. "This is not too much. You are not too much. We're going to figure this out together—and honestly, after this conversation, I do feel much better about it. I'm just . . . tired. We've been through a lot lately, and the thought of all this on top of it . . ."

Asa nodded in understanding. "We could take a break?" they offered.

"Maybe." Kennet sounded grateful for the suggestion. "Let's hear what Lange has to say about our next moves. I'm sure we'll find time to move at our pace."

With Kennet's concerns put to rest, the two began to head back to the tower, but Asa's head had started to swim again. Now that they'd admitted it out loud, it wasn't sitting right with them anymore. And they were beginning to find themself anxious about the very things they had told Kennet not to be anxious about—and more, at that. They almost wished they hadn't come here. They almost wanted to tell Kennet to forget everything, and live in the momentary relief they'd found at the idea of running away.

Always running.

But this time, what would they be running from? Themself?

Was that what they'd been running from this whole time?

It had always been a push and pull, the curiosity and the running. And now they were further from escaping than they ever had been—it was finally time to embrace that curiosity and face whatever was waiting for them. Even if it was painful, they would see this through. For once, there would be no running.

They were going to face themself, and the questions, and the doubts and the fears.

And they were going to win.

∼

When they returned, Kennet and Asa found Lange exactly where they had left him. He was absentmindedly braiding his own hair and when they entered, he looked up with slight interest.

"Everything all right?" he asked.

"I'm fine," Kennet replied, correctly assuming that the question had been mostly directed at him. "Just overwhelmed."

"That's understandable, I suppose." Lange yawned. He gave up on his hair partway through, tossing the half-formed braid over his shoulder and waving to his guests to take a seat. "While you were gone, I found what I was looking for."

"And what's that?" Asa asked as the two sat.

"Your next move," Lange said. He pulled a loose sheet from one of the books that was lying in front of him. It had been tucked between two of the pages, and he unfolded it carefully, smoothing out the creases. "When you've been doing this as long as I have, you begin to forget details—misplace a few, mix them up. Sometimes you forget entire stories. I hadn't even thought about Essaim and Helice for . . . well, for a long time. But when we were talking about it, I thought I remembered that there was something more concrete. Like I said, most of what I know about them is cobbled together from different myths and customs. Their individual domains—figuring that out was all guesswork."

"Are you going to find the point anywhere in that paper, Lange?" Kennet asked. With his anxiety settled, it seemed like his wit had found itself again. Lange didn't react to the jab—he barely even paused to let Kennet speak.

"I have one story about them that addresses the two as one unit. It addresses them as the gods of marriage, so without knowing their unique domains beyond that, I probably wouldn't have thought to connect it to Asa. But it may come in handy even without a direct connection."

"Why's that?" Asa asked.

"It gives an example of a human summoning the two gods—mind you, it would summon both of them, but I don't think that would be a problem. It might even be beneficial to have Order there for your conversation with Chaos."

Asa saw Kennet tense up again. So Lange hadn't just been implying it, he'd really been genuine. They were going to try and contact these gods. Asa hadn't thought that was possible, but then again, perhaps it was just that nobody had tried. It was, like Kennet said, part of the agreement between the gods and humanity. They would stay out of human affairs. Humans would not meddle with gods. But if Asa was a prophet, then human affairs had already been meddled with. There was free rein to meddle back.

"Is that the only way? Summoning, I mean. It sounds rather final. I thought in Gethinism it's taught that Gethin can hear prayers addressed to him no matter where he is. Does it not work the same with other gods?" Kennet asked.

"Gethin can only hear us because he's listening," Lange explained. "That's how we understand it, anyway. He cares to listen to humans, he's made it his business to hear us when we call. He's made himself available. The same can't be said for the other gods."

"Then why would they listen to a summoning?" Asa interjected, beginning to catch on to what Kennet was getting at.

"Well, I'm getting to that. The story I'm about to tell you takes place after the time of the gods—if you let me tell it, perhaps you'll understand."

Asa and Kennet apologized in clumsy unison, and both fell silent. Lange waited, perhaps expecting one last interruption, but when that interruption didn't come he referred to the paper and finally began his story.

"Long ago, in the mountains of Byvar, just after the time of the gods had ended, there were two lovers. One was of the Darach people—like me," Lange interjected with a gesture to himself, "the nomads who wandered far north. The other was of the Kingdom of Byvar. The two peoples were at war at the time. Byvar's king was pushing north, trying to integrate the lands previously wandered by the Darach into his kingdom. Because of this, hatred had begun to form between the two peoples. This, naturally, affected the two lovers in our story. Neither culture allowed for them to marry one another—and after the way each of them had seen their lover treated by their own culture, neither of them wanted anything to do with those cultures, anyway."

"Even more than that, they no longer felt safe in their own homelands. With nowhere to turn, and no safety to be found outside of each other's arms, they became desperate. They decided to call out to the gods—two gods, in particular. They figured that the only people who would understand them were two lovers even more mismatched themselves, the gods of love and marriage." Lange paused, and squinted at the paper. "Things get a little muddy here—all accounts say they climbed the highest mountain available to them, but there's some disagreement on the exact day. Some say the two summoned the gods during an eclipse, while others say they did it during the sun's peak on the solstice. They don't even say *which* solstice. Maybe it doesn't matter."

"I hope it doesn't matter," Asa said, "I don't think we can wait for an eclipse. I don't even know how to find out when the next eclipse would *be*."

"I think there are some who study the night sky that might be able to predict it, or at least get close. But you're right, that's a lot of work, especially when the winter solstice is right around the corner."

"So the solstice it is. On a mountain. What next?"

"Right." Lange continued, "Now, like I said, this was after the time of the gods. The gods, who had been pretty explicit about not wanting to be bothered, as Kennet brought up. So these two lovers needed a way to show that they were serious, that they weren't wasting the gods' time. So, together, they held a candle." Lange clasped his hands together in demonstration. "And they tied their joined hands together with twine. Some accounts say it was red string specifically, but I can't see why color would be important. Then, they lit a candle, and let it burn down. Even as the hot wax dripped onto their skin, even as the fire and heat grew closer to burning them, they showed that they were willing to brave the pain of life for each other. And as a response, the gods answered their call."

"I see." Kennet nodded seriously. "You think that repeating this specific ritual will do it?"

"I think it's the best chance you've got," Lange replied.

"It seems simple enough," Asa murmured as they considered the idea. "And even if it doesn't work, I don't see the harm in trying."

"Precisely. Even if it doesn't work, what have you lost? Some time, and maybe a few hairs off the back of your hand to the candle flame," Lange said cheerfully.

If it didn't work, they would have tried, at least. If it didn't work, they could give up, and perhaps live knowing they'd done their best. Peace was still an option here.

Frankly, they were more frightened of the version of their life where it *did* work.

Kennet was watching their face, and it was almost like he could see their decision from their expression, because he didn't wait for them to say anything before he turned to Lange with a sharp, decisive nod. "So we'll do that, then. Go north to the mountains for the solstice, light a candle, off we go. Nothing to it."

Lange looked thrilled. He gave a little shiver of joy, and slapped the paper down on the book, standing so quickly he almost knocked one of his stacks over. "Right! Then you'll need some things. Hold on." He had the decency to announce his departure this time, disappearing into his room before returning with a few things in his hands.

As he approached, Asa could discern a bit of what he was carrying. There were a few sheets of golden-yellow material with a little sheen to it, and a bundle of thick white thread. Asa craned their head to get a better look, and asked, confused, "What's all that?"

"Beeswax," Lange said. "And wicks. I figure if you're going to need a candle, it might as well be a beeswax one. We'll make it small—then you won't be sitting on a mountain in the winter for longer than you have to be."

"You make your own candles?" Asa was impressed, examining one of the sheets as Lange held it out to them. They took it and turned it over in their hands—it was almost translucent, and seemed very stiff. They wondered how you were supposed to make a candle out of this.

"I try to make sure I'm as self-sufficient as possible. The

bees and I have an understanding—they let me have some wax, and I promise to use it well. I think they'll approve of this use."

"I hope so, wouldn't want to anger the bees," Asa said half-seriously. "How does it work?"

Lange held out his hand to take the wax back from them. "Let me show you."

CHAPTER 4

COMING TO TERMS WITH CONDITIONS

Asa held up the small, golden candle, and inspected it from all angles. It seemed like they had made a million attempts—warming the wax by holding it just the right distance away from the fire, to soften it. Dipping the wick in a small mug of hot wax that Lange had set on the hearth to melt. Rolling the wick in the soft sheet of wax until it was a tightly wound little candle. Some of their first tries had been . . . less than desirable. Misshapen, a little warped—Lange had seen their dissatisfaction and promised that they could keep going until they were happy with one. He would keep their defects and use them around the house.

This one, though, was much better. It stood up straight on Asa's palm, and though it was only the size of their index finger, it stood strong. They nodded in satisfaction.

"I think this is it." They turned to Kennet with a proud smile. He was fumbling with an attempt of his own and stopped to look up at theirs. His shoulders sagged when he saw it, and he gave a sigh of relief.

"I think it is," he said. "Thank god, I was beginning to think we'd be at this all night."

"Let's give it a finishing touch," Lange said, and he held

his hand out to Asa. The bard was hesitant to hand it over. They'd worked so hard on it, and they didn't want to have to start over. Nevertheless, they relented, and gave him the candle, curious to see what he would do.

Lange took a small penknife out of his pocket and carefully held the tip to the flames. After a moment, when the blade was suitably hot, he gingerly pressed it into the candle, working for a few minutes to carve something into its surface. When he was done he held it out to Asa again.

He had carved a sun and moon into the candle. They were small, and simple, but lent an undeniable charm that Asa couldn't help but appreciate.

"Thank you," they said warmly. "It's perfect."

"Happy to hear it. I'm glad I can be part of this—wish I could come with you," he added, staring into the fire. "It would really be something, you know. To see a god."

"I thought you said you were a high priest," Asa said as they took the candle from him fully and watched him stare absentmindedly at the flames.

"I was."

"So don't high priests get to see Gethin? I thought that was . . . well, their whole thing."

Lange laughed, though his face didn't show any joy. Really it was just a sharp puff of air leaving his nose as his gaze stayed fixed on the hearth. "I guess I wasn't counting Gethin," he said, half to himself.

"Wasn't counting? Why wouldn't he count?" Asa hadn't ever wanted to talk about Gethin before, least of all with a priest. But Lange felt different. He felt safe. There was something in the way he talked about his religion that told Asa they were closer to his opinion than anyone who had ever been a priest should be.

Lange sighed. He finally looked back to his guests, smiling sadly. "Well. I guess because he's not very godly. At least when I read the stories of the other gods—even the god that

Gethin *used* to be, I think that's what a god should be. And then I think of the Gethin I know and . . . well, it's not the same."

There was a longing in his voice, similar to the longing Asa had been willing into him when they'd shown him their powers. It was deeper this time. That's how they knew it was genuine. However much he longed for the past, he longed for this more. He longed to meet the god he thought he deserved, the god he wanted to worship. Not whatever he had seen.

"What was he like?"

"I thought you didn't like talking about Gethin," Kennet said from beside them. He had set aside his failed attempts at candles and seemed like he was beginning to nod off. They had no doubt that their constant talk of gods and myth was exhausting to him. Even if Kennet was the religious one of the two of them, his faith had always seemed practical, and his description of myth had been personal. It wasn't that he was incurious—just that he had other things to worry about. Like rest. They thought he deserved to rest.

"I don't, usually," Asa replied. "But I don't think I mind it from Lange."

"Hmm," Kennet mumbled. Between his own interjection and Asa's answer, he had already slipped halfway into slumber. "Well, good for you."

"Do you want us to move so you can sleep, darling?"

"Mmm." His reply was unintelligible.

"Let's move." Asa interpreted the reply in his favor.

"I know just the place," Lange said, and he gestured to the door. "Sleep well, Sir Peders."

Kennet opened his eye just a sliver and smiled just a hair. By the time they had made it out the door, he had fully fallen asleep where he sat.

The stars shone brightly overhead as Asa and Lange sat on top of the roof of his room. It was a sturdy, flat surface with similar tiles to the ones on the conical roof of the tower, but it was clear from the pattern of wear that Lange often came up here to sit. He brought two thick wool blankets with them, laying out one to sit on and offering the other to Asa, which they accepted. As they wrapped the blanket around their shoulders, they wondered if he would sit. He stood with his back to them, hands clasped behind him as he stared up at the sky.

"I think Gethin is finished with humanity," he said when he finally spoke. Asa blinked. It hadn't been the kind of thing they were expecting, but it intrigued them even more to hear from someone who used to be a holy man.

"What makes you say that?" they asked, and he shrugged.

"He never gave us input. We would go to meet with him and he seemed, to put it bluntly, disinterested. He would ask stupid questions—it felt like he was *trying* to egg us on. The plague—are you old enough to remember that?"

Asa nodded, then realized that he couldn't see the gesture since he still wasn't facing them. "Yes."

"A lot of people think we were taking that thing one day at a time, no plan to speak of. And they're right—we were. I saw many of my cohorts arguing day after day, and do you know what happened when I suggested that we take the issue to Gethin? They *laughed*. They said it would be a waste of our time. Our own god! A waste of time! And you know what's worse? They were wrong!" Lange gave a desperate, baffled chuckle at how unfortunate it all was. "He told me what he wanted us to do, he really cared. At that moment, I realized he'd been waiting for us to ask the right questions. And when I asked, he answered—open your doors to the needy. Don't charge fees for your medical assistance. Collaborate with Lucien, distribute recipes for the cures they had found. That was the first we heard of them having cures at all, actually. I took all of that back to the others. And they refused to listen." He turned to them finally, and Asa saw a somewhat forlorn look on his face.

"Why wouldn't they listen? Isn't he their god, too?"

"You said you don't like the church."

"No, I don't."

"Then I think you already know the answer. His words didn't suit them. It would cost too much money, put too many priests in danger. All selfish, heartless reasons. And as I heard them, I realized how many times before—how many times his words hadn't suited *me* and I'd ignored them just as my cohorts were ignoring him during the plague." He paused, almost as though to sit with his mistakes for a moment. "That was the last time I heard him try. After that, he gave up completely. I left not long after."

Gave up? Gave up on what, the priests? On humanity? They felt horrified by the implication. "Then what is he still here for?" they demanded. "What is the church there for, if he's given up?"

"I don't know. Perhaps he hopes they'll find their way back eventually. Back to the creed."

"Damn his creed," Asa replied sharply, and Lange raised his eyebrows in surprise.

"Pardon?"

"It's too vague. Too easy to twist. They can use it for their own motives."

"Who's they, then?" Lange wondered aloud.

"The priests." Asa waved his question aside with the answer that they had considered to be obvious.

"You're right. We did twist his words. I suppose it's our fault that he gave up on us, after all."

"No. No, it's not your fault. If he wants to give up on humanity, you're right: he's not very godly, is he? If the priesthood is broken beyond repair, why bother with it? Why not go back to doing what he did before? There was a time when the priests didn't exist at all, and he did just fine helping humanity then. So help humanity! Damn the church and damn the priests! What are they good for? Look at you, for example. You're more good without them than you were with them. Perhaps the same is true for him."

"Are you saying a god should abandon his church?"

"From what you were saying, it sounds like he already has."

The two fell quiet after that. Asa felt their blood running hot. They were talking on things they knew nothing about, of course. Things they'd even made a point of not getting involved in. But something about this, all these excuses Lange was making for Gethin, it made them angry. If Gethin cared so much about humanity, about life and death, why did he keep trying to bail out the sinking ship that was the church? It seemed like he cared more about his own ego than the actual well-being of his self-proclaimed domain.

They didn't know what else to say. They had asked the question—about Gethin and what he was like—but then they'd gone and thrown their own ideas of the answer into Lange's face instead. They wanted to ask again, but they felt like things were too tense. They had ruined it.

Lange looked at them critically. "It sounds like you think you'd do a better job in his place," he said, and they could detect a hint of laughter in his voice.

Asa snorted. "Maybe I would," they said.

"If it turns out that you're a prophet of Essaim, they might form a whole new religion around you, you know. Maybe you'll get a chance to show Gethin how it's really done."

Asa laughed. "I hope not! I like attention, but not that much."

"Then if you get the answers you're looking for, maybe you'd best keep them to yourself," Lange suggested. "I get the feeling you're only doing this for your own self-gratification, which is how it ought to be. I had to do a lot of thinking when Kennet and you went out to the barn. I got to wondering whether I should even help you at all. Some of Gethin's prophets—their gifts from Gethin led them to be less-than-stellar people. Some of them let it get to their heads."

"My head can't get much bigger than it already is."

"I figured that out pretty quickly," Lange said laughingly. "I can see why Kennet got involved with you. You're very interesting. I wish I could see this through to the end."

"That's the second time you've said that. Why can't you? It seems like the kind of opportunity you shouldn't miss, especially given how many of your accounts you've been forced to record second or third hand."

"Sixthhand, sometimes," Lange agreed, but he held fast. "But no, it's tempting . . . but it's not my place. The ritual is meant to be private. So you and Sir Peders . . . I think you'll have to do it alone. I don't want to risk ruining it just by being there."

Asa felt their cheeks flush, but they nodded in understanding. "I see."

"You'll have to come straight back and tell me all about it, though," he added quickly. "I won't forgive you if you don't."

"I promise you," Asa said, "if everything goes to plan, or even if it doesn't—you'll be our first stop the moment it's over."

That seemed to satisfy Lange. He stood up again, and stretched. "Well," he said, "if that's all settled, I think it's time to get to bed."

"Let's," Asa said. "Now that we've finally got all this out of the way, maybe I'll actually be able to sleep."

∽

EVEN WITH THEIR plan in place, Kennet and Asa had realized fairly quickly that they were in no rush. They had time for the break that Kennet had sounded so eager to take—and what better place to start taking it than with Lange? Asa had no complaints about it. They enjoyed Lange's company very much, and Lange seemed ecstatic to have guests for longer. Asa wondered how such a personable man could be a hermit like he was. Not one to leave things to the imagination when they could get the explanation straight from the source, they asked him.

"I have limits," he answered, starting to gather the books that had begun to overflow into the walkways around the ground floor. "At some point I'm just done with company. Trust me—you'll know when it happens."

Asa couldn't imagine what he meant by that. They liked their alone time as much as anyone—in fact, they needed it. But they had never really been desperate to leave company to find that quiet. They wondered if living in isolation had done anything to help or hinder his tolerance for other people. Asa imagined that if they ever lived alone for very long, they'd either go mad from boredom, or they'd lose patience for other people entirely.

Lange seemed to keep himself busy, though. Besides the books there were the bees, and the plants, and the house itself, which seemed to have undergone extensive upgrades and repairs.

He began to load up the pulley bucket with books, then looked toward Asa, who realized that they'd been staring at him. "I do leave now and again," he added. "I used to a lot more. Recently I've started to only make local trips. I think it's the age, but worldwide travel seems a lot less practical, these days."

"Does that mean your work is complete?"

Lange laughed. "It never is," he replied. "It never will be. When I die, I'll have left nothing behind but perhaps a solid foundation for the next person with an insatiable curiosity for this kind of thing."

Asa considered that. "How will people find it all, then?"

"I'm not some kind of recluse. Plenty of people know that I live out here. I've got people who come by every few months, just to make sure I'm still alive, and bring me some things I can't make for myself. They have instructions should they turn up and I'm gone for good."

That made more sense. For all that this man seemed to be a mess, it was all just a result of not having to put on airs for others. When it came down to details, he had plans, and he had strategies. There was a system, which was apparent by the way that he carefully arranged the books in his bucket. Asa had no idea how things were organized in the tower, but Lange seemed to know each shelf by heart and had refused any help in putting things back.

"Why don't you get comfortable?" he said. "I have chores to get done, it'll take a moment before I can get back to being my wonderful, entertaining self."

"Is there some way I can help?" Asa prompted him for what felt like the tenth time that morning. "I won't touch the books, I promise."

Lange thought over the offer this time, which was an improvement. "You and Kennet have come a long way. Don't you want some rest?"

"He needs the rest, that's certainly true, but honestly I'm unscathed. Just had some poison, but I'm pretty sure that's all out of my system by now." Asa straightened their posture a bit. "You've been a wonderful host. It's rude not to help out a bit."

"Hmm. Lucien hospitality." Lange muttered, almost bitterly, though he laughed after he had said it. "Turning up unannounced for dinner is fine as long as you do the dishes after."

Asa wasn't sure why he was making a joke of it. It was just

as he said. They'd always been taught that as long as they didn't add to a workload, they were welcome wherever they'd land. It had worked out fine for them most of the time, even if it had been a bit awkward when they'd first arrived in Bladland. What was more frustrating was Byvarans—always so protective of their routines. What was wrong with a little help, if it meant they got more time to spend with friends later? What was so important about doing everything at the same time every day?

It seemed like they had gotten through to him either way, though, since he gestured for them to follow him out the door.

"I'm all right with a little help, I suppose," he mused. "But you'll have to do something else for me in return."

"The chores *are* something in return, Lange."

"No no. You misunderstand. I mean something *fun*." He grinned at them. "I don't know what exactly, just yet, but you'll have to trust me."

From what Asa had seen, they felt confident in trusting his definition of "fun." So far, fun had been tales, drinking, and good food. They nodded enthusiastically in agreement. "I feel like it'd be foolish not to."

The two made their way out into the garden behind Lange's room, where he pointed out various late-harvest vegetables with pride. "These gourds are far too big to eat," he said as he gestured to one particularly massive specimen. "But I like to hollow them out and dry them for storage."

"Storage in a gourd?" Asa asked skeptically with a snort.

"Yes." He looked unimpressed by their attitude. "You cut off the top, you hollow them out—sticky business—fill 'em with sand, they dry up all hard."

"So you're asking me to hollow this thing out?"

"Are you going to say no now that you know what it is?" He was challenging them, they knew. Did he want to be left alone that badly?

"Do you want me to leave you alone? Is that what this is?" they challenged him back, and he looked startled.

"Oh! No. Ha. No, not at all. Truly, this is what I had on my agenda for today."

There was a moment of tension before, seemingly because he simply didn't know what else to do, Lange walked away again. Not far away, just to the nearest gourd, which he severed from its vine with a hardy knife he took from his belt. Straddling the gourd, he cut a neat, even ring around the stem and with a solid twist, an inch of the top came clean off.

Asa gave the guts of the gourd a calculating look. Then they unbuttoned their gloves with determination and gave Lange a nod. "All right then," they said as they rolled up their sleeves. "Off we go."

Lange took an even larger gourd for himself, and the two settled on the soft grass to do the dirty work of hollowing them out. The first step was to dig the innards out by hand, a step that Asa found as enjoyable as they found it uncomfortable. The feeling of the slime in their hands wasn't unpleasant, but it was certainly new. A few times, they paused in their digging just to squish the pulp between their fingers.

For a while, the squelching of this process was the only sound that the two made. Asa felt like they'd been talking a lot—so had Lange, but it was his house. If he preferred to work in silence, they would work in silence.

Of course, this didn't last for long at all.

"Had a lot dropped on you, haven't you?" Lange asked without looking up from his work.

"Yes," Asa agreed as they pulled a particularly long clump of stringy slime out of the gourd.

"How are you feeling?"

Asa paused. They had thought about that a great deal but hadn't reached a conclusion they were happy with. "I'm not sure. I was thinking more about what we talked about last night, though."

"Oh? Which part?"

"Gethin." They resumed their work, busying their hands to match their busy mind. "How you've met him. Well, less about Gethin specifically, I suppose. More about . . . gods in general."

Lange looked in their direction, raising a bushy eyebrow in questioning.

"I've never met a god before," they elaborated when he didn't ask them anything specific. "Obviously. We've been over that. But now I'm going to, and I'm . . ." They struggled to find a word that felt accurate. "Afraid?"

"That's likely a rational reaction," Lange said quickly after they had voiced their concern, as though he'd known exactly where they were going with it.

There was another long pause. Asa looked up and Lange had completely refocused on the gourd. ". . . so?" they prompted.

"Hmm?"

"So, what's it like? Meeting a god?"

"Oh!" He sat back on his heels. "I'm sorry, I forgot. Like I told you, I don't really consider him a god anymore. Too . . . familiar. But, if I take myself back to the first time I ever faced him, I think I can get back to what you're asking for. I was pretty young for a high priest, all things considered—it was me and a friend of mine, we got appointed at the same time. Well . . . I use the term 'friend' loosely. A colleague, more appropriately. She and I never got along until the day I left. Having someone I actually *liked* there with me might have made things easier. Luckily, you already have that advantage over me."

Asa laughed. "That's true, I do rather like Kennet."

"I can tell. Much more than I ever liked Harriet, that's for certain." Lange laughed along with them. "No, we had this kind of combative relationship so I guess I probably looked as confident to her as she did to me. I know, at least on my part, that it was all fake. I was scared as hell. He's Death, you know, and they've done well to shroud him in mystery so you're in no way expecting the absolute dunce he actually is. So I went in expecting a god, a god that could potentially snap his fingers and I'd drop dead right then and there."

"And instead?"

"Well, to his credit, he did manage to keep the façade up for that one meeting." Lange scratched his chin. "He was . . . tall. Very tall, tall enough to read the titles on the books on the second story of my house with his feet planted on solid ground. I'd seen paintings of him so I thought I knew what to expect—paintings like the ones I showed you of Helice and Essaim. But it was larger than that, physically and metaphorically. So don't expect something literally like what you saw in the art."

"I wasn't."

"No, you're smarter than that, I suppose. Storytellers like us recognize metaphor better than others. But back to Gethin—the paintings show him in black and white, in sort of striped robes similar to the ones we wore as priests. That wasn't right at all. His robes were . . . alive. They writhed and twisted at his will. Since a god's touch bestows prophethood, he used the cloth as hands to avoid accidentally brushing up against us. In carvings he has a skull for a head, but in reality there's often no head there at all. He speaks in your soul—my ears have never heard his voice, but he spoke to me nonetheless."

"And all this from the god that *knows* humanity?" Asa felt their curiosity and anxiety heightening in unison with each other.

"Right, so how must the gods who never talk to us look? Perhaps even less human than him." Lange nodded seriously. "Or perhaps not. I wish I knew." He paused. "So like I said, you'll have to come straight back and tell me."

Asa fell silent again, turning their attention back to the

gourd as they pulled the final stringy remnants from inside of it. They threw the glob at the ground, letting it hit the pile they had been making with a wet, sticky slap. Should they say it? It would sound defeatist, but this was the second time he'd mentioned them returning. Last night it had seemed like the obvious thing to do, but today, they were clouded by other, less bright possibilities.

Lange noticed their silence, and their lack of enthusiasm, and he didn't let them sit in it. "What's wrong?"

"What if I don't come back?" they asked, their tone suddenly blunt as they looked up at him. "What if this is it? No matter what I learn from them, it's going to change everything for me. What's the best case scenario? That they don't show up at all, and nothing changes?"

"Are you afraid of change, my friend?" Lange cocked his head to the side, like a dog when it receives an unfamiliar command. "You left Lucien at your age, and you're afraid of change?"

"Surely you of all people can understand the difference between this and that."

He conceded their point with a small grunt and a shrug. "There is no best case scenario, but there certainly is a worst one."

"Certainly. And that's that I've set my own death-date."

"I didn't want to say it, but that's exactly right. Gods are dangerous, and Essaim is potentially the most dangerous of all. She's unpredictable." He set his gourd upright and crossed his arms over the opening as he leaned on it. "Is it worth that to you?"

There it was, the question that they'd been refusing to ask themself. Was it worth it to them? Finding out the truth was scary, death was scary, but were either as terrifying as the reality they were living in—a reality where they could never truly know themself?

"It is," they answered.

"Thank the gods." Lange breathed a sigh of relief. "I didn't want to sway you either way, but if I never hear the end of your story, I might waste away from curiosity."

"If I die, you'll never hear the end of the story either," Asa pointed out.

"So it's a life-and-death situation for both of us," Lange replied.

Asa snorted. *Gods,* they thought to themself, *storytellers are so dramatic. I hope I'm not this insufferable.*

Deep down, though, they rather figured that they were.

CHAPTER 5

A MOMENT OF RESPITE

"I've never braided hair this straight before," Asa complained as their fingers worked Kennet's hair, intertwining it with itself.

"You don't have to braid it," Kennet told them from where he sat at their feet, between their legs on the rug in front of the fire. He started to look up at them, but they gave him a playful shove and took his head between their hands to level it again.

"I want to, shut up," they said, and he laughed.

They loved his hair. It was straight, certainly, but it was thick and soft. As much as it took some getting used to, after a while the braiding came more easily to them and they settled into a rhythm. Kennet sighed contentedly as they worked, and leaned back against the chair.

Lange was still working on various chores, leaving the two of them alone. At one point he had ducked in to fetch his beekeeper's robes, and then again to return them. When he'd come back he'd been wearing the robes and apart from a few stray curls of red hair peeking around the sides of the mask, Asa wouldn't have known it was him in there at all. It was even more unnerving to see the costume in action.

They weren't sure what their host was up to now, but it was nice to have some quiet.

Kennet had been very right. They did enjoy Lange as a person, as much as he overwhelmed them. The only thing that still stuck with them was the fact that he and Kennet had once spent a lot of time alone together. Asa found that hard to imagine—the entire time that they'd been here, Kennet had mostly kept to himself, asleep at that. While Asa knew that was partially due to everything they'd gone through recently, they also knew he'd been through a good lot the last time he'd been here, too.

And Lange hardly seemed the social type, either, as much as he claimed otherwise. He had gotten tired of Asa's company quickly though he hadn't said as much. He'd politely insinuated that they'd done enough to help him, and that perhaps now they should worry about Kennet. That was enough for Asa to know that they were no longer wanted.

So they figured that when the two men spent any time together without a third party around, it must have been mostly silence, mostly the two of them each doing their own thing, intercut with bouts of depressing philosophical talk and Gethinism. Sounded miserable.

"I'm excited to move on," Asa expressed aloud, and Kennet hummed in agreement.

"To where, though?" he wondered, scratching at the side of his face absentmindedly.

Asa slapped his hand—he'd developed a bad habit of scratching near the wound, and while it had healed a lot, they were still worried he'd undo that healing if he wasn't careful. "I've been giving that some thought, certainly."

"We have plenty of time, but I'm sure you'll want to get where we're going quickly, so perhaps we should linger near the mountains? There's a good few interesting places we could visit in that area."

Asa went silent, wondering if they should mention their

concerns to him. They didn't want to worry him—they could do enough worrying for the both of them. Just the same, perhaps it would be best for the two of them to be on the same page. They took a deep breath, and began with honesty. "I'm not really in a rush to get to the mountains," they said slowly.

He looked up at them—the braid was long enough now that he could—and tried to read their expression to no avail. "You're so close to everything you've been looking for, and you want to bide your time?" he said, slightly confused.

"It's more that I'm not quite sure that we're that close after all—and in case we aren't, I don't see why we should rush toward disaster."

"Oh dear." He patted the rug next to him, and moved so that Asa could slide down to join him on the floor, their braiding fully abandoned. "I hope I didn't force my fears onto you with all that worrying over the time of the gods and whatnot."

"No, no. This is entirely me." Asa scooted so they were sitting closer to him. They lifted his arm and positioned it around their shoulders to his amusement, then pressed their cheek to his chest, letting themself settle into his embrace as it tightened. "I just feel . . . even though I don't know for sure, I feel almost certainly that things are going to change drastically—and maybe not for the better. And I'm excited for that, certainly! But I like . . . now. I like where we are *now*. I like this."

Kennet nodded slowly, beginning to understand, and he softly kissed them on the forehead so quickly that they couldn't even think about giving him any emotion through the touch. "I see," he said. "Well, there's time for more of this. Whatever you like about this—I can make sure we get more of it."

"That's precisely what I'd like."

They sat, enjoying each other's company for a good moment longer.

"Where should we go?" Kennet said eventually, when he had tired of silence. "The mountains are all well and good, but there's a lot of Bladland you've yet to see."

Asa considered the question. "It's your home. I'd hoped you would know the places worth visiting."

"That's the problem, I've lived here so long that it's all entirely unremarkable to me. The lake pass—completely boring, everyday stuff by my standards."

That was a good point. "Well, it doesn't have to be remarkable. I would almost prefer if it wasn't. Surely you have a place that is special to you—something that nobody else would find remarkable, but you do?"

Kennet pondered this, but gave a frown when apparently nothing came to him.

That wouldn't do at all, Asa decided. They knew that he'd have plenty of time to come up with something, but part of them wondered if that kind of happy memory had fled from him a long time ago. It was a terribly sad thought so they combated it immediately.

What if they could draw it out again? They could, they realized, if they could repeat what had happened with Maryska and Lange a third time.

"Can I try something?" they asked, determined now more than ever to obtain permission before moving forward.

"Try what?"

"Well, when I talked to Lange about everything, he asked me to try and give him an emotion, and when I did I got a memory with it as well. The same as with Maryska, but calmer. I was in control of it. So now, I think it's just a new facet of what I could already do. And I think, if I tried it with the right emotion, I could find somewhere—somewhere special for us to visit."

Kennet raised an eyebrow at that. "Well, I suppose it

couldn't hurt," he said. "Hopefully it's not an embarrassing memory, though."

"I don't see why it should be if I do this right," they said.

Their gloves had already been off to allow them to braid his hair more easily, and at first their hand hovered above his where it rested on his leg. They changed their trajectory, though, slipping their hand up around his shoulder and running their fingers over his cheek, down to his chest. With their touch, they gave him a feeling similar to the longing they'd given Lange, but more specific. They drew from their own experiences—their own place that felt special to them, their favorite place to perform in their hometown. They brought to mind the type of people they saw in the crowd, the drinks they were served, the smell of the food. The warmth they felt as people sang along in their native language. They felt an ache in their chest—homesickness, far stronger than they'd felt on this journey so far.

Then the picture shifted, though the homesick feeling lingered. They were no longer inside a warm room—instead, they felt a soft breeze on their face and smelled the sea air. They stood on the coast, on a rocky beach as grey waves lapped at the shore. There was a thick, dried green kelp lining where the tide settled when it rose. The sun had just begun its descent, tinting the entire coastline a beautiful orange-gold. They could see where the beach faded into tall grass, then into trees that broke the sunlight into a dappled carpet of light across the forest floor.

They realized they weren't alone in this memory. Someone was standing next to them, and he casually scooped up a flat rock. He looked familiar—and Asa realized they had seen him in one of these memories before. In Maryska's memory. He looked just the same, only his head was squarely attached to his neck this time. He didn't really acknowledge them, considering the rock, then flicking his wrist to send it across the surface of the water.

As the rock skipped once, twice, three times, the memory dissolved in the ripples of the water's surface.

As soon as it was gone, Asa wondered if that was the best place to go after all. If Isak had been there . . .

"Where was it?" Kennet asked eagerly though, completely unaware of what he had projected. "Where to?"

"It was . . . it was a coastline, a rocky beach at sunset," Asa replied, and though Kennet's enthusiasm didn't fade, they saw recognition flash across his face. They decided it was in their best interest to continue to be honest. "Isak was there," they said.

"Yes, I did take him there. It was one of the best days of my life—and I'd love to share that with you." He didn't linger on the sadness. It seemed like he was refusing to. "It's beautiful, there's a spot with some pools in the beach that collect all the strangest creatures."

"That sounds lovely," Asa said. "I haven't seen the sea properly in so long—unless this isn't the sea? Is it the lake again?"

"No, no, it's the ocean. It's not far from here, either, all things considered. It's just a bit southeast."

"Then it's settled. I'm excited." They snuggled in closer, happy to have something to look forward to that wasn't as life-shattering as the solstice.

Though, they hoped that even after the solstice, there would be plenty of time for much, much more of this sort of thing.

∼

ASA HAD FINALLY FIGURED out what Lange and Kennet did when they weren't pointedly spending time being silent around each other—and that was that they were getting very, very drunk.

Lange burst in as the sun set, his arms full of bottles of various sizes. "All right!" he crowed. "This will do, I think!"

"Oh, you think?" Kennet wondered, though he sat up

straighter with interest. "Gods above, man, that's quite the selection you've got there."

"The thing about bees, you know—you get honey, lots of it, what do you do with all that? Mead, that's what. And the mead you don't drink, you trade for barley wine, and ale of all sorts, and suddenly you have a properly stocked cellar all for the price of a few measly stings," he said triumphantly. "More of a cellar than I could ever properly drink myself, but that's what having company over is for."

"Well, we're certainly more than happy to help you thin it out some," Asa said as Kennet took his arm from around them and pulled himself to his feet, taking Asa with him. "I'm never going to turn my nose up at mead."

"Good. Excellent." Lange nodded sagely, setting the bottles down on a table where there was a gap between the books, then throwing open a cupboard. He grabbed three mugs in one hand, then turned his attention back to his guests. "All right. Each of you pick a poison, and we'll head out."

"Out?" Asa echoed, and when they turned to Kennet they saw that he was grinning as well. "Out where?"

"I built a bit of a fire on the yard. Nothing huge, but certainly more festive than being around all these books. Come on." Lange gestured for them to follow, taking a big bottle of mead with him. Kennet considered the cluster of alcoholic offerings for a moment before selecting two bottles and handing one to Asa.

"I think you'll like this," he said, and followed Lange out the door.

The three made their way down a small trail to an area behind the house with a fire that was already roaring away. It bordered on being a bonfire, blazing high yet still manageable, and its light gave Lange an eerie look as it lit him from behind. He motioned for his guests to join him closer to the flames.

"Let me show you one last little piece of Gethinism, if I may," he said, handing a cup to each of them. "I know you must be exhausted from it by now," he added to Asa, who shrugged.

"I don't mind it from you," they said.

"I wonder why!" he said with a laugh. "Nevertheless—there are some things I could never quite leave behind. The robes, for one. I tried to go back to trousers after I left the order, and heavens that never did suit me. And for another, there are a few traditions that it feels . . . wrong not to observe. I suppose I still see the merit in them, even if I disagree with the church as a whole."

"Like what?" Asa wondered, and Lange shrugged.

"Meditation. Respect for the dead. The creed. Everything I passed on to Kennet, really. There's a lot of good to be found when you strip it all down to its bare essentials."

Asa figured they probably agreed with that, but they didn't want to give it too much thought at the moment. They just wanted to drink. "So what's this one, then?"

"Pour yourself as much as you want to drink," Lange instructed, and did so into his own cup, "but don't sip it. Instead, think about how lucky you are to be alive. Think of all the people who never had a chance to see this night, or these drinks. It can be a specific person or just the concept of humanity as a whole. Then, when you think you're good and depressed enough—HA!" He turned and flung the cup full of mead into the fire.

The blaze flared up with his action, and Lange whooped. Asa laughed in surprise before they followed his example. They poured a hearty serving of liquid into their own cup, and considered it as it bubbled and foamed before them. They thought about what Lange had said, and honestly, they had never felt more lucky to be alive than they did at this moment. Everything they had done had led them here—and it was going to take them even further. There was still plenty to go, but for now, they were here. They could have died so many times—on the voyage over, in their journey to save Marna, when they had faced Maryska—but here they were, alive still.

Kennet threw his drink into the fire before they did, giving a shout as he did, and Lange whooped again when the fire flared. Finally, Asa followed suit, lashing out with their cup and shouting. They felt like a weight lifted off their chest, and when the fire flared so did their heart, a smile taking up on their face.

"Spectacular!" Lange shouted. "Now pour another drink! Enough of death! Now we serve life!"

When Asa finally got a sip of the drink Kennet had picked out for them, they found that it wasn't mead at all but a much more sour, bready-tasting ale. It was fruited, that much was for certain, but they'd never had anything like it before. They liked it, though, and it certainly packed exactly the punch they all seemed to want out of their drinks tonight.

As the fire roared and the three continued to drink, Asa watched Lange and Kennet transform into a completely new pair of people, a pair who were much closer to friends than they had been even moments ago. Where it had taken much coaxing to get Kennet to sing a few nights ago, now all it took was for Lange to sing the first few bars of a folk song, and Kennet would quickly chime in.

Even as their night filled with music, Asa never felt pressured to play for them. They joined in the singing with equal indifference to skill or tone, purely reveling in being a part of the festivities and not a performer for once.

"Have I told you," Kennet said suddenly, fully drunk and fully relaxed as he came to stand next to Asa where they had calmed down for a moment to stare into the flames, "that I thought you were beautiful, from the very moment I saw you?"

Asa, not quite as inebriated as Kennet, couldn't help but

laugh at his declaration. "No, you hadn't told me that," they said warmly.

"Well, you were—you are! And I couldn't believe—can you believe how lucky I was to see you the next day at the gates? I thought I was dreaming, because I never thought I'd see you again, I thought my luck had worn out just getting to see you one time. And I would have been happy with that, you know."

"I believe you," Asa snorted, but he wasn't finished. He leaned closer, and they could smell his sweet, mead-scented breath. Gods how they wanted to kiss him, but they'd let him finish his thought first.

"And then I saw you again! Even after all that, I was blessed to see you one more time, and you even agreed to come with me. And then to stay with me, after everything. The most beautiful thing I've ever seen in my life and you're mine."

"All yours," Asa replied, and they leaned in, finally getting the kiss they'd wanted since the moment he walked up to them. He was smiling so wide it was hard to get a proper kiss in, and they couldn't help but start to smile too at the sensation. Two idiots, smiling against each other—couldn't even kiss properly.

"You two look so stupid," Lange broke in from where he stood, a near-empty bottle dangling in his hand. Asa and Kennet both laughed, with nothing to say to defend themselves. "Here, Asa, try this," their host interrupted them further. The remaining liquid in his bottle sloshed slightly as he held it out toward them, and they raised an eyebrow.

"I'm not sure I can drink much more," they warned him, but he didn't seem to take them seriously.

"Come on, try it. It's like nothing you've had before."

"Isn't it just mead? I've had so much mead since I got here, Lange. I think I've drunk more mead than I've drunk water."

"Drink."

Asa gave in and accepted the bottle from him. When they raised it to their lips, they caught a familiar scent. They paused to give the older man a skeptical look. "What's in this?" they asked, but he didn't reply. Of course not. They couldn't place the scent, but it wasn't one that brought danger to mind, so they caved in and tipped the contents of the bottle into their mouth.

The sweetness of the mead was instantly highlighted by something that made their mouth tingle with bright heat. Asa was no stranger to heat, but since they hadn't been expecting it, they coughed in surprise. Lange cackled at the look on their face—they were sure it must have been quite amusing. When they had recovered, they took a moment to try and identify the flavor.

"That was hot pepper!" Asa said. "I think I know which one, too, but gods help me, I can't remember the name."

"Me either!" Lange said through his laughter. "I brought them over from the Isles but I don't know if I ever knew what they were called. I have a lot of them—all dried, of course, but I don't eat much spice so I took a chance and threw them in a batch of mead one day. The locals *hate* that one. They won't even trade me for it. But I have a couple more bottles—if you like it, please, take it with you and get it off my hands."

"I'll happily relieve you of a bottle or two," Asa said, and they drank the rest of the bottle. It was less unwelcome when they were expecting the spice, and the flavor of the pepper was complemented by the honey. They nodded, deciding that they liked it. "Yes, I'll take one."

"Perfect, don't let me forget."

Their conversation continued—they talked about the peppers, about other things Lange had brought with him from the eastern shore, about the difference in climate. He bored of such topics quickly, however. It seemed that he had no particular fondness for recounting his own lifetime, and preferred to linger on times long ago. In fact, it was only a matter of time before he began to relate every conversation back to a tale or a myth.

Some of the stories had nothing to do with gods at all, which intrigued Asa. These, strangely, seemed even more far-fetched than others. Tales of the stars being the souls of men, tales of the world ending in fire and being reborn to what they knew today. If Asa hadn't been fairly certain that the gods had existed, they wondered if they would believe something else, if they would believe in these stories of rebirth and of destruction. They wondered if maybe the gods weren't the only things out there to believe in—if everything were necessarily true on its own, or if more things could be true at once.

Their head was beginning to spin, and they realized they had certainly had too much to drink, especially if they were going to try and comprehend what Lange was talking about.

Eventually, he noticed their discomfort.

"I think that's enough for tonight," he said, and Kennet gave a loud sigh of relief.

"Thank heavens," Kennet declared. "I forgot how dizzying you are."

"I'll take that as a compliment." Lange gave a light cackle. "Why don't you two turn in?"

Asa looked to Kennet, who had taken a seat on the grass and had his head between his legs in an attempt to cling to some level of sobriety. They extended a hand to him and helped him haphazardly to his feet. As the two walked toward the tower, Asa noticed that Lange wasn't following them. They turned and addressed him.

"What about you?"

"I'll be in when I'm good and ready. Thank you." He said it with a smile, but Asa detected something underneath the expression. Some sorrow.

They didn't argue, though. They were too drunk and too

tired to do so. Instead they made their way inside, and lay Kennet down on the rug. He murmured something—probably thanks, likely also something sweet they would have liked to hear if they weren't still distracted by their host.

Lange's voice was still audible through the door. He was talking to himself—that was fine, a man who lived alone for most of the time was bound to talk to himself now and again. But then they caught a word that surprised them—Gethin, the name of the god that he longer served. Curiosity began to get the better of Asa, and they inched back toward the door, opening it just a crack to watch him.

It was hard to understand anything. They weren't able to get a full phrase from what he was saying, but here and there they picked up on words. The name was in there several times, with other phrases, all in a slow, quiet murmur that was almost melodic. Asa realized with some surprise that he was praying.

One sentiment did reach Asa in full over the crackling of the fire, and the soft evening breeze.

"I'm sorry," he was saying, "I only ever seem to talk to you when I'm drunk these days, don't I? I miss you." He paused and added tearfully, "I hate you. I'm sorry."

CHAPTER 6

STICKS AND STONES

ASA PULLED KENNET'S COAT TIGHTER AROUND THEIR shoulders as they sat next to him on a small wooden barge that was slowly making its way across a narrow channel toward the island from Kennet's memory. They hadn't realized it was an island from the vision that they'd seen, but when they'd gotten to the mainland beach and Kennet had begun to walk toward the docks, they'd put two and two together.

The island was so small that it didn't have a name, and according to Kennet it didn't have inhabitants either. Being entirely alone on an island like that might have seemed unpleasant to some, but Kennet spoke of the place fondly, and Asa was looking forward to seeing it for themself.

The water was grey—that was something that Asa had never quite gotten used to about Bladland, along with the rockiness of the beaches. Everything seemed washed out of color, especially in the colder months, and though their journey to the coast hadn't taken them very long it had chilled remarkably in that time. But even in this chill, and with the grey, and having been convinced to leave their vihuela at the inn, Asa couldn't find themselves anything other than happy.

Perhaps a bit anxious, but that was to be expected when they were planning on meeting a god in under a month.

The man who was rowing them across to the island was quiet, and in an effort to respect him, Kennet and Asa had been quiet too. The only exception had been when Asa had asked Kennet for his coat—he didn't seem nearly as bothered by the cold as they were, so they didn't feel bad taking it from him.

The coat was so heavy and thick—the leather of it smelled old but was clearly well taken care of, and the spray of the water didn't even sink into it, rolling off instead. The fur collar, on the other hand, collected the droplets on its surface. It was comfortable and warm, and Asa wished they could keep it—but it was clearly very special to Kennet, and the only thing that he wore that seemed to be a choice in the way of style. The off-white shirt and brown vest he wore underneath were both utilitarian, simple things. But this coat was like him—scarred, and dark, and mysterious.

And old, they added internally as a joke, though they knew that Kennet wasn't all that old. The grey in his hair had come from stress, not the passage of time, they were certain. No other part of his body showed that level of age. He was the opposite of Lange, who appeared utterly untouched by time.

Kennet noticed that Asa was staring at him, and raised an eyebrow.

"I know what you're doing," he said with a slight smirk.

"What do you mean?"

"You're looking at my grey hair."

Asa snorted. "And if I am?"

"Stop it. I don't need you to remind me that they're there."

"I just think they're unique! Gorgeous, even. What, so you're allowed to come up to me drunk and tell me you thought I was beautiful the moment you saw me, but I'm not allowed to admire your hair?"

"No, you aren't, because it makes me feel old."

Asa laughed. "How old are you, then? I don't think I even know."

"Thirty-two."

Asa pursed their lips and nodded after they had considered that. "That's about what I thought. Your hair is the only thing that ages you, you don't look that old otherwise."

"You're only saying that to spare my feelings."

"As if I would *ever* spare your feelings."

Kennet laughed now, too. "Right, you never have before," he agreed. "I suppose I'll just have to disagree with you on this one."

Asa blew a raspberry and gave him a gentle shove before noticing that they were closing in on the shore. "Oh, I think we need to get ready to get out."

"Indeed. Here, put the coat on properly, you can keep wearing it. It's not going to get any warmer." He held the coat open so they could put their arms through the sleeves—sleeves that were still just a little long for them, so they rolled the cuffs up and nodded with satisfaction.

The boat's underside scraped the rocky beach as they came to a stop, and Kennet got out to pull the boat farther up onto the shore. Then he helped Asa step out onto the beach without their boots even grazing the water. When they were solidly on shore, they turned back to the man still in the boat.

"I'll come back for you around sunset," he said. "If that's acceptable."

"Thank you very much," Kennet replied appreciatively, and fished a few coins out of his pocket to hand to the man, who nodded at the gesture. As quiet as he was, Asa was relieved that it didn't seem as though he felt inconvenienced by the couple. They always hated that about quiet people—

never knowing if they were quietly being judged or not. It was something they'd never quite gotten used to about Bladland. People as a whole here were a lot quieter than on the Isles.

With a hearty push back from the shore, the man began his journey back toward the mainland, and Kennet and Asa were left to their own devices.

"Come on," Kennet said immediately, and began to make his way away from the beach, toward the tree line.

"Okay!" Asa cheerfully followed. They were confused for a moment—they'd been under the impression that the beach was the destination. But then again, the island was small enough that he likely knew it like the back of his hand. They would just have to trust him on it. They caught up to him, and tried to match his long strides even as they reached the unpredictable terrain of the forest floor. "So, how did you find this place?" they asked as they caught themself mid-trip and stumbled back into a normal pace.

Kennet chuckled. "Watch your step," he told them, then considered the question. "One day I was just walking on the beach on the mainland and I saw this place from there. I thought, 'I wonder what's on that island?' I asked the townsfolk and nobody had an answer for me, so I decided to find out for myself. Turns out, there's not much. But it was quiet and borderline untouched by human hands. It became kind of a solace for me—and beyond that, once I started coming here regularly, nobody else dared to come near it."

"Ah yes, because nobody wants to be on a deserted island with a known assassin." Asa nodded seriously.

"Except you, apparently," Kennet pointed out.

"If I can't trust you at this point, then I can't trust anyone," Asa said brightly.

"With what I know you're capable of, I'd have to be a fool to try anything."

Asa became more solemn at that. "I hope she woke up,"

they said, referencing Maryska. "I'm afraid I did something... awful to her."

Kennet shook his head, stepping up onto a large rock and offering them his hand to come up after him. When he had pulled them up to join him, he sighed. "I hope so, too." He added softly, "I wish I could offer any kind of comfort, but other than the fact that she was breathing and seemed physically unharmed, I have nothing to add."

"It's terrifying to know I did all that without even knowing I could."

Kennet nodded grimly. Then, he cleared his throat. "Let's not worry about that," he said, forcefully cheerful. "We're here to have a lovely day and not worry at all. Right?"

"Right, of course."

He hopped down off the rock he had just climbed on top of, and continued to lead them into the woods. As Asa followed him, they forced themself to do as Kennet had asked them to and stop worrying. But even as the thoughts faded from their mind, the lingering discomfort was still there, as it had been since the day they had hurt her.

∽

"A WATCHTOWER!" Asa breathed in surprise as they realized what they were standing in front of.

"It used to be," Kennet agreed, stepping toward it. "Gods, it looks worse every time I visit it. Still sturdy, though!" He kicked the foundation, and the stone building didn't budge—of course it didn't. It towered several stories over their heads, weathered and worn by wind and time. The years hadn't been kind to it, but if it had lasted this long it wasn't going to collapse at a meager kick.

"How long has it been here?"

"Since before I used to come and visit," Kennet replied.

"Whatever they built it for must have stopped being an issue."

"Is there anything inside?" Asa wondered, peeking through the doorway. There was no door in the arched frame, but it was too dim inside to see anything clearly from where they were standing.

"I'm glad you asked," Kennet said. He gestured for them to follow him in.

Just within the door was a small chest that had a few dry leaves settled on its lid. After brushing them off, Kennet opened the chest to reveal a small bundle of blankets, which he pushed aside to access what was underneath. It was a spyglass, copper and slightly dented, and Asa let out a little squeak of delight.

"You just leave that here? What if someone finds it?" they asked, and he shrugged.

"I told you, nobody would dare," he said, and stood up, telescoping the spyglass to its full length and putting it up to his good eye. "Yep. Can't see a thing, too close," he said brightly before snapping it shut again. "Up we go, then."

A staircase spiraled up the side of the tower, luckily made mostly of the same stone built into the walls. If it had been wood, Asa was certain there would be no stairs to climb at all at this point. Soon they reached the top of the tower—there had been a hatch here, Asa was sure, but like the door it had rotted away long ago.

When they stepped out onto the roof, Asa's breath caught in their throat. Even before they were handed the spyglass, the view was something to behold. They could see the mainland, and the outline of the town they had come from, and then to the north the outline of a much larger city. Beyond that, they saw forests stretch into the distance. Lange's home was nestled somewhere in there, they knew, and then beyond that was the mountains. In the late autumn light, they were almost blue in color, creating a jagged horizon that was as intimidating as it was beautiful.

"Wow," Asa breathed.

"I know," Kennet agreed. "Here, take this." He held the spyglass out to them.

Through its lens they were able to see the ships in the foggy docks of the large city, vessels of all shapes and sizes. They were still so small that Asa couldn't see any detail, but they were surprised they could see the ships in the first place. "What's that city?" they asked excitedly.

"That's Guldfjord, the royal city," Kennet said. His voice was right next to their ear. He was looking over their shoulder, following their eye line. "If you thought that Grankoping was busy, Guldfjord is twice as much. But it's also very, very stiff. Everyone's quite full of themselves. They all act like just because the king lives there, they're somehow not still just peasants under his rule."

"What a shame."

"I'll take you there someday."

He was so optimistic about what was coming next—or perhaps he was faking it. They were leaning toward the latter, given his initial reaction to this plan. Though they appreciated the attempt, it was like there was a thick fog over their life, just like the one they could see through the spyglass. The furthest they could see was the solstice. After that—nothing. They didn't want to make plans that would never happen. But they forced themself to smile, and nod. Even if both of them were faking their calm, there was really no use in sharing panic, especially when a negative outcome was equally as probable as a positive one.

"I'd like that," they said.

"Look over there," he added. They took the spyglass down to see he was pointing toward the horizon. "Pick a mountain now; we're not going to get a better view."

"Do you think it really has to be the highest peak?" Asa wondered.

"I don't know. I think the point is just to take a risk—all stories have a measure of exaggeration."

"I'd had the same thought. Surely the mountain in the tale wasn't the highest peak in the entire world—there are so many mountains we may not even be aware of, beyond the western border. Perhaps even just north of us."

"So let's just be realistic, then." Kennet nodded in relief and agreement. "I think that's the best way of interpreting it."

"I think it's the ritual itself that's most important, anyway," Asa added, hoping deeply that they were right.

"If there's one thing I've learned from Lange it's that the gods aren't as detail-oriented as people think. At least, Gethin isn't, and I sort of assume the same is true of the others."

"It's all about a show of effort, then. Well, we'll be putting in effort, that's for certain." They didn't want to make any stupid mistakes—they'd be climbing a mountain no matter what, and even if it wasn't the highest, it was still going to be treacherous. "I can't wait until we're done and we can stop having adventures like this."

"You and me both."

Asa lowered the spyglass and turned to where Kennet's face still hovered only inches from theirs. They darted in for a quick kiss on the cheek, leaving him startled with no way to react other than a soft chuckle.

"Come on now, is that all I get?" he teased, and at his prompting they shared a longer, sweeter kiss. Asa held back any influence—they'd found that while it was impossible to refrain from sharing their feelings through kisses entirely, they could limit it somewhat, and keep from giving him anything overwhelming or evoking any memories. This was a relief to them. They didn't want to have to keep away from him, especially now.

When they pulled away from each other, Asa sighed contentedly. They noticed a little shiver from Kennet—even he couldn't ignore the chill in the wind at the height they stood, above the protective barrier of the trees.

"Let's go down," Asa suggested. "Something tells me you still have plenty more to show me."

∽

BACK ON THE BEACH, Asa and Kennet walked side by side. Every now and again, Kennet would bend down and pick up a rock, examine it, and then toss it into the ocean. Once or twice, he managed to make them skip, but never more than a couple times.

The rocky beaches never ceased to interest Asa, who was used to beaches of fine sand and blue water. Certainly there was sand to be found here, but it was much closer to the water itself and it was only filling in gaps between the stones. Stones, and other things—shells, seaweed, and most interestingly to Asa, wood.

Lots of it, white and weatherworn, in all shapes and sizes. Kennet called it "driftwood."

"We used to make forts out of it when we'd visit the beach as children," he'd said as they came across a particularly large log.

"We?"

"My brother and I," Kennet replied.

"You have a *brother*?" Asa asked, blinking rapidly in surprise.

"Oh, damn. I suppose I've never mentioned him."

"No, you haven't!"

"We aren't really close anymore. I never really visit home, and he stopped seeking me out for relationship after I joined the Hawks. Most of my family did, actually."

"But you used to be close?" Asa asked.

"Decently close, yes."

"What's his name?" Asa found their interest piqued, and Kennet rubbed at his eye a little, surrendering to the fact that he was going to have to talk about this for a while.

"Mathias."

"Older or younger?"

"Older."

"By how much?"

"A good deal." Kennet scratched his beard. "Five years? He had fully taken over my father's business by the time I left."

"What business would that be?"

"He was a cobbler."

"A shoemaker?" Asa repeated to clarify, and Kennet nodded. "You're the son of a shoemaker?"

"And the brother of one. See, this is why I haven't brought it up. It really shatters my image, doesn't it?"

"It does a bit," Asa admitted. "But that's not what shocks me. I'm just surprised I haven't bothered to ask these things before."

"They're not really important." Kennet shrugged. "It feels like another lifetime—I was a different person back then. Really, that boy is . . . more or less, I feel like he's dead now."

It was a sentiment that Asa could relate to. When they looked back to who they were as a child, they saw a stranger. And at the same time . . .

"I don't think he's dead. Just different," Asa said reassuringly as they came up beside Kennet and laced their gloved fingers between his. "After all, I think that's the boy who wants to wear a dark, threatening cloak and sweep around towns as a mysterious drifter."

Kennet laughed and squeezed their hand, then thought about what they had said. "I think you're right," he said. "I think if he were to see me now, he'd be impressed and a little scared."

"That's your goal, isn't it?" Asa teased. "To scare and impress people?"

"It might be. Never worked on you though."

"I may never have been scared or impressed, but I was intrigued," Asa said. "And I still am. Every new thing I learn about you makes me want to know more."

"There's not much more to know," Kennet protested. Asa shrugged.

"I don't think *that's* true at all," they said. "For instance, I don't know how you'd make a fort out of those logs." They pointed toward some driftwood, and raised their eyebrows meaningfully.

"Oh, do you want to make a fort?" He looked surprised, but then a smile of childish joy grew on his face. "Do you?" he repeated with a tiny bit of pleading in his tone.

"I absolutely do."

That was the only encouragement he needed, and he as much as dragged them toward the most promising of the logs. He began to outline his plan, collecting different sticks and logs of varying widths and sizes, telling Asa what he wanted and needed. Almost immediately their job became to collect smaller branches with Y shapes in them to act as supports.

They wandered up and down the beach as he set to work, and every now and then they glanced back at him. It was very hard to keep a smile off their face at his excitement, so they grinned like a fool the entire time they looked for sufficient sticks.

After a while, they paused, and knelt down to examine something they saw on the ground. Among the grey and brown stones, nestled carefully, was a black stone with winding cracks filled with white. Their fingertips dug underneath the stone to pry it out, collecting grains of sand in the seams of their gloves as they did. Eventually they managed to dislodge it, and pulled it up from the ground—it was much larger than they had thought it would be, and the half that had been buried was dark from the damp earth. Asa dusted the remaining few grains of sand off and examined their prize—it was shaped like a heart, they realized now, and immediately their grip tightened on it. They slipped it into a pocket, and nodded in satisfaction as its weight settled.

No sooner had they done this than they felt a large, wet splatter on their nose, followed by another and then a few more. They heard Kennet shout from down the beach, and when they looked up at the sky they saw that more rain was only inevitable as dark clouds had suddenly rolled in. They wondered if they should have seen them from the top of the watch tower—but they hadn't been paying much attention to that at the time.

Their boots slid over the sand as they scuffled back toward Kennet and the sad beginnings of the fort he had been working on. There was not even the slightest hint of a roof over the thing yet, and it would offer no shelter from the rain.

"The watchtower!" he shouted over the sound of the ever-strengthening rainfall.

"Yes!"

The two tore through the forest, with Asa holding Kennet's coat up over their head to shield themself from the rain as they blindly followed him. The tower was farther than they remembered, but they made it there just as a loud crack of thunder echoed overhead. When they had ducked into the shelter, Kennet gave a long, relieved sigh.

"That was fun," he said, beginning to wring water out of his hair.

"So much for the fort."

"Yes, well. Maybe it was a silly idea anyway."

"Hardly," Asa said, and they leaned on the wall of the tower.

"And now the rest of the day we'll be stuck in here,"

Kennet added with annoyance, giving up on wringing out his hair and instead untying it, unbraiding it, and shaking his head violently like a dog. Asa laughed as his action sprayed them with water. "Sorry," he said when he noticed.

"Don't worry, there are far worse places to be stuck," they assured him. "Here, I bet I can cheer you up."

"I bet you can too," Kennet replied, "but please, do share."

Asa dug around in their pocket and pulled out the stone that they had found. They held it out to him and he took it with a low whistle, turning it over in his hands.

"Pretty little thing, isn't it?" they said proudly. He nodded.

"It's a find for sure," he agreed. "I do enjoy a nice rock."

"Keep it, then," Asa said, "a reminder of today."

"I'll cherish it forever," Kennet said, and he pressed the rock to his chest for a second before putting in one of the bags around his waist. Then he came to rest against the wall with them.

"This has been a lovely day," Asa said after a moment of silence, and Kennet hummed in agreement.

"I'm glad we did this," he said.

"Me too. I think I feel more ready now, for whatever happens next."

Kennet reached down and squeezed their hand. "I'm ready too," he said, "though it's going to be a lot easier for me."

"Well, perhaps. But you don't have to bring that up."

CHAPTER 7

FIRE, PAIN AND REBIRTH

"So is it true that the air is thinner on mountaintops?" Asa called ahead to Kennet as they rode up the mountain path. Emilio and Starling were not enjoying the narrow, rocky and uneven trail, but they had left the wider path long ago—the day before, even on their first day of travel up the mountain. The trees became farther apart, and the trail wound through them and back into itself constantly to make the way up less steep.

"There's definitely something wrong with mountain air," Kennet replied, leaning back in his saddle to help Starling balance. "I've only ever been very far up one once, and I felt lightheaded constantly. Isak and Maryska grew up on a mountain—they say that the air down with us feels heavy and thick. So perhaps there's something to that."

"Then I guess we should try not to talk too much," Asa said. "I've never been up on a mountain before at all, much less anywhere near the top."

They still had a long way to go, but with each step Asa's heart beat just a little faster. It felt like rather than them getting closer to their destination, the destination was creeping steadily closer to them. Although they'd had plenty of time to prepare, they wondered if there wasn't a way they could have done that more appropriately. For the fifth time that day, they checked their saddlebag—the candle was still there, along with the twine, and the bottle of mead Lange had given them. They sighed and shut the flap again.

"What can I do to help you calm down?" Kennet asked from in front of them. He must have heard them rustling around in the bag.

"I'm completely calm," Asa lied.

"Ah, and yet, I can only assume there are ways you could be *more* calm," Kennet said.

"Perhaps. But I can't think of anything."

Just then, Starling stopped walking. Emilio almost walked into her hind, but stopped just in time, and both stood still in confusion.

"Is she just . . . done?" Asa wondered.

"I thought for sure she could go a little farther," Kennet replied. He tried to nudge her on but her only response was to paw at the ground. "She might be done."

"I guess we were going to have to start walking sooner or later," Asa offered, and Kennet grumbled to himself.

"Damn. I'd really hoped she'd go farther." He began to dismount. "But there's no forcing her if she doesn't want to."

"Stubborn girl." Asa laughed, dismounting as well. The two led their mounts off the side of the trail, where they hitched them to two trees in a flat-ish clearing. Asa patted Emilio's flank. "We'll be back soon," they assured him, and they wondered if he could tell how nervous they were. If he did, he showed no signs of it. Asa turned to Kennet. "Will they be all right?"

"They should be," he replied. "There are bears out here, but, uh—" They must have made a face, because he paused, and backtracked. "They'll be fine. I've tied a kind of knot that if they really need to get out of, they can. And if we come back and they're gone—hopefully that just means they've got away."

"I'd rather walk down a mountain than come back to dead horses," Asa said. They dug the candle and twine out of the saddlebag and held them out to Kennet. "I think you'd better hold onto these."

"I do have a little more room," he agreed, and slipped them into a bag on his waist. Then he watched as they took down their vihuela and slung it over their back. To his credit, he didn't ask if it was necessary to bring it with them. After the conversation about horses escaping, it was obvious that the idea of coming down to see their instrument missing—well, that clearly wasn't an option.

"All right," Asa said as they tightened the strap around their chest. "Let's go."

～

THE PEAK of the mountain seemed comically out of reach, even as they continued to climb. At one point, the two had taken a break, but the pause had only served to make Asa even more anxious. As the sun rose over the sea, their goal threatened to arrive long before they were ready.

"The gods have a lot of nerve to make us do these rituals to summon them," they muttered to themself half-sarcastically as they leaned on a smooth, straight branch they had taken up to use as a walking stick. "It would be nice to just have some sort of signal. Something easy and quick."

"Isn't that what a ritual is?" Kennet said as he tipped the waterskin to his lips. He drank greedily, then wiped a few stray droplets of water from his beard before he held the skin out to Asa.

"No, a ritual is a lot of steps," Asa replied, accepting the water and pausing to drink a bit themself. "I was thinking something more . . . one step. Like a special word or something."

"I think that'd be abused pretty quickly. The whole point is to show that we mean it—that we're desperate."

"Well, I *am* that. Or else I wouldn't have even bothered to climb this far," Asa said.

"Then hopefully that's good enough. Because saying we'll climb a mountain is one thing—actually doing it . . ."

"To our credit, neither of us have climbed all the way up a mountain before."

"We might not even do that yet," Kennet pointed out, "especially if we keep stopping."

"Right, we should continue."

"Let's."

∼

THIS WAS the part that Asa had been dreading. They actually had to climb.

There was still a kind of path. And this was far from the steepest thing they had ever seen, with the cliffs of Hagertrask in mind. Why had those cliffs looked so easy to scale? Why had they imagined that it would be like walking up a set of stairs, but this was so intimidating? Likely it was because nobody had actually expected them to climb up the cliffs.

They felt their breaths come shorter. Perhaps they couldn't do this. Perhaps they never could have. Kennet noticed their heaving chest and stepped between them and the way forward, placing his hands on their shoulders.

"Hey," he said calmly. "Hey, we don't have to go up farther."

"What do you mean?" Asa said, nearly struck dumb by the task before them. "Of course we have to go farther, we have to get to the top."

"You aren't built for this, my friend." Kennet kept his

voice steady as he tried to catch their eye, but they hardly even noticed him, looking right past as their chest thundered with their heartbeat.

"We can't give up now," they said, but he stopped them.

"We aren't giving up. We're being realistic. You're barely able to breathe as it is, I can't have you passing out. If you aren't conscious there will be no ritual either way."

Asa frowned, and finally they were able to focus on his face. They saw deep concern written in his eye, and their shoulders slumped under his touch. He was right. Each breath felt like it was yielding a fraction of the air they needed. If they were going to do this ritual, it would have to be here. They couldn't have anticipated this—not the way it was affecting them, even if they had heard warnings. They'd thought they could do it, but now . . .

The gods would have to understand.

"All right," Asa said, and stepped back from the incline. "All right," they repeated, more firmly.

"Good. Good. Then let's figure this out." Kennet tapped the bag at his hip. "I suppose that it's impossible to know whether the candle will burn out exactly as the sun reaches its peak."

"Honestly," Asa agreed, looking up at the sky. It seemed like the sun wouldn't be at its fullest for some time yet. "It's another one of those things, like the 'highest mountain top.' It's just a folktale—we'll just have to do our best. I have an idea—hold on."

They had crossed a snow line at some point, and now their footsteps crunched against the slick wet surface as they walked away from the hill and down to a flatter spot. There were still a few trees even at this height, and as they slid a little they used one of these trees for support before settling.

They tapped their walking stick against the top layer of the snow that had frozen into a fairly thick sheet of ice, moving out of the shade of the tree and into the sunlight, then slamming the stick through the ice and embedding it deep into the snow. The stick stood up straight, creating a fairly effective sundial. Asa planted their hands on their hips with satisfaction.

"There we go," they said. "I say we light the candle when it gets close to midday, and hope it burns out as close as possible to the sun's peak."

Kennet slid down the hill to join them, landing with similar grace to how they had. "This is likely far more scientific than the couple in the tale did it," he said, "if you think about it."

"Perhaps we should write down what we did for future attempts."

"Lange would probably like it if we did that, whether it works or not."

The two backed away from the sundial and settled down under one of the trees. Asa took their vihuela from their back and propped it up. They stroked its side wistfully—if they ended up somehow not coming back from this, it dawned on them that one thing they would be saddest to leave behind was this masterpiece of an instrument.

"If this ends up . . . going poorly, will you make sure that my vihuela gets down safe?" they asked Kennet, and he gave them a confused look.

"Wait, this whole time—have you been assuming that somehow I'll make it out even if you don't?" he asked.

"Well, yes."

"We're doing this *together*. Why would you be the only one to go down?"

"The better question is why wouldn't I? There's no reason they'd have an issue with you—you're not the one who's outside natural order. I keep considering it, and I think it's a real possibility that their solution will be taking me away forever if they realize that I was never supposed to exist."

Kennet's expression turned from confusion to distress. "You think I'll lose you like that?"

"Oh, no, this is why I didn't want to talk about it." Asa buried their hands in their hair.

"No, no, it's all right." Kennet took a deep breath. "It . . . It'll be all right. No matter what happens, I'll be here. I'll wait for you to come back."

They considered him after he'd said that. "For how long?" they asked.

"As long as it takes. I'll summon them again and talk to them myself. I'll bring you back."

"But—"

"I'll take your vihuela down, I'll get Emilio someplace safe. And then I'll come back." He took one of their hands, pressing it between his. "I'll come back every solstice if I have to—no, I'll build a house a little ways down the trail, and I'll come look for you every day."

Asa was stunned by the passion in his voice. He meant it with his entire soul. "You would really do that?" they said, unable to keep the awe and affection out of their voice as they said it—the idea that someone would wait for them like that made their heart ache. The idea that he would think they would come back, that he wouldn't give up on them. They felt tears prick at their eyes.

"I would, of course I would," Kennet said softly, reaching up to touch their face when he noticed the tears. They leaned into his touch, forgetting to hold their feelings back from him—too late, they noticed a tear roll down his cheek from the corner of his eye, as well. "I love you too," he said.

"Too?"

"You don't have to say it," he said. "I can feel it."

∼

When the sun was near its peak, the two began their preparations to summon the gods.

Asa took their gloves off and laid them to the side. They wondered—if this went well, would they ever need those gloves again? The thought of abandoning them was alluring. Could a god take their gift away after it had been given? Is that what they wanted?

They supposed they wouldn't know until it happened, but in the moment maybe that's what they'd ask for. Probably it would be. They felt like this influence had already done all the good it would be capable of, at this point. They were ready to be relieved of it.

With the gloves carefully laid out, they turned their attention to Kennet, who held the candle in one hand and the twine in the other.

"All right," he said. "Here we go."

The two sat down across from each other on Kennet's coat, using it to keep themselves off the snow. Kennet reached his hand out with the candle in it, and Asa took it in theirs. They kept their emotions back for now—they knew that with the effort it took to suppress their influence they wouldn't be able to hold it back forever, but the least they could do was wait until the candle was lit. As it stood upright in their grasp, Kennet wound the twine around their joined hands, leaving one end for Asa to hold as he used the other.

"Is it too tight?" he asked as he finished.

"Fine for me," they said. He nodded.

"All right. Help me tie it off."

Carefully the two used their free hands to tie a knot in the twine. Then, Kennet handed Asa a matchbox and as they held it open he removed one of the matches. They'd discussed this part, but Asa was only now struck by how funny it was that they had to each operate half of the match lighting process, and they couldn't help but laugh as their first two attempts failed.

"Hey, hold still," Kennet said, but he was laughing as well. The nerves and stress all bubbled over as the ridiculousness of the task at hand set in for both of them. "Stupid hell-blessed ritual," he muttered, and struck at the matchbox a third time. This time, the match was lit, and he was so startled by his success that he almost dropped it. Luckily, he managed to save himself in time, and held the match to the candle's wick. When the flame had made its way onto the target, both parties let out a relieved sigh.

And so the candle was lit.

And it burned slowly.

For the first few minutes, Asa focused the entirety of their energy on keeping their emotions back from Kennet. It wasn't painful, but it took focus, and they watched the flame flicker as their mind stayed trained on managing their feelings.

"I'm not feeling anything," Kennet remarked after a while.

"What?"

"Surely you're frightened by now. And stressed. Why don't I feel any of it?"

"Oh, I wasn't—I didn't want to make you feel that way."

"I knew what I was getting into when I agreed to this, Asa. Please don't keep yourself from feeling things just to spare me. It's a big moment."

They exhaled, and let the flood of emotions flow. Immediately Kennet gave a nervous chuckle.

"Ahh, that's more what I expected," he said, leaning back a little, as though the physical distance would lessen the impact. It wouldn't; they were still touching. "Damn, are you sure you want to go through with this?"

"I think you know that I am," Asa said solemnly, and he nodded.

The silence resumed, and a particularly heavy breeze tipped a small bit of wax out of where it had pooled at the top of the candle. It rolled down the length quickly, but solidified before it could reach either of their skin. Asa cringed, mostly out of anticipation.

"Beeswax candles don't drip much, usually," Kennet said, observing the bead of wax that had hardened. "But the wind is going to change that."

"I suppose it's just part of the experience."

Another stronger breeze sent more hot wax spilling over the edge. With the direction the wind was coming from, the wax would only roll down the side facing Asa. One of the drops hit their hand—hot, but not burning—and they winced. Almost immediately, so did Kennet.

Asa's eyes widened. "Did you . . . feel that?" they asked.

"As if it had hit my own skin," he replied, equally awestruck.

"I didn't know I could do that," they said. "Let me try something."

"Are you going to pinch your—"

They pinched their hand. Kennet gave a small yelp. "Well!" Asa said. "I guess that's one thing we learned today, if nothing else."

"I can't imagine this is a skill you're going to use for good."

"Oh I've never been known to use my skills *only* for good," Asa replied, and pinched their own hand again, laughing when Kennet reacted. "Sorry, I'll stop."

Another bead of wax dripped onto them, and they both narrowed their eyes in the momentary pain.

Hours went by—only a couple, but they crawled by and came with more dripping wax and more slipping emotions from Asa to Kennet. When their mind wandered, so did their emotions, which quickly turned into a game between the two of them. Asa would imagine something, and Kennet would guess what they were thinking of.

"Food," he said now, after about thirty minutes of playing this game.

"Right," Asa replied. They'd been thinking of a warm, sticky sweet roll from a bakery in their hometown.

"That one was easy. We're both hungry," he said, and used his free hand to dig around in his pack and take out some strips of dried meat. He held one out to Asa.

"Thank you." They tore off a bit with their teeth, and chewed thoughtfully as they watched the candle continue to burn. It was getting closer to their hands—only about an inch away, almost two thirds gone. They looked over to the sundial—it was hard to tell the exact time, but it was very close to noon. Their heart fluttered, and when they tried to swallow, they felt their stomach churn.

"Hey, hey." Kennet snapped his fingers on his free hand. "Calm down, if you throw up I'll certainly join you."

"Sorry," Asa said sheepishly and forced themself to steady their breathing, lowering their heart rate. "It's just . . . we're so close."

"I know."

They tried to finish eating what they'd been given, and were proud when they managed to get the whole thing down. When they finished, their focus settled on the candle again.

As the last hour burned down, they couldn't bear to look away. They felt as though if they diverted their attention and missed the moment the candle went out, they'd somehow forfeit all of their efforts.

The flame began to sputter, and their heart leapt. The moment was finally upon them. They wondered how they should react—was there a way to address a god? Would they know it when they saw them?

"Here we go," Kennet breathed across from them. "Are you ready?"

"Not in the slightest." Asa squeezed his hand.

"I'll be here the whole time. Don't worry."

Asa nodded. The candle flickered again—

And went out.

And everything went dark.

∼

Kennet Peders sat with his hand outstretched, holding thin air.

As the candle had gone out it was like the sun had blinked out with it.

When he could see again, he was alone.

∼

At a glance, nothing had changed when Asa was able to see again. Slowly, though, they became acutely aware of a few key differences. Most notably they seemed to be completely alone. Kennet wasn't there, though they seemed to be on the same mountainside as they had been on before. It surprised them—they hadn't even had a chance to say why they were there, so they'd expected that the gods would want to talk to both of them, at least until their intentions were made clear. But instead, Kennet was nowhere to be seen. They forced themself to be calm. They hadn't even met the gods yet. Perhaps there was an explanation for this.

They looked around them—the scenery was familiar but hazy, and felt surreal by the way it was lit. When they turned their eyes to the sky, they saw the cause of this. The sun and moon both hovered above them, larger than they should be, as if they were closer to the ground. As Asa looked into their light, the bright forms began to morph.

The sun's rays became more defined, splaying out in all directions before forming into a few sharp points that flickered like flames even in their definition. The moon, which appeared full and round in the sky, split into three, like eyes staring down at them. They grew larger and Asa realized they were descending toward them, and with that descent their heart raced faster and faster.

The sun and moon thundered to earth at a breathtaking pace and landed with a flash of light so bright they had to shield their eyes.

And when it had died down—

The gods were giants. They stood at least ten feet tall each, and as Asa peered up toward them they thought that they looked nothing like their illustrations from Lange's books. Nevertheless, seeing them now, Asa was only more certain that they knew them.

Essaim was the first to notice Asa—her hair and eyes burned with fire. Real, actual fire in the case of her hair, which was flame licking at the sky from her scalp. A cape flowed down her back like the wings of a dragonfly—or, Asa thought it was a cape at first, but quickly realized that the wings flicked as the god looked them over. They were a part of her.

Helice was markedly less intimidating, but only at first. When she looked toward Asa, they felt a chill under the scrutiny of her three eyes as they were set like glossy pearls in her deep, black-purple skin. She held herself regally where Essaim almost leered. Like Essaim's, Helice's hair morphed with life of its own, a thundercloud in the sky—the sky, which was represented in a floor-length gown of stars in twilight, cascading down her form as if made from an impossibly light fabric.

The two stared at Asa in silence, and they felt the gaze of the gods burn into them.

Essaim spoke, after what seemed like an eternity, her voice raspy and harsh. As Lange had described, they didn't seem to hear it through their ears, but instead in the depths of their very soul. **"Who is this?"** she said to Helice, cocking her head sharply. An arc of flame shot from her head as she said it, catching the nearest tree branch on fire.

"It's a mortal," Helice replied patiently as she extinguished the flame with a wave of her hand. Her voice was softer but held the same critical air that Asa had felt when she first looked at them.

"I figured that. But only one?" Essaim considered Asa again, then giggled loudly. **"Oh, how interesting. Why only one?"**

"It's odd indeed," Helice muttered. **"It seems there was another one who took part in calling us here, but it's not come with this one."**

"I wonder why . . ." Essaim began to pace, walking around Asa. Neither of them had addressed Asa directly, and they still didn't now, continuing to talk among themselves.

"I think the other one didn't want us. It was only there for this one." Helice gestured to Asa, and Essaim paused in her pacing.

"How romantic," she said brightly.

"Indeed."

"So then, if it's some grand act of love, shouldn't we listen to what it has to say?"

"But if it was a grand act of love, why is there only one here? No. I think this one is here for another reason."

They both turned their burning gazes back on Asa.

"I—" Asa felt their words leave them. Every prepared statement died on their lips. "You don't . . . remember me?" they said weakly. It was all they could think to say.

"Remember you?" Essaim repeated. **"I haven't seen a human in eras! Not since the first ones who did that silly little ritual you just finished down there."**

Asa's heart sank further than it had back at Lange's hut. Then they felt themself get angry. Their face scrunched up involuntarily, and tears sprang to their eyes.

They had not come all this way for nothing.

They would get what they had come for.

"You have to have made me," they said, surprising themself with their boldness. "There's no other option! If you didn't, then who did? Then why am I this way?" They heard their voice break, but even this wasn't enough to stop them. "And then why do I recognize you if I've never seen you before?"

The outburst took the gods aback, that much was clear. They were speechless, and they both tilted their heads to the opposite sides.

"Did you make a prophet, dear?" Helice said finally.

"I don't think so!" Essaim replied. **"I think I would have told you about that."**

"Perhaps you forgot to."

"It's not the kind of thing I think I'd take lightly."

"Oh? Like the time you caused the sun to go out in the middle of the day and sent mortals into a panic for a full decade?" Helice said. Asa was surprised to detect amusement in her tone.

Essaim cackled with delight. **"I forgot about that."**

"Then perhaps you forgot about this one, too."

Asa wished the gods would stop looking back to them. It burned every time, both in their intentions and the physical feeling. They wondered if they'd come away with some kind of sunburn.

Essaim circled back around to Asa's front again, and dropped down into a squat, putting her much closer to Asa's eyeline. Asa felt that breathless feeling again—so close to a god that they could feel the heat radiating off her skin. They could now make out the smattering of freckles over her face, various shades of orange that speckled and marbled the pale skin of her face like granite. A soft circular glow of light flickered behind her head, a glow that should have been dimmed by the brightness of her hair, yet somehow it wasn't.

"What's your name, then?"

"Asa."

"Well, Asa. What makes you think you're my prophet?"

"I . . ." They held up their hands helplessly. "I can change people's emotions, just by touching them. I can make them feel what I feel. And sometimes . . . I can see their memories when I do it."

Essaim raised her eyebrows at that, pursing her lips in thought. **"Well, that does sound like a prophet,"** she said.

"It certainly does," Helice agreed, joining Essaim in front of Asa by kneeling gently on the ground. The hem of her skirt absorbed into the earth as she did, creating a pool of starlight around her knees. **"Are you positive that it wasn't your god Gethin that did it? He's much more likely."**

"Gethin wouldn't do this. He's too much like you—needs to play by the rules," Essaim interrupted her wife. She rested her elbow on her knee and her chin in her hand. **"No, they're right. If it was anyone it was me, but I swear I don't remember doing it."**

"And you say that you know us? Interesting," Helice murmured. **"Well, if she doesn't remember it, then I suppose this is something to keep in mind for the future. An odd anomaly, to be sure."**

"Wait," Asa said as Helice began to stand up, motioning for Essaim to follow her. "Wait, no. I won't—you can't leave! I need answers!"

"We don't have any answers for you," Helice said, genuinely apologetic. She gestured again for Essaim to follow.

The god of the sun didn't budge. She stayed where she had knelt, staring at Asa intently. Even as her wife beckoned for them to leave, the look only intensified.

"You . . . do look familiar," she whispered, her voice like the soft crackling of a newborn fire. **"No. . . but I've never seen you before today."**

Asa felt hope surge in them again, and they nodded excitedly. "Surely there's some way we can find out for certain," they prompted, and Essaim seemed to be seriously considering them. Another jet of flame shot out from her head, this one going directly over Helice and into the sky where it dissipated harmlessly.

"**. . . there may be a way,**" she said slowly. "**But it's all or nothing. Are you in, all or nothing, Asa?**"

Helice's eyes widened as she realized what Essaim was proposing. "**This is not a prophet of yours,**" she said sharply. "**And if you were to make one, much less out of an already powerful human, there's no telling what may happen.**"

"**Oh, but now I *must* know,**" Essaim said deviously.

"**No, you mustn't,**" Helice reprimanded, but the Sun was already set in her path.

"**I'm going to touch you,**" she said to Asa, "**and if you are my prophet, I believe that will be revealed. And if you aren't . . .**"

"**Then I'll kill you where you stand,**" Helice interjected sternly. She looked to Asa with a challenging expression. "**Understand that. If this does not go exactly as you think it ought to, I will bring you down. The world is fragile, and something like Gethin's prophets have already threatened the natural order several times. We made a pact when the gods left—nothing like that will happen again. Do you hear me?**"

Asa allowed themself to fully consider things, every aspect, one last time. This truly seemed like the only way forward. It wasn't that they hadn't considered the possibility —and they might have hesitated, if they hadn't felt so strongly that they were doing the right thing. Something in them, the same thing that had recognized the gods, the same thing that had driven them this far—it bade them to continue forward.

"I understand," they said firmly, and Helice sighed in disappointment.

"Then carry on. I'm sorry that you came all this way just to die." Once more she sounded deeply, unexpectedly sincere.

Essaim, on the other hand, just became more giddy with this permission. **"I have no idea what's about to happen,"** she said brightly. **"Are you ready?"**

They hadn't been ready, moments ago, when the candle had burned out. They certainly shouldn't be ready now. But they nodded seriously. "I'm ready."

The god gave a wide smile, showing wickedly sharp teeth. **"I like you,"** she said as she reached out her hand. **"I hope this doesn't kill you."**

Asa hesitated. Their hands seemed glued to their sides, like their survival instincts had finally decided to kick in. It took every muscle in their body to reach out and shake the god's hand.

The instant their fingers touched hers, they felt fire spread over their entire body. Hot, and bright, like touching the sun should feel. They felt it rip through them, and they wondered if Helice would even need to help them die.

The feeling overpowered them. They were unsure if they were losing consciousness, or losing life, but either way their vision began to fail them. It was impossible to tell exactly when it happened—the only thing they knew for sure was that they had blacked out.

CHAPTER 8

THE ONE TO MAKE IT

DEEPER, ANOTHER LAYER IN, ANOTHER LAYER FURTHER from reality. Not dead—at least, Asa didn't think they were dead. Though their eyes could see nothing but darkness, their other senses served them slightly better. They could smell dankness, dampness. They could hear their own heartbeat, and their heavy breathing, and then when they listened harder, they heard someone else in the same room. They heard soft, light sobs.

They strained their eyes, desperate to see anything. When they held their hand up in front of their face, they could see the vague forms of their fingers.

"Hello?" they called out, abandoning their reliance on their sight once again.

The sobbing didn't wane or get louder. It was steady, only interrupted by long, ragged deep breaths.

"Hello?"

Still nothing. Luckily, their eyesight was beginning to adjust, and when they looked in the direction of the sobs they could barely make it out—small, with heaving shoulders. A child.

The child sat in the middle of the room they were in, a

room that Asa could now see was fairly large, with dingy wooden floors that creaked as they got to their feet. There were no windows, and they couldn't decipher any walls, neither near them or behind the child as they approached it.

The child did not look up or acknowledge Asa's approach in any way. That was fair enough. Asa wondered how long it had been there, how it had gotten here. Had it been touched by Essaim as well? She said she hadn't seen a human in eras, much less touched one, but perhaps this child was from a time long gone by. Or perhaps she had just forgotten the child, as it seemed she had forgotten Asa. Perhaps it was something else entirely, but regardless, they could hardly ignore its cries.

"Hello there," Asa ventured in a softer voice, continuing to get closer slowly.

The sobs faltered only slightly. The child looked up at Asa through scraggly blonde ringlets that were matted near its scalp. Big, sad, brown eyes. It was so small. Asa felt a throbbing in their chest when they looked at it, dressed in rags and with dirt smudged across its face. When they didn't move to speak further, the child began to cry again with renewed energy.

They would have to take it with them, they decided. They couldn't leave it here. But first, they would need to find a way out.

As they backed away from the child again, they began to notice a few more details about their situation. For one thing, they were not wearing their own clothes. Instead, they were wearing a plain white gown, one without sleeves or even seams. It was seemingly a single piece of cloth with holes cut in it for their arms and their head. They found it odd that they weren't concerned about where it had come from, or who had undressed them, and put them in the gown. They weren't concerned about it at all.

In fact they were barely concerned about anything. When

they tried to feel anxious or upset about their situation, nothing came to them. The only thing on their mind among the overwhelming numbness was the child, and the way forward.

They found the latter quickly. With their eyes fully adjusted to the lack of light, they found the border to the room—a room that was circular, with the child at the center, and smooth walls that felt cold like stone. Asa pressed a palm to the wall, and slowly began to drag their hand across it as they walked around the edge of the room. They hadn't gotten far when they brushed up against a new texture—wood. The frame to a door.

Relief washed over them. A way out—or at least a way to something new.

With their path set out for them, Asa turned back to the child.

It was still crying as they returned to it, and with each step the cries only seemed to intensify. Asa had never had any parental instinct, but this was what they imagined that must be. There was a deep longing to make the child's pain stop, to calm it down, by any means necessary. To make it feel safe, and loved.

They knew one easy way to do that.

Carefully, with the intention to give the child peace through their influence, they knelt down in front of the child and reached out a hand.

The child reacted the moment their hand entered its field of view. Its eyes snapped up to meet Asa's, and the cries turned into a frightened scream as it reached up and grabbed their hand to force them away from it. When their hands touched, Asa felt something they had never experienced before.

They didn't give. There was no overflowing, no exchange of emotion from them to the child. It wasn't like Maryska, no backflow of anything residual. It was far more intense than that.

They were being given to.

The child was influencing them.

Fear.

It was the only strong emotion to occur to them since they had woken up, and it surged through them like a lightning strike.

Asa screamed, falling backward away from the child, and the two scrambled back on their hands and knees in unison. They both stopped about five feet away from each other, their breaths heaving in sync, their panting screams interrupted in alternating intervals, a broken staccato of confusion and terror.

The fear barely subsided when Asa had gotten away from the child's touch. When they were finally able to stop screaming, their thoughts turned to running. They forgot any notion of taking the child with them as they stumbled away toward the door, as fast as they could. In one swift motion, they had thrown it open, and dashed inside, slamming it behind them.

They faced the door and leaned against it heavily as they tried to recover their breath and restructure their thoughts.

There was no mistaking it. They had been doing this long enough to recognize it when they were on the other end. That child had been like them.

As they calmed down, they wished they hadn't run. But then again, the child had hardly seemed in the talking mood. Perhaps it hadn't even known how to speak. Perhaps it wouldn't have mattered.

Before they could decide one way or another, a voice interrupted their thoughts.

"Now what do we have here?"

They turned around to see who had spoken, but were faced with many other things to take in. It was a whole new room—

this one brighter, with a single window letting sunlight stream in. It was a simple bedroom of a simple house, with tile floor, and plaster walls. There was a dresser painted a lovely pastel green, to complement the yellow walls. A small wooden table was set up near Asa, with a simple vase on it full of colorful flowers. Then, in the corner, there was a bed. And on that bed sat a man.

He was old. Old, and balding, though he maintained a thick mustache on his upper lip of striped black and silver. His eyes were dark, with clouded pupils, and they watched Asa closely. Unlike the child, he seemed calm. The only thing that struck Asa as odd was his clothing—it was Lucien in style, but incredibly old-fashioned. Asa felt like they had only ever seen this specific style worn in costume for plays and historical lectures at the local university. Their curiosity growing, they examined him closer. His skin was leathery and spotted with age, and a warm tan from years spent in the sun. He seemed kindly. Asa didn't allow themself to be put at ease, not after what had happened in the last room.

"You've made it all the way here," he said before they could get any words out. "You've made it farther than any of us. How did you get here, and so young? I never imagined to see someone so young."

"What are you talking about?" Asa asked in bewilderment.

"I'm talking about you. Being here. So close. And you are so, so close my friend. It's just beyond this door—or the next one. Just a little farther, my friend, you are so close to the answers to all our questions." He began to stand from the bed, coming closer to them. His tone was bright with an enthusiasm that only served to confuse Asa further.

"Our questions? But—my question—my question is, who are you?" They stumbled over their words as rather than finding answers, they only found new gaps in their knowledge.

"Ah, I am happy to answer you. If only someone like me

had been here to answer my questions when I came. Perhaps I would have gotten farther—but perhaps it was only my destiny to get this far, so I can help you do what I could not."

"If you're so happy to answer me, then why don't you?"

The man stopped advancing toward Asa, only a few steps from them. He gestured to himself with both hands, then to them, as he said calmly, "I am you."

Asa felt their lips part in shock, and their eyes widened, but it was all involuntary. They were frozen and only their eyes moved as they looked over the old man in an attempt to make sense of everything. He looked nothing like them—their brown eyes were similar, but the little hair that he had was straight and fine. His skin, though tan, was a few shades lighter than theirs. He was a man.

"You are not me," Asa said, but even as they said it, they knew they were wrong.

"I am you," the man repeated. "We all are."

Asa looked over their shoulder to the door they had just come from. "The child?" they asked.

"I suppose so. I don't know who else is here. I don't know how far they got. If there is a child—well, I doubt they got far at all. How sad, that one of us died so young."

"Dead?" Asa repeated. It was a lot, but they felt they were starting to understand. At least, they hoped they were. "Dead—then you are dead, too."

"Yes."

"And I'm not?"

"I assume not. You're moving between us. You can see and speak to us. I can't do that—I've never seen anyone else here. Come to think of it, I don't even remember being here until I saw you."

Asa pressed their hand to their chin, trying to think logically. "How do you know we're the same person?"

"That's all I found out—that's as far as I was able to get."

"Then you don't know why, or how? Does everyone in this world do this—die, and become someone new?"

"I don't think so. I think this has to do with us specifically —with what we are."

"And what's that?"

He shook his head mournfully. "I don't know. I never found out." The sadness was suddenly replaced by the same eagerness he had expressed when they had first entered. "But you can! You will! You have to keep going—through this door, and the next, and however many it takes. You will succeed where I failed."

"And if I don't?" Asa asked, looking beyond him to the door in question, a simple door with the same pastel color scheme as the rest of the room.

"Then you will end up here too, forever, until one of us does."

That didn't seem agreeable at all. And if he was right—if they were that close—then they simply had to continue on.

"I'll go," they assured him, "for you. For the child, for me."

"Good. For all of us."

"For all of us."

He stepped aside, allowing them to walk forward. The room seemed smaller when they began to move through it, and before they knew it, they were at the door—even more, they had already opened the door, and moved into the next room.

This room was even more interesting than the last.

The walls were made of a painted paper that cast the entire scene in a golden glow. Deep red and green wood with intricate carvings broke up the ceiling into tiers, so delicate and intense that Asa felt their head spin as they looked at everything. The floor was warm, and the entire place, while dizzying, radiated comfort. They looked around the room for its inhabitant, until they finally saw him: a man sitting on a soft cushion to their left, watching them intently.

Like the old man in the room before them, he was not wearing the simple white robe that Asa was. He was clothed in rich silks, with golden trim, and his thick black hair was tied up out of his face. He was also young—maybe only a little older than Asa. When they looked at him, he smiled.

"Welcome, friend. Where have you come from?"

"The last room," Asa replied, not sure how else to answer.

"Ah. Of course."

"I guess you're me, too, aren't you?"

"Am I? I suppose that's right."

Asa's brow furrowed at his response. "You suppose?"

"It sounds correct." He shrugged, not moving from where he was seated. "I haven't given it much thought."

"Why not? It's all I could ever think about," Asa said as they came around to face him from the front.

"Oh, the gnawing, empty feeling? The hole you could never fill? The strange desires, the strange fears, the things you could never justify? The things you remembered but had never done? I'm familiar with that."

"But you haven't given it much thought?"

"Why would I? It's terrifying."

That was true. It had always been terrifying, but that terror had only ever drawn them in. It wasn't the knowing that scared them—it was the thought of never knowing at all. They had never even thought to be scared of knowing. Knowing was the relief that they were promising themself.

"More terrifying than never knowing?"

"I never knew, and I don't know if you noticed, but I'm quite happy." He gestured to their luxurious surroundings. "Happier than you, I wager."

"We're the same person," Asa pointed out to him again, with annoyance this time.

"Oh, I suppose we are."

"If we never find out, we may never truly be happy. We

may always stay lingering in fear, always afraid of whatever is behind that door." Asa gestured to the other end of the room.

"Or we may only find more to be afraid of," he replied. It seemed that only now did he notice the door. His eyes widened ever so slightly, and when he spoke again there was a slight tremor to his voice. "Don't go through the door," he said softly.

"Why not?"

"Go back the way you came." He didn't provide an explanation. "Don't go any farther."

"But if I go back, we may never know."

"We may never want to know what we may never know what we may never want to know what we may never know what we may never want to know what we may never know what we may never—"

His voice lost its tremor as he began to drone, his eyes only widening with each word as he pointed toward the door beyond them. Asa backed away slowly—as they got closer to the door he got louder and louder, until he was screaming after them.

"WE MAY NEVER KNOW WHAT WE MAY NEVER WANT TO KNOW WHAT WE MAY NEVER KNOW WHAT WE—"

Asa's heart raced and their hand shook as they fumbled to slide this newest door open, only getting it open enough for them to slip through before they quickly dashed into the room beyond. They closed it behind them with as much haste as they could, and as the crack began to shrink, so did his voice, until the door shut and they found themself once again in silence.

This new room was the most unfamiliar yet they felt much calmer just for being in it.

The walls were not made of wood or stone, but of animal skins stretched over a wooden frame. A pit sat in the middle of the room with a fire roaring in it that bathed the room in flickering, comforting warmth. Asa leaned against the door slightly, savoring the moment of quiet. Perhaps they should turn around, they thought to themself. Perhaps it wasn't worth it. But at the same time, the words of the old man echoed in their mind.

They were so close.

They owed it to him, to the child, to everyone they'd ever been to continue on.

"You don't, actually."

Asa turned, surprised, to see a woman with pale red hair and a kind face smiling at them from near the fire.

"I don't what?"

"Owe it to anyone."

Asa squinted. "How did you know what I was thinking?" they asked.

"I don't know. I suppose I just feel like you and I have a lot in common. I suppose I just . . . knew." She shrugged, and gestured for them to join her by the fire.

They did, coming around beside her and kneeling on the bearskin rug that was laid out a small distance away from the edge of the pit.

Neither of them spoke for some time. Asa stared into the fire, and found themself mesmerized by the flames. With the flickering, they felt their thoughts fall out of the circular pattern they often got caught in. They felt themself forget to be worried and remember to breathe.

After a while of this, they glanced over at their latest host. They could tell from her face that she was older—not quite as old as the old man, but not young. Her clothes were warm and hearty, thick with fur that her hair tangled in as it cascaded down her shoulders, some loose and some in several delicate braids. She had a motherly atmosphere to her, one that grew stronger when she noticed them staring, and smiled.

"I have to move forward," they told her.

"Why?" she asked. "Who told you that?"

"I did," Asa sighed.

"I see."

"But I also told myself not to go any farther at all."

"Well, you've already done that."

"I guess I have."

They went quiet again. This time, it was the woman who broke the silence.

"Listen to your heart," she said softly. "You don't need to know for anyone else. If you want to know the truth, truly, then continue on. But know that it's not the only way."

"The only way? For what?"

"To feel whole." She turned to them, then gestured to the room around them. Asa noticed now that this room was larger than the old man's room, and while it was smaller than the rich man's room, it was less empty. There were two pairs of small shoes near the door to the next room—children's shoes.

"You never looked, either," they said slowly, in realization. "Like the last man, you never looked. Were you afraid?"

"No," the woman's tone was thoughtful. "I wasn't afraid. In fact, I was curious, like you are. But I didn't know where to start. And eventually, I found something that mattered more to me than knowing ever would." She looked Asa over. "Do you have anything like that?"

They pondered that. Previously to this year, the answer would have been a fervent "no." But now they wondered—could they give up now, and still feel full? Kennet meant more to them than anything. If going forward was the end of them, the end of whatever this chain of lives was, would it be worth it? To leave him behind, if that's what it took?

They had done so much together, and yet Asa still wanted more. They wanted every moment they could get with him.

"I think I might have something," Asa replied to the woman, and she smiled.

"Then you have a choice before you that is all your own. You can go forward, for yourself. Or you can stop, for yourself. Don't listen to the others. Hell, don't listen to me. Do what's best for you. Do what's true to you." She reached out, and pressed her hand against Asa's chest and the cold white fabric that covered it.

Asa felt warmth spread over themself at her words, and they nodded seriously. "I will. Thank you."

"I have nothing more to say to you. Rest if you want. Both doors will open to you whenever you want to move on."

They took her up on the offer. The flames continued to calm them, and the fire never died down even as the two sat motionless in the room, making no attempt to tend it. Asa chose not to think further about things—about where they were, how they'd gotten there, what it all meant. There was only the way they had come from and the way they would go next.

Eventually they settled on the latter, and stood up.

"Good luck," said the woman, without looking away from the fire.

"And the same to you," Asa replied, and they stepped up to the next door. They would move forward.

With their resolve fully settled, and the risks taken into account, something about this door seemed different when they opened it.

They were back in the dark, circular room.

But there was no child this time, and when the door shut behind them, there was no sound. It was eerily still—at least they could see where they were going, though. Or at least, they could see what they had come to find.

There was someone in the room with them again, but this someone was not quite . . . like them.

It was formless, warping with each footstep Asa took toward it. It vibrated like it was moving to the sound of their footfall itself, but there was no sound to be heard. It was colorful, shifting colors through the rainbow, but not like it was shining. It was like it was breaking the light apart into tiny, colorful particles, like it was made of a precious gem.

When Asa spoke, they were surprised that their voice made any sound at all. It sounded muted, like the walls refused to echo them. But they were able to speak to the creature, nonetheless.

"Can you hear me?" they asked.

The form shivered. It became rounded, and on either side of it, its surface rippled. Two small disks began to protrude, then wrinkle like fabric, then solidify again. Ears. Human ears, on the iridescent surface of the thing. Asa felt repulsed and intrigued simultaneously.

"Can you . . . see me?" they ventured.

Again the form trembled. The surface split twice in the front, two slits that opened to blank, convex shapes underneath. The orbs under the slits spun, and rotated, and rolled back and forth in their sockets until Asa was looking into two eyes. The whites were shiny, slick like the rest of the form, but the irises were bright and saturated with color. They took Asa in hungrily, the first thing these eyes had ever seen.

As it looked at Asa, it began to shift again, more violently this time. It rippled down from the top of the sphere—arms, legs, a torso, all smooth and featureless, formed under what was now becoming a head. Two feet touched down on the floor, and Asa stood before someone new. They still had no face besides the eyes and ears, but they seemed to have consciousness. They were watching Asa expectantly.

Asa took a step toward them. They stepped toward Asa. The movements were mirrored, but unnervingly stilted, delayed as they waited for Asa to lead them. Something in Asa told them that they shouldn't get too close.

They stopped a few paces away, and faced each other.

"What are you?" Asa said finally, awe seeping into their voice.

The creature stared at them blankly. It held Asa's gaze, but no clear emotion showed.

Asa decided to try something else, something more directed.

"Are you me?"

The creature blinked for the first time. Their stare didn't waver but the longer that Asa looked into their eyes, the clearer they could see them—tears had started to form. The creature was crying.

Asa felt something stir deep within them at these tears. They felt the same compulsion they'd had to reach out to the child. The same voracious curiosity that they had felt from the old man, but more desperate. The same fear that they'd felt from the rich man, but more hopeful. The same reassurance as from the woman, but more of an invitation.

The creature reached their hand out toward Asa. Long, slender fingers hesitated ever so slightly as they extended to their fullest, and the eyes seemed to implore Asa. To beg them.

Almost without meaning to, Asa reached back.

Their fingertips met, and Asa shouted. It was like touching the sun all over again—this time they only lasted a second before they jerked their hand back, but they were surprised to see that the creature had done the same thing. Then, they were surprised to see that the creature wasn't so unfamiliar anymore. In fact, it was far more familiar than any of the other people they'd met so far.

Asa of the Isles. A bard, a child to their parents, a traveler, and a lover. It was them, standing right across from themself, feature for feature. Every freckle, every curl, right where it ought to be, down to the gap between their front teeth.

This new Asa seemed just as shocked as the Asa who had entered the room.

Suddenly they doubted themself. Were they the one who

had come in? Had they been looking for themself the whole time? Was there any difference between the two of them?

They met their own eyes, and saw that there was nothing unusual there.

"What are you?" they repeated, longing for a simple answer, to finally get the only answer that they'd ever wanted.

The Asa across from them smiled. It was the most joyful, pure smile Asa had ever imagined they could smile. "I am you!" they replied with elation. "You are me!"

"And what are we?" Asa prodded desperately.

Their smile only grew. "We . . . are a god."

They reached their hand out toward Asa again, and Asa reached back this time, perfectly mirrored. They didn't hesitate. The words they had heard didn't fully sink in until their hands touched for a second time.

And then they became undone.

Their consciousness unfurled like a scroll. They were gone—both of them, completely gone. The room was gone. The questions were gone, as Asa could look down on themself for once. Every life they had ever lived was laid out before them in detail. They couldn't comprehend it all at once—countless births and deaths, more unique joys and sufferings and experiences than they could ever hope to imagine. But all of them were familiar. Every moment they saw was like a memory, and not a distant one. It was like it had all just happened, like it was about to happen, and like it was currently happening.

They could see even before their first breath, they realized. The very first life they had ever lived—there was something before that. They could go back further, and so they did. As they turned their attention toward the beginning of the story, they saw it.

Godhood.

They reached out with invisible hands toward the end of that scroll, toward godhood, their heart soaring. They knew that if they took that moment in their hands, it would all end, this continuous cycle of not knowing, of gnawing emptiness.

But then, there was a moment they observed that made them stop.

You think I'll lose you like that?

I'll come back every solstice if I have to—no, I'll build a house a little ways down the trail, and I'll come look for you every day.

They faltered.

He was waiting for them. And though this wasn't the only love story they could read in the scroll, not even the only unfinished one, it was still worth something to them. It hadn't been worth stopping before now—it hadn't been worth more than knowing the truth, but was it worth so little that they could just leave him behind?

Wasn't that the only outcome they hadn't wanted from this?

They stopped short of godhood. The scroll stretched out to its limit before them, as if offering them one more chance.

And then, it snapped shut.

$\sim$

When Asa awoke, they were right where they had been last.

On the mountainside, in front of the sun and the moon.

But one marked thing had changed. All three of them had tears in their eyes.

Helice had pressed her hands over her lips, and when Asa looked from one to the other, they understood why. They didn't remember everything, not even close, but they knew one thing for certain.

". . . It's me," they said, breathless.

"Ceri?" Essaim said it, hesitantly.

That was the name. *Their* name, the first one they'd ever had. "It's me!" they repeated, with more certainty this time.

"Ceri," Helice breathed.

The two gods got down on their knees, the Sun collapsing completely into sobs as she reached her arms out to Asa. In an instant, they found themself wrapped up in the embrace of gods—gods, a thing which they were. They were a god, a god who had been lost.

And now, a god who had been found.

CHAPTER 9

THE HEART OF THE MATTER

"**We haven't seen even a sign of you since humanity was born.**"

Helice and Essaim sat in front of Asa. Their demeanor had completely changed with the revelation that Asa was neither a prophet nor even a human—which was to be expected, of course. Essaim was a distraught mess, hardly able to speak at all. She kept reaching out to touch them, taking their hand in her massive one, letting it go, then reaching out again. Tears dripped down from her face and into the snow, hitting with puffs of steam. Though Helice was more composed, she hadn't stopped crying either. Periodically she would pause and stare at the ground in an attempt to contain an outburst similar to her wife's.

"**Where have you been?**" Helice demanded, and Asa shook their head in surprise. Unlike the other gods, their eyes had dried since they'd returned to the mountaintop, and they were more confused than anything else.

"My memory is . . . incredibly hazy," they said slowly. "I know I've been cycling through human lives, living them until death and then forgetting everything and starting anew. Over and over and over."

"And you didn't know . . . you forgot completely. That's why you never reached out." Essaim broke through in sobs. She pressed her palms against her eyes for a moment, attempting to suppress her tears, but it hardly worked. **"We thought . . . At first we thought it was something we did. That you'd just left us."**

"Why would I do that?" Asa wondered aloud. Their recollection of their life as a god was the most unclear of any memory right now. It seemed like there were vague bits and pieces of various human lives, but godhood . . . it was more of a feeling than anything else.

"We don't know," Helice muttered, **"and I suppose we still don't. But that's not what matters—you're back now. Still a human, somehow, but we can fix that, I'm sure. We can find a way to get you back to your old self, and then—"** She paused, and seemed to realize something. **"Why are you still human, exactly? I would think you would have returned to being fully god the moment that you realized what you were. A touch from Essaim—surely that should have been enough to bring you back? Are you trapped like this?"**

"I . . . ah." Asa winced, then admitted, "I actually . . . did have the chance to."

"And?"

"And I refused it."

Essaim and Helice were stricken silent.

"I'm sorry," Asa continued, "but I . . . I don't think I'm ready."

Essaim opened her mouth, then snapped it shut again. She looked helplessly to Helice, but the god of Order didn't have the answers either. After taking a deep breath, Essaim tried again. **"I think I understand,"** she said slowly. **"It seems like you're still human in spirit. It might take you a while to come to terms with all of this, we shouldn't expect you to jump back into it right away."**

"No, we shouldn't," Helice agreed. "But Ceri, you have to understand something. It seems by the way you described it that after you die, you forget everything you learned during your life. By remaining human, it's entirely possible that if you die before you're able to reclaim godhood, you'll forget everything. You'll have to start over—we'll have no way to find you."

"We don't want to lose you again, dear heart," Essaim added.

The way she said "dear heart" was so familiar. She had called them that before, they were certain. It was like a warm hug, or a favorite meal—hearing it brought a smile to their face involuntarily. "I don't want to lose you again, either," they said. Despite not remembering much, they knew one thing. Not only did they know Helice and Essaim, they loved them dearly.

"You have to stay alive long enough to come back to us," Essaim said, and Helice nudged her gently.

"There's no guarantee of that," she chided softly. "It's a risk we're going to have to take."

"All alone in the world . . ." Essaim bemoaned.

"Not all alone," Helice murmured, and Asa saw that she was staring past them, toward the foot of one of the trees. She narrowed her three eyes, then returned her attention to Asa. "Ceri, the man you came here with. Do you trust him?"

Asa's heart leapt. Kennet—they hadn't forgotten about him, but they definitely thought that the gods had. "I trust him more than anything," they said fervently.

"Is he loyal to you? Would he give his life for you?" she prompted, somewhat forcefully.

"I . . ." Asa looked at the ground, confused as to how to answer. "I've never asked that of him. I don't want to put him in that position."

"You may not ask that of him, but I will." Helice drew herself back up to her full height, beckoning for Essaim to do the same. The god of the sun wiped a lingering tear off her cheek and nodded. She stood to join her wife, and when she had done so, Helice snapped her fingers.

Kennet Peders materialized in front of them.

"Hell!" he yelped, taking a step backward and frantically looking around him. When he saw Asa his shoulders relaxed, but only slightly.

"It's all right, Kennet," they said with a step toward him, "I'll explain everything."

"First," Helice said, her voice booming, **"I have a question for this one."**

"For me?" Kennet repeated. He gave Asa another worried look. They attempted to reassure him with a smile and a nod, but it was hard to tell if it worked.

"Yes, for you," Helice replied without expression. **"Firstly, what do you call yourself?"**

"Kennet. Kennet Peders."

"Very well, Kennet Peders." Helice nodded. **"Ceri tells us that they trust you. We want to trust you as well, if we are to leave them in your hands."**

"C-ceri?" Kennet repeated.

"The one you call Asa. A god of the world. Ceri, god of the Heart," Helice said patiently.

"God?"

Helice and Essaim both looked at Asa with different expressions. Helice looked tired, annoyed at having to repeat herself. Essaim, on the other hand, was completely charmed by Kennet and was beaming. Asa shook their head.

"I promise," they said again to Kennet, putting a hand on his shoulder as they stepped up to stand directly beside him. "I'll explain later."

"You're a god?" he said to them, apparently not registering anything after what Helice had said.

"Please, Kennet Peders." Helice commanded his attention again, and he looked back toward her. **"I need to know that you will protect Ceri with your life. They are not ready to return to their rightful place as a god of the world, and though we respect that, we are hesitant to leave them alone. We would feel a lot better knowing they were in capable hands. So, answer me this—do you care for them?"**

Kennet swallowed, and Asa felt his posture change under their hand as he drew his shoulders back and nodded firmly. "Very much," he said.

"How much?"

"I love them," he said, and Asa's heart fluttered. They wished they could kiss him, or hold him, but they knew now was not the time. They settled for giving his shoulder a reassuring, loving squeeze.

"You love them." Helice raised her eyebrows. **"I see. Then you would do everything in your power to keep them out of harm's way?"**

"Anything."

"You would die for them?" Essaim broke in.

Even Asa was caught off guard when Kennet replied without hesitation. "I would."

Essaim and Helice looked at each other, impressed. **"I believe he would,"** Essaim said.

"I think I believe him too," Helice agreed. **"And Ceri."** Helice turned her attention to Asa. **"Do you love him?"**

"I do." Asa nodded seriously.

"I knew that without asking," Essaim said with a slight tone of bragging.

"I just wanted to hear them say it," Helice replied, **"but I am satisfied."**

"Yes, I think they're in good hands."

Kennet threw Asa a look of wide-eyed relief and lingering

concern, but all Asa could do was shrug. ". . . Thank you?" he said to the gods, and Essaim laughed.

"Very good hands," she repeated. **"My my, what will Gethin think when he sees that you've replaced him?"**

"Gethin?" Asa felt a sudden wave of panic. "Oh, no—no you can't tell him."

Essaim and Helice exchanged another look. **"What do you mean?"** Essaim asked. **"He's taken your disappearance harder than anyone. He thought it was his fault, that he did something to anger you. To know you were alive would be a huge weight off his shoulders."**

"Please, not yet," Asa pleaded. The thought of facing him —no solid memory came to their still-recovering mind, but they knew the feeling well from their time as a human. It was the feeling of dread that came with the potential of running into someone that they used to be in love with. And with the way that they were talking about him, they were sure—Gethin had been something to them, when they were a god.

It made sense now, with the way they had hated hearing his name the moment they knew he existed. Something had lingered in them over every lifetime. Even in the few memories they had of their other lives, they'd felt the same dread at his presence. It wasn't hate, or disgust, just . . .

"I'm not ready," they said. "I'll . . . I'll reach out to him in my own time. Please don't tell him about this."

"It's a bit too late for that, I'm afraid," Essaim said. **"When you and I touched hands, I felt your presence immediately. I knew it was you, even before you told me. Helice felt it too—didn't you, dear?"**

"Immediately. It was as if the universe said it in unison. Ceri is alive," Helice confirmed, and Asa ground their teeth.

"That's fine," they muttered. "That's fine, just . . . if he comes to you, don't tell him where to find me. I hardly know who I am right now, much less how to talk to him."

"Once more . . . I suppose I understand you," Essaim sighed. **"It will break his heart, but . . ."**

"We'll make sure he understands too." Helice nodded.

The four of them stood in silence, with nobody quite sure what to say next. There was a lot to be said, but Asa knew that none of it would make sense yet. They needed time, and a lot of it. Right now they wanted nothing more than to get back to the real world, and just be alone with Kennet. Talk with him, process things. He was good at helping them process things.

"Perhaps . . . perhaps we should leave now," Essaim prompted. **"I feel like they have a lot to think about."**

"I agree," Helice said, but she hesitated. She knelt down in front of Asa again, demanding their attention and holding it. **"As much as I believe this man's intentions to be true, I don't want to leave you to the world again. Let us give you something to contact us without all this . . . pomp."**

"Oh, I agree." Essaim nodded, and joined her wife one more time to kneel in front of the humans. **"Here— together, then."**

Helice nodded. The two gods pressed their hands together, and through the gaps in their fingers, Asa saw a faint glow. It started out white, but as their grip tightened, the light flashed gold, and then silver. Eventually it faded away and each god held out a hand toward Kennet and Asa.

In Helice's hand was a simple golden hexagon of thin, delicate metal. It hung from a golden chain—there were no marks of human touch on it, no dents from a hammer or scrapes from a file. It was completely perfect in shape and form. She offered it to Kennet.

In Essaim's hand was a similar pendant on a chain, but in the form of a bee. In fact, at first Asa thought it was a live bee, still squirming, but as they watched it stilled and became solid gold. When they looked to Essaim, unsettled by its moving, they saw that the god was grinning at them again. She held the pendant out to them with a wink.

"Wear these at all times," Helice instructed them as they each accepted the jewelry and began to fasten it around their necks. **"And should you ever need us—for any reason—press the two pieces together. If you do that, we will come."**

"Thank you," Asa said. The gods smiled, but the smiles were sad.

"We will miss you, Ceri," Helice said, **"but it's so, so good to know that you're safe."**

"Please come home soon," Essaim added, and before she stood up, she opened her arms to Asa for another embrace. It was a request they filled eagerly—and where her presence had threatened to burn them before, now it was warm and inviting like an early spring's day. They felt filled with comfort as her massive form enveloped them. They didn't want to let go.

Eventually, though, they forced themself to pull away.

"I'll see you both again soon," they said. "I promise."

∽

THE WORLD SEEMED SO MUCH MORE REAL now.

Asa stood under the trees, looking out from the mountain over the world below. It seemed so much smaller and yet so much larger than it ever had before. So much more beautiful. They tried to remember—had they been there when it was made? They assumed they must have been. They remembered what it looked like before plants and animals, when Seok had been the only one to take initiative and put anything down. He'd been so very passionate about stone. Nobody had ever matched his passion for his creation.

And Cobb—they put a hand on the tree nearest them,

and inhaled the clear, mountain air that still burned their lungs. They remembered how he'd worked with Seok to think of different trees for different earth, different elevations. This pine had been a work of art in of itself.

They had been there at the beginning of the world.

What a thought.

Kennet cleared his throat, and Asa snapped out of their trance.

"I'm sorry," they said.

"Don't be. You've been through a lot today," he replied. He was sitting down and appeared to be breathing manually, taking deep and purposeful breaths. Asa shook off the thoughts of the trees and the earth, and put their focus on him. They stepped away from the view and sat down beside him.

"I'm sure you have questions," they said slowly.

"I do, but . . . I'm not sure if you have the answers," Kennet replied.

"It's true, I don't have much to go off of—almost at all. Even now that I know, I don't remember everything. It's almost the opposite, like I'm more confused than I was before, but in a more hopeful way."

"I do have one question, actually." Kennet leaned forward, propping his elbows on his knees, and considered the ground in front of him. Asa could see his hands knitting together and realized he was turning over a rock between his fingers—the rock they had given him on the beach. "If you're a god, if you have been this whole time . . . why are you still here?"

"Kennet . . ." Asa scoffed in slight disbelief. "What do you mean? Where would I go?"

"Back to wherever the gods go, I suppose. It's clear that the Sun and Moon care about you very much, that you have some kind of history or family waiting for you. Were you unable to?"

Asa shook their head. "No," they answered. "Not exactly.

I was able to, for a moment. I saw it in front of me, all I had to do was reach out and take it." They reached their hand out toward the horizon, closing it around nothing and pulling back.

"Why didn't you?" Kennet demanded.

"Please. Why else wouldn't I?" They turned and ducked down, attempting to make eye contact with him, to turn his face away from the ground. He didn't look up right away. "Kennet. I stayed for you. I love you."

Kennet winced at their words, still refusing to look at them. "I don't mean to insult you," he muttered, "but that was a stupid decision."

"Hey!" They tensed up, annoyed at his attitude. "No, listen here. I'm still me. I'm still Asa, I still have a life here. Why would I just . . . drop everything I have, leave you, and go live some life I have no memory of?"

"You seem to have a propensity for making the wrong choice when it comes to these things. You left your home when there was nothing waiting for you. And now that there's everything waiting for you, the literal life of a god—now? Now you decide to stay?" He laughed bitterly.

"You know what both of those choices have in common?" Asa said. "Both of them gave me more of you—even if I didn't know it when I left the Isles."

This broke Kennet enough to make him look up. They thought they saw more defiance on his lips, another outburst, more self-doubt. But instead, when he met their gaze, all those words died out.

"Asa . . . your eyes," he whispered.

"My . . . ?" They reached up to touch their face, half expecting to feel some difference in the texture of their skin. When they felt nothing, they turned to Kennet questioningly, but he was already rustling in his bags. Eventually he gave up and pulled the sword from his side, unsheathing it and presenting the blade to them.

When they looked into its slightly scuffed but still polished surface, they saw their own brown eyes reflected back. But just as Kennet had said, something was different. Their pupils were no longer black—they glowed like a cat's eyes in the dark, a brilliant and glorious gold. They blinked hard, as if that would make it go away, but when they opened their eyes again it was still there.

"How odd," they murmured to themself, pulling their eyelids open between their fingers to get a better look.

"Very," Kennet agreed. "But think of how lovely they'll look with your eyeliner."

Asa looked at Kennet in surprise, and tried to think of how they felt about his point. Then they snorted—scoffed—and burst out laughing. They took the sword from Kennet's hand, putting it aside, and threw themself into his arms. He caught them haphazardly and the two of them tumbled to the ground. Asa kept their hands from his skin, didn't give in to kissing him, as much as they wanted to. They held themself up above him as they lay on top of him, pushing themself up on their palms.

"I love you," they said. "It would take a lot to get me to leave you, even for godhood."

"So you're staying, then? Until you're sick of me?"

"I'm here until the end," they said. "I have a lot of feelings right now, so I don't want to kiss you."

"No, by all means." Kennet reached up and carefully pulled them down toward him. "Don't hold back."

∼

IT WAS MUCH EASIER to fill the silence on the ride down the mountain than it had been on the way up.

"Should we even *tell* Lange?" Asa wondered aloud presently. "I feel like he might lock me in his tower to study me if we do."

"Didn't you say you don't remember anything though?" Kennet asked.

"There's bits and pieces. I could probably be made to remember more, if details presented themselves. It's like this—I see things, and they remind me of more things. Like the trees on the mountaintop. Just looking at them, I remembered how they were made, when Cobb decided to make trees with spines instead of flat leaves." They were remembering even more now, just by talking about it.

"You were there when the world was made?"

"It's the strongest memory I have, actually. But not the parts I'd think I'd remember." They considered it deeper. "I remember the others and what they made, but . . . not what I did."

"Helice called you the god of the Heart," Kennet offered, and Asa nodded slowly.

"She did. I suppose with my influence it makes sense. But how would that even work? Humanity are the only ones besides the gods with complex emotions. And as far as I know, Gethin is the one who . . ." They trailed off and their eyes widened.

"Asa?" Kennet urged Starling to slow down, dropping back alongside them. "Asa, what's wrong?"

"I remember now!" they said, somewhere between confused and excited. "It was us—together!"

"What was?"

"You! Humans!" Asa grinned widely at the memory. "Oh, right—because Gethin, he'd been making so many beautiful animals. And I thought to myself, what if I gave those animals something different? I tried with a few of them—horses, dogs, some of the others. They all took . . . kind of. Right, they all had feelings, but not . . . not the way we did." They rubbed Emilio's neck. "I mean no offense, Emilio."

"I mean full offense to Starling."

Asa laughed. "Anyway, I had asked his permission before

fiddling with life. The other gods, they never saw him the way I did, I don't think. They thought he was too stiff, too logical. It was like he was my polar opposite, no feelings at all. But he was open to me—like he was curious about the way I did things."

"I can relate to him in that," Kennet said warmly, and Asa paused in their speech to let his words sink in with a smile.

"Well, it turned out much the same way for him as it did for you. The two of us became closer and finally I felt like I could ask him—what if we made something together? Something from scratch? Maybe then, maybe my creation would stick."

"And he said yes. And you made humanity."

"I . . . think so." Asa's smile slowly melted away again. "See, that's where things get *really* fuzzy."

"How so?"

"We had a plan, we agreed on what we were going to do, but then . . . nothing. That's where my memories of godhood end, and the little snippets I have of my various human lives begin."

"Do you think something happened when you created humanity?" Kennet asked.

"I have to imagine so," Asa muttered. "But I don't know what."

"So why not speak to Gethin then, if he helped you make humanity?"

It was hard to explain what Gethin's name brought to them. It was the same as it had always been, but intensified now. In fact, their knowledge of their past relationship only made those feelings make more sense. "You . . . you remember how you felt when you had to go see Hana again after so long?"

Kennet nodded solemnly.

"That's it. That's how I feel. Except, maybe it's more how she felt about seeing you again. She told me that she'd heard so much about what you'd become after you left the Hawks. It all conflicted with what she knew you to be—especially with what you'd done." Asa realized they sounded a bit down on Kennet, and so they brought it back around to them sharply. "And that's how I feel. Every life I've led, he's been there for it. We didn't know that each other existed, not on the level we used to. But I would hear about him in every life, and he . . . he's changed."

"How can you tell?" Kennet asked.

"The church. The Gethin I know never would have . . . the way they act, the harshness behind them. The way Lange spoke about him—callous and dismissive. None of that fits with the way I remember him. He was awkward, and sweet, and . . ." They were surprised to find a tear in their eye. "He wouldn't hurt a soul. This 'death' business was just a necessary function of the way he had designed life. But 'if I must kill, I will kill'? Those are not the words of the one that I"—they paused, the word "loved" on the tip of their tongue—"knew," they finished hesitantly.

"I understand," Kennet said softly.

"Besides that, even if he hasn't changed . . . I have." They said this more firmly, and gripped their reins with determination. "And I want to—no, I need to figure that out before I speak to him. I don't want to know who *he* thought I was. I want to know who *I* thought I was. And who I am now."

"Then we'll find that. Together."

Asa nodded, then paused. "You know," they said, a sudden thought occurring to them. "You asked why I stayed, but I should ask you the same thing. Helice and Essaim asked you some very intense questions, and I can't expect the answers you gave in that environment to hold true."

"It was intense," he admitted. "I felt as though I was being judged, but . . . to be held up against my love for you? There are far worse ways to be judged. Especially for me."

"But now that we're alone—"

"Asa. I still mean everything I said. I mean it even *more* now that we're alone. I promised them that I'd take care of you, but even more than that I promise you—I promise you. I will never leave your side, as long as you'll have me."

That was more than enough to soothe Asa's lingering concerns, and they finally smiled again. "You know," they said, "I've written a good many songs I'm quite proud of, but now that I know I made you . . . I think that you're my finest work of art."

∽

THE TWO HADN'T BEEN in a proper town since before they visited Lange. Not that this town at the foot of the mountain could be called a proper one, but it was larger than the village by the sea, and it certainly beat camping on a mountainside. Asa let out a long sigh of relief as they set foot on the paved streets.

"I'm so glad we get to eat a warm meal tonight," they said excitedly.

"Was the stew I made last night that terrible?" Kennet teased. Asa knew he had no misgivings about how terrible the stew had been.

"I'm excited to eat some real food," they repeated, pointedly ignoring what he'd said while giving him a knowing grin.

Kennet sighed in surrender, and motioned for them to follow him. For once, they were in a town that neither of them had been to before, but even still Asa trusted Kennet far more than they trusted their own instincts. They trailed behind him, taking in the little mountainside town with its various trappings. A soft sprinkling of snow had fallen the night before, just enough that it hadn't quite melted from the streets by the time Asa and Kennet arrived. It crunched under their boots as they walked.

Asa tugged their gloves tighter again. Despite the fact

that Kennet had assured them that the change to their eyes wasn't noticeable from far away, they felt deeply self conscious. They had no idea how common folk would react to the way they looked. And their gloves—always a source of comfort—seemed even more necessary now.

They felt like everyone was staring at them.

Nothing to do but keep their head down, though. There was no reason for anyone to stare at them. It was only their nerves, still on edge from everything that had happened on the solstice.

But it still felt like . . .

No, they were definitely staring.

But not at Asa.

"Oi." A gruff voice commanded the pair's attention, and they turned in unison to see a man taller than Kennet and twice as wide. He was holding something in his hand. "This you?"

He held the paper out in front of them. It was a poster, on weatherworn paper, with the words REWARD—CAPTURE ALIVE written in bold black ink. Above the nerve-wracking announcement was the portrait of an unmistakable face with an eyepatch and long, streaked hair. Asa's breath caught in their throat.

They realized now that those who had been staring were closing in. As Kennet seemed to be trying to make sense of what was going on, he noticed them too, and stepped between Asa and the large man. His hand went to his sword.

"It *is* him!" another voice declared. "Shorter than I thought he'd be."

"Less impressive, for someone who's meant to be delivered straight to the king himself," the big man agreed. "Well, I saw him first. That means I get—"

Asa's heart pounded as the townspeople talked. Without thinking, they raised their hands, still gloved, and threw them out to their sides.

The entire street full of people collapsed, screaming.

Kennet and Asa were left standing above the writhing mass of townspeople. There had been no sign of anything—no light, no sound, nothing as Asa had willed their fear to leave them and enter the bodies of those around them. There had just been their movement, and then the screams.

Kennet's eyes were wide as he stared at Asa, but the god wasn't looking back at him. They were staring down at their hands—their hands, which had started to shake. He rested a hand on their shoulder with an attempted calm, tugging at them gently, not saying a word. Numbly, they nodded, and in the midst of the screaming, the two began to back out of the town. Slowly, at first, until they had cleared the square, and the edge of the crowd.

Then they turned their backs on the screams, leaving them in their wake as the god and the killer tore off through the town and out into the woods.

END OF PART 3

EPILOGUE

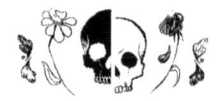

On the winter solstice, on a different continent, in a massive marble cathedral, the prophet of Gethin was idly minding her own business. She sat in a large high-back chair in the office of the Exarch, the leader of the church. The two had weekly "meetings" they upheld without fail, but in truth, those meetings were just a time set aside for both of them to have a moment of silence. As the highest points of authority in the church, they were both in constant demand, but if they had urgent "meetings" scheduled nobody would dare interrupt them. These had become their only moments of peace, where they would sit in this office, read books, play music, or just talk about nothing in particular.

The Exarch, however, was late to this meeting.

This was especially odd since it was his office. Usually, he was here when she arrived, but today the only person waiting for her had been his flat-faced fluffy white cat, Luci. The cat had seemed equally annoyed. She had settled into the prophet's lap, purring in a way that sounded almost huffy, if a purr could be huffy.

The prophet pet the cat absentmindedly, staring blankly at the empty chair that was usually occupied by her friend, then at the door. Just as she turned her head toward it, the door was flung open. The Exarch had finally arrived.

"Quincy," he said breathlessly. He was uncharacteristically disheveled—his thinning blond hair had been mussed by his hands running through it, an action which he repeated now as he looked around the room. Quincy sat up straighter, causing the cat to jump from her lap.

"Is something wrong?"

"Gethin wants to see you."

Quincy drew back in surprise. She hadn't ever been summoned to the throne room—not since the day she'd become prophet. Usually if the god wanted to speak to her, he chose to do so in the garden, under a lilac bush. It was their spot. Something *was* wrong.

"Did he say why?" Quincy said, rising to her feet. The Exarch picked up his cat and began to pet her, trying to calm his nerves as he frowned at her question.

"He was vague," he said slowly.

"What else is new?"

"Well, even for him. He seemed . . . confused. I think he wouldn't have even asked for me first if I hadn't been nearby with some novices, giving them a tour. He said it's urgent, though."

"I'll go immediately." Quincy nodded, and she made her way from the room with one last pause to give Luci a final scratch between the ears.

The halls were buzzing with energy. As the different priests in their black and white robes went about their business, they seemed on edge. They must have seen the Exarch rushing toward his office—a good reason to be nervous. That man rushing anywhere was never a good sign.

Quincy tried not to panic them any further, forcing herself to smile at anyone who met her eye. A few of her friends smiled back, but most of them eyed her with caution. They could tell where she was headed, and they would have to be as confused and concerned as she was by it.

She entered the outer chamber of Gethin's throne room, and waited. She was supposed to get permission before moving on, she knew, though she hadn't done that the first time. Then again, the first time, she'd been thrown into this room in chains. A lot had changed.

"Come in," she heard from the other room.

She pushed aside the plush curtain door and stepped into the inner chamber, where she saw her god. He stood at his usual towering height, but his posture betrayed uncertainty, with his hands clasped behind his back. He had placed a skull —a deer's skull, this time—over the empty collar of his robes. He knew that Quincy usually liked to have a face to look at when they talked, but she had learned that it didn't make much of a difference. With or without a head, Quincy had learned that his body language was the only real way to read him, and now she could see that he was . . . nervous?

"Are you all right?" she asked. To some, it would be an odd question to ask of a god. But this wasn't just any god, this was Gethin. This was her god. Her friend. And she was worried about him.

"I'm sorry to have summoned you so suddenly like this," he said, gesturing for her to come closer.

As she walked down the narrow room toward him, she frowned. "You didn't answer my question," she told him, and he sighed.

"I'm . . . I don't know yet," he muttered. **"I'm hoping that after this conversation, I will be."**

"I'll do my best to help with that."

His shoulders relaxed a little, and his robes shifted slightly in their usual unseen breeze. He turned his back to her for a moment to walk back to his throne and sat in it, slumping down and sighing deeply again. Quincy followed him toward the back of the room and when he sat, she did the same on the floor in front of him. He stayed silent for a moment as he absentmindedly reached up and touched the horns on his skull.

"I received a message from the other gods," he said finally.

There was no correct way to react to that. Previously, when she'd asked him about the other gods, he'd been very cagey about their existence. There were stories and myths, tales of a time before the gods, some of which were even written into their holy book. But Quincy had never known for sure, or even really suspected, that they were completely real. She took a moment to compose herself before replying. "Is something wrong?" she asked.

"No. Yes. Hmm," he answered too quickly, then stopped. **"Do you remember how long ago, I told you that when you all call me the 'god of Life and Death,' it's not quite true?"**

"I do, yes. God of Who-in-the-Hell-Knows."

"Right." There was no laughter in his voice at their shared little joke. **"And you know that in the Compendium they say I created humanity, along with every animal—all life."**

"Of course. I learned that when I was ten, or even younger. What are you getting at, Gethin?" Quincy prodded, and he shook his head again.

"That's . . . also not quite true." The skull turned a bit, looking toward a rack of human skulls that decorated the death-themed half of the dual-colored throne room. **"Half true, more like."**

Quincy kept her focus on the god, but she was having a hard time following him. This was an odd time to drop revelations, when he seemed so anxious. "What you're telling me contradicts the very foundation of this church," she said slowly. "Why is all of that based on some half-truth?"

"Because the truth didn't matter, at the time. It . . .

hurt too much to tell. Humanity assumed that I alone had created them, and to tell them otherwise . . ." He trailed off. **"I . . . you never made sense to me, you know."**

If he'd had a face, Quincy thought maybe he would have been crying. "Gethin . . . ?"

"You never made sense to me. So . . . irrational. So willing to do the stupidest things for love, or even to die for it, when there was no benefit to you. All other life had common sense. They would only fight if they could win, and if they couldn't, they would run. You were different. You were like them, and I couldn't . . ." He paused, hopefully to collect his thoughts, because Quincy was terribly lost.

"Like who?" she prompted, but he didn't answer. "Gethin, what are you talking about?" Her second question came a bit more forcefully as she leaned forward and tried to examine him for some clue of where he was going with this.

"I'm talking about the other creator of humanity. Ceri, the god of the Heart. I gave you life, and they gave you . . . everything else that makes you special." He looked down at Quincy now, who was staring back at him with bewilderment.

"There was another creator?" she repeated, trying to wrap her mind around it. "But why—"

"They disappeared. The moment the first human heart started to beat, they were just . . . gone. It felt like some kind of cruel joke—they left me. I was always afraid that they would. They flitted from passion to passion so easily, I knew in my heart that their interest in me wouldn't last. I had just hoped—I had hoped it would last for longer. I had hoped they'd talk to me about it, when they decided to leave me. But they didn't. And they left me with you—you beautiful, confusing creatures." He chuckled ruefully.

"It seems like you've done fine with us," Quincy tried to encourage him. He didn't seem to want to hear it.

"I did my best," he said, **"and it's greatly in part to you—humanity, that is. You were as lost without them as I was. So I stepped in. I learned from you, and you from me. Together we grew, and changed. I began to recover from Ceri, and love humanity for what you are."**

"But why tell me?" Quincy wondered. "I can see that this hurts you to talk about. Why bother bringing it up at all?"

"Because they've returned," Gethin replied. He paused, looking away from Quincy again, then back to her. **"That's the message I received from the other gods, like a memory or some kind of a thought that wasn't my own. 'Ceri is alive.'"** He said the last words slowly, almost bitterly.

"That's . . . a good thing?" Quincy attempted, but he laughed at her.

"Well, it could be. No, no, it is. But it's also . . . not. I went to the others and I learned two things—Ceri never left me. They didn't even know who they were from the moment humanity existed, it was like . . . it was like it absorbed them. Like you couldn't be born without taking some part of them with you. They've been living among you, not knowing, dying and being born over and over until now, until they finally found out the truth. When that happened, it revealed them to the rest of us."

"That's still good news, though, isn't it?" Quincy was still deeply confused. Nothing about this warranted his tone, or the way he was fidgeting. None of it warranted this conversation. What was he hiding from her?

"It would be good news," he agreed, **"if it weren't for the second thing. They . . . don't want to see me."**

"Why not?"

"They didn't say, exactly. From what I heard, it seems like there was some sort of misunderstanding. I . . . I'm sure if they heard my side of the story, they'd understand. Which is where you come in."

And there it was. "You want me to . . . what? Go find them?" she asked. "I'm sure they'd understand your side if they heard it, but it sounds like they need space. I think I know what they're feeling, and if so, they'll come to you in their own time."

"No, no, you don't understand." He got down from his throne now, stepping closer to her and crouching down to force her to look in the skull's eyes. **"Quincy, if Ceri dies while they're still a human, they'll be born again into humanity with no memory of their identity. I'll lose them again—perhaps for good this time. I understand that they need space. But I can't risk this. It's my one chance in eras to make things right, to say everything I've wanted to say since the birth of humanity. So I'm asking you, Quincy. I'm begging you, as your friend— and I'm commanding you, as your god."**

The gravity of his words was not lost on Quincy. He so rarely asked things of her. Her entire role as prophet had mostly been at her own whim this entire time, from the very beginning. She felt a chill run through her veins, and forced herself to nod, with as much certainty as she could muster.

"I'll find them," she said. "I promise."

THE END

SHORT STORY: THE NEW HIGH PRIEST

The following events take place directly after the story told in The Unwanted Prophet, *but before the events of* Book Three: The Friend of Gods. *Knowing what happens here will not be instrumental to understanding the upcoming third book, but I wanted to share them with you anyway, as a moment with our friends Quincy and Marlowe, and an introduction to a new friend. I hope you enjoy it.*

Quincy had lost the Exarch.

This happened often. Both of them were constantly moving, and although Quincy tended to be trying to avoid people, Marlowe was seeking them out. He tried to get her to do the same, to take part in the side of things he called "diplomatic." Though she could be useful in those settings from time to time, she was also known to run her mouth. So usually, he went about those things without her. That was fine.

She did wish that he'd leave a note in his office or something, though, so she could find him when he wasn't there.

But he never did that, so she was resigned to wander the abbey alone, looking for him in all the usual places. The courtyard and library were only good bets when she knew he was trying to hide, but recently he'd been very busy, so he likely wasn't trying to get any downtime. She knew how anxious he got when he wasn't working during a busy season. It was impossible for him to relax.

He usually turned to blowing off steam, instead. So this time, Quincy made her way through the courtyard toward the back of the abbey, through a narrow stone passageway that amplified the echoing sound of staves clashing together. The training grounds mirrored the garden courtyard in their layout, similarly lined with offices, classrooms, and halls of worship. This area, however, was not as peaceful.

Sand lined the ground, creating a soft landing for any falls. There were a few different "arenas" fenced off, with benches set up in tiers for bystanders to watch from. Quincy had begun to spend increasingly more time here herself—the few priests who had dared to foster friendships with her often challenged her to fights. She didn't know how to fight, of course, but she found that in these casual sparring matches she didn't need to. She would either lose, or her gift from Gethin would come into effect and she would overpower her opponent easily.

Today, though, the training grounds were surprisingly empty. Only one of them was active, but she was happy to see that of the two people using it, one was Marlowe.

Neither combatant noticed Quincy's approach, so she didn't interrupt—she felt that would be rude. Instead, she made her way to the fence, and propped herself up against it to watch.

The first thing that caught her eye was how Marlowe was moving. She'd never really watched him fight before, not since their first trip to find the Sycamore in the south. Not that she'd been able to properly pay attention back then, but still, she remembered him being more reserved back then, not as outgoing as Harriet or the others when it came to fighting style.

This was different, though. Here he moved fluidly, still favoring his left leg as he always did, but with less caution and more strategy. He stayed mostly stationary while his opponent circled, attacking as Marlowe pivoted and defended. Another thing Quincy noted was Marlowe's expression—he was almost smiling. He looked determined, of course, but where there would often be a scowl on his face there was now a look of glee, like he was enjoying himself.

That made Quincy wonder what was different. She turned her attention to the other fighter—and realized that this was a man she had never seen before. Most of the priests in the abbey had made a point of introducing themselves, so she wasn't used to seeing strangers around. What was even more interesting were his clothes. His robes were both black and white, the robes of a high priest. There weren't many of those, so Quincy knew all of them—that is, she thought she did.

She felt that if she'd met this man, she'd remember it. He wasn't extremely memorable by looks, necessarily. His head was bald, his features broad and stern, like a fighting dog's. Not particularly memorable, no, but then there was the way he moved. He attacked with ferocity, but with the same playfulness that Quincy saw in Marlowe's defense. Though the two priests were hardly holding back, they were clearly still enjoying the sparring.

Then Marlowe caught Quincy in the corner of his vision and faltered.

He was barely able to deflect the staff that was coming in fast toward his shoulder in the moment of his distraction. Luckily, he raised his own staff in time, glancing his attacker's weapon off his own and narrowly missing a nasty bruise.

His opponent noticed his mistake and stopped his advances, allowing Marlowe to let down his guard.

"Distracted, Your Excellency?" he asked, glancing over at Quincy. She felt a chill as his eyes traveled over her—his expression was calculating. She felt like she'd been looked at this way before, but she couldn't tell by who. His voice contradicted the cold stare, though, with a warm deepness to it and a light accent that she couldn't place.

"Sorry, yes, Brother Aleki." Marlowe paused, breathless. He wasn't wearing the full regalia of the Exarch, so it caught Quincy a bit off guard to hear the other priest use his formal title. Sometimes she forgot that Marlowe was in charge.

"There are plenty of distractions on the battlefield. To lose focus can be fatal," the newcomer, Brother Aleki, pointed out. There was a wry smile on his lips, though. He knew Marlowe already knew all that.

"Good thing you weren't trying to kill me," Marlowe replied, and Aleki conceded with a shake of his head. Marlowe turned his attention to Quincy. "Quincy! Just who I was hoping to see!"

"I am?" Quincy spoke up for the first time now, perking up from her spot at the fence. "What did I do this time?"

"Well, for starters, you completely abandoned me at the council meeting this morning, and if you hadn't, I wouldn't need to do this now." He stood up a little straighter and composed himself fully before he gestured from Quincy to Aleki, then back again. "Brother Aleki, this is the prophet Quincy Sauer. Quincy, this is Brother Aleki. He's our new master of combat."

Quincy's eyebrows flew up. "Oh really?" she asked, unable to disguise her surprise. Surprise not at the fact that this very apparently capable man was going to be taking up a place of high station, but at the fact that Marlowe was so enthusiastic about it. After all, the previous combat master had been Harriet, and she knew Marlowe had been very close with her. That was, in part, why it had taken nearly a year to find a new combat master at all. That seemed to be the last thing on

Marlowe's mind right now, however, so she didn't dare bring it up.

"No need to sound so shocked." Aleki took her tone to mean the obvious. "I may be old, but I can be very dangerous."

"Oh, I can see that. I'm sorry, I didn't mean to be rude," Quincy said with a nervous smile. She didn't even mention that she didn't think he looked that old. Best to just let it be. "I was just surprised that I hadn't heard about this sooner."

"Like I said, if you hadn't skipped out on the last . . . what is it now, three? Three council sessions you've abandoned me for? If you'd been to at least one, you'd be aware of our new brother's arrival."

"Did he transfer in from Lucien?" Quincy guessed. The robe style told her as much, but his accent still evaded her. Perhaps he was from a different region.

"Correct," Marlowe said.

"I was a high priest of the church in Figaroa," Aleki added, "but I'm from one of the Isles, originally. Farther west than most ever venture."

Quincy felt her interest growing at that, but she could tell that Marlowe wasn't enthused by her attempts to get answers out of Aleki when all that information had been readily available months before. Well, let him be mad at her. It wasn't her fault that those meetings were incredibly boring. She had always relied on Marlowe or Ethel to fill her in on the important parts—though, apparently Marlowe had given up on that. Maybe he'd been hoping that leaving her out of the loop would encourage her to attend more.

There would be time to argue about that later.

"Well, thank you for coming so far north to be part of our Order," Quincy said, attempting to win back some points by sounding official.

"Thank you for welcoming me. I look forward to working with you all—and you, specifically," he said, tilting his head back. A smile grew over his face, and he added, "In fact, His Excellency is exactly right. You're just who we were hoping to see."

Quincy sensed a condition coming. "Because you were so eager to meet me?" she asked hesitantly.

"To meet you, and to assess you," Aleki elaborated. "I've been doing the same with every priest so far, and the only one who's evaded me is you."

Ah. "Assess my . . . what, fighting skills?"

"Or lack thereof," Marlowe interjected with his lazy smile, an expression she hadn't seen from him in a while. It seemed to only come out when he had the distinct upper hand in one of their conversations.

"As His Excellency says," Aleki said, though he seemed to be taking the statement seriously. "I want to get a good idea of what you need to improve on, how you fight, what sort of style you favor. I hear that you know some level of fighting art?"

"Not really," Quincy said, erring on the side of honesty. She had fallen even further out of practice now that they were in a time of peace. Part of her had hoped that she could fully escape the rigid combat training the Order usually underwent. "I don't . . . well, I don't know that I see the point in training like that. I'm not a priest."

"No, you're not," Aleki admitted, "but His Excellency explained to me how your gift works. It seems like combat is in your nature as a prophet, and as such, you should know how to fight properly."

Quincy cringed at that, but nodded in surrender. "I suppose so," she said with a sigh.

"Good." Aleki seemed pleased by her agreement. "Get into the ring, then."

"Now?"

"Now."

His voice was commanding, something that intrigued

Quincy as much as it unnerved her. Nobody, not even the high priests, were comfortable telling her what to do. Even Marlowe seemed to hesitate a lot of the time, though he was very quick to passive-aggressively tell her what he wished she *had* done. But this new priest . . .

She obeyed almost instinctively, vaulting over the fence and landing on the soft sand with a thud. Aleki nodded, satisfied, and to both her and the Exarch's surprise he began to walk away toward the benches.

"Aleki?" Marlowe called after him, and without turning, the priest responded.

"I've been fighting too much," he said calmly. "It can be useful to observe one's fighting style firsthand, but your prophet seems guarded. I don't know if I'd get the information I need from fighting her myself." As he finished talking, he reached the benches and turned, fanning out his robes before taking a seat with his arms crossed at his chest.

"So . . . " Marlowe seemed to realize what was going on before Quincy did. "Ah. You want me to fight her."

"If you would. Your Excellency."

The way he added the title almost as an afterthought made Quincy snort. It seemed she wasn't the only one whose authority was being entirely ignored. The exchange reminded her of Marlowe's own interactions with the Exarch that had preceded him. He was getting a taste of his own medicine.

Marlowe turned back to Quincy. "Will you use your gift on me?" he asked suspiciously.

"If I get the chance to," Quincy replied. She still didn't have a handle on her gift—still couldn't activate it on command. But it did come easier, and in more opportune situations. It was entirely possible it would come into play during this match.

"I hope you do!" Aleki called from the stands. "I'm counting on it."

Marlowe sighed with some amount of dread, but steadied

himself, positioning his staff and assuming a fighting stance. Quincy did the same across from him, and for a moment, they stood there.

Aleki's voice came again, this time thick with disbelief. "Do you both default to defense?" he said, incredulous. "Stop that! One of you needs to attack."

Quincy locked eyes with her friend, her expression easily readable. "Is this guy serious?" it said. Marlowe made a face that said "dead serious." Then he lunged. He swung his staff around from the side, and Quincy dodged easily, as she had learned from fighting numerous priests over the past year.

Most of the priests had very easy-to-predict fighting styles, which made sense. They trained as a group and rarely had to face the same threat twice, so there was no real concern for their enemies learning how they fought. Quincy, however, had become frustratingly used to it. And this frustration became evident in Aleki's tone as he called out over their sparring.

"Your evasion is good," he shouted, "but I need to see you fight!"

"Sorry! It'll come to me!" Quincy shouted back as she dodged another of Marlowe's blows. He was tired, she could tell—he'd already been doing this for some time even before she had entered the field so he was at a slight disadvantage. She caught his eyes again as he took a pause, panting for air.

Quincy took this moment to try and strike—and she almost got him, too. But he blocked her with his staff, the crack sending a shockwave of ice down her arm as he hit a nerve.

"Ah, hell!" Quincy cried as she reared back and took another defensive stance. She could hear Aleki sigh from the stands.

"Your Excellency, I understand you don't want to injure the prophet," he said, "but I've seen you fight. You're holding back. Please, once more."

"It's not her I'm worried about getting hurt, it's me," Marlowe said jokingly but Quincy knew that Aleki was right. Marlowe was definitely being half-hearted with his swings. Though the fighting style may be familiar to Quincy, she was still able to tell when it wasn't being used to the fullest.

"No, Marlowe, it's okay," she said, adjusting her stance. He raised an eyebrow at her. "He's right, let loose. Don't hold back."

"I—"

"I really thought the Exarch would be more of a challenge," she teased, and finally saw a flash of fierceness in his face. There was that competitive streak.

"Oh, is it a challenge you want?" he chuckled and shifted his own stance, tossing the flap off his dressed-down robes over his hip and tucking it in at the belt. "If you insist."

"I do." Quincy grinned, and smacked her fists together to prove it. He laughed.

Quincy glanced to the benches to see Aleki was leaning back on the bench behind him, his arms still crossed. His gaze was as stern as ever, but she could tell he was pleased that it finally seemed to be going in the right direction.

"At your leisure," Quincy prodded Marlowe, then added with dripping insincerity, "Your Excellency."

"Oh-ho." Marlowe took her taunting as intended, and lunged once again. Where before he had been slow, calculated, she recognized the ferocity of his new attacks. She felt a shiver run down her back at the familiarity of his anger, but pushed it down.

Relax, she told herself, *Marlowe is your friend. You're just sparring.*

She continued to dodge as he lashed out at her. As usual, she watched for an opening, but an opening didn't come.

"You can't keep waiting," shouted Aleki. "You have to attack."

"I need an opening!" Quincy called back, but in the

moment it took her to reply she lost focus. Marlowe's staff smacked into her side, knocking her off balance. He immediately stopped his barrage—only to be reprimanded.

"Your Excellency. Stop favoring her." Aleki sounded tired of repeating himself. "Please, if I'm going to get any idea of how you fight, I need you to take this seriously."

"Sorry," the Exarch and the prophet said in unison.

"So again. Fight."

Quincy should've taken the opportunity to attack, but she missed it. Marlowe began to advance on her again with renewed fury, and this time, she felt like he was taking the advice as seriously as Aleki was hoping he would. His swings became more unpredictable. As Quincy found it harder and harder to dodge, she heard Aleki's voice over the whooshing of the staff over her head.

"Good job, Your Excellency. Prophet, you need to fight back."

She didn't respond to him, focusing on dodging, on trying to find a way to do what Aleki wanted her to do, but she just wasn't finding it. And what was worse was as he shouted, she felt her heart racing, her breaths coming faster. It felt wrong—something was wrong, not just the normal fatigue of battle. But she didn't know what.

She was beginning to shake.

As she dodged, she caught Marlowe's eye again. She realized she was backed against the fence, as she saw the glimmer of victory in his expression. He had been slowly advancing on her, driving her back as she dodged. She rolled out of his way to the side, but in a circular arena, she was only prolonging the inevitable.

"You have no way out, Quincy!" Aleki shouted. "You have to fight back!"

WHY WON'T YOU FIGHT BACK?

Quincy stood up, covered in sand, but was only able to take a second to breathe before Marlowe came at her again.

"Come on, Quincy, you can do it. I'm already tired out, I should be easy to take down," he said between attacks, trying to taunt her the way she had taunted him.

But there was something about how he said it.

It hit harder than any of the glances of the staff that she had caught so far.

I'm out of practice. Surely I, you can bring down!
Hit me
HIT ME
I'm wide open
What's WRONG with you?
Something snapped.

Suddenly, like a horse with blinders, Quincy couldn't see Aleki anymore. She couldn't hear his voice, or even see Marlowe as he stood before her with confusion overwritten on his face as he recognized the fear in hers.

She could only see Marlowe as he had been in her darkest moments, standing above her. She could hear him shouting at her. Calling her worthless. Calling her pathetic.

He had been right.

But he wasn't anymore.

The absolute terror of that night came back to her like it had never left, and with it came her gift. Never came when she wanted it to, that gift. She could've used it back then.

Quincy caught Marlowe's next blow with her bare hand, her grip wrapping around the staff as a ripple of terror shot out from her. She wondered if it would hit Aleki. Maybe not. It wasn't meant for him. Neither was the anger she felt, still blinded by the emotion—all aimed at the man whose staff she was now holding in an iron grip. She wasn't shaking anymore.

"Quincy?" Marlowe asked, after one attempt to yank the staff back from her. His voice was worried.

She didn't answer him, instead wrenching the staff at an awkward angle, causing him to cry out as it was ripped from his hands. Then, without giving him a moment to think, she whipped it around again and there was a sickeningly loud crack as the staff connected with his brow. He collapsed on the ground in front of her.

It sounded like someone was shouting at her.

But she couldn't make out the words, and she didn't want to. All the hurt, all the fear and helplessness. They wanted her to fight back so badly, did they? He wanted her to take him down?

All right.

It was high time she finally gave him what he wanted.

Marlowe was trying to stand but failing; the blow to his head had disoriented him. He was lucky that was all it had done. He stumbled, then resorted to trying to crawl away from her, frantic in his movements. She didn't let him. She brought the staff's tip down on his back between his shoulder blades and slammed him into the sandy ground. When he looked up through hair that was caked with sand and sweat, she saw in him the same pure fear that she had felt when he'd threatened her brothers.

She raised the staff, unfettered by his weak pleas for her to stop—

Another staff intercepted her.

Aleki stood over Marlowe, bracing his staff with both hands as he quickly and deftly knocked Quincy's blow aside just in time to spare Marlowe the impact.

It only took a moment, but that moment was enough time to bring Quincy back. She stood, gasping for breath as her strength faded and Marlowe's staff dropped from her hand. Aleki held his weapon at the ready until he was sure Quincy was no longer a threat, then lowered it to his side. He turned to Marlowe, who still lay cowering in the sand.

"Your Excellency," he said, concern obvious in his tone, and held out a hand.

Quincy seemed to finally realize what she had done.

"Marlowe." Her eyes were wide. As Aleki brought the

Exarch to his feet, Quincy stood with her hands awkwardly at her sides. "I'm sorry," she said, and tears sprang to her eyes. "Oh god, I didn't mean to."

Marlowe's gaze avoided hers for a moment as he regained his bearings and accepted his staff back from Aleki, who had picked it up. Then, once he had collected himself, he laughed nervously. "I suppose that's what I get," he said. "I did ask for it, after all."

"I just . . . " Tears were still streaming down her face, mingling with the dust.

"Should I leave you two alone?" Aleki asked slowly.

Marlowe considered Quincy quietly. She couldn't bring herself to meet his eye, gingerly lowering herself to her knees as she realized that she didn't think she could stand anymore.

"I think that would be best," Marlowe replied. "Thank you, Brother Aleki. I'll . . . come and find you when we're done."

∽

The two had been sitting in silence for a long time. He hadn't gotten near her—she knew he didn't like being close to people, so as much as she needed some sort of physical comfort, she hadn't asked him for it. But him being there, even though he had been the provocation, was greater help than she had realized it would be.

Finally, Quincy spoke. "You know I forgive you," she said, still tearfully.

Marlowe didn't respond right away. If she had looked at him, she would have seen a look of surprise on his face, then one of understanding. "Oh," he said. His voice was very quiet. "I see."

"I do, you know, I do forgive you. I just . . . when he was yelling at me, and you were hitting me and I wasn't fighting back, it was so familiar . . . I couldn't breathe. I . . . " She had to stop talking to keep herself from crying again.

She was unsurprised when he didn't say anything to that at first. In fact, he didn't say anything for a while until eventually Quincy felt a hand on her shoulder. It was hesitant, and she didn't look up when she felt it. After a moment of his hand resting there, Marlowe began to gently rub Quincy's back in small, circular motions. The gesture wasn't monumental, but it brought a new cascade of sobs from the prophet.

Marlowe let her cry until it seemed like the sobs were ebbing again, then ventured to speak. "I know you forgive me," he said softly. "But that doesn't mean you've healed from everything I did to you. And I understand that. That's not your fault—what happened just now wasn't your fault. It was my own."

"I shouldn't—you're my friend! And you're trying so hard, and I know that, and I care so deeply about you, I would never want you to come to harm. I don't know why—"

"You never told me you were angry," Marlowe said. "I mean, you did initially, the night I lied to you about your brothers. But after that, I never gave you the chance to tell me how you felt. I tried so hard to avoid it—I intercepted you, badgered you into forgiving me, and no matter how much you meant it . . . I kept you from being able to mean it fully. Because I was afraid . . . of how much it would hurt to hear it from you. That was incredibly selfish of me."

Though Quincy didn't say it right away, she agreed with him. She couldn't count how many times she'd thought about those first few months of her prophethood, and how much she wished she could tell him earnestly how much that had hurt her. How much it had set her back in her recovery from her own past, her own pain. But she'd always felt like he already knew. It had never occurred to her that even though they both knew, she just needed to . . . say it.

"I don't want to keep being mad at you," Quincy said, "and usually I'm not. But sometimes, deep into the night, when I'm the only one awake in the abbey I think about it. I think about what could've been if you'd really advocated for me, if you'd listened to me. If you'd worked with me and treated me with kindness. I think about how we're friends now, and I wonder. . . how much closer we'd be if you hadn't done all that to me."

Marlowe bowed his head in shame. She wondered if this was really going to be helpful at all—she didn't like making him feel bad. But now that the words had started flowing, they wouldn't stop.

"It's even worse because of how much I care about you!" she said, with an incredulous laugh. "I'm not mad at Harriet anymore, because she's dead. Or at Arvin, because he stopped being what he was, he might as well have died. But you—you're still the same, passionate, smart-ass religious nutcase I met on day one. You're still the same man who was willing to do that to me."

This seemed to hit a nerve enough that Marlowe almost interrupted her. "I'm not—"

"No, you're not. You're not that man anymore. I know." She looked down at the ground. His hand steadied on her back as the two sat quietly once more. "And I'm not angry at the man you are now. I'm really not. It's like you said, I just never got to . . . to say it. And it's useless to tell you that you hurt me, because you know."

"God, don't I."

"But I think . . . I think this helped." Quincy took a deep breath as she pushed past the lingering sobs.

"You don't have to pretend not to be angry at me," Marlowe added. "I understand why you are. I won't hold it against you."

"We need to be a team." Quincy drew squiggles in the sand as she talked, finally finding her train of thought returning to her. "You and I. We need to work together. I can't be angry at you anymore. I don't want to be. I want to be the way people see us—powerful friends who have the world's best interest at heart."

"Is that how they see us?" Marlowe raised an eyebrow, his voice thick with doubt.

"I think so. Remember when we visited Lucien together? Remember how that felt, us working as a unit? That's what people see, that's what I want us to be. I want us to run this church together as equals, and if I don't get over this, I'm worried . . ."

"We make a wonderful team, Quincy." Marlowe patted her on the back, somewhat awkwardly. "And I'm sure we will continue to. Hell, if we were going to let one of us trying to kill the other stop us from being god's perfect duo, we would've failed on day one."

"That's true," Quincy laughed, then sighed. "Thank you," she added, "for staying with me."

"I wasn't about to leave you crying in the sand."

She laughed again, harder, at that, and turned to embrace him. In the past, any attempt at a hug like this would go largely unreciprocated, but not today. The arm that had already been resting around Quincy's back tightened, and the arm that hadn't came around to join it. It was a brief embrace, but tight, and when the two drew back Quincy felt worlds lighter.

"Guess I'd better go find Aleki," Marlowe said, almost immediately business again—probably to avoid any awkwardness that he might feel in spite of himself. "I should explain to him that everything's okay." He gave Quincy one last wary once-over. "Everything is okay, right?"

"Absolutely," Quincy replied with feeling. "I'm going to go take a nap now, though." She got to her feet and extended her hand to pull him up to join her. He accepted, then gave a small yelp as her strength proved greater than he had expected and he almost overshot and fell onto his face again.

"I wish I could nap," he grumbled when he regained his balance. "But no, I have to go be in charge. For a team, you certainly make me do all the dirty work."

"The benefits of being blessed."

∽

Quincy knocked on the doorframe to the supply room, and Aleki looked up. He had been taking stock of weapons—that's what she'd been told when she asked where to find him. She had been hesitant to interrupt him, but decided that sooner was probably better than later with what she had to discuss.

"Hi," she said, standing in the doorway awkwardly.

"Hello," he replied, his deep voice saying even the simple greeting with an overwhelming amount of gravitas. He didn't prompt her further.

"I wanted to talk about what happened earlier," she added and took an emboldened step into the supply room when he inclined his head in response.

"I would also like to talk about that," he said, leaning back on a crate. "Do you always lose control like that?"

"No. This was the first time. Usually I get . . . emotional, but never to the point where I'd hurt someone I care about."

Aleki raised an eyebrow, and Quincy noted that there was a thick scar running through it. "So what was different this time?"

"I . . . it was like I was pulled into a different situation, a time where I was truly helpless, and Marlowe . . . Well, he had been there at that time. I couldn't differentiate between that horrible memory and the present, and that's when I lost control. The yelling, the hitting . . . it was all too similar."

Aleki considered this. "I heard they beat you," he said

matter-of-factly. "His Excellency was one of those who took part?"

"Yes."

His expression softened. "You are a stronger person than I to remain in his presence, then. These priests—much has changed since I was last in Bellion, but I heard everything that happened to you, and I was unsurprised. I'm sorry if my methods brought the same feelings to you." He seemed deeply troubled by the last statement, as if the idea had only just occurred to him.

That was encouraging. Though Quincy hadn't wanted to seriously consider it, she'd had the fleeting fear that any combat master would have the same mean streak as Harriet, and Aleki's attitude earlier hadn't done much to temper that fear. But now . . .

"You and I will train one on one," he said decisively. "I understand why you find safety in evasion, but we will find you a way to feel safe in attacks. You will feel confident, you will find security in your abilities—both your gift and your natural skill."

The way he said it left no room for argument, so Quincy didn't try. "And what happened today . . . ?"

"Will not happen again. I will do everything in my power to help you learn how to fight without that feeling of desperation." His eyes darkened, and he continued with sadness in his voice. "You've learned to rely on that. I'm sorry that you were made to feel that only your last resort was good enough."

Quincy felt uncomfortable with the change in tone, and shrugged. "Ah," she said, trying to be lighthearted, "it kind of was, at the time."

"It no longer is." He stood up straighter, and retrieved the inventory list from the top of the crate where he had set it. "We'll take a week off. I don't want that incident in your mind when we begin to work again. But after that—every day. You and I. We'll go slow, and if you need to stop you'll tell me. But we *will* make you feel safe, and we *will* make you secure. I promise you that."

Safety, security—things that felt so out of reach when it came to combat. Things she had been led to believe were antithetical to the way her gift worked, and yet . . .

When he said it, she believed it was possible.

That was something she never would have expected, especially coming from the master of combat.

She smiled, and nodded. "All right," she said. "Thank you, Brother Aleki."

"Thank you, Quincy. I look forward to working with you."

Leaving the room, Quincy knew it was awful what she was thinking—but still there was only one thought on her mind.

As terrible as it was . . .

She was very glad that Harriet was dead.

ACKNOWLEDGMENTS

To Bas – I can't express how much I value the readings we get to do with each other. Thank you for giving Kennet his voice.

To Lynda – I'm so glad our relationship goes beyond editor and author, and we can be frank and excited with each other. I'm also glad this one was easier to edit.

To Bekah – Oh heavens, the typos we find. Thank you for being honest with me about what did and didn't work in this one. I think the book is so much stronger overall for that. I'm glad we get to be family.

To Noah – Thank you for listening to me ramble, for coming up with headcanons, for doing goofy voices with me on long drives to work through character development. I love you so much.

To Ruthie – I'm so glad I found you! Couldn't have asked for a better sensitivity reader for this project, and I'm looking forward to your thoughts on the third one. Thank you for helping me make Asa and the whole book the best it could be!

To All My Artist Friends Who Cheer Me On – The fact that ya'll gave me a chance and picked up *Prophet* means so much to me. Everyone has stories they dream about but you guys helped make mine a reality by reading it. I'm glad you liked it, and I hope you liked this one too.

ABOUT THE AUTHOR

Carolina "Nina" Cruz is an author and artist who grew up in Seattle, Washington. Nina grew up with a strong connection to her Puerto Rican heritage, as well as a love for comic books and the Narnia and Redwall series. This love for fantasy manifested into a full-blown obsession as time went on.

Growing up, Nina often tried to write and illustrate her own books from scratch, from the adventures of the superhero bird Captain Chickadee, to a book about puffins that was heavily inspired by the Warrior Cats books. What initially seemed like a harmless hobby very quickly became a serious venture during college, when *Unwanted Prophet* began production in the middle of a different project for National Novel Writing Month. Sometimes, our projects choose us.

Nina enjoys gothic horror, drawing her characters in cool action poses, and paying other people to draw her characters in cool action poses. You can see her artwork on her twitter or instagram @Ninawolverina

ALSO BY CAROLINA CRUZ

The Creed of Gethin Book I:

The Unwanted Prophet

Made in the USA
Columbia, SC
04 September 2024